Peter Olaf

Peter Olaf

Richard H. Grabmeier

Writer's Showcase
presented by *Writer's Digest*
San Jose New York Lincoln Shanghai

Peter Olaf

Writer's Showcase
presented by *Writer's Digest*
an imprint of iUniverse.com, Inc.

For information address:
iUniverse.com, Inc.
5220 S 16th, Ste. 200
Lincoln, NE 68512
www.iuniverse.com

ISBN: 0-595-15744-0

Printed in the United States of America

To Mary Kay.

Contents

Chapter 1

The New World at Last

Peter Olaf Hokanson stood bewildered on the rough-plank depot platform. With a slow chuffing sound and belches of steam, the locomotive tightened the train's couplings and inched down the track, continuing its trip westward. It was cold and he was hungry. Snowflakes drifted lazily down in the dim light of that early November morning in 1895. Minneapolis, Minnesota was thousands of miles away from his home in Huskvarna, Sweden. Peter Olaf, at age seventeen, was lonely and frightened. He looked at the depot and saw the glow of lamplight. Shivering violently, he picked up his only luggage, a worn, secondhand suitcase, and walked into the depot. The building was still deserted, except for a ticket clerk reading a newspaper, and a baggage handler sleeping on a bench next to a huge pot bellied stove that glowed dark red with burning coal. Peter warmed his hands, then removed his coat and turned to let the heat penetrate his lean frame. At five feet, nine inches and a hundred forty pounds, he was not large, but he had become rawhide tough logging in the pine forest of Smaland. After his chills had subsided, he put his coat back on and went to the ticket counter. The clerk glanced at him over the top of his paper.

"Can I help you, young fellow?"

Peter struggled with the unfamiliar language, bringing the English out in a broken drawl. "Sir, could you please tell me when there is a train to Grand Rapids?"

The clerk listened closely and grinned. "Another Swede, eh? I bet you're going up to the logging camps."

Peter nodded. "Yah, my cousin is up there, somewhere near a place called Remer."

"Remer eh? That's almost fifteen miles from Grand Rapids. I hope you can find a ride, that's a long walk in the cold."

"He said there are wagons in the daytime. Will the train get there before dark?"

"Yeah, you'll have to stay someplace tonight though. Next train up there is tomorrow morning at six."

Peter thought about his diminishing funds. "May I stay here?"

"Suit yourself, no law against it. Wanna buy a ticket?"

"How much money for the ticket, Sir?"

"Let's see, it'll be...a dollar and twenty."

Peter had felt rich when he converted his kronor to dollars at Ellis Island. But the forty dollars he started with had shrunk to sixteen dollars and seventy five cents. As he paid for his ticket, he prayed he would find work at Remer.

"Is there somewhere near, that I might buy food?"

"Sure, just go a couple of blocks straight south, there's a restaurant and a grocery store." The clerk saw Peter's confused look—he pointed south. "That way, young fellow."

Peter walked down the cobble stone street as heavy freight wagons lumbered by. The city was beginning to awaken. The smell of food guided him to a small cafe where he sat down at a long, plank table, next to a man dressed in rough clothing and a leather apron. The man was eating a plate of sausage and eggs. Peter looked at the food hungrily. "Excuse me sir, would you tell me how much that cost?"

"What's the matter kid, can't you read?" The man looked at him from under bushy eyebrows. "Oh hell! You just got off the boat, didn't you? Sorry I got so growly, kid. Sausage and eggs is twenty five cents, pancakes is fifteen, coffee's free. What do you want?"

"I think I'd like the pancakes."

"Joe! Give the kid a stack of pancakes! So where you heading, kid?"

"Up to Remer, my cousin's at a logging camp up there."

"You don't look like no logger, kid. You need some meat on your bones."

"I worked at logging at home, in Sweden, all right."

"Well damn, I bet you did. The north country's rough though, you got a gun?"

Peter shook his head. "I didn't know I need one."

"All kinds of roughnecks up there, kid. And Indians, you could get scalped if you got no protection." The man laughed.

Peter's eyes widened. "Do they really do that?"

"Naw, I was just kiddin you. But there's really some bad characters floating around. If I were you, I'd get me a pocket pistol, a little 38 maybe."

"Where would I get a gun?"

"Down the street there's a gun shop. But don't let them charge you too much. You can buy a used one for maybe three or four dollars. Well, I gotta go, good luck kid."

After he had eaten, Peter walked the streets of Minneapolis. The snow flurries subsided and the sun came out, turning the scant accumulation into slush. It was invigorating to be walking after the seeming endless travel he had endured. First the weeks on board the old tub of a ship that ferried immigrants across the Atlantic, then the relentless lurching and clanging as the trains from New York to Minneapolis slowly crept from town to town, through farm land and forest, around the bottom of Lake Michigan, through Chicago and Milwaukee and finally up to Minneapolis. Peter had been awed at the sheer size of this country. "Is there no end? " He said to himself. "It is no wonder that everyone who comes here can become rich."

He looked out the window of the drafty passenger car. Rows of corn shocks waited to be stripped of the golden ears that would fatten big, lardy hogs for market. The sight filled Peter with dreams. From the time he was just a boy, growing up in a family of five children, Peter had listened to the stories of the new country. Sweden was alive with these stories, told by fathers and mothers, sisters, brothers, cousins and friends of those who had made the great journey.

It seemed that everyone he knew could tell of letters describing the new 'Sweden' that waited for the brave and ambitious. It was a vast land, with prairies and and forests so great that it would take weeks for the settlers to cross just one grassland. He listened with awe as he heard stories of the hardships and triumphs of his hardy kinsmen. There were fields so rich, he was told, that potatoes grew nearly as large as a man's head. Wheat grew so tall that a man could scarcely see over the shimmering stems.

And there were the hardships that only the bravest and strongest could endure. Winters were so fierce that the snow piled high over the sod huts of the prairie settlers, with a cold so deep that any animal left out, unprotected, was frozen into a frosty statue overnight. There were the stories told by the kin of those who had gone before Peter was born. Tales of the Indian war at a place called New Ulm, a town in Minnesota where many Swedes had settled. His young eyes had grown round as he heard of whole families being murdered, and imagined the scalpless corpses lying bloating in the sun. As he dreamed on, the boy could see the war painted Indians stealthily creeping up on some hapless settler's cabin, then bursting out of the forest with terrible cries, their tomahawks held high to crush the skulls of the unwary Swedes. In his dreams, the settlers were always Swedes, for in his youth, Peter could not imagine the diversity of nationalities in the new land.

Peter's obsession with the new land had become a trial for his parents, Hokan and Helen Johannson. His father, a cabinet maker, grew weary of the boy's questions, and despaired of teaching him the wood joiner's trade. When Peter was with his father, he would stop sanding the piece that he was working on, and ask questions.

"Father, is the president of the United States a Swede?"

"I don't think so, go about your work."

Peter would continue smoothing the piece. "Father, why don't we go to the United States?"

"Because all our people are here, I can't take your old grandmother, and we can't leave her. Besides, my business is here, and all our friends are here. We are Swedes, and this is where we belong."

"The Larsons went."

"Yes, but Gunnar was a poor laborer, he had nothing and his people were mostly gone already, and his parents are buried."

"I think that when I am grown, I will go."

"You may as well, you will never be a cabinet maker. Your brother is only two years older than you, and already he can make a table nearly as well as I."

His brother Johann joined the conversation. "Peter, you will never go, all you do is dream about it. If you learned how to do something, you could have a good life here, like father."

"But, I don't want to make cabinets, I want to have my own farm, with lots of cattle, and horses, and a fine house."

Johann laughed. "You dream. With what will you buy this land, and this fine house? You don't even have money for passage to the new land."

Peter looked at his brother, his young eyes flashing. "I will get the money, and I will go! In America they give the land away—here there is nothing for a poor man."

Hokan chided his elder son, "Johann, your brother is different than you or I, he has the wanderlust like your cousin Sven, who just left for the new land. I think that Peter will some day follow him, as much as I want him here with us, if he must go, he will go."

"Just the same, I think he is foolish to want to go so far away," Johann said. "I will stay here with you and Mama and the girls."

"I am thankful for that, Johann. I think that others may go too, and I need someone to care for your mother and I when we are old. Already, your older sister, Ingrid, talks of marrying. A man cannot depend on his daughters. They fall in love with a young man and they think of nothing else."

Later that evening, after the family had eaten, Peter approached his mother. "Mother, will you hate me if I leave you and father when I am grown, and go to America?"

His mother put her arm around him and drew him to her chair, where she sat knitting. "No Peter. I know that your dreams are of America. And if you must go when you are grown, I will still love you. A mother always loves her children, wherever they are." She looked at Peter, and her eyes misted, for he was her favorite child, and the thought of losing him was almost more than she could bear.

From that day on he planned of how he would go to the new land, and when letters from his cousin, Sven Thorson, were shared, Peter read and reread every word. He dreamed of Minnesota, where Sven worked for farmers who had gone to that country years ago, and were now growing rich on the new land's bounty.

When Peter was a gangly youth of fifteen, he went to work in the pine forest of Smaland south of Huskvarna. There he learned the logger's art. At first he served the lumberjacks, carrying tools and water, fixing ropes and chains, and caring for the sturdy oxen used to skid the timbers to the small rivers that served as a highway to the mills. Later, as his muscles grew and hardened, he began to work with the double edged axes and long, two man saws used to fell the pine and spruce trees. Peter gloried in the work in the forest, where the air was clear and crisp. It was so much different from the dusty atmosphere of his father's wood shop. Working with the hardy timber men, he developed the discipline and self reliance he lacked as a boy. Then too, his attitudes changed, and the dreams he indulged in as a boy developed into plans backed up with a fierce determination. He no longer wished he could go to America, he knew he would go, and soon. With that in mind, he saved almost every krona he earned, depriving himself of the trips to the nearby towns that most of the young loggers indulged in. Instead, he occasionally went to visit his parents, enjoying his mother's food, and long games of chess with his father and brother.

Young Peter was a handsome youth. He was lean and muscular, with dark kinky hair, a handsome face and brown eyes that twinkled with humor. It was only natural then, that the sixteen year old youth would meet a girl on one of his infrequent visits to the nearby towns.

Julia, the youngest daughter of Emil Thorgeson, a successful blacksmith, was a beauty. The moment he saw the blond, blue eyed girl, Peter was stricken with infatuation. From that moment on, his trips to his parents' home became less frequent. Every hour he could get away from the logging camp, he spent at Julia's home. He was well accepted, despite the fact he was more than a year younger than Julia. The girl was flattered by Peter's ardent attention, even though she was much sought after by local young men superior in age and resources to him. The couple spent many hours talking and walking the village streets on Sunday afternoons, and Peter even went to the Lutheran church with Julia and her family.

At this time, he said nothing to Julia about his plans, fearing that he would discourage the home loving girl's affection. Instead, he continued to save his money, until at his seventeenth birthday Peter had enough money for a ticket on an immigrant ship to New York, and a small sum to see him to Minnesota.

One evening, Peter was sitting in the parlor of her parents' house with Julia. Her parents had gone to the neighbors' in order to leave the couple to themselves for a short time. Peter put his arms around Julia and kissed the unresisting girl. Her lips were warm and passionate, and Peter was filled with a storm of enthusiasm for the life he saw in the future. He drew back from Julia ever so slightly, his face radiating the passion of his vision.

"Julia, I must tell you something, something wonderful!"

The girl looked at him, a smile on her face. "And what do you have to tell me, my lumberjack. You look like someone has just given you a thousand kronor."

"We are going to America, you and me."

The smile froze on her face. "What do you mean, Peter? You have never talked of going to America."

"I know, I wanted to keep it a surprise! I have saved money, I will go and get a job. Then I will send for you and we will have a life in a new land."

"But Peter, I don't know if I would want to go to America."

"Why wouldn't you? We can have a wonderful life there. It is a new country, and I can become rich if I work hard. I can give you everything you want in America!"

"All I want is a home and children—you can give me that here. In America my children would never see their grandparents."

Peter waved the thought away. "When I am rich, you can come home to visit, and bring our children. I will come too."

Julia was uncertain about what to do, she loved Peter, but she had always thought of the two of them in a little house near her parents.

"Peter,do you love me?"

"Of course I love you, Julia. How could you ever doubt it?"

"If we love each other, is it so important where we go? Can't we just stay here?"

"It is important Julia, I have dreamed of America ever since I was a small child."

"But why? It is so far away!"

"Because there I can be somebody. There I can be more than a lumberjack. There I can have a big farm with fat cattle, and a fine house. We will be rich!"

The gleam in his eyes told Julia that trying to dissuade him would be useless. She wished that her mother were here to tell her what to do.

Peter continued, his enthusiasm undiminished. "We can get married before I leave. That way your mother and father and my mother and father can be at the wedding and give us their blessings."

The poor girl was in shock—this wasn't at all the way she had imagined her wedding. "But Peter, you haven't even proposed, I need to think about all this."

For the first time, he hesitated. "But, don't you love me, Julia? What is there to think about? We can be married, and I will send for you as soon as I have the money."

"If we were married, and something happened to you, I might never know. I love you, but I must think about it."

Nothing he could say would persuade Julia to say yes, so Peter said he must go back to the logging camp. He kissed Julia good night, and started the long walk back, not really knowing whether her kiss had been less passionate, or whether he was simply tired.

Julia went to bed disturbed, and try as she would, she could not take her mind off the terrible black ocean, and the land so far beyond it. She resolved to talk to her mother in the morning. It was, she thought, too soon for a wedding. If Peter would only stay another year, so they could do it right!

In the end, Julia's mother convinced her to wait and see what success Peter would have in the new land before marrying him.

"After all," she said, "he is still a boy. You are a full year older than he. You should marry a man who is steady and established in a trade or business. I worry that he will not be able to care for a family, and in America, who would help you?"

Julia loved Peter, but she was not an adventurous girl. The thought of leaving all of her loved ones was terrifying to her. She told Peter when she next saw him, that she must think about it before making such an irreversible decision.

"Go to America if you must, but I will not come until you have a home for me," she said.

So, Peter got his papers for immigration, bought his ticket for the passage, and prepared to depart for America alone. On the day of his departure, Julia and her parents and Peter's entire family saw him aboard the ship at the dock in Goteborg. It was a tearful parting. All of Peter's sisters were weeping pitifully, and his mother held him so tightly that he was tempted to stay for her sake. His father, and Julia's father shook hands gruffly, saying their goodbyes hastily as men do. They tried not to betray their emotion, but looked all the more pitiful for the lack of it.

Johann was more direct, he held his brother close, and asked, "Will I ever see you again, little brother?" Whereupon tears flowed down the faces of both of them, and Peter had to blow his nose before he could answer.

"Yes brother, you will."

Julia's mother hugged him, then looked into his eyes and said, "Be careful Peter, and come back to us all."

"Julia, my love," Peter said as he embraced the sobbing girl, "write to me. I will send for you soon. I love you so, you will be on my mind every minute."

"Oh Peter, don't go! We can be happy here!" she said, crying as though she would never see him again.

Peter pushed her gently away and walked quickly up the gangplank as the steam whistle blew its last warning. As the tugs moved the ship out into the channel he looked at his mother and father for the last time, as they waved their tear wet handkerchiefs at him. Peter waved his cap in return, and suddenly he felt an aching aloneness and his first fear of the unknown.

Now that he was here in Minneapolis, Peter pushed these memories into the back of his mind. He walked farther down the street and saw a sign that displayed a painted rifle. He couldn't read the English—it had been all he could do to learn a little of the speech in the two years that he had been preparing to come—but he assumed it was a gunshop.

A man in a white shirt and tie stood behind a counter loaded with guns of every description. Peter said, "Sir, I need a gun, a 38 I think."

"You do, huh? What do ya need it for?"

"I'm going up to a logging camp, I need it for protection."

The man chuckled. "I reckon ya do all right. Know how to use one?"

Peter shook his head.

"Hm…m, I guess I can show you the basics. Ya want a pocket pistol?"

Peter nodded, not having the slightest idea what one looked like.

Not much of a talker, are ya? How much ya wanna spend?"

"Can I get one for three dollars?"

Hm—m, not much of one, I've got a nice one for four an a half. Ya wanna see it?"

Peter started to nod his head, but stopped and answered. "Yes sir, I would."

The man turned to the case behind him and picked out a revolver. "This is a five shot Bulldog, a guy traded it on a rifle. It's nickel plated, and it's got a folding hammer so it won't get caught in your pocket, …see."

"How do you put the bullets in it?"

"Ya see this little door on the side? Ya flip it aside and ya put them in like this." The man deftly slipped five bullets into the cylinder. "Ya wanna try it out?"

Peter looked at him hesitantly.

"Ya don't have to buy it if ya don't like it. C'mon with me." He turned and walked into a storage room. "Ya see those bags of sand?"

Peter nodded, "Yes?"

"Ya hold the gun like this, with both hands. Then ya pull the hammer back, and aim over the top of the barrel at that block of wood on the center bag. Hold your breath, and when the sights line up squeeze the trigger like this." The gun made a sharp report and the block of wood split into two pieces. "Now ya try it." The man put up a new block of wood, and offered the revolver to Peter.

Bravely, he took the gun in both hands as the man had shown him, aimed the gun at the block and pulled the hammer back.

"Wait!" the man shouted, as he grasped Peter's arm. "Ya always keep your eyes open, ya could shoot somebody that way!"

Sheepishly Peter raised the revolver again, this time taking care to keep his eyes open as he squeezed the trigger. The little gun bucked in his hand, and a little stream of sand trickled from the bag about a foot over the block of wood. "It is very nice," he said, grinning with pleasure.

The man shrugged. "Ya'll get onto it—just need a little practice. Ya want the gun?"

"I want it very much," Peter grinned.

"Four fifty, and bullets are twenty five cents a box. Ya need practice, better take about four boxes. That'll be five dollars and fifty cents."

He gave the man the money, and proudly placed the revolver in his inside coat pocket. "Now I'm safe," he said.

"If anybody else is," the man said dryly, as he waved Peter out the door.

Peter walked back up the street toward the depot. He stopped at a store long enough to buy some bread and cheese to eat that day, and on the way to Remer on the following day. Then he wandered the streets and roads as far as he dared go, for fear of getting lost, until the autumn sun was low in the west. He returned to the warmth of the depot with his confidence renewed, and a comforting lump in his coat pocket.

A different ticket clerk was on duty when he returned, a young man near Peter's age. Peter quickly struck up a conversation with him, whiling away the hours by learning as much as possible about his new country.

Later in the evening, he took a tablet and pencil from his suitcase and began to write in Swedish:

My very dearest Julia,

I have come at last to Minneapolis, Minnesota, and I am very near my destination. After all these many miles, I feel like I should be arriving home instead of these thousands of miles from it. Already I miss you terribly. I wish I could hold you close this minute as I sit in the train depot writing to you.

If I didn't have this dream, if I didn't know that we can build a wonderful life here in this country, I could never have left you. Knowing that you love me, and the thought that you will be with me again soon, drives me on. I will succeed, I will make the life I have dreamed of for us.

The weather here is much like home. Though I am further south, it seems that the air is a little sharper, but otherwise it is much the same. It may be that the cold is a little dryer, because Minnesota is so far inland. There is no humid breeze from the ocean as we have in Sweden. This morning we had a little snow, just enough to hang on the branches of the trees, so that the entire landscape was coated in white. Minneapolis was so much like Huskvarna that I felt homesick. The difference though, is that the city is so much newer. There are no grand old buildings here, everything is new. And while there are some very nice new houses and stores, much of the city is built of rough boards and logs.

I walked many miles today, as far as a great river that is called the Mississippi. It is nearly as wide as the Kalmarsund strait, and certainly as large as several of our rivers in Sweden put together. It had some large barges on it that were loading at what I was told are flour mills and wheat shipping buildings. I also saw a great saw mill, with logs still floating in the river almost as far as I could see. There were great strings of railroad cars loading with lumber, and also great barges in the river doing the same. The river, the ticket clerk told me, starts in the north where I am going, and runs all the way south through the nation to the ocean. It must surely be the biggest river in the world when it reaches the ocean, more than a thousand miles south. Even here, a strong man cannot throw a stone across it.

Many of the names here are taken from the Indians who were in the land when the white men came. Mississippi means 'Father of Waters', Minneapolis means 'City of Falling Water', and Minnesota means 'Cloudy Water'. What a grand country! It is like a newborn calf now, still wobbling about on its young legs. But one day soon it will be a strong bull, challenging everyone with its power. And when that day comes, Julia, we will share in the wealth of this new country. We will be rich, and we shall go home to Sweden to visit, dressed in fine furs and jewelry. You will be very proud of me for doing what I do now.

I almost forgot to tell you that I have bought a gun for my protection in the wilds. It is a revolver that I can carry in my pocket, so that if the need for one arises, I will always have it with me. I tell you this, so you will know that I am always safe.

Now I will have the ticket clerk help me post this letter. I am tired, and I must rise early to ride the train to the timber lands. I love you much, and I miss you greatly.

Your Peter Olaf

In the morning, Peter was awake long before it was light. The ticket agent of the previous morning was again on duty, snoring loudly as he lay back in his chair, with his feet on some boxes of freight. Peter tore a piece of bread from one of the loaves he had purchased, and took out the pocket knife that Julia had given him, to cut a slice of cheese. He looked about as he munched the food.

Another young man had arrived during the night, and lay sleeping on the bench behind him. He was dressed in a heavy Mackinaw coat and wool trousers with the tops tucked into high lace boots. His blond hair stuck out from a knit cap with a long top and a tassel on the tip. His sparse beard was about an inch long and formed a fringe around his square jaw. Peter thought that he too must be heading for the logging camps. Presently, Peter heard the sound of a steam whistle rip through the silence. The ticket clerk started, then opened his eyes sleepily. He stretched and got to his feet.

"Morning young fellow, ready to start your adventure? Want to wake the other kid? He's going with you."

Peter returned the greeting, then reached over the bench to shake the young man sleeping there. To Peter's astonishment, the young man grabbed Peter's arm and jumped to his feet with his other hand pulled back in a fist, ready to strike. He stood there for a moment, as he gathered his wits, then let go of Peter's arm.

"I'm sorry," he said sheepishly, "I thought you were trying to rob me. My name is Gustav, are you Swede?"

"Yes, I am from Huskvarna," Peter said. "My name is Peter Olaf." He stuck out his hand, overjoyed at meeting a countryman.

"Good," the stocky young Swede grinned, "let's get on the train, then we shall talk."

As the locomotive began its rhythmic chuffing, and the train began crawling away from the station, Gustav turned to Peter. "Then, are you just in from the old country?"

Peter blinked at the strong odor of whiskey the other exhaled. "Yes, I'm going to Remer to find my cousin. And you?"

"I've been here for more than a year already. I just took a holiday from the camp. You say you're going to Remer? I work up there, what is your cousin's name?"

"Sven Thorson, he has been up there for a long time."

"You say, Sven Thorson!," Gustav shouted, "he is my foreman! We will go to him together." He slapped Peter's back in high glee.

"In truth you know him? I had worried that I might not find him, they tell me that it is a great forest."

"Millions of acres, and few roads, it would be difficult for a greenhorn."

"What does "greenhorn" mean?"

"Just someone who is new to the country and its ways. They will call you a greenhorn, they did me."

"But Gustav, are there jobs in the camps?"

"It depends if you know how to do anything. Logging has just started, there are jobs."

"I know how to fall trees, I did it in Sweden."

"Then you will have no problem. When I first came I had to clean the bunkhouse and help the cook. Then when another greenhorn came, they made him do it, and I got to go out with the timber crews."

"I bet your hands got sore, I know mine did when I first started swinging an axe."

Gustav grinned. "My hands, my arms and my back. I had blisters so big I could hardly make a fist. The other loggers laughed at me a lot, until the next greenhorn came along."

"Are there many Swedes at the camps? The ticket clerk thought there were."

"A lot, and some Norwegians and a few Finns. But there are French, Germans, Poles, Irish and even a couple of Chinese too."

"Are they hard men? I mean do they fight and steal and things like that?" Peter looked at him anxiously.

"Naw! Most of them are just like you and me, just honest men trying to make a living. It's not easy though, most of them drink and gamble when they can get to town. Most of the things we need we buy at the commissary, that's the company store."

"You mean the logging company has a store?"

"Sure, they all do. We work too hard and long to walk into town very often, so if we need something we buy it from the store. They charge us more than it's worth, but what can we do?"

"Do you make much money logging? Sven said he saved almost a thousand dollars since he came."

Gustav snorted and grinned. "Sven maybe saved that much, but most of it is from teaching greenhorns how to play cards. Sven is a good one at that, all right. That's how he got his scar."

"What scar? Sven wrote nothing of a scar."

"I don't expect he would—he was playing cards with a couple of greenhorns, only Sven didn't know this one kid worked in a hotel in Chicago. Anyway, this skinny kid knew how to play cards, and Sven, he got a little careless dealing. The kid caught him taking cards off the bottom of the deck, and accused him of cheating. Well, you know how big and husky Sven is, he picked the kid up by the front of his shirt, and threw him across the bunkhouse so he skidded up against the stove. Then he went to picking up the money from the table. Next thing he knew, the kid was coming at him with the big old poker from the stove. Nailed Sven right across his forehead, he went down like a pig hit with an axe. He didn't come to until the next morning, and then he wasn't much good for about a week."

Peter was laughing now. "But what became of the kid, Sven would kill him for that, I think."

"The boss gave him ten dollars because he was a good worker, and told him to go to another outfit. Even so, Sven still watches for him every time he gets to town. Mostly he's mad cause the little runt put him down, and everybody kids him about it. The tougher guys will shake the poker at him and laugh whenever they tend the fire."

"I'm glad you told me, otherwise I would have asked him about it."

"You'll have to anyway, Peter. Otherwise he'll know I told you about it, and he'll be mad at me. If you ask, he can lie if he wants to."

Peter shook his head, "Sven never lies."

"I suppose not, and he doesn't fight, or cheat at cards, or drink, or go to loose women neither. And I suppose he leads at prayers every Sunday, and gives a tenth of his wages to charity too." Gustav pulled out some plug tobacco and chewed off a chunk. "Fact is, your cousin is a might different than he was in the old country, I expect."

"In Sweden, Sven always went to church on a Sunday… me too."

"Well, you might as well forget about that, unless you like real long walks in the cold. Once in a while a preacher will stop by—nobody much listens to them though."

"Doesn't anybody up here believe in God?"

"It isn't that, they just don't need anybody preaching to them about God. What with guys getting hurt or killed by 'widow makers' and runaway logs, or drowning in the river, we're all plenty close to Him all the time."

"I suppose so, but what's this 'widow maker'?"

"A tree or a big branch that hangs up on another tree. They can fall at any time, guys get dead when they do."

Peter nodded his head. "I have heard of that happening up at Smaland in Sweden. Gustav, I hope I can get a job that pays good, I want to bring my girlfriend over soon. How much does an axman make?"

"Depends on how good he is, if you're real good, ask the boss if he'll wait until after your first week before he sets your wage. Axmen make thirty to thirty five dollars a month generally. They'll give you thirty the first year and thirty five the second, but if you're real good, he might give you thirty five the first year."

Peter was silent, thinking about how much he could make in his first season. "How long will they log?"

Gustav shifted his chew. "Depends on the weather, maybe till the end of March."

Peter was dismayed. "But that is only five months from now, I can't earn enough to bring Julia here in that time."

"Not if you quit at the end of cutting, ever ride the logs?"

Peter shook his head.

"You can get an extra couple of months if you go down river with the logs. I do, but it's dangerous as hell, especially at first."

"I don't care, I will do it if they'll let me."

"No trouble there, not too many guys like being river pigs, it's cold and wet, and the hours are awful long."

"Gustav."

"Yeah?"

"Do you have a girl?"

"Used to."

"Why, 'used to'?"

"Had a girl back home, just like you. After about a year, she married one of my friends that stayed in Sweden. Said she couldn't wait til I had the money to bring her. Now I think I'll sleep a little, I've got a fearsome headache from the cheap whiskey I drank last night."

"But why do you drink it, if it makes you feel bad?"

"Peter, after you're around the camps a while you'll understand that good enough." Gustav pulled the collar of his Mackinaw up around his ears and soon was snoring softly.

Peter watched out the window as the train passed the scattering of farms that thinned out gradually, until the landscape became an almost continuous wall of trees and brush. Then he fell asleep, and dreamed of Julia in her wedding dress, standing next to his best friend.

The train braked to a stop amid clouds of steam and a clattering of couplers. The conductor shook Gustav and Peter awake.

"Grand Rapids boys, time to pick it up and move it," he said in a heavy Irish brogue. "Good luck now, and may the saints walk with you."

They stretched themselves awake and picked their gear from the rack, then stepped out into the crispness of a November afternoon in northern Minnesota. With the many stops on the route, most of the shortening day had already slipped away. The sun was sinking low on the horizon, and they must go another twelve miles to the camp.

"By damn, I wish we had a team," Gustav complained. "Let's go over to the stores and see if the tote wagon might still be in town."

They walked down the street, muddy yet from the melted snow that had fallen the previous day.

"Winter is in the air, by damn," Gustav said, as he looked at the murky clouds beginning to move in from the northwest. "We best get to the camp fast, or we're going to freeze our asses off."

A quick check of the business section of the little town revealed no tote wagon from the logging camp.

"By golly," Peter said, "it looks like we've got a long walk ahead of us."

"It's not the walk I mind so much, it's the damned wolves," Gustav said. "They're not very hungry yet this early in the winter. But they still make me nervous, always following behind a body in the dark. And I ain't got a gun either."

Peter's eyes grew round with fright. "I've got a gun, Gustav," he said, and drew the little 38 from his jacket pocket.

Gustav looked at the revolver with contempt. "That ain't no gun, it's a damned toy. Those wolves would have us et before you could stop them with that. Besides it's gonna be too dark to shoot with them clouds rolling in."

"C—can't we stay here tonight, and go out in the morning?"

"Could, but I ain't got no money left for a room an something to eat," Gustav said, eyeing Peter speculatively. "If I did, I'd sure enough stay in town tonight."

"I've still got some money," Peter said. "I'll pay for you if you'll help me get a job tomorrow."

Gustav had already decided to help his new friend do just that. "Okay, you've got a deal."

The new hotel at Grand Rapids was plain, but it was clean, and had good food, reasonably priced. After dinner the two young men went to their room and stretched out on the double bed.

"By Golly, this is the first decent bed I've had under my back since I left Sweden." Peter luxuriated on the new mattress.

"Better enjoy it, it'll be spruce branches and lice from now on."

"Lice?"

"Yeah, those little bugs that get in your clothes and itch like hell. Every logging camp has them. Didn't you have them in Sweden?"

"Maybe, but not where I was, everybody washed, and the bunkhouse had a woman who took care of it. Everything was very clean."

"Well, it won't be that way now. The bunkhouse reeks, nobody ever takes a bath less'n they fall in the river. Anyway, this is the last soft bed we'll see for a long time. I think we should go to sleep and get up and start walking real early. No telling what the weather will do with them clouds coming in from the northwest like that."

They slept like little children that night, but long before light, Gustav, who was accustomed to rising before dawn, woke Peter.

"Peter, wake up, we must leave for the camp. It has snowed, and the wind is starting to blow. Put on your warmest clothing."

When they reached the street, they found that six inches of snow had fallen, and more was coming, driven by a light northwest wind.

Gustav looked worried. "I hope that wind dies down when the sun comes up, we gotta walk about twelve miles to the camp."

The two young men started walking, first across a crude bridge across the Mississippi River, then to the north around the tip of Lake Pokegama and then southwest into the the rich pine forest. The logging company tote road meandered around ponds and swampy spots, going ever deeper into the virgin stands of white and red pine. Walking was hard. The snow was slush at the bottom that slipped under each step, while the increasing depth dragged at their feet, making them step ever higher. The wind was broken here by the massive trees, but the snow drifted down from above heavily, obliterating everything but the closest trees from sight. They walked for several hours, trusting to the stand of timber on either side of the roadway to keep them on the narrow trail. Finally, they came to an area where there was no more timber at the sides of the road, only great stumps and tree tops laying in the snow. Here the wind attacked in pulsing gusts, driving the snow before it in a blinding fury of white.

Gustav stopped and faced Peter, his beard and mustache were caked with snow and he looked like a piece of sculpture Peter had once seen in a museum in Stockholm.

"I have lost the road in these cuttings. We will never find it again in this blizzard, it is what I had feared."

"Are we lost, then?" Peter asked.

Gustav nodded soberly. "We will never find the camp by just walking in what we think is the right direction. We will walk in circles, and when the storm is over someone will find us frozen in the snow."

"Then what can we do, shall we try to make a shelter?"

"I think not, we have no axe to cut branches, and we have nothing with which to make a fire. We would just grow tired, and eventually we would freeze. Don't you feel that the wind grows colder?"

"Yes, my hands and face feel numb."

"That is the first warning, soon you will no longer feel them, soon after that, you will be dead. We must find the camp, it is not much more than a mile away."

"But how, if we will walk in circles? We have no compass."

"No Peter, we have no compass, but we have the wind. It blows from the northwest, the river is there. The camp is on the river. Follow me close, we will walk into the wind. Wrap something over your face so you do not freeze it."

Peter took a big bandanna from his suitcase and tied it over his face.

Gustav laughed. "You look like a robber, but there is nothing for you to rob, except snow and pine stumps. Come, let's find the river."

They struggled through the snow that was building up in drifts behind the tree tops and stumps. Now and again one or the other would hook a foot in some branch hidden beneath the snow and fall headlong, then come up swearing at the snow, the wind and the cold.

"By damn, this is one son of a bitch." Peter sputtered in exasperation, after picking himself up out of a snowbank.

"What, have you lost your "by golly" already? I think we may make a lumberjack out of you," Gustav laughed. "Listen, do you here that?"

Peter strained to hear above the whistling of the wind. "I hear nothing but the wind."

"You are a tenderfoot. Can't you hear the water? It is the river."

The gurgling of the river along its banks cheered the two as they struggled through the drifted snow. They now would become close friends, welded together by their first joint battle with the elements. They fought through the hardening banks of snow with renewed enthusiasm. After what seemed like hours, Peter slapped his friend on the shoulder.

"Did you hear that?"

"What?"

"Listen, you tenderfoot!" The sound came again, a warbling ring.

"It is the cooks bell!," Gustav howled. "We are home!"

They ran then, stumbling through the storm in the direction of the sound, until a great, low, log building emerged from the curtains of blowing snow.

A bearded figure in a mackinaw jacket was vigorously beating on a triangle of steel. Peter took one look and ran to embrace the burly young man. Slapping him about the back and shoulders as though he meant to break his very bones.

"Sven! Sven! It is me, your cousin Peter!"

Peter Olaf's long journey had ended.

Chapter 2

Christian's Logging Camp

Elias Oberg was twenty-four and the son of an affluent banker. At this moment, he was sitting in the Lutheran church just behind Julia Thorgeson and her parents. Though Elias's father was Jewish, his mother was a Swede, and Elias had grown up in the ways of his mother's people. How like an angel she is, he thought as he watched Julia sing from the hymnal. For a while she had been coming to church with a curly headed bumpkin, but now she was alone. Elias knew her father, Emil Thorgeson, quite well, since he had seen to a small loan the blacksmith had needed. Emil seemed to like him, and Elias had done well for him, saving him a few kronor by giving him a slightly lower interest rate than other bankers had offered. Elias resolved he would meet the girl.

As the Thorgeson's chatted with friends on the steps of the church, a tall, blond, young man approached them.

He extended his hand and shook Emil's as though he were a long lost friend.

"Emil Thorgeson, how are you?! I haven't seen you at the bank for some time."

Emil smiled his recognition, and was bound to make introductions.

"Elias, it is good to see you. I have not needed money of late, but I am undertaking a considerable project for a logging company, I may be in to see you soon. May I introduce you to my wife, Christine, and my daughter, Julia? Elias Oberg is the young banker that gave me such a favorable loan."

Christine smiled warmly, as she extended her hand to the handsome, and notably affluent young man.

"Oh, how very nice to meet you, Elias. Are your parents in church today?"

"No, they went to Stockholm for a fortnight—a bit of a holiday."

"Then are you all alone, or do you have someone to keep you company?"

"Only the servants, I'm afraid, and this Sunday is a holiday for them, so I must make do as I can."

Christine pursued the situation like a hound on the scent of a hare.

"You poor man, men should not have to do for themselves for a Sunday's dinner. We have a fine roast waiting for us, do join us. Julia and I insist, don't we Julia?"

The girl was surprised and a little embarrassed by her mother's sudden invitation. But she had noticed the handsome young man before, and a little company on a Sunday afternoon could do no harm. Besides, Peter had been gone for almost a month, and she was lonely.

Julia smiled demurely. "Please do come, Mister Oberg, Mother is the best cook in the neighborhood, and it would be so nice to have company."

Elias bowed slightly to Julia. "I am very pleased to accept your invitation, Miss Thorgeson. Perhaps you would guide me, as I do not know the way to your home." He offered Julia his arm, and led her down the pathway to the hitching yard, where his milk white horse and shiny black carriage waited.

Christine Thorgeson watched as they walked away.

"They make such a nice couple," she said.

Her husband nodded and smiled.

Dinner at the Thorgeson's had never been more splendid. Christine put out her best china and silver—the pieces that she usually reserved for the holidays. And she lavished Elias with attention, urging him to have another slice of the roast or a little more pudding, and yet another cup of tea, until the young man swore that if he ate another bite he would have to be carried from the table. He joined with Emil in animated conversation on the art of blacksmithing, and asked whether he might bring his horse to be shod.

"It is so difficult to find a smith who knows the proper way to fit a shoe," he said to Julia. "Your father is truly an expert in his trade."

If at times Emil or his wife had to repeat a statement or question directed to Elias, they did not mind, for they saw that the cause of his inattention was their daughter seated across the table from him. It seemed that he saw a great deal more than they did in her blue eyes, for that was where his attention was directed. Near the end of the meal, Elias cleared his throat nervously and spoke to Julia.

"Miss Thorgeson, on Friday next, my parents and a few friends are having a little party at our home. There will be a few young people there, and I wondered if you might do me the honor of attending? With your parents permission, of course."

Julia looked at him with a sparkle in her eyes, then quickly turned them down to her hands, which she began clasping nervously. "I would like that very much, but Peter is..."

"Peter wants you to have a little fun, Julia." Her mother quickly interjected. "I'm sure he doesn't expect you to sit here like an old woman while he runs around in America. There can be no harm in being with a few young people like yourself."

Julia was hesitant, she loved Peter, and she didn't want to do anything that would be unfaithful to him. "Daddy?"

Emil looked at his daughter, the father's love showing in his eyes. "My little angel, God meant for the young to be happy. Go and have a little fun. It makes me sad to see you sitting by your window all alone. Peter can't fault you for continuing to live while he is gone."

Julia looked up at the blond young man in front of her. "I would like to meet your family, but you must understand that we can only be friends."

When Elias left later that day, there was a noticeable spring in his step that had not been there before.

In Minnesota, Peter had just awakened from a sleep in which he had walked through an endless land of stumps and swirling snow, where great gray wolves stalked him, watching expectantly for him to fall exhausted in the drifts. The man in the bunk below him was pulling on his boots.

"Come on Svensk, it's time for breakfast."

Peter dropped to the floor and pulled on his pants and shirt. It had been too hot in the top bunk to sleep in them, as the men in the lower bunks did. The bunkhouse was already almost clear of men, so he didn't have to wait for a place at the long, plank sink, in order to throw some water on his face. He ran to the cook house through great banks of snow, and looked for a place at the long tables where over a hundred men ate daily.

Gustav was already seated between two other men. He hollered at Peter and pointed at a kid who was scurrying around with platters of pancakes and bacon.

"Pete, ask the cookee for a place."

The cookee gave him a plate and a tin cup at an empty spot near the door. "This is your place at every meal, and no talking while you eat."

Since talking was forbidden, Peter dug into the platter of pancakes and helped himself to a liberal supply of bacon and began to eat. He had not seen the boss when he and Gustav arrived in the snowstorm. Rather, he was content to let the big barrel stoves of the bunkhouse drive the chill from his bones, as he renewed his relationship with his cousin, Sven.

Peter, Sven, and Gustav had talked of Sweden and Minnesota until it was time to douse the bull lamp for the night. Then Peter crawled into the upper bunk and fell into an exhausted sleep, even though he had no spruce boughs for a mattress and had to make do with a blanket loaned him by Sven for a pad, and his coat for a pillow.

This morning he would have plenty of time to talk with the boss, since it was Sunday, and the men were not at work. He spooned stewed apricots into his tin bowl and poured canned milk over them. In Smaland, he had not been used to such delicacies, the fare for breakfast had always been great bowls of porridge.

Some things would be better here, some worse, he had already deduced, remembering the heavy air near the ceiling of the bunkhouse. It had smelled of unwashed bodies, wet clothing, pipe smoke and the peculiar odor that a diet heavy on beans lent to human digestive gases. He felt at home though, since this bunkhouse was inhabited primarily by Swedes, Norwegians and Finns. He was told that the Germans, Poles and Slavic men were mostly clumped together in the other bunkhouse. The French Canadians were scattered throughout, they were gregarious, and didn't give a damn who they had for neighbors.

Peter became aware that the rest of the men were no longer eating, but were sitting quietly, picking bits of bacon from their teeth or just observing him. Uncomfortably, he put his spoon down, and wiped his mouth with his sleeve. As though some prearranged signal had been given, the men rose from the table and began filing past him, talking among themselves as they walked through the wide doorway of the cookhouse.

Sven was laughing as he grabbed Peter by the collar of his wool shirt and dragged him along.

"You didn't know they were waiting for you, did you?"

Peter shook his head, looking puzzled.

"It's one of the cook's rules, just like the one about not talking. Nobody leaves until the last man is finished, it prevents dawdling. I think it's because the cook and cookees want everybody to eat and get out, so they can clean everything up for the next meal. Nobody complains though, the cook is a big Frenchie, and hot tempered as hell. Besides, he's a damned good cook, and that's the main thing. Ain't no logging camp worth a damn if the cook ain't good. Now, if'n you're ready, we'll go talk to the boss. Here comes Gus, reckon he might like to go along, he's always ready to shine up to the boss a bit."

Peter was just a little scared—in Sweden the boss was almost a deity, one saw him, but rarely spoke to him without a purpose. "What kind of a man is the boss? What should I say to him?"

"He's a big Norwegian by the name of Christian Halvorsen," Sven said. "Stands maybe six foot and a couple of inches, he's a lean, wiry kind of guy. He moves like a cat, some say he's part Indian, but that ain't true. More likely, he got to move that way from ridin logs down the rivers."

"But damn, the guy can fight—course he couldn't be boss if'n he couldn't," Gustav said. "But I seen him kick a guy a couple of inches taller'n him right in the jaw, as he was standing there making out like he was goin to punch Chris. The guy went down like he was hit with an axe, stayed down too. Course Chris was wearing iron caulks on his boots at the time, bein' it was during the log drive. One taste of them caulks is generally all it takes to discourage even a tough guy."

The boss was relaxing in a battered wooden rocker next to the stove in the commissary. It was part of a log complex that included the company office and the boss's room. Christian Halvorsen was a lean, rangy man in his early forties. His short-cut hair was blonde with traces of gray sprinkled through his side burns, which he wore just below mid-ear. He looked up from the account book in his hands, as the men entered.

"Mornin Sven, Gus. What's that you got with you, another of your Svensk orphans?" The man smiled good naturedly, blue eyes twinkling, as he chewed on a short pipe jutting away from his square jaw.

Sven took a bite off a plug of tobacco before answering. "This here is a genuine Swedish trained lumberjack, just like me. And he come here to make money for you."

Christian grinned, he always had liked the blocky, braggy Swede. And he looked forward to their constant Norwegian versus Swede sparring.

"I spose that means I'll have to show him how to take a shit Norwegian style before he can get it right. You damned Swede blockheads always think you know everything, so you fuck everything up until I retrain you."

"Yeah, yeah, I suppose that's why you'd marry a Swede, so you could teach her how to screw," Sven said. "Fact is all the Norwegian women are so ugly, you couldn't do it without puttin a bandanna over your eyes first."

Both men laughed, but Peter was standing there with his eyes wide. In Sweden no one would have talked to the boss so. He was terrified that Sven would get him driven from the camp, much less get him a job.

Christian turned to Gustav. "What're you standing here for, you puny runt? I suppose your going to say that this kid is your long lost brother, and I should hire him too."

Gustav showed no sign of irritation, which puzzled Peter. "Naw, I met him on the train and he says he can swing an axe, so I thought maybe I'd get me a new partner bein' that the German got sluiced." (The man Gustav referred to had been killed by a tree which split and fell wildly, crushing him against a nearby stump.)

"Yeah, too bad about Herman, he was a good sawman." Christian looked at Peter, judging the build of the young man as he would a tree. "What can you do, Kid?"

"I can fall trees fast, and so they go where they should. I can swing an axe or pull a saw all day without getting tired. I can rig chains and cables, and I can drive oxen, skidding logs."

"Well kid, if you can do all that, it looks like I've got me a lumber jack. What's your name?"

"Peter Olaf Hokanson."

"Well Peter, I can put you on with Sven's felling crew. I'll pay you first year axeman wage, being I don't know how good you are. That'd be thirty dollars a month, but if you don't produce you go down the trail."

Peter swallowed hard and gathered all the courage his seventeen years could muster. "Mister Halvorsen, Sir, I am very good....Could you maybe try me out for a week, and if I am good enough, pay me second year wages. That would be thirty-five dollars a month, I think."

Christian looked at the young man before him with astonishment, then he laughed heartily.

"By God, Sven, we've got a Swede with brains here, and I've always said there was no such creature!"

Abruptly he stopped laughing and spoke in his most threatening voice to Peter, who was beginning to wish he hadn't been so brash.

"So you think you should get second year pay, just because you swung an axe on your pissant Swedish trees, do you? Well, I tell you what Kid, I'll do just that if you can perform. But you better be God damned good, or I'll send you down the trail so fast you won't have time to kiss Sven and Gus goodbye."

With that he stood up and shook Peter's hand. "If you need stuff, you better get it now, we charge it against your wages. If you go, the stuff stays."

Peter bought a blanket, some woolen underwear, and the usual personal items, including a pipe. He didn't smoke, but he had seen that most of the loggers did, so he resolved to learn. The thing that most excited him though, was the new double bit axe.

The company supplied axes and saws for those who didn't have their own, but an axe was a very personal thing to a logger, at the same time the tool of his trade and his badge of office. No self respecting axman would use a company axe, his tool must be tailored to his needs. The haft must be just the length and size to fit his hand and swing, and the head must be ground to what he considered the perfect edge.

So, that morning Peter spent some time honing his new axe to a perfect edge, with his new friend Gus turning the grindstone for him. When he was through, he went into the snowy forest and cut some spruce boughs for his mattress. That act settled him in as a resident of the logging camp. Tomorrow he would begin earning Julia's passage to Minnesota.

"It's daylight in the swamp, drop your cocks and grab your socks," the boss of Willow River Camp One of Northwest Timber Company shouted. It was five in the morning, and there definitely was no daylight in the swamp or anyplace else, save beneath the eastern horizon.

Nevertheless, the lumberjacks piled out of their bunks and sat in a long untidy row on the deacon's bench at the base of their bunks, as they laced their tallow greased boots for another day in the snow. Already, the cookees were carrying huge bowls of oatmeal and piles of pancakes to the long tables in the cookhouse, where the teamsters were straggling in for breakfast, having risen earlier to feed and harness their horses.

Peter finished lacing his boots and folded his long, thick, woolen stockings over the tops of them. (This kept twigs and brush from snagging the laces and untying them.) He raced to the cookshack and took his place at the table where he began bolting oatmeal, washed down with honey sweetened tea, and fortified with greasy bacon.

The morning was cold, with the big thermometer on the cookshack reading ten below zero. The first cold front of the winter had followed on the heels of the first snowstorm. The men walked in little groups to the woods, following in the trails of the teams of oxen and horses used to skid the great pine logs from the woods to the haul roads. Sven, Gustav and Peter, along with several other men Peter did not yet know, trudged through the snow far back into the forest. There, Sven's crew had begun felling a stand of white pines that stood well over a hundred feet in height.

"Now you're going to do some real logging, Pete. Drop her," Sven said, pointing to a pine with a butt that was about four feet thick.

Peter walked away from the tree, circling around it to judge where he could best fall the huge log. Satisfied that there were no overhanging branches that might change its direction, he tramped an escape path in the deep snow, then began swinging his axe. He felt an exultation rise within him as the keen edge bit great chips of soft wood from the ancient tree. The fact that this great pine had stood here for centuries did not occur to him. He was a logger, and at last he was doing what he had traveled thousands of miles to do. His young muscles drove the axe with a rapid steady rhythm that brought admiration from Gustav.

"By damn, you keep that up and the boss will kiss your ass, he'll be so happy."

By the time the lunch sleigh came at ten o'clock Peter had notched a second pine. He had stood still only when the sawyers cutting the first great pine called ,"Timber—r—r—r!" and he watched it go crashing to the ground. Now, as he ate his bowl of thick beef stew, he was content. He would one day be a rich man in this new country, and Julia would share it with him.

As the days passed into weeks, Peter worked with a will, and he became a favorite with the men, and with Christian Halvorsen. Peter had not talked to the boss about his wages again, he had not needed to. One day when the boss saw him at the camp, he walked up to Peter and put his hand on the young man's shoulder.

"Sven tells me you do well for a second year man. Your pay will be as I promised.... You know Kid, this is a big company. There is a future for a young man who works hard and uses his brains. Always say what you think, if it'll do some good for the company. And always think before you say something. Work hard, but don't be afraid to grab when an opportunity comes. It's not necessary to be swinging an axe when you're an old coot. Nobody ever made more than a measly living swinging an axe. Learn everything, then make sure the right people know what you can do." He patted Peter on the back and walked away.

Peter never forgot what Christian said, and in later years he often wondered how his life would have been if he had never met Christian Halvorsen.

Soon after he started work, the tote sleigh brought mail from Grand Rapids. Peter waited anxiously as the letters and packages were handed out. He received two, one from his sister, Ingrid, and one from Julia. He stuffed his sister's letter in a pocket, and slit the other envelope open with his sheath knife. In the light of the bull lamp he began reading with happy anticipation.

Dear Peter,

I hope and pray that you are well. I miss you terribly and wish you were here with me. I love you very much, and every day I read the letter you sent from New York. I sometimes cannot believe that you are so far away from me. It makes me a little angry once in a while, that you left me alone in order to go to America, and then I cry. But then, I know that you are doing it to make a life for us, and I forgive you and think of when we will be together again. Still, it is hard not having you here, and I wonder if it wouldn't be better for us to make a life here at home.

Mother and Father send their warmest regards and best wishes to you. They both love you, and miss you at Sunday church and dinner. They both are well, and father's business goes good. He has much work from the lumber company, and he must hire help now and again. Father wishes that you would come to work with him, and some day take over his business, since he has no son of his own. He has made a good deal of money in the past few years, and he thinks of having a young partner so that he will not have to work quite so hard. I know you have your heart set on being a rich farmer in Minnesota, but I beg you to think of me. I love my family and friends here in Sweden, and I do not understand what is to be gained by going off into the wilderness to live alone. Perhaps after you have been there a while, you may decide that you do not like it so well, and may wish to return.

The weather is cold now, as it must be there. The ice in the little pond in the park has frozen and all the children go to skate. I went on Sunday afternoon and it was fun. Some of my friends were there also, and we had a grand time together. Harold Olson skated with me some. He wanted to come to visit me, but I said he could not since I am in love with you. He was very disappointed, and said that if he had such a girl as me, he would never leave.

I have a Christmas present ready for you and I will send it this week, so that it may get to you by Christmas. I made it myself, so you will know that it brings much love to you. This year, we will have Christmas with my aunt and uncle and cousins in Goteborg. There will be good fun, since there are six children, and they are all within a few years of my age.

I pray for you every day, that God will protect you and bring you back to me.

I love you.

Julia

Peter read and reread Julia's letter. Her reassurance of her love for him was comforting, but her lack of enthusiasm for America disturbed him. He wondered for the first time whether she would be happy here. He folded the letter thoughtfully and put it in his pocket. Almost as an afterthought, he opened his sister's letter and read:

Dear brother Peter,

I very much hope that you are well, and that all goes well with you in Minnesota. We got to read cousin Sven's last letter which came as you were crossing the ocean. In it he said that they were starting logging again, and that he was watching for you day by day. He said that he was sure his company would have a job for you, since they have much more timber to cut than their crew can handle. I hope you have made the trip with no adversity, and that you are happy in your new life.

Father and Johann are very busy now, as they have a contract to do the woodworking for the vicarage at the new church outside Huskvarna. They scarcely sleep, they work so much. The work must be done before Easter, when the new house is to be dedicated. Father says he wishes you were here now, even though he often said you would not make a good wood joiner. It is difficult to find help that can be relied on.

Mother asks that I tell you that you are always in her prayers, and that if she could write well enough, she would write to you herself. Peter, mother has become sad and quiet since you left. You were always her favorite, and I fear that your absence bears too heavily on her. Father has been increasingly kind and attentive to her, but he cannot replace the happiness you brought her. Please do write often to her, for that may ease the pain of missing you, the rest of us try to cheer her, but always she becomes so lonely again.

Wilhelm and I plan to marry in the spring, in May we think. Everything will be fresh and green then, and it is a good time to start a new life. Wilhelm has been promoted to foreman at the tannery, and that gives him a few more kronar every month. Between that and the money I make from my needlework, we will be able to rent a small place for ourselves, and we will not have to live with his parents. That is a relief to me, because though his mother is a good woman, and I like her well enough, she is somewhat overbearing. That would not go well with your stubborn sister.

Johann goes to pubs of a Saturday night as always, and sleeps in church on Sunday. Mother chides him for it, and says he should find a nice girl, though she despairs that he ever will. He is a good craftsman, but I fear he likes liquor and wild girls overmuch. But he is a comfort and great help to father, and that is good.

Your younger sisters give you their greetings, and say to tell you that they miss their brother at the skating pond. They spend most of their free time there since the ice froze. I think it is because there are a number of boys there, and they are getting to that age.

Again I wish you well, we all miss you very much. Please write to us, especially Mother, often.

Your loving sister,

Ingrid

That night Peter was very homesick. He sought out Sven and Gustav and asked them if they might play a few games of cards before bedtime.

Noticing Peter's sad expression, Sven said, "You are lonely for home, my cousin. It always comes with the letters."

Petter nodded dejectedly. "They all miss me, and wish I would return."

"I know, they all want you to know that you are missed and that they care for you, to cheer you up. And so, they make you feel bad that you have left them."

"Have I done the right thing, Sven? Maybe I should have stayed with Father in the wood shop."

"Naw, you would be at each other's throats by now. Your father knows that the two of you could never get along, he has Johann, and that is enough."

"Yeah, I guess so,...but Julia,...I think she doesn't want to come here."

"Peter, that is another matter. A young girl's blood runs hot when she is with her man. But if you are not there for her, her passion cools soon enough."

"You think she no longer loves me?"

"She loves you alright, but you are not there, and others are. Don't worry about it, there is nothing you can do. If you are to be together, you will be."

"But if I had not gone, she would be happy."

"And you would not be," Gustav said, "and that would make you both unhappy. It was that way with me, I had to go, and so I did."

"But you lost your girl."

Gustav nodded. "But it need not be the same with you. You will find out in time."

"Enough of this talk!" Sven said. "I have something that will make it all look better. But you must not breathe a word, I could get fired for having it. Come!" He went to his bunk, with Gustav and Peter close behind him. He crawled into his bunk and removed something from under his blankets and poured into a tin cup. After taking a drink he offered it to Peter. The strong odor of whiskey hit Peter's nose.

"I have never touched liquor."

Sven grinned. "You can't start any younger, and by God, it'll make you feel better." He motioned for Peter to drink.

Peter put the cup to his mouth and took a swallow as Sven had. He coughed hard, but the burning liquid had gone down and was beginning to warm the pit of his stomach.

"How can you drink that stuff?"

"Much practice cousin, it will get easier." He took the cup from Gustav and added to its contents. "Soon you will be a happy man."

"But I don't feel anything, except for a warmness in my stomach."

"That is only because you haven't had enough." Gustav said as he took another drink and passed the cup to Peter.

Since the whiskey had such a little effect on him, Peter took several swallows before passing the cup back to Sven. "It warms the body," he said, "but I don't feel any different." He wondered at the grins on the faces of his friends.

"Let's play cards," Sven said. "You will feel better soon."

They sat down, and soon Peter was feeling a strange giddiness. He talked rapidly and with good humor, laughing loudly at his friends' jokes, and at those he himself made.

"By God," he said, "I feel much better. I don't know what I was so worried about."

Later, after a few more drinks, Sven and Gustav laid Peter in Sven's bunk, not knowing how to get him into his own top bunk. Peter slept peacefully, and in the morning awoke to a severe headache and a peculiar queasiness of his stomach.

Shortly before Christmas, Peter was introduced to the hardness of the logging life. It was very cold, and a strong wind was blowing from the north. As he walked up the logging road, Gustav listened to the snow squeaking beneath his boots.

"The trees are frozen hard now, and the wind is strong," he said. "I don't like it, the pines will split easily."

Sven nodded his concern. "Take care, boys. Make sure you have a good path tramped away from the tree you are falling."

As the morning progressed, the wind increased, blowing in strong gusts that whipped the tops of the great pines like so many wheat stems in a summer breeze. The air was filled with the sharp snapping sound of breaking wood, and occasionally the men would be forced to dodge a branch that came crashing down from the heights.

"We should not be in the woods on such a day," Gustav complained after a branch struck the ground near him. "A coffin never did any man good."

"I know," Sven said, " but we can't go in, the boss would dock our pay."

"It's not Chris that's the fault, it's the greedy owners in Saint Paul," Gustav said. "They care more for their purses than they do for men."

"And why not?" Sven returned with a sarcastic laugh. "There's always more dumb Swedes to take the place of the ones that get sluiced."

"If we must work we've got to be careful, not like those Germans." Peter pointed to a crew a little way down the slope. "They're not notching deep enough, and they don't have trails tramped away from the tree."

"They've got a lazy axeman," Gustav said. "It's easier to saw through six inches of timber than it is to chop it out."

"And easier for the trunk to split off with that shallow notch," Sven said.

He had scarcely spoken, when a loud cracking sound came from the tree the German sawyers were cutting. As the two men jumped away from the tree, the trunk split from the end of their saw cut and off to the notched side of the tree. The huge tree spun crazily in the air and crashed to the ground. The Swedes looked on with horror as the top of the massive pine recoiled from a standing tree and drove the butt skidding and bouncing toward the unfortunate sawyers.

"My God,...it's got him!" Peter shouted as the trunk made a final leap and came to rest on top of one of the men.

The forest suddenly came alive with running men, axes and saws in hand, racing to see whether by some stroke of luck their comrade might still be alive. Sven was the first to reach the scene, followed by Gustav and Peter.

The tree had fallen squarely on top of the man, its three foot thick trunk had driven his head and shoulders deep in the drifted snow. Only his legs protruded, and the muscles contracting in death moved them sickeningly as the three men watched. As other men arrived, the second German sawyer came out of the paralysis that had seized him. He dove down to the body of his partner, digging frantically in the snow with his hands, as if to loose him from the grip of the tree. And all the while he screamed, "Wilhelm! Mein brudder! Wilhelm!"

Two men gently raised the distraught man to his feet and led him off in the direction of the camp.

"They were brothers," Sven said, his voice choking. "Bring the saw."

Gustav and Sven were silent, their faces set in grim masks, as they whipped the eight foot saw through the log. The other men stood quietly in little groups until they were finished. Then they advanced and rolled the severed log off the German's body. When they turned the German over on his back, Peter turned away and bent, retching miserably. The man's face had been crushed and flattened so that it had no resemblance to a human countenance. The little knot of men stood frozen by horror until an older Swede stepped forward.

"We can't let him freeze like that, I once worked for an undertaker," he said. Then he knelt down beside the man and carefully began forming his features back into something like a face.

They laid the German's body on the cook sleigh when it came up to feed the men a few hours later. But no one except the driver accompanied it back to camp. It would never do to stop felling timber because of the death of one man. That afternoon the carpenter made a coffin of pine planks, and the bull cook laid him in it so his brother could take him back to town with the tote sleigh. The company lost a few hours of time because of the accident, but Christian Halvorsen didn't tell his bosses so in his report.

CHAPTER 3

FOREST AND FROSTBITE

Just before Christmas a package for Peter came with the tote sleigh. It was from Julia and Peter opened it eagerly. Inside was a woolen sweater, knit in white and green. The note with it said:

Dearest Peter,

I knit this for you so that you might be covered with the warmth of my love.

Blessed Christmas, I miss you and love you,

Julia.

He was exuberant in his joy. And when he showed the sweater to Sven and Gustav, his pride was great. "I am so happy, that on Christmas I want to celebrate. Can we do something,...just us three?"

"We could go to Grand Rapids," Sven said. "I know some women who might be lonely at Christmas."

"Yeah!," Gustav said. "We could go Christmas Eve and stay until the next afternoon."

Peter looked at them dejectedly. "You know I can't do that. It would be unfaithful to Julia."

"I swear, sometimes you are such a little boy, Peter," Sven said. "Just how in the hell do you think she would ever know?"

"She wouldn't, but I would. My conscience would bother me. Besides, I don't want to lay with one of those hussies, they are just a bunch of old whores."

"The hell you say, mister man of the world. Constance is only eighteen, and as nice a girl as you ever laid eyes on."

"She's still a whore!"

"And you're a Goddamn, louse bitten logger, does that make you better?"

"It's honest."

"And so is she, and the others. If you were a woman and you had to whore or starve to death, I bet you'd be on your back soon enough!"

"Just the same, I can't do it."

Sven and Gustav looked at Peter in exasperation. "Then what would you like us to do? Maybe we should go to church, and invite ourselves to dinner at the Pastor's house," Gustav said. "Or maybe we should borrow one of Freidrich's oxen and make a nativity scene. Sven could be Joseph, and you could be an angel."

"No, you farthead, nothing like that," Peter said, reddening slightly around his ears. "Maybe we could go hunting, there are fat deer, and lots of rabbits. It would be good to have a change on the table too."

Sven turned the idea over in his mind, he had always loved hunting, but in the logging camp there was little time for it.

"Chris has a shotgun and an old rifle, I think he would lend them to us."

"And I know where there are some fat does down by the spruce swamp," Gustav said, his eyes brightening with anticipation. "Some venison and a bunch of snowshoe rabbits would taste awful good. And maybe the bunkhouse wouldn't smell from bean farts for a day or so."

"Then it's settled. I'll ask Chris about his guns, and have the cook pack us some food. He'll be glad for something different to cook. After breakfast on Christmas we go hunting!" Sven had warmed to the idea, and now he took out a cup of 'Old Crow' to celebrate.

On Christmas morning, the three friends ate breakfast with gusto, and soon after, they walked back into the woods. This time Sven and Gustav carried guns instead of axes on their shoulders, while Peter carried some rope and a canvas bag for the rabbits. The day was warm for winter in northern Minnesota, and the sky was overcast with clouds, but not threatening. They walked, joking and laughing, down the skid roads for a few miles, until they reached the spruce swamp.

"We should get a couple of deer before we hunt for rabbits," Gustav said. "Else the deer will run so far into the swamp we won't be able to find them."

Sven directed the hunt, much as he directed the cutting of trees.

" We should split up. Gustav, you go down a way to the south. I will go to the north. And Peter, you wait a while, then walk straight into the swamp. That should send the deer to us. If anybody gets lost, shoot three times. We will fire twice from the logging road, so you can find your way out. But Peter, you don't have a gun to shoot."

Peter smiled proudly, holding up his nickel plated revolver. "I brought this, I thought I might shoot a rabbit or two with it."

Gustav laughed. "If you shoot anything with that pea shooter, I'll eat it, hair, hide and bones. But, after I get my deer, you can use the shotgun and I'll take your revolver for signaling."

Peter sat on a stump and watched his friends walk along the edge of the swamp until they disappeared from view, then he started into the brush that bordered the spruce trees. He had scarcely walked a hundred yards when the road and pine stumps were obscured from view.

The branches of the spruce trees formed thick canopies that in some places were so dense he was forced to turn aside and find an easier route. The stillness was so complete, that he felt as though he been transported to a world far distant from his own world of swearing lumberjacks and crashing trees.

As he walked through the knee deep snow, he wished that he had a pair of snow shoes. But still, the going wasn't all that hard for a young man in the prime of life. The snow in the swamp wasn't drifted, but lay as it fell, soft and loose. He was seeing the tracks of different creatures as he walked. The zig-zag trails of snowshoe rabbits were everywhere. Sometimes they were overlaid with foot prints of a fox or bobcat in search of a meal . Now and then, he would come on a deer trail and follow it for a way, finding relief in walking on the packed snow.

On one of these trails he found a place where three deer had bedded. The snow was packed and melted in dished circles from the body heat of the animals. Peter bent over and touched the surface of one of the depressions. He found that it had not yet frozen. Apparently he had disturbed the deer in their sleep. He began following the trail the deer had taken, it swung south, deeper into the swamp.

In a short while, he heard the dull boom of a shotgun to the south. Excited now, he quickened his pace, running along the trail where it was hard enough. He crunched along with determination where he broke through the packed skin of the trail, each step a major effort. As the trail turned into a field of dried cattails and swamp willows, he came on Gustav. His friend was grinning broadly as he waited for Peter. He had stripped off his coat and rolled up his shirt sleeves. He held his sheath knife in his right hand and was bloodied to both elbows.

"By God, I've got a fine fat doe," He said. "There'll be deer meat on the table tomorrow!"

Peter looked at the animal, lying in the snow, its insides in a bloody heap beside the trail

"By golly, she's a big one alright. Should we drag it out now, or wait for Sven?"

"Let's take it out now. If Sven shoots, we'll hear it, and we'll go back to help him."

They dragged the carcass out to the skid road, a feat which took them hours in the deep snow. When they had finished, they sat down on a pine stump and ate some of beef sandwiches they'd brought along.

"Sven is having bad luck, by God. I thought we would have to pull his deer out by now, but nary a shot from him." Gustav observed.

"He's probably lying in the cattails sleeping," Peter laughed. "He's got a lazy streak in him."

"Well, I guess we'll have to show him how to hunt deer. Let's go in again. This time, you can take the shotgun, and I'll drive them for you. But you better go a little further south to the edge of the pine woods. And we'll have to hurry, there's only about four hours more of good light."

Peter did as he was told, and walked along the edge of the swamp for nearly an hour until he came to a series of hills rising from the swamp. There he swung west, taking a course between the massive pines and the spruce trees of the swamp. Some distance in he approached a dense copse of swamp willows. As he neared the clump, there was the crashing sound of breaking branches, and a huge buck broke into the relative openness of the pines.

Peter reacted immediately, bringing the shotgun to bear on the bounding target, he unleashed a load of buckshot. The deer went down, its legs thrashing in the air. Peter broke open the action of the single shot, and pushed another shell into the chamber. To his dismay, the buck righted himself and scrambled into the pines, though he was dragging one hind leg. Peter cursed himself silently for his incompetence, and dashed into the pines after the wounded animal.

A trail of blood spots in the snow led him on, and he fully expected to come on the buck over the next rise or in the next little willow swamp. So he followed the animal ever deeper into the forest until, at last it staggered up from its resting place behind a fallen pine. Stiffened from its wounds, its power spent from loss of blood, the splendid buck made an easy target.

Peter dropped it with another shot, and ran forward with his knife to sever its jugular artery. The deer had made his last spasmodic kick, and his eyes were dulling when, Peter bent to count the points on the huge rack. "Sixteen points, by golly! The boys will be jealous of this buck all right," he said to himself as he began gutting the deer.

The sun had dropped below the treetops, and large flakes of snow had begun to fall when he had finished. He wished his friends were there, as he tied his rope to the massive antlers and slung the loop around his chest and shoulder. He began to drag the deer, using every bit of his strength to move the weight.

"This will never do, by God! He said after a few hundred feet. "I'd best signal to the boys." With the first tinges of concern, he fired three of his handful of shells.

Gustav and Sven were standing on a hummock in the swamp when they heard the first, far off boom of the shotgun. They had met in the woods and decided to join Peter and shoot a few rabbits before dark, since Sven had not yet seen a deer.

"By God, Pete is onto a deer," Sven said. "But he is far away, if he's killed one we'll be hard pressed to get it out by dark."

"It sounds like he's on the far side of the swamp," Gustav said. "If he goes into the pines he'll lose his way. There are thousands of acres out there."

"Yah, we better trail him in a hurry, we'll never find him otherwise."

The two young men struck off to the south, in the direction they knew Sven must have gone. They reached a small lake in the middle of the swamp and began crossing the expanse of drifted snow on its surface. Despite the lack of brush, the going was harder here, with every step they broke through the hardened crust, sinking to their knees in the powdery snow beneath. They took turns breaking trail, and had reached the far shore when they heard Peter's second shot, it was farther away and sounded muffled. They stopped, looking at each other with concern.

"He's back in the pines ," Sven said. "And look!"

Large flakes of snow had begun to fall. At first they came in a gentle flurry, but within a matter of minutes the air was filled with a thickening mass of white. They hurried into the spruce trees at the edge of the lake, forcing their tired legs into renewed vigor as they pressed through the snow in the direction of the pine forest.

They were nearing the first pines that appeared as a shadowy image in the falling snow, when they heard three muffled booms. The sounds were indistinct, and vague in direction. Sven stopped and fired two shots from the lever action rifle he carried. The sharp crack of the high powered cartridges echoed into the thickening gloom. The two pressed on, their faces now growing grim.

Peter heard the reports of the rifle, the shots were distant, and unclear in the exact direction from which they had come. The falling snow muffled the sounds that echoed through the pines, making them indistinct and confusing. It was growing dark rapidly, the last rays of light obscured by the cloak of snow that now surrounded him.

He dragged the deer to the base of a huge white pine and left it, hurrying off in the direction of the rifle shots. About a half hour later, he stopped and fired his shotgun again. The answering report of Sven's rifle came back even more distant, and to his rear.

"By God, I'm walking in a circle," he muttered to himself. Then he turned around, and began retracing his steps in the dim light.

Sven and Gustav heard the solitary boom of the shotgun and Sven answered it with the rifle before turning to face Gustav.

"He is walking away from us, he is walking in a circle."

"We will never find him in the dark," Gustav said. "We must return to the skid road or we will all be lost. We will fire a shot every little while, so he can follow us."

They turned around and began following their footprints to the lake, pausing to fire the rifle when they reached the spruce trees.

"Look! Our tracks are nearly filled with the new snow," Sven said. "If we cross the lake we won't be able to see anything. We'll lose our direction for sure."

Gustav nodded. "We better follow the spruce trees around to the skid road. It'll be harder for Pete to follow us, but we have no choice."

They walked more slowly now, as they followed the edge of the spruce trees around the swamp. They were tired, and they hoped Peter would somehow catch up with them. Neither of them admitted that they knew he would not.

Somehow Peter was able to follow his trail in the falling snow and gloom of the pine forest. He heard the occasional report of the rifle and knew from its faintness that Sven and Gustav were returning to the skid road.

He was alone, and he suddenly felt the cold wash of fear envelop him. He was lost in the pine woods at night with nothing to guide him except the fading distant report of a rifle. He took stock of his situation. He had a little food, and a tin of matches that every woodsman carried when venturing into the wilderness. If he could get back to the swamp, he could find some cattails and dried brush and make a fire. It would be better to stay by a fire until morning than to freeze to death stumbling around in the snow. He thought that he must be near the deer carcass, and stopped for a moment to rest.

A peculiar sound reached his ears, a growling, snarling sound that caused chills to run along his spine. He peered into the falling snow, but could see nothing. Quietly he crept ahead. The sound became louder, and Peter could make out indistinct shadows moving about near the base of a big pine tree. He stopped walking, suddenly frozen with fright. He felt new fear wash over him like an invisible sheet of ice.The realization came to him that the shadowy forms were timber wolves!

One of the group broke away and trotted up to within a few feet of Peter. It stood there eyeing him curiously, making no movement or sound. Even in the darkness, Peter could feel the animal's pale, yellow eyes staring impassively at him. The rest of the pack stopped tearing at the buck Peter had left at the base of the tree. They began moving silently toward him like sinister, silent shadows. He felt panic grip at his gut, but resisted the impulse to run. He instinctively knew that to run would cause these creatures to chase him, and the result of that would be certain death.

With his shotgun before him, Peter began slowly backing away from the pack. He had passed a small dead pine that had fallen at an angle against a much larger one a little way back, if he could just make it there!

The wolves followed him curiously, their interest in the deer carcass temporarily diverted. Peter saw with horror that the wolves on the outsides of the pack were separating from the main group and moving as though to flank him. Damned wolves would make good generals, he thought grimly. But they're not going to get this Swede without a fight. He aimed the shotgun at the lead wolf on his right and pulled the trigger. The wolf jumped into the air with a surprised yelping sound, then ran a few steps before it fell whimpering in the snow.

The rest of the pack ran away in obvious terror. Peter was able to gain the fallen pine, before the wolves regained sufficient courage to come back and sniff their fallen comrade. He stuck the shotgun through the belt of his coat and began climbing the sloping trunk of the pine. As he reached the safety of the tree's branches, the pack gathered below him and milled around as though they were unsure what course to take. A big male stood up against the tree, and looked at Peter curiously. Then he dropped to all four, and lifted a leg to urinate against the tree trunk.

Peter was tempted to raise the shotgun and drop the insolent creature where he stood. But he had only a few shells left, and he might need them on his walk back to the camp. The walk back to camp, he thought, that won't be until daylight. In the distance he heard the report of Sven's rifle.

"Damn!" he cursed, "damn! damn! damn!"

After a while, the wolves lost interest in him, and began drifting back to the deer carcass. Peter counted the dark shapes in the snow as they left, one, two,...twenty, twenty-one, with the dead one,...twenty-two wolves! What if they'd been really hungry, or if this little tree hadn't been here? he thought. The wolves were tearing at his buck again, growling and complaining to each other. Why not?, he thought, and he got out his last beef sandwich. The food would help keep him warm, if that were possible.

The snow continued to fall heavily for several hours, covering him with a thick layer of white as though he were a statue in the park at Stockholm. The wolves had completed their meal and were resting. Occasionally one would throw its head back and howl, followed by several others, much like a soloist and chorus. The eerie sound raised the hair on Peter's neck. He tried not to think about the trapper in Wisconsin he had heard about, who had supplied the banquet for just such a pack of wolves as this.

Sometime in the middle of the night, the wolves left, and Peter was alone on his frigid perch. He was afraid to come down, but he was more afraid that he would freeze to death in the tree. He had tried to keep his hands warm by pushing them inside his coat, but the necessity of holding on to a branch to keep from falling made this less than effective. Despite the heavy gloves he wore, his little fingers were numb and the pain in the rest of his fingers told of oncoming frostbite. He could no longer feel his feet, and he knew that if he didn't get down and start walking, he would never leave the woods alive. The snow had diminished to a few small flakes fluttering down, and the moon was becoming visible between patches of clouds.

In the distance Peter heard the solitary report of a rifle. "By God," he said aloud,"I'm going to walk in!"

Sven and Gustav had gathered dead pine branches and built a beacon fire at the skid road. Then Sven went back to the camp for help, while Gustav kept the fire going and fired the rifle. It was he that heard the last shotgun discharge, and he wondered why Peter would be shooting in the dark. Perhaps he is injured, and is signaling where he is, he thought. But when no more shots came in the following hours, he feared worse. In time, Gustav saw a flickering torch appear on the skid road, and he ran to meet it. It was Sven, and next to him Christian Halvorsen leading a long column of men carrying lanterns and torches.

"Peter fired his shotgun," Gus told them in a voice that was too loud.

"When?" Christian asked.

"Just after Sven left."

"And not since then?"

"No, just once and then nothing."

Christian's face was serious. "Do you know about where he is?"

"I think west and a little south of here, into the pine woods on the other side of the spruce swamp. We crossed the lake to get close to him, but he must have been another mile or more west."

Christian raised his voice so all could hear. "About fifty of you guys light your torches and spread out south until the end of the spruce swamp. The rest of you spread out to the north, then go through the swamp, holler and listen as you go." To Gustav he said, "here's another box of cartridges, you go right down the middle, and keep on firing that rifle."

Peter was cold through and through. Even the exertion of walking didn't warm him up, he didn't know why, it always had before. He didn't know his body had used up its energy reserves, and now could barely supply enough to keep moving. He wanted to sit down and rest, he was so very tired. But he forced himself step by step toward the insistent sound of the rifle reports. At last he came out of the pines at the edge of the spruce swamp. He lifted one feelingless wooden foot at a time. He had to get through the swamp, and he'd be safe. The spruce branches were endless, he had to sit down to rest. Crack! came the rifle's report, shattering the silence of the forest.

That damned rifle, he had to go to the rifle. He staggered on, too tired to duck under the spruce branches that clawed at his face. There is no end, he thought, it is all a fantasy. He was really sleeping in his bunk. He had to lie down for just a minute. "Crack!"

The rifle again, why don't they quit firing that damned rifle? I'm really in the bunkhouse he thought, I can see the light of the bull lamp, it's just ahead. He stumbled and fell, too tired to rise. But then strong hands were lifting him from the snow and carrying him. Voices were talking to him, but he could no longer understand what they were saying. He fell into a deep sleep.

Peter awoke to an agonizing pain in his hands and feet. He was lying in a bunk covered in blankets, the nearby stove was glowing bright red. Sven and Gustav were watching him anxiously. God, how my feet and hands hurt, was his first thought.

"Pete, you're back with us again," Sven said. "You gave us an awful scare. We were afraid you wouldn't wake up. You were so cold your heart was barely pumping."

"Yah, we ran with you all the way across the lake and down the skid roads. We were afraid you'd die before we could get you here," Gustav said.

"Did I lose Christian's shotgun?" Peter asked. The question was ludicrous in view of his close brush with death, and his friends laughed good naturedly, relieved that he was becoming himself again.

"Nah," Sven said, "you couldn't have lost it if you wanted to. We had to pry your fingers loose from it."

"What time is it?"

"Ten in the morning, the day after Christmas."

Peter sat up. "But it's a work day, we must go out! Chris will be angry."

"Lie back down," Gustav said. "Chris told us to stay with you until you awakened. Now, if you are all right, we will go to the woods. Edgar, the bull cook, will tend to your needs. As for you, it will be some time before you go into the woods again."

"But why? I must earn money, to get Julia!"

"Look at your hands."

Hesitantly Peter held up his hands. The fingers were swollen to twice their normal size. The tips were of a dark color that would soon become black, and blisters had formed where his right hand had grasped the cold steel of the shotgun. He was shocked and dismayed.

"But what will I do? I must earn money!"

Sven put his hand on his cousin's shoulder. "For now Pete, you must get well, and hope you don't lose your fingers. Christian will get someone he knows to attend to them, he is very good with medicine. Be glad you are alive, because you survived by a hairbreadth. If you had fallen among the spruce trees, we might not have found you in time."

The two young men returned to their duties in the forest, and Peter was left alone to consider his situation. He was about to put his feet on the floor and walk about, but stopped when he saw them. They looked much worse than his hands, horribly swollen and blistered beyond imagination. He felt crushed and depressed—his plans to bring Julia to America seemed so badly damaged that he couldn't conceive of how he was going to achieve them.

The door of the bunkhouse opened, and Christian Halvorsen strode in. He sat down on the deacon's bench at Peter's bunk, and took a deep pull on his pipe. "How's the deer hunter? Did you get him?"

"Yes sir, Boss. I got him all right, a sixteen point buck. But then the damned wolves drove me up a tree and ate him."

Christian smiled. "Better they ate him than you. You're a pretty lucky kid. I've seen men die under better circumstances than that."

"Yes sir, Boss, but I don't feel so lucky. I can't cut timber to earn money. And without the money, I can't bring Julia."

"I know, kid. Sometimes these things look awful bad, but usually they turn out for the best. Did you ever hear of predestination?"

"No sir, Boss."

"First of all, quit the 'yes sir, no sir' bullshit. You can call me Chris like everyone else. Predestination means you are meant to do something, and things happen to make you do it."

"Like I froze my hands so I can't swing an axe?"

"Could be, maybe you're supposed to do something else."

"But what could I do?"

"After you heal up a bit, you could drive a skid team, pays the same. Anyway, we've got to take care of your hands and feet. Got a guy coming that's real good, name's Wise Otter."

"An Indian?"

"Yep, and better at healing than any quack sawbones from Grand Rapids. I've seen him heal up a gangrened leg the doc was going to saw off."

"Gangrene? What's that?"

"That's when a part of your body starts dying when it's still attached to you. Like your fingers and toes, if we don't get them treated real quick."

"You mean I could lose my fingers from having them frozen? They hurt real bad."

Christian nodded gravely. "If you don't get good circulation of the blood in your hands and feet you'll lose them. But the hurting is a good sign, means the limbs are still alive, give me your hand."

He took Peter's hand and felt it gently. Peter flinched at the contact.

"Touchy, ain't they Kid? Seems like the blood's flowing in most of the fingers. Little ones are cold though, might lose them. Don't worry about it, the medicine man should be here any minute, he'll take care of you. Meanwhile, Edgar will bring you some grub, you must be getting hungry."

"Thank you, Sir…I mean, Chris. I haven't eaten since the damned wolves treed me, and then I ate more poorly than they did."

Christian grinned. "They might have eaten a lot better, Kid. I got to go, a logging camp doesn't run itself."

In a little while Edgar, the bull cook, came in with some food for Peter. He was an old man of about forty five, (in the logging camps that was old for a lumberjack) and he walked with a bad limp. A log had rolled off a load and crushed his leg several years before. So he was relegated to the job of bull cook. (Nobody knew where the term had come from, since the position was that of a handyman-custodian rather than a cook. It was usually given to an unskilled laborer, or a lumberjack who was too old or infirm to continue working in the forest.) Edgar sat down on the deacon's bench with a pot of beans, some bread and a tin cup of tea. He handed a bowl to Peter, who immediately dropped it, his fingers being too swollen to grip the container.

"You got a bad dose of the frozen burns, hey Lad?," he said with a grin that displayed a row of yellowed, pipe worn teeth.

"Well, you just open your face, an old Edgar will stuff some beans in it. I remember when I was your age, a guy stepped through the river ice a long way from camp," he said, as he spooned beans into Peter's mouth. "He didn't have nothin to start a fire with, an it was colder'n a landlord's heart. Pore feller had to walk all the way back to camp in them freezin wet boots."

He paused to sop some bread in bean juice and stuff it into Peter's mouth with his grimy fingers.

"Well Lad, when he got back to camp, his boots, socks and feet was frozen into solid lumps, specially the right one, which had got dunked the worst.They had to stick his legs into buckets of warm water to get them thawed out enough to where they could cut his boots off. That was the only way they could take em off, on account of they was afraid his toes might break off, bein froze so bad."

He offered Peter the tea cup, and after Peter drank, resumed spooning beans into his mouth.

"Anyway, the poor guy went through some awful miseries when his feet thawed out. The boss gave him some of his own whiskey to help him stand the pain. But the worst come later, cuz all his toes went rancid an stinky on his left foot, an his whole right foot went dead. The boss knew he had to do somethin if the guy was to live, so he got together with the blacksmith and the cook to figger it out."

He offered Peter some more bread.

"They took a bottle of whiskey and got that feller plumb drunk, then they had four men put him on top of the table under the bull lamp. The cook took his boning knife and commenced to cut off all them rotten toes. The pore guy come to with that, but he handled it purty good when they give him a chunk of harness leather to bite on. Only he didn't know about the bad foot, and when the cook took his meat saw to the leg, jus' above the ankle, he started screamin somethin fierce.

It was all them four lumberjacks could do to hold him down until he passed out, an they could finish the job decent. They had a belt twisted tight around the leg so's he wouldn't bleed to death while the cook was cuttin. An when he was through, the blacksmith took a chunk of iron he'd heated red hot an seared the end of the stump real good so's it couldn't bleed."

Edgar took a swig of the tea and resumed his story.

"The feller got kinda sullen like after that, even though he healed up real good. The carpenter measured him up, and made him a peg out of white pine. Did a real nice job of it too, fitted like a glove. They strapped that peg onto him and in a few weeks he could hobble around fair to middlin.

The boss told him he could work with the cook, since he didn't see as how he could be a lumberjack no more. The feller didn't take it none too good, bein that he was a big strappin young feller. Anyway, the next morning they found him hangin from a tree next to camp. Damned shame too, after all he been through."

Peter told Edgar that he didn't want any more to eat, and thanked him for the company, but he'd just as soon rest a while.

Edgar patted the youth on the head like an indulgent uncle. "Well Young Feller, you jus take yore rest. I'll be around to feed you, an if'n you get to feelin down, jus you holler an I'll come to cheer you up."

Peter turned in his bunk to face the wall, idly watching a spider as it crawled over the logs in search of prey. By golly, if he eats lice, he will be fat soon, he thought. Though there was no sound, a flood of light from the doorway announced another visitor. Damn! he thought, I wish they'd leave me sleep.

"You are Peter?" The questioning voice was distinctly feminine.

Peter turned toward the door so quickly that he banged his swollen hand on the side of the bunk, causing a fiery pain. He winced as his eyes focused on the forms in front of him.

"You are Peter?" the feminine voice repeated.

"Yes, I'm Peter," he managed, as he pushed himself up on an elbow.

"I am Sarah. This is my grandfather, Wise Otter. He has come to heal you. I came with him, because he speaks no English, only the language of the Chippewa and a little French."

Peter looked at the pair. The young woman looked back at him with black eyes that seemed to laugh, as though she knew some secret joke that she wanted to tell him. Her features were more Caucasian than Indian, and her skin was not much darker than his own. Her black hair was pulled back behind her neck, and tied by a bit of red ribbon. She was only slightly shorter than Peter, and shorter than her grandfather by several inches. She wore a heavy coat made of some kind of animal skins with the fur inside, and high winter boots made of deerskin with the hair left on.

Wise Otter was gaunt of frame with graying hair in two braids which hung forward over his shoulders. His face was weathered and lean, his black eyes were piercing. He wore a white man's coat of worn blue wool, and rough black trousers stuffed into deerskin boots similar to those worn by his granddaughter. On his head was a shapeless black felt hat.

Peter said, "I welcome you and your grandfather. My hands and feet are badly frozen, and I fear I may lose my fingers and toes."

Sarah spoke to Wise Otter in a language Peter had never heard. The old man replied, and removed his coat, revealing a shirt of deerskin decorated with colored quills. He approached Peter and looked at his hands, then moved to the foot of the bunk and and pulled the blanket from his feet. As he examined the swollen limbs, the old Indian spoke to Sarah.

"He says they are very bad, but he has strong medicine, and he thinks he can heal them. He also says your bed stinks and crawls with vermin, we must clean it first. Do you have clean blankets?"

"No, but Chris has some at the store."

"Good, I know Christian Halvorsen, he is a good man. He will give me what I need."

She left, and Wise Otter began removing little packets from a large, birch basket he had brought with him. Then he turned to Peter and began a strangely stirring chant, sometimes raising his hands upwards, and sometimes placing them on Peters head and limbs. When Sarah returned, she stood aside quietly and respectfully until he had finished.

"What was that all about?" Peter asked.

"He was invoking the spirits of healing to help you."

"Does that really work?"

"I don't know, I'm Catholic. But I'm trying to learn of the old religion, it doesn't hurt anything, and his medicine is good."

There was a rattling at the door, and Edgar appeared dragging a big bundle of fresh spruce branches. He looked mildly irritated.

"I don't know what a clean bed has to do with healing frozen feet, but Chris said to get em, so I did."

He and Sarah lifted Peter bodily from his bunk and laid him in another until they had removed the old branches and washed the bunk with a solution of hot water and wood ashes. Then Sarah directed Edgar as he replaced the branches and fitted the new blankets. When all was ready, they lifted Peter and placed him on the deacons bench in front of the fresh bed. He was about to crawl into the bed, when he felt a strong hand on his shoulder restrain him.

Sarah waved a finger at him. "You don't get into that clean bed with those filthy clothes on,...you stink!"

She began unbuttoning his shirt and trousers.

Peter wrapped his arms tightly around his waist, trying to evade this invasion of his privacy.

"What are you doing?"

"Helping you take your stinking clothes off."

"You can't do that!"

"Why not?"

"You're a woman."

"And you're a man who is acting like a small boy. Be still if you can't help!"

She took a small knife from Wise Otter's bag, and began slitting his trouser legs.

"Do you have to do that?"

"Yes,...your feet are too swollen."

She deftly pulled off his trousers and shirt, then began the same procedure on his underwear.

"You aren't a bad looking man, even if you are a little puny. I don't know what you're so ashamed of."

Sarah turned to Edgar. "Wash him, and don't spare the soap. And you could use some yourself, you stink too."

When the newly clean Peter was safely deposited in his fresh bed, Wise Otter approached with a plaster he had been preparing. He applied it to Peter's hands and feet, and covered it with a damp moss he had gathered in the forest before the snows of winter. Sarah worked with her grandfather, wrapping the poultices with cotton bandages procured from Christian's stores. When they had finished, the old man spoke briefly to Sarah. Then he left to go and visit with his friend, Christian, who had learned a little Chippewa as well as some French during his years in the timberlands.

Sarah remained with Peter, mixing something in a tin cup.

"This is a tea made from plants that grandfather picked in the summer. It will help you sleep peacefully." She said. "And when there is too much pain, chew on these willow twigs and swallow the juice, it will help."

She raised Peter to a sitting position and put the cup to his mouth. "Drink all of this, and when you awake, you will feel better."

Peter lay in his bed with the young Indian woman gently stroking his face. As a warm sleepiness overtook him, he wondered why he had never seen a picture of a black eyed, raven haired angel.

Every day Wise Otter and and his granddaughter returned to check on the condition of their patient. They replaced the contaminated poultices with fresh dressings and gave him a fresh supply of willow twigs to reduce his pain and fever. It was not until his limbs had healed, that Peter knew Wise Otter had removed the tips of his little fingers, and his two little toes. They were a sign of remembrance of the old healer, that Peter carried with him until his death.

Every day, Peter and Sarah sat and talked. It was during these quiet hours that he learned that she was the daughter of a French trapper, whom she had never known, except as a small child. And that her mother and her wise grandfather had sent her to the Catholic mission school to be educated.

"This is the white man's country now," her grandfather had said. "She must know the language and ways of the white man if she is to survive."

So, she went to the mission school. She learned English and some French in addition to her native tongue. She learned to spell and write well and was a superior student in arithmetic. After her graduation from the school, Father Goebel, who headed the mission school, enlisted Sarah's aid in working with the Indian families of the area. It was a position which had greater returns in prestige than in monetary reward.

Her intelligence and curiosity also led her to question her grandfather endlessly about the art of healing. So that finally, lacking a male heir to carry forward his knowledge, Wise Otter began teaching the girl the many secrets of the medicine man.

By the time she was eighteen years of age, Sarah was a respected member of both the Indian and white communities. She was frequently sought out by individuals of both races as a scribe and tutor for those whose language skills were inadequate. And her constant presence at the side of her grandfather as he attended to the sick and injured, brought her recognition as a nurse and healer in her own rite.

Sarah was quite content with her life as it was. But, her mother was concerned that she had no suitors. Indeed no young men had approached her grandfather with respect to matrimonial possibilities, and it seemed unlikely that any would appear. Sarah was a half breed, a segment of society held in limbo by whites and Indians alike. And though she was highly respected for her abilities, she was not given the same solicitude on a social basis.

Peter, however, had not become a member of either society. Lumberjacks lived in a world of their own and were themselves sometimes viewed as rather an undesirable lot. In addition, his friends were immigrants not yet established in the area culture, who tended to stay in a close ethnic group. For those reasons, he had not yet assimilated the prejudices common in white society at that time.

In the weeks of his disability Peter came to regard the half-breed girl as a close friend. His simple devotion to Julia prevented him from considering the comely young woman in anything approaching a romantic basis. However, a bond of sorts did form between the two. The young Swede looked forward to the daily visits by Sarah, and he spoke of her much to his friends. This was a situation Sven and Gustav greatly appreciated, since they had grown quite tired of Peter's endless mooning over the absent Julia.

As the middle of January approached, Peter's hands and feet were healing well. He was able to move about with the use of a pair of crutches, that the carpenter fashioned from the forked branches of ash trees.

Though Sarah's visits were less frequent, a second purpose had evolved. She began tutoring the young Swede in spelling and writing in English, and was delighted with the ease with which his quick mind accepted the subjects. On Sundays they spent the entire day together talking and studying books borrowed from the mission school.

The bunkhouse was filled with restless and rather love starved men on Sunday, who tended to hover around Sarah. So Christian Halvorsen allowed Peter and Sarah the use of the accounting table in his office as a work place for

Peter's studies. Christian had a small library of much used and cherished books. It was these books that now gave Peter much pleasure, and honed his sharp mind for the future. Christian had proudly shown Peter the volumes.

"Read, Peter. All of the knowledge of the world is at your fingertips. A man can learn to do anything if he can read the right book. Read and learn, then use what you've learned. *The Declaration of Independence* and *The Constitution*, *The Bible*, Shakespeare, Thoreau, Jefferson, Franklin, Twain, Poe, they've all got something for you. You might not understand everything they're telling you at first, but read them again, and you'll understand them.

You see, Peter, these books all have messages. The authors are trying to tell you something, and the more you learn to understand them, the more you understand ordinary, everyday people. You understand people, you can help them, or you can use them. Depends on the kind of man you are."

Peter read and studied every moment he could, and when he wasn't reading, he wrote. He practiced his new language by writing letters home. Arduously he formed the words with his still stiff fingers, writing voluminous letters that described in careful detail every event that took place at the logging camp. He smiled inwardly that his dear ones would require the services of an interpreter in order to read his letters, but he continued to write in English.

Chapter 4

Sarah and Her People

Sarah lay staring at the crackling flames in the fireplace of Wise Otter's cabin. The old man had been one of the first Indians to adopt the white man's ways, and what he did , he did well. The cabin was tight and warm, and cheerfully lighted with candles made by dipping wicks of hammered birch bark into a melted blend of deer tallow and beeswax. A large bearskin provided a carpet near the fireplace, it was on this warm black fur that Sarah lay as she half heartedly read a book.

Star Flower had noticed her daughter's malaise these past few days. "You are not well, my daughter?" she asked. "Does your time go hard with you?"

"No mother, it is not that. I don't really know what it is, just a feeling. I am not happy, my work with the children no longer interests me. I have never felt this way before."

"It is that you are a woman and you are lonely. You are no longer a child Sarah, your grandfather and I are no longer enough for you. You need a man to be your own, it is ordained so by the earth mother."

Sarah laughed. "Mother! Every time there is something you can't explain, you say one of the 'old religion' spirits is responsible. You have been without a man for many years."

"I have not been without a man, Sarah. I just have not taken a man to my spirit. I have chosen it to be so, for there is already one in my heart."

"My father?"

"Yes, Sarah, your father. Others have satisfied my earth needs, but no one but he can fill the hunger in my heart."

"But he has been gone so long. He left when I was a little baby. Why don't you forget about him and find another man? You are not yet old."

"Because he said he would return. He left in the spring with another trapper in a big canoe. They had a load of furs to take to 'The Place of the Falling Water.' Some said that he drowned in the spring wildness of the great river, 'The Father of Waters'. But I would have known—his spirit would have visited me."

"You think that he still lives, my mother?"

"Yes, I think your father still lives."

"But then,...he is not someone for us to love, Mother. He deserted us if he is still alive! I think that he died in the Mississippi—I think he was a good man who drowned—and we can remember him with love."

Her mother nodded her head slowly, her own eyes focused on the firelight. "Perhaps you are right, Daughter. Louis was a good man. He was kind to me, and he loved you. His 'Little Mouse' he called you, because you were so tiny. He would not have left us. Perhaps the spirit of the river took him and would not let his spirit return to me."

"Mother, why did you take a white man to you? Why did you not take one of your own?"

"Because he he was a handsome man who was good, and he loved me. He made my spirit laugh with joy. I did not think of him as a white man, neither did your grandfather. Wise Otter took the hand of Louis, as men do, and he misses him also. That is why he cares so much for you."

"But, why has Grandfather never spoken of him?"

"Because he is of the old religion. He believes that to speak the name of the dead will cause his spirit to return from its rest."

"You don't believe that, do you, Mother?"

"No. I have called his name many times."

"Mother..."

"Yes, My Daughter?"

"There is a young white man, that I have been tending to. We talk much, and it makes me feel warm inside. I feel sad when I am gone from him."

"Does he feel the same?"

Sarah looked confused. "I don't think so,...he talks of a white woman across the ocean. Yet,...his eyes talk to me, his spirit talks to me."

Star Flower gazed at her daughter. "It is the way of men to not know what is good for them," she said quietly. "Show him gently, Sarah, and if you are patient, he will come to you."

During the last weeks of January Peter felt well enough to want some work to do. He could walk fairly well, but not well enough to return to the forest. He went to

Christian and asked if there might be something to do that would let him earn his keep. The boss drew on his pipe and blew the smoke to the ceiling.

"I could use some help with the stores. We need to count what we have left on the shelves and order goods for the spring log drive. Then you can take the tote sleigh into town if you can handle a team, and make the purchases. If you do well, you may one day become a purchaser for the company. It is an opportunity—use it well."

Peter was ecstatic, to have such trust put in him was more than he had dreamed. He was glad now for the many hours that he and Sarah had spent studying his writing and arithmetic. By Golly, he would make something of himself in this country. Perhaps Chris was right, there might be such a thing as predestination.

In the weeks that followed, he worked with enthusiasm. When the inventory of goods was completed, and the long list of pike poles, peaveys, rope and chain, dynamite, nails, iron for the smith, canvas and a host of other items had been made, he was put to work accounting the logs being brought to the river.

Each day, the logs arriving at the river were branded by stamping a big NT on both ends with a special chisel-like hammer made for the purpose. It was the duty of Brian Fry, a bookish middle aged man, to do the branding and estimate the board feet of lumber in each log.

As the huge loads of logs came down to the river bank in ever increasing numbers, Fry was hard pressed to keep up with the estimating and branding. Normally, after the last load of the day had been dumped at the river bank, he would go to the office, and enter the results of the day into the company ledger.

But now, the days were beginning to lengthen, and the company had sent in additional lumberjacks and more haul sleds and teams. Fry now had to work long after the last lumberjack had eaten his evening meal, in order to list the last loads of logs coming to the river on any day. The man was exhausted, and told Christian so, a feat difficult for the mild mannered Fry to accomplish. He prided himself in the meticulous efficiency with which he kept the records and it irritated him that his books were now less than perfect.

"But, damn me for a lazy incompetent, if you can see any way I can do this job by myself," he told Christian. "I have hardly eaten and seldom slept in these two weeks. If Northwest Timber is going to kill me with work, I might as well do it myself with a bottle or two in Grand Rapids."

Christian knew that the man was greatly overloaded. He also knew that on rare occasions he took to the bottle as a form of recreation and relief. This always resulted in a bout that lasted several weeks. But Fry was usually able to postpone it until the log drive, when his work at the riverbank was completed. The fact that he mentioned it now worried the boss, and he made haste to find him help with his duties. For if Fry quit work to go on a binge in the midst of logging, the result would be chaotic. He was the only member of the encampment who knew how to estimate timber, with the exception of Christian himself.

So now, Peter spent much of his time recording in a thick ledger, the information gathered by Fry. And with the help of Christian, he made up the weekly reports of production which were sent to the headquarters of Northwest Timber in Minneapolis. So the reports that were received in Minneapolis were signed by Christian

Halvorsen, but now bore the byline: "As prepared by Peter Olaf Hokanson," a fact that did not go unnoted by the chief accountant.

When Peter's work on the ledger was completed each day, he went down to the river bank and assisted Brian Fry with the branding of logs. His strength was returning, and he climbed the loads of timber with vigor, measuring the diameter of the logs and swinging the six pound branding hammer with might, to impress the NT brand in the soft pine.

If his efforts resulted in pain from a bumped foot or a sore hand, he didn't complain, though he might pause for a moment to vent an oath under his breath. He wheedled Fry into teaching him how to calculate the board feet of lumber in a log—something that the man was reluctant to do, because he was the only one of the men who knew the formula and it was this that made his job secure.

Christian watched young Peter with approval, and took every opportunity to teach him about the operation of the company. A bachelor himself, he would tell Peter; "Since I have no sons of my own, at least none I can lay claim to, you can carry on for me some day. Learn, and when you are my age you will be a big man in this company. If I had someone to teach me when I was a kid, I'd be sitting in a fancy office now, instead of just being a camp boss."

Peter was proud, and when he visited with Sarah of a Sunday, he eagerly told her of his progress in the company. If in his excitement, he spoke of his renewed confidence in bringing Julia to America, she shared in his happiness, or so it seemed to Peter. The days with Sarah were more important to Peter than he realized. She was his tutor, friend and confidante, and her firm, yet gentle guidance reinforced his inherent ambition and confidence.

On the second week of February 1896, Christian told Peter that the time had come to go to Grand Rapids to purchase supplies for the spring log drive. Peter hitched a team of Belgians to the tote sleigh in the early hours of Monday morning and set off. It was a clear, moonlit morning, and the air was crisp. Peter whistled and sang Swedish love songs to the horses as they trotted briskly, their sharply calked shoes throwing chunks of packed snow in the air. In a little over two hours he had reached Grand Rapids.

The shopkeepers were just opening their places of business, and they smiled broadly and hollered their good mornings as he drove the big "Northwest Timber" sleigh down the street. The arrival of the tote sleigh meant sales and profit for them. A welcome thing at a time of the year when most of the residents of the area were staying warm in their homes, rather than doing anything that would require purchases from the merchants.

Peter began his purchasing with the heavy hardware items for the log drive, haggling long and hard with the owner of the hardware store. His zeal in acquiring the best possible prices for the goods he purchased was such that the exasperated merchant finally threw up his hands and said, "Why don't you tell Halverson to buy my store and let me work for him? I'll make more money than what you allow me for profit."

Peter smiled good naturedly and said, "But he too must make a profit. If I pay too dearly for equipment, he may discharge me from this duty and hire someone more frugal than I."

The merchant rolled his eyes. "That would be most unlikely, Lad. I swear you are more frugal then old Angus, the barber. And he insists on lighting the fire, the lamp and his pipe, all with one match."

Several hours later, when he had completed his acquisitions, Peter left the various shop owners counting their hard won profits, and went to the post office to pick up the mail for the camp. He sorted through the bag of letters and packages and found two for himself. There was one from Ingrid and another from Christine Thorgeson, Julia's mother.

Peter hurriedly returned the rest of the mail to the bag and put it in the padlocked mail box on the sleigh. Then he hurried to the restaurant across the street, and seated himself at a table where light streamed in through a frosty window. He ordered hot tea and a bowl of stew before opening the letter from Julia's mother.

Peter was perplexed at receiving a letter from the woman, especially since she did not seem to have much enthusiasm for having him as a son-in-law. He was anxious lest Julia was ill or badly injured and so could not write to him herself. He unfolded the single sheet of paper, and read:

Dear Peter,

We all hope that this letter finds you well and in good spirits. It must be terribly lonely in that wilderness so far from home. We are all well, and Emil sends you his best regards.

Julia wanted to write to you herself, but the poor girl couldn't bring herself to do so. I insisted that it must be done, so at her pleading, I am writing for her. It is not a happy thing I must tell you, and doubtless will cause you some pain and suffering. I feel sorry to bring you such ill tidings, but in all honesty, it was your own actions that created this situation, so you must bear up and live with it.

Julia will marry Elias Oberg, the son of Banker Oberg, on the fifteenth of May. Her betrothal party was held last Sunday afternoon at the mansion of the Obergs. Though she knows that her marriage will cause you some pain, Julia hopes that you will wish her well, and not be bitter toward her. She continues to have a deep affection for you, and wishes to be your friend always.

Emil and I wish you well in your endeavors, and fervently hope you will find happiness. Perhaps one day we will all meet again and this momentary unhappiness will be forgotten.

May the peace of God be with you and strengthen you.

In friendship and best wishes,
Christine Thorgeson

At first Peter stared blankly at the paper in his hands. He could not bring himself to believe the words it carried. Then he sat reading and rereading it for a long time, wanting to believe that it he had somehow misunderstood its content. At last he crumpled the piece of paper and threw it on the dirty plank floor. He paid for his uneaten dinner and walked down the street to the tavern, the burning tears of his anguish blurring the piles of snow beside the walkway.

Peter tipped the first glass of whiskey as though it were tea, desperately wanting to feel the flow of warmth it would bestow. He looked at the second one, and saw the trap it held in its amber fluid.

"God damned bitch," he said under his breath, "God damned unfaithful bitch."

Slowly he drank the contents of the glass, allowing the alcohol to take effect as it should, numbing the sharp edge of his pain.

"I'll show that damned old hypocrite," he said to himself of Christine. "One day I'll show the damned old bag."

He got up and bought a bottle of Old Crow for the nighttime, then walked out to the Belgians. In the hours that it took to return to the camp, Peter nipped only lightly on the whiskey. In his thoughts he developed a new resolve—despite Julia and because of her—he had to become a success in this new country. He would do whatever it took to show Julia that she was wrong.

"Someday," he said to the wind, "someday." The trust of the boy was dead, the determination of the man had been born.

In the days that followed Peter's trip to Grand Rapids, he never spoke of Julia, or the letter he had received from her mother. If the brightness and innocence of his youthful smile had disappeared, no one mentioned it. He did his work with a quiet determination that was noticed by Christian, but no one else. The older man also noticed the new reticence of the youth. One day he put his hand on Peter's shoulder and pressed it firmly.

"Something troubling you, Pete?"

Peter turned to Christian and shook his head. "Nothing important." But the hurt in his eyes showed through the attempt at deception.

"How about you tell me about it?"

Peter shook his head uncertainly.

"It's Julia, isn't it?"

"How'd you know?"

"Because a woman is the only thing that can make a man pull into himself like you have. She's not coming, is she?"

"No, she's getting married." Peter said the words much like he would have said, "I'm being hanged."

"Hm...hard to take when you really love a woman."

"Did it ever happen to you, Chris?"

"Yep, it happened to me all right."

"How did you get over it?"

"Didn't, not really."

"You mean you still love her?"

"Yeah...I guess so, never could forget her, doesn't hurt so much anymore though."

"And that's why you haven't married?"

"Kinda, I could never find a woman I loved as much as Sue, I was always comparing others to her."

"But, you've been with other women, haven't you?"

"Been with lots of women, but she kinda spoiled me for getting married. I'm always afraid it will happen again, I guess."

"You think I should go out and find another woman?"

"Yep, it's the fastest way to get over the miseries—If your dog dies you get another dog—It's the same with women, if one quits you, you got to find another."

"Why do they do it Chris?"

"Do what?"

"Say they love you...then marry someone else."

"Can't really say, I think they've got a thing in them about home and family. If you don't measure up with that, they'll find someone else."

"Even if they love you?"

"Love means different things to men and women. To most men it means they want to have a woman. They'll bust their asses to give her everything they can, just so they can have her. Men are more romantic, women are more practical."

"But, what can you do if you never know what a woman is thinking?"

"All I can say is, take what comes to you, and hope sometime it'll work out right. There isn't any safe way when it comes to love, Peter."

That Friday evening Sarah came to tutor Peter on writing business letters. When she sat beside him at the accounting table, he saw her in an entirely different way. Her face was pretty, and her long black hair was glossy and flowed over her shoulders in pleasing waves. He noticed the gentle swell of her breasts, where before he had only seen a deerskin shirt. When she spoke, he noticed a sensual tone in her soft, low voice, that he now found to be deeply exciting. Peter wondered why he had not noticed any of this before. The warmth of her body next to his was more than he could withstand—he took her hand in his and raised it to his lips.

"What was that for?" Sarah looked at Peter with surprise, for had never before shown that he considered her to be anything but a friend.

"I just realized something I should have been aware of a long time ago."

She said nothing, but sat beside him, with her lips slightly parted, a quizzical expression on her face.

"I just realized what a wonderful, beautiful woman you are. I want to know you that way…as a woman, not just a friend."

"But what of your woman in Sweden, do you not love her?"

Peter's face became cheerless. "It is over, she is marrying someone else."

Sarah read the despondency in his expression. She pulled her hand away, a shadow of hurt dulling the brightness of her eyes.

"She has thrown you away, so you come to me? Before you saw nothing in me—but now I'm good enough for you to consider as a woman? Peter!… that isn't a compliment, that's an insult!"

"I did not mean it as such, Sarah! I just meant that I see now what I was too blinded to see before. I need you as a friend still, I will always need you as a friend. But now, I see so much more in you that I want to know. Don't be angry with me for that."

Sarah thought of what her mother had told her. "Show him gently, Sarah, and if you are patient, he will come to you." She put her hand on Peter's.

"I will be your friend for a while yet, but before we think of anything more, the hurt that clouds your face must be gone. For, now I would be holding her man, and not my own."

Peter nodded his head sadly. "You are right, Sarah. But I want to spend a little time with you. You can help me forget, help me lose the pain in here." He pressed two fingers against his breastbone. "Can I come to see you on Sunday?"

"Is that not too soon? Your hurt is still fresh."

"And if I were bleeding to death, would you wait to bandage me?"

"It is not the same."

"Sarah, I need your help, that's what friends are for."

"Oh, all right! but just as friends, and you must come early enough to go to Mass with me."

"But I'm Lutheran!"

"And when did you last talk to God?"

"I talk to him often."

"But when did you last honor him by going to church?"

Peter shook his head in exasperation. "If it will make you happy, I will go with you."

"Good, be at Grandfather's cabin by nine. Now let's get some work done."

On Sunday morning a freshly washed and shaved Peter arrived at the cabin of Wise Otter at eight-thirty. He didn't know how long the four mile walk to the tribal village would take him, and he didn't want to be late. Sarah met him at the door and escorted him into the cozy warmth of the cabin.

"Come, we will talk to Grandfather first, as is the custom of the old ones."

She led him to where Wise Otter sat on a chair beside the fire, and spoke to the old man in the Chippewa tongue. He smiled and answered her, putting down the piece of wood he was carving to extend his hand to Peter. He took Peter's hand and shook it, then looked at it carefully. He spoke to Peter, and Sarah interpreted.

"He says he remembers you well, and how you were so badly frozen when he first saw you. He is pleased that you have healed so well, and welcomes you to his home."

Peter said, "Tell him I am grateful to him for his healing, and that I have brought a small gift to thank him."

He took a sheath knife from his pocket and offered it to Wise Otter.

"It is made from good Swedish steel, and was given to me by my father. It is fitting that he who made my body whole should have it."

Sarah spoke to her grandfather, who turned the knife over in his hand, examining the carved reindeer antler haft and the engraving of a sea otter on either side of the blade. He touched the edge with his thumb, then put it to the piece of maple he was carving. He smiled broadly and spoke to Peter enthusiastically.

Sarah smiled at Peter. "He says it is a fine knife, and the edge is sharper than the one he carves with. He thanks you and says he is glad to know a white man who has the manners of the Chippewa. You have pleased Grandfather greatly, he will not forget."

Sarah turned to her mother, who had been watching the exchange quietly.

"Mother, this is Peter, the man I told you about....Peter, this is my mother, Star Flower. She has been anxious to meet you."

Peter bowed to Star Flower in the way of the Swedes. "I am honored to meet the mother of Sarah. You have raised a wonderful daughter who has helped me more than I can hope to repay."

"Receiving thanks for what one has done is the only payment that is important," Star Flower returned. "You have thanked my father properly, that speaks well of you. Come, let us have a cup of tea before you and Sarah go to Mass."

"Won't you come with us?"

"No, I will stay with Wise Otter. He is of the old religion, and I will stay and honor the spirits with him. I go also to the church, but then Sarah stays with Father. We do this to properly honor him. He is an old warrior as well as a medicine man, and he should never be dishonored."

"I didn't know that he was a warrior. I thought he was always a healer, a medicine man."

"No, he was a warrior first, when he was young and full of hot blood. He became a healer and counselor later, when he learned of his gift. He says the great spirit showed him the way. Sarah can tell you about it. She learned all of it from Blue Waters, my mother, when she was just a child."

They spoke of small things as they drank their tea, though Peter wanted to hear more about Wise Otter. Star Flower said it was impolite to speak of one's past when that person is present.

"One should not speak of another's past in his presence, when he has grown old. The past is dead, and to speak of it makes him feel that his life is gone, and he should go to the land of the spirits. I will not do that to my father."

How true that is, Peter thought. He remembered how his grandfather's eyes would grow misty when he spoke of his youth. He thought that it must hurt to think of all the things that one could do, and know you can no longer do them. It must be like a prison, one from which there is only one escape.

"It is time for us to go to the church," Sarah said. "We can talk of this later, when Mass is over and after our noon meal."

At the church Peter did his best to follow Sarah's example, as the priest led the congregation through the Mass. But he felt strangely out of place. It was much the same as if he had joined Wise Otter in his worship of the Great

Spirit. He understood no more of the Mass than he would have understood the Chippewa's chanting.

"Why do Catholics have their worship in Latin?" He asked Sarah as they walked to her home. "I felt uncomfortable, as though I were intruding on someone's private prayers."

"I don't know, it has always been that way, I think. We learn what it means in our religious training, but I know it would be completely strange to someone else."

"I suppose it would be the same for you, if you went to a Swedish Lutheran service."

"Yes, but I could not."

"Why not?"

"Because it would be a sin."

"What would?"

"To worship in a church that is not of the true faith."

"Why? We worship the same God."

"I know, but it is what they teach us."

"What do they teach you of your Grandfather?"

Sarah looked uncomfortable. "That he is in danger of eternal damnation, because he heard the true word of God, and refused to believe."

"Do you believe that? It is the same thing our pastors teach us. I don't know if I can believe that an honorable man like your grandfather would be condemned to hell."

"I know, I feel the same way. It would be different perhaps, if I hadn't learned so much from him."

"What are you speaking of?"

"His reverence for life, he believes that all living things are sacred, even things that are not alive, as we know life. He believes that everything has a spirit of its own, a man, a deer, a bear, the great river, the ancient pines. Once all of the people believed as he does. Then the white priests came and told us that we were wrong, and that we must worship their God."

"And did your people believe what the priests told them?"

"At first there were many who did. At first there were not so many white men, and all could live together. So it was easy to believe the teachings of the white priests. They taught us not to steal and lie, not to take another man's wife, not to kill each other. These were things we already knew, so it was easy to believe.

But then more white men came, and they lied to us and cheated us and stole our lands. And so many wished that they had stayed with the old religion—but it was too late.

Most of the strong ones like my grandfather were members of the Midewiwin, the secret spiritual society. They kept their old beliefs, but their numbers lessened and they could not get back the strength they once knew. The spirit of the people was changed. They went to the religions of the white men, but still they keep some of the old beliefs and mix them with their new religions."

"Your grandfather," Peter said, "kept his life pretty much as it always was, didn't he?"

"No, he did not!" Sarah spoke with a sudden bitterness that surprised Peter. "They destroyed his life, and destroyed his world. That is why I sometimes hate the whites so bad that I could kill every liar and murderer among them!"

"But Sarah, how can you hate whites, when your own father was white? I am white, do you hate me? "

Sarah stopped walking and took both of Peter's hands in her own. He could see confusion and pain mirrored in her face.

"Peter, my father was a special man. He was different from the whites in the way he lived and in what he believed to be right. You are much like him. I can feel the honor in you. I do not hate you, but what you do is not right either."

"How can you say that? I do nothing wrong. I'm honest and I work hard for a living. I hurt no one!" He was filled with righteous indignation, and the reddening of his face showed it.

"Oh Peter! You are a white man, and you do not understand yet, but one day you will. I am talking about the earth—my people lived with the earth from the beginning of our time and we changed nothing. We took from the forest, the prairie, the lakes and rivers that which we needed to live. And always there was enough for everyone. We lived, but so did the deer, elk and bison. We took the ducks and geese, and the fish, and always there was more than we could use. Wise Otter and those like him never killed a deer or elk without thanking its spirit for the food it provided.

But the white man came, and he plowed over the prairies and killed the bison. He shot the pigeons that came in flocks that blotted out the sky, until they came no more. He killed game he did not need, until there was so little left that in the winter our people starved.

And now you cut the great pines and float so many down the river that the fish are killed by the taint in the water. The whites will not quit until every ancient pine is gone. Where there were great forests there will be nothing but waste-land, and my people's way will perish."

Peter said nothing, but he turned from Sarah and continued walking. It was inconceivable to him that these endless forests could ever be cut. In later years, he would remember Sarah's prediction. But now it made no sense to him to worry about forests so great they extended beyond the horizon.

The noon meal was excellent, a roast cooked with wild rice. Peter asked what it was, thinking it might be an elk or forest caribou.

Sarah laughed. "You eat this all the time, Peter. Christian Halvorsen gave us a haunch of beef for taking care of you."

Peter reddened, he had not known that Christian had paid Wise Otter, and he felt stupid and ashamed for not having asked about it.

"I didn't know, it is so much better than we get at the camp." He changed the subject and asked about Sarah's work for the mission school.

"I work with Father Goebel," Sarah said. "I teach the little children, and he teaches the older ones. Sometimes when he must go to someone sick, or bury someone, I take care of all of the children. When I must go to heal someone, he takes care of all the children. It works well."

"I'd like to see the school sometime," Peter said, "could I?"

"There is no reason you couldn't this afternoon, do you want to?"

"Yes, I would like that if it isn't any trouble."

"It's no trouble, I would like to show it to you."

After dinner, the two walked to the school. The sun was shining and they strolled slowly, enjoying its warmth.

"You said your grandfather was a warrior first, than a medicine man. Would you tell me about it?" Peter asked.

"I will tell you what I know, as my grandmother told it to me. He was born and grew up in the land you know as 'Wisconsin'. Like all Chippewa children of his time, he received his name in a ceremony especially for that purpose, just as we receive ours during the rite of baptism today. His uncle, who was a well respected warrior of the time, had a dream. From that dream came grandfather's name. This is the story of that dream:

"There was an otter who lived by a small stream, where he and his kin caught fish for their livelihood. One summer the skies didn't bring forth rain, and so the stream dropped and all the fish were caught in a small pool.

"All the otters, except for the one, were very happy because the fish were easily caught, and they gorged themselves. But the first otter worried that no rain would come and the small pool would dry up. The fish would die, leaving the otters nothing to eat. His kin laughed at him saying, 'It always rains, and there are always fish, come eat!'

"But the first otter went down the stream to where some beavers were chewing at aspen trees. The trees were very large and far from the stream.

'I know where there is a little pool surrounded with young, tender aspen trees,' he told the beavers. 'Come and I will show them to you.'

"So the beavers followed him to the pool and began cutting the young aspen trees. With them the beavers built a dam below the pool, and the waters grew deep as the trickling stream ran into it. The rains failed to come, and the stream went dry. But the otters had fish to eat because of the dam that the beavers built. That otter was very wise, because he looked beyond today. So my grandfather was named 'Wise Otter', and he has always been as the name he was given.

"Grandfather grew up as a hunter and warrior. At an early age he learned to make very good bows from the wood of the ash tree, a craft that made him popular with the young men of the tribe. When he was eighteen winters old, he went into war for the first time against the Sioux.

"The Sioux and my people had long been enemies. Their feuding became all the more bitter because the Chippewa were continually moving westward. They were pushing the Sioux from their hunting grounds around the great lake that you call 'Superior'. This wasn't a desire for more land, but a necessity. Because the movement of the whites from the east was forcing my people off their ancient homeland. The land around the great lake had many shallow waters that were abundant with wild rice, waterfowl and game of all sorts. And so it was very desirable to both the Sioux and the Chippewa. For many years both used the land, and battles between the two peoples were common.

"On one autumn day, a small group of Chippewa women were gathering rice on one of the small lakes. They were seen by a party of young, Sioux braves who were hunting in the area. The Sioux knew that the women would have a camp nearby, so they searched quietly until they found it. The camp was set up for the parching of rice, so there were no young warriors with it, only women and a few old men as escorts.

"The braves stole up to the edge of the camp with drawn bows, and in a few moments the old men of the camp were dying with arrows in their bodies. The Sioux quickly captured the women of the camp. They killed the old ones with their tomahawks and bound the younger women and girls to prevent their escape. Then they took a canoe that was on the lakeshore and went out to capture the women who were gathering rice.

"Unknown to the Sioux, a young woman had gone away from camp to relieve herself. As she returned, she heard the women's cries at the camp. Seeing the Sioux braves, she ran into the forest and made her way back to the main Chippewa camp several miles away. When she told what had happened, all the Chippewa warriors who were in camp took up their weapons and ran to the rice camp.

"When they reached the camp, the Sioux had gone, taking the young women and girls with them. They left only the murdered old women, and the scalped bodies of the old warriors. One of the old warriors was Grandfather's uncle, the one who had bestowed his name on him.

"The Warriors swore a blood oath to avenge their people. They cut their arms so the blood flowed, then dripped it on the bodies of the murdered ones. Then they went into the forest, swiftly trailing the Sioux. Wise Otter led the party despite his youth. He had the greatest right of vengeance because his name bestower had been murdered.

"In the early afternoon, the avengers were brought to a halt by the cries of a pair of ravens a short way ahead of them. Wise Otter sent several of the swiftest young warriors into the forest on either side of the trail they were following. They ran stealthily through the trees until they had passed the Sioux, who could not move as rapidly because of their prisoners. Then they waited in ambush beside the trail.

"Wise Otter and the rest of the warriors followed behind the Sioux. They stayed far enough back to avoid warning them of the Chippewa's presence. When war cries ahead gave notice of the beginning battle, the force to the rear dashed ahead and fell on the Sioux from behind. The battle was short, and none of the Sioux escaped. Wise Otter received a tomahawk blow to the shoulder, a scar he carries today. But he himself dispatched two of the enemy, and hung the scalps outside his mother's lodge as evidence that he had properly avenged his uncle."

Peter was impressed. "I can see that your grandfather is a very brave man, if he did such a thing when he was the age I am. Was he in any other battles?"

"Yes," Sarah said, "there were many, and always with the Sioux. The Chippewa never fought the whites, as the Sioux did. The greatest battle was at the Brule river two winters after his uncle was murdered.

"The Sioux had come to attack the Chippewa with a war party of several hundred braves. A large party of warriors was gone from the Chippewa camps. But a wise old chief was there, and he gathered together a force of about two hundred, including young, inexperienced braves and many of the older ones. Wise Otter was one of the few proven young warriors there.

"In the evening of the day that the Sioux came, both banks of the river were lined with warriors. But the battle did not start because it was nearly dark, and it was believed that a warrior killed in the dark would wander forever in the night in the spirit world. That was fortunate for the Chippewa, because the Sioux force was of strong warriors and the battle then would have gone badly for the Chippewa.

"During the night, the wily old chief had all of his best warriors hide themselves at the edge of the river bank, which dropped steeply into the water. Then, at dawn he had the remaining number stand in full view higher on the bank. When the Sioux started into the river, these braves fell back, as though to retreat because of their lesser strength.

"The Sioux warriors became overconfident of an easy victory. They charged into the river in a great mass, shouting their war cries and waving knives and tomahawks. But when they reached the steep bank on the Chippewa side, the hidden warriors rose up and slaughtered the Sioux as they tried to climb out of the river. On that day, Wise Otter took many scalps, and he became one of the great warriors of our people. But from that time on he fought fewer battles, and spent most of his time making bows and hunting."

"When did he marry?"

"He married soon after the great battle, and had two sons and a daughter with Quiet One."

"That was not your grandmother though, wasn't her name Blue Water?"

"That is right, when they had shared a lodge for perhaps ten winters, the whiteman's sickness came to them. It was the one called 'smallpox'. It came when Grandfather was gone on a long hunt, and he returned, the children were already dead, and Quiet One was dying. Though he stayed with her until her death, and buried his whole family, grandfather never became sick, except in his heart."

Peter thought about the old warrior, now perhaps in his seventies, and still strong and straight. He was gaining a new respect for these people, they had suffered great hardships, and still kept their quiet dignity.

"Wise Otter married again? And that was your grandmother?"

"Yes, he took another wife, but not right away. After Quiet One and his children died, he left Wisconsin and wandered for a few winters. It was during that time that he had the dream in which the Great Spirit told him to become a healer:

"He was far to the north in Minnesota, hunting alone on the shores of the great Red Lakes. One day he saw a big she-wolf of pure white standing near the freezing water. Since it was nearly winter and her pelt would be thick and soft, he aimed his rifle at the wolf. She watched him quietly and without fear as he pulled the trigger. The cartridge did not fire, and by the time he was ready to fire again, the she wolf had disappeared.

"Grandfather decided that the wolf's manitou had protected her, and therefore he decided to quit hunting and make camp for the night. He cut some long willow wands and set up a small wickiup covered with marsh grass. That night he heard the wolf howl three times before he fell asleep.

"When his spirit was quiet in sleep, the wolf came to him in a dream. She carried a pup in her mouth, and laid it at his feet. The pup was sick and whined pitifully, and he was about to kill it in his dream, when the she wolf spoke to him. 'Do not kill it, but lay your hand on it.'...He did as he was told, and the pup got up and ran in circles with the joy of health. Before the she-wolf left with her pup, she looked into his eyes and said, 'So you must do with your own kind, from this day.'

"Grandfather woke with fear, and looked about him for the wolf, but she was not there. In the morning there was a powder of snow on the ground, and near his wickiup he found the tracks of a wolf and a pup. From that day he never again went to war, but began to learn the ways of the healers."

"What a wonderful story! How did he learn all he knows, did he find it all out by himself?"

"No, when he left the Red Lakes, he traveled back to the western shores of Gitchi-Gume, which you know as 'Lake Superior'. There he lived with another Chippewa tribe, and it was there he joined with my grandmother.

"She was nearly as old as he, having shared a wigwam with another man for many winters. They had no children, and her man drowned in the great lake, so she was living alone with her mother when grandfather found her. They joined their lives together and had two children, my mother and her brother. Blue Water's mother was a healer, and it was from her that my grandfather learned much."

"I didn't know you have an uncle, what of him?"

"It is one of the sadnesses that make me hate the whites sometimes." Sarah said quietly. "White Buck was grandfather's only son, and the pride of his heart. He was two winters older than my mother, a brave man and a great hunter. White Buck was very dear to me when I was a little child. He played with me and treated me like a daughter of his own. I looked up to him, since my own father was gone. To me he was more than an uncle, he was like a father who was always kind and happy with me."

"You say 'was'. Is he then gone too?"

Sarah nodded wearily. "It was when I was about ten, he was trapping for furs and had been gone for more than a month. He had told us that he would return for Christmas, which he and Mother both celebrated, since they were both Christians. When he didn't return, we didn't worry at first. We thought that the trapping might have been very good, so that he could bring in many more furs.

"But he didn't return, and it wasn't until two French trappers came through our village in the late winter that we found out what had happened to him. They came by his camp and found what was left of his body after the wolves had finished with it. There was a bullet hole in the back of his skull, and everything he owned was gone, except the cup he had been drinking tea from."

"But if the wolves ate his body, how did you know it was him?"

"The trappers brought back what was left of his winter moccasins. Every Indian woman knows her own work, my mother knew the minute she saw them that they were her brother's, because she made them for him."

"And you blame the white trappers for it? How do you know it wasn't an Indian?"

"By many things, the French are like Indians. They looked at footprints still frozen in the snow, and saw that the toes pointed out. An Indian never walks so. A Chippewa would never rob and kill one of his own, and if it had been some wandering Sioux, they would have scalped him. They were white."

"Oh Sarah, now I understand why you sometimes hate the whites. I too would hate such men."

"But that is enough of this talk," Sarah said. "we are nearly to the school, and I am anxious to show it to you."

The school was a log structure about twenty feet wide and thirty feet long. Sarah opened the door and they went into a large room filled with benches and tables of large pine planks. The sun was streaming in through windows set all along the southeast wall, so that the room was bright, and almost warm, despite the cold weather.

Sarah opened the big, round, iron stove at the center of the room, and began taking finely-split, pine kindling from a large, wooden box near the door. Peter took some of the larger chunks of wood and helped her build a fire. As he looked about, he was impressed by the neatness of the room. A large table was placed at the front, which obviously belonged to the teacher. It carried a load of books and teaching supplies. On the wall at the center of the room hung the flag of the United States of America with forty-four stars. It was flanked by a large crucifix and a picture of Jesus teaching the children. Lower on the wall there was a large slate board with the the alphabet neatly lettered along the top in a feminine hand. Beside it there was a map of the United States and its territories, showing the date 1890.

"If you teach the younger children, and Father Goebel teaches the older ones, how do you do it in one room?" Peter asked.

Sarah laughed. "We don't teach them all at the same time, silly. I teach the younger ones for two hours while the older ones work on their lessons. Then Father Goebel teaches the older ones while I help the younger ones with their lessons. Sometimes I take the little ones in there." She said, pointing to a door at the front of the room. "Come, let me show you."

They went into a long, narrow room at the front of the main classroom. It had a small table with a kerosene lamp set on top and a pair of chairs. There were shelves on the walls, and a narrow bench along one side. At the far end of the room was a chest of drawers and a bed neatly covered with a patchwork quilt.

"This is the teacher's room" Sarah said. "When the weather is very bad, sometimes I sleep here. That way I don't have to walk all the way home, and I can tend the fire to keep the school warm."

"But then, where do you eat? I don't see any place for food."

"At Father Geobel's house, an old woman cooks for him and we have had many pleasant meals together. Come, sit on the bed with me, it is more comfortable than those straight backed chairs. I want to show you some of my favorite books." She took several volumes from the shelf and settled back close to him to read.

Peter was acutely aware of the young woman's body next to his. It was not a conscious thought, but rather a sensing of her own attraction to him. He took the book that she had begun to read from her hands and laid it on a chest beside the bed. Then he turned her to face him and tenderly yet firmly placed his lips on hers.

Sarah's resistance was momentary, and was followed by an urgent return of his kiss. They held each other desperately, their passion fueled by the long denial of their true emotions. Peter lay back on the bed and drew Sarah to him. He buried his fingers in her flowing black hair and pressed his lips to hers, hotly, in a storm of demanding passion. He undid the fastenings of her jacket and brought his hand to rest on a firm breast, the soft cotton of her shirt did nothing to mask the hard nipple beneath. The effect on Peter was immediate and dramatic and he pressed her body to him as if to consummate their love through the heavy clothing he wore.

Sarah's breathing became deep and she felt a strange giddiness, a deep and consuming feeling that she had never known before. It was insistent, driving her against her better judgment, against the sensible promises she had made to herself. She pressed Peter gently away, then stood up to strip off her heavy outer clothing. Peter watched her as though hypnotized, then suddenly jumped up to pull off his own coat and boots, not entirely sure where she was leading him.

Sarah answered the pleading of Peter's eyes by taking off her remaining clothing, and slipping beneath the patchwork quilt to escape the chill that was still in the air. In a moment he joined her, his own clothing now resting in an unkempt pile on the rough, wood floor. Again he drew her body to him and kissed her with a passion he had never known, with the unleashed hunger of his pent up desire. They made love then. And when it was over, they lay together, kissing and murmuring to each other in a manner possible only when it is the first time for each. It was the indescribable newness of young love.

Later, Peter walked Sarah back to her grandfather's cabin. They held hands, despite the bitter cold that engulfed them as the setting sun dropped below the trees. They were both silent, their love flowing through the touch of their hands, both thinking thoughts private to their own souls. And when they said good-bye, it was with a tender lingering kiss that spoke more of the gentle nature of love, than it did of passion.

From that day on Peter was a frequent visitor at the cabin of Wise Otter. He was warmly accepted by the old man because of his respectful attitude and his friendly, good natured manner. For his part, Peter had developed a genuine liking for the old warrior. He liked nothing better than to coax him into telling stories of the Chippewa people, which Sarah dutifully interpreted.

He understood now why Wise Otter and Christian Halvorsen were friends. They were men cut out of the same cloth, wise men and warriors, one red and one white. The bonding between Peter and the two older men continued to strengthen. It was their influence on his young personality that decided the outcome of many of the exigencies of his life.

Sarah's mother, Star Flower, was fond of Peter but was reluctant to encourage a deeper relationship between him and her daughter. The memory of her own white-man and the uncertainty of his fate haunted her. It was this that prevented her from encouraging her daughter toward joining with Peter in a life bond. So if she questioned the necessity of the trips Sarah made to the school with Peter, she gave no indication of it. She preferred to allow the relationship to continue in a casual manner. She did not wish to force a marriage of the two by objecting to their clandestine affair.

The last weeks before the spring log drive were joy filled for Peter and Sarah. The pain of Julia's betrayal had dulled in the ecstasy of Peter's new found love. But still, in private moments of bitterness he promised himself that one day she would regret having so easily forsaken him for another. And that promise, he swore, he would one day carry to fruition.

Chapter 5

A Teamster Now

One Sunday evening, when Peter returned from seeing Sarah, Gustav was waiting for him.

"Pete, Chris is looking for you, he wants you to go and see him right away."

"Did he say what for?"

"No, just that it was important."

Peter went to Christian's office wondering what was so urgent it couldn't wait for morning. The Boss was sitting in his old rocker reading a book when Peter entered.

"There you are, Pete. I was afraid you'd stay with Sarah all night. Is she good?" Christian grinned.

Peter colored, but ignored the question. "Gus said you wanted to see me. Have I done something wrong?"

"No, no, nothing like that. How about a swig of schnapps to warm yourself? You must be cold after your long walk." He offered a bottle to Peter and Peter took a healthy pull of the sweetish liquor.

"You know Hjalmar Olsen, don't you?" Christian continued.

"Yah, he's one of the big sleigh teamsters, he drives the four big, sorrel Belgians ."

"Yep, he's the one. His kid came and got him today, wife's awful sick."

"That's too bad." Peter said, and waited for the rest of the story. He knew Christian hadn't call him over just to be sociable.

"That puts us one team short for tomorrow, unless we can find a teamster who can talk Swedish to his horses. You know how to harness a team and drive them?"

"Yes, but I've never driven a team of four. We didn't have such big sleds in Smaland where I worked." Peter said, wishing that Christian would find someone else. He watched the twelve foot wide sleds with their towering loads of logs, and he feared them.

"Well Kid," Christian said, emphasizing 'Kid' (a habit he had when he was daring Peter to do something.) "When you started driving two horses, you didn't know how to do that either, did you? You're a smart fellow, you'll get the hang of it soon enough. Just don't wreck the sleigh and kill the horses." He offered the schnapps to Peter again, signaling an end to debate.

"I'll have the bull cook wake you the same time he hustles the other teamsters out."

"How long will I do this?"

"Til the log drive, unless you kill yourself first." Christian laughed and took a pull of the schnapps. "Now you better get some sleep, Pete. Four o'clock comes quick."

At four the next morning one of the cookees shook Peter awake. He pulled on his clothes and walked out into the squeaking crispness of a February morning. Soon it would be March and the air would begin to warm. But now it was still frigid, and the snow squeaked beneath his feet as he went to the stable to feed and harness the four Belgians.

The other teamsters were already there, having slept in their clothes, thus saving precious minutes. Peter gave each horse some oats, then stuffed the manger full of hay. He fitted the sweat pad and collar on the first horse, then hoisted a harness onto his shoulder from a hanger beside the stall. As he swung the unwieldy mass of leather straps over the face-high back of the Belgian, he remembered why he had chosen to be an axe-man rather than a teamster. (The lumberjacks were still sleeping.) He fitted the hames bars to the collar and cinched them tight, then dropped the harness over the horse's rump and lifted its tail over the rump strap. He was tightening the girth (or belly band) when he heard a voice.

"Hey Mon, would you like a little help?"

It was Jacque, the diminutive Frenchmen who was known to haul the biggest loads of all the teamsters. He took a sweat pad and collar from the rack and started to harness a Belgian.

"I heard that Hjalmar had to go home, wondered who the boss was going to put on his sleigh—ever drive a haul team?"

"Yah, but only a single team, and not such big loads," Peter said. "I'm afraid I won't be able to handle it."

"Don't worry Pete, driving is the same. Just have to watch the loaders so they get the logs settled straight and tight, then check and recheck your chains. A loose chain will kill you. And don't forget to talk to Hjalmar's horses in Swede, that's what they're used to."

"Jacque, I don't know how to load and chain these big loads. I'm afraid that I'll break a chain, or that one will come loose. I don't want to kill the horses, and I don't want to get killed either."

"Tell you what Keed, when we go up to the timber, you go ahead of me and behind Hans. Then I can show you how to chain up your load, and you can follow Hans down to the river. That German is a good teamster and knows how to handle a load. You can watch and do what he does. We'll make your first load small so you can get the feel of it. Hokay?"

Peter was grateful for the Frenchmen's concern, and went to breakfast feeling a trifle reassured. He was afraid, but he remembered Christian's admonition to learn all he could, and to take every opportunity and make the best of it. He was determined to succeed in this opportunity to prove himself at something few men ever learned.

After breakfast, he and Jacque took the big Belgians out of the stable and hooked them to the logging sleigh, a huge, four runnered sled that had runners eight feet apart and load beams (bolsters) twelve feet across. Then they led out Jacque's team of dappled gray Perch's, or Percherons, and hooked them to his sleigh.

Hans had already broken his sleigh free of the frozen snow by swinging his team first to one side and then to the other, and was heading up the haul road. Peter talked to the Belgians, duplicating the maneuver, and turned the horses toward the twin iced furrows that were the haul road.

The Belgians trotted briskly between the runner grooves of the road, their sharp caulked shoes beating a steady rhythm on the icy surface. The horses seemed to feel an exhilaration in the crisp air of early morning, a feeling that spread to Peter. Despite his concerns about the challenge he faced, he felt a certain pride as he guided the mighty creatures along the road. Heads high, harness metal jingling, they ran, the behemoths of the horse family. They were his team, these giants, and he would be a teamster, a member of the aristocracy of the logging camp.

Peter watched as Hans positioned his sleigh carefully in front of a log deck in the forest. This was a pair of huge logs laid out with their butts to the haul road, on which the logs to be hauled were stacked crossways. Hans set his sleigh so that its load bolsters were close to the two deck logs. Next a hired farmer positioned his team near the sleigh, but opposite the pile of logs. The groundhogs, or loading men, hooked a chain to a log and guided it with their cant hooks as the team of horses rolled the log onto the sleigh. This continued until the load was too high to roll the logs up a pair of heavy poles used as a ramp.

At this point the "top loaders" took over, using a forty foot high "A" frame built of two poles and a pulley or tackle block to lift the logs to the top of the load. As the team of horses pulled on the line, the logs were swung up onto the load, and guided into place by the "top loaders". The job of top loading was the most dangerous job in the logging camp. It was said there were no old top loaders, as they were killed or maimed by falling logs, or developed enough common sense to quit and do something else.

When Hans had enough logs on his load he chained it down to the sleigh. The pile on top of the sleigh was about ten feet high, and weighed about twelve tons. It contained as many thousands of board feet of lumber.

Hans and Jacque were supremely confident of their abilities, and not a little daring. They had the habit of riding atop their loads, rather than walking by the side as some drivers did. It was true that they didn't grow leg weary, Peter thought, but he shuddered at what would happen to the men if they had the ill fortune to break a binding chain.

Peter watched as Hans, atop his load of logs spoke to the four horses. In unison they threw their bodies into the harnesses, squatting slightly as they strained with their hind legs to start the massive load moving. Imperceptibly at first, the sleigh broke free, gaining momentum as it moved along on its bed of ice until the horses were moving in an easy, quick-walk along the road.

Once a load started moving, it moved easily, much the same as a skater on a pond. The weight of the load, and the friction as it moved, caused a film of ice to melt and act as a lubricant to the runners. As long as a driver kept his load moving, his team of four could pull it easily, despite the tremendous weight.

As Hans moved off, Peter spoke to his horses and moved into position at the deck. The groundhogs were young men like himself who were not adept enough with axe and saw to be on the felling crews. They began by hooking chains and horsing logs with a canthook and their backs, hoping to someday get one of the higher paying jobs driving a team or felling timber.

Some of them graduated to "top loader" which paid better, but also had a generally short longevity. Now, a short, blond kid hailed Peter.

"Hey Pete, how'd you get onto Hjalmar's sleigh? You got pull with the boss?"

"Nah," Peter hollered back, "he just knows a good man when he sees one. I didn't ask for it, but I got it all right.... Hey Jim, do me a favor and load me light, it's my first load and I need to get used to the rig and the road."

"Sure Pete, we'll just skip the top loading first time around. After that we'll add a couple of logs each time until you got a real load."

Peter watched as the big white pines were rolled onto his sleigh, then threw the chains across and pulled them tight with iron binders. He spoke to the horses and they heaved into their harnesses, easily breaking the light load loose.

The deck was about two miles from the rollway at the river. The road wound along the ridges so that the horses never had to pull on an upgrade of more than a foot of rise to one hundred feet of distance. The iron edged runners of the haul sleigh slid easily on the ice bottomed furrows of the haul road, and the fresh horses made good time.

Peter was hard pressed to keep up with the long strides of the Belgians as he half walked, half ran alongside his load. Soon he weakened in his determination to walk with his team, and stopped the horses for a moment, so he could scramble up the log butts to the top of the load. For as long as he hauled logs, that is where he rode, in spite of the danger he knew was always present.

As he neared the river the haul road began a gentle decline, and the horses no longer had to pull on their harness tugs. Rather, the rear team had to hunch back on the neck yoke (cross bar at the end of the sled's steering pole) of the sleigh to check its speed.

As the road became steeper, the sleigh crossed over bunches of marsh hay that had been pitched into the furrows to act as a brake for the loads. Were it not for this friction applied to the sleigh runners, the heavy loads of logs would overtake the team, the results of which would be killed or maimed horses and wrecked sleds.

To be sure that the braking effect was just right, unskilled laborers called "road monkeys" accompanied the loads down inclines, throwing hay in front of the runners of the sleds whenever the teamster demanded. A few of these men stood along the road as Peter brought his little, eight ton load down. They leaned on their fork handles as he passed, making good natured derogatory remarks.

"Hey Swede, my sister hauls heavier than that." Or, "Hey Pete, everybody hauled pissant loads like that, we'd lose our jobs. Wouldn't need no hay, just run em down."

By the time Peter reached the rollway at the river edge, his ears were a ruddy red. And he still had to meet Fry, the log scaler, who was none too happy with Peter's efficiency in writing his production reports.

"My, my, what have we here?" Fry sneered. "My office boy has become a teamster, and look at the load you have. It must go all of nine thousand feet, did you lose some of your logs on the way down, Pete?"

Fry's comments were less than good natured, and Peter felt the bite of the man's sarcasm.

"At least I can do my job by myself, Fry. I don't have to cry for help like some people I know."

Fry's face reddened and he retorted angrily, "Don't get too big for your britches, just because you' re the boss's flunky. There's those as would like a chance to trim you down a bit."

Peter was about to make an angry retort, but he realized that antagonizing the man further would end his usefulness. There were still things he could learn from this man.

"I'm sorry, Sir. I was out of line, and you are right about the load. But I'm a greenhorn at driving, and I didn't want to take a chance of wrecking the rig on my first load."

Fry was mollified by the apology and Peter's respectful demeanor. He handed Peter the branding hammer, and began to measure logs.

"And right you are Lad, better safe than sorry I always say. And if you are the first team back to camp, I'd take it kindly if you had the time to help me enter the figures for the day. Not that I can't do it, you understand, but there's only twenty-four hours in a day, and a man needs to sleep some of them."

Peter had learned another lessen in judgment that he would not forget. He could have made an enemy in Fry, instead he had preserved a relationship that could prove useful to him. He hauléd logs all that day, each load bigger than the one before it. Finally his loads were of a substantial enough size to avoid the harassment of the road monkeys and the groundhogs at the rollway. That night, after he had cared for his team and filled his own stomach with beans and beef, he helped Fry with the big ledger of production,while the log scaler prepared the company report.

Christian Halvorsen entered the office after visiting with the blacksmith about making some shackles for the "wanigan" or cooking raft that would soon be built. The wanigan would travel with the logs on the spring log drive, and the shackles were chain assemblies that held the corners of the log raft together. He looked at Peter with surprise.

"Pete! I thought I had you hauling logs. What the dickens are you doing here when you could be jawing or flipping cards with the rest of the jacks?"

"Mr. Fry can use a little help, and there are things he can teach me. It's much better than sitting around picking at lice." Peter gave Christian a boyish grin.

"Can't argue on that. I 'm not paying you extra wages though, in case you were figuring on it." Christian regarded Peter with shrewd eyes, and thought that the kid just might own an outfit one day. "Anyway, don't work too late, Kid. You need your wits about you on that sleigh."

The days of driving the four big Belgians passed swiftly, and Peter became one with his team. He now was hauling loads that equaled those of Jacque and Hans. Gradually a friendly rivalry grew between the three, a competition to see who could haul the most board feet of timber to the rollway on a load.

Fry entered into the spirit of the contest, and kept a piece of pine slab outside his scaling shack with a running total of timber hauled by each of the teamsters every day. At first, the young Swede trailed the German and the Frenchmen, but gradually he closed the gap on Hans. The veteran teamster was driven to take ever bigger loads, and ever bigger chances.

The logs were loaded on the twelve foot wide bunks or cross members of the sleigh, three or four tiers high, with the outer logs stacked slightly higher than the inner ones, forming a cradle shaped load. Four oak stakes were set in sockets at the ends of the two bunks and served to keep the logs in place during loading. Then a pair of heavy chains were fastened over the load and to the bunks.

Since the outer logs were higher than the inner ones, the chains fastened over the load were suspended loosely over the inner logs. Several logs were then dropped onto these chains, forcing them down into the cradle thus formed, and tightening the binding chains on the entire load. These binding logs were not chained in place but rested securely in the depressed center of the load by their own weight.

It was such a load that Hans was hauling this morning, five tiers high, with three thirty inch binder logs, and two massive forty two inch pines as a cap.

"Gott damn!" He said to his team. "We got eighteen thousand feet at least, let that Swede kid and that skinny Frenchman try to beat that." He was grinning broadly as the road monkeys gaped at him, then ran to pitch hay under the sleigh's creaking runners as he started down the incline.

Over fifteen tons of logs swayed gently as the sleigh groaned its way over the slight unevenness of the ice road. Then, a sound like a rifle shot rang out as one of the over-burdened maple runners snapped, dropping the right front bunk to the ground. The load swayed perilously, threatening to roll over on its side and cast logs and team-ster down from the ridge along which the road was built. The left runner of the sleigh raised off the ice, then returned to its track as the huge load settled back. It came to rest at a crazy tilt that caused the stout oak load stakes to give off little snapping sounds, as the weight of the logs broke their fibers one by one.

On top the load, Hans was standing on the two big logs as he began maneuvering his sleigh down the slope. When the load tipped, the sudden lurch rolled the unchained timbers apart, and Hans fell, his right leg dropping between the logs. The return lurch of the load slapped them back together, crushing Hans's leg with the tremendous pressure of several tons of wood.

Hans felt the shock and heard the sound of bone breaking, but it was fear for his life not pain that stunned him into a paralized silence. He sat there pinned by the huge logs, as the load stakes crackled their complaints. He knew he would be crushed into a mass of broken bone and torn tissue by the torrent of logs that would thunder down the slope when the last fibers of the oak stakes parted. Hans thought not of himself or even of his dear wife. Alone in his mind's picture was little Elke, his little blonde, blue eyed five year old Elke. The thought of never holding her on his lap again brought tears to the tough German's eyes.

The road monkeys saw it happen, as did Peter on the return trail a hundred feet away. The two road men ran to control the great horses who were rolling their eyes and threatening to bolt, which would certainly seal Hans' doom by causing the immediate collapse of his load.

Peter saw the logs slap together like the jaws of a great trap, and he knew no amount of lifting by men would raise the huge timbers. Immediately he turned his team in a circle and brought them to a stop with the tail of his sleigh to the tilting load. Oblivious to the snapping sound from the far side of the logs, he threw a heavy chain over his shoulder and climbed the slowly shifting log pile. Swiftly he wrapped the chain around the butt of the great pine and dropped the other end to one of the road monkeys.

"Hook it onto the sleigh and pull!" He yelled.

But Jacque, who had also seen the runner break, already had the reins, and at his urging the great Belgians laid into the load. The huge log rolled up and away as Peter pulled Hans from his trap and passed him to waiting hands below. As he leaped from the load there was a final cracking of wood and the dull snap of parting chain. Eighteen thousand board feet of logs tumbled and bounced down the ridge.

They laid some poles across Peter's sleigh and padded them with the soft needled branches of the pines, and this was the ambulance that brought Hans from the woods. At the camp, he was loaded into the tote sleigh on a bed of blankets and was taken to the hospital at Grand Rapids. Christian himself drove the team and delivered Hans to the doctors. He stayed to learn of the man's condition, and to send word of his injury to his wife in Mankato.

When Christian returned late in the night, he told the men in the bunkhouse that Hans's leg was badly broken. And while he would probably keep it, it was not likely he would ever return to the woods. He made a little speech thanking Peter for his unselfish heroism, which brought a round of applause from the jacks.

Then Christian returned to the business of running the camp. A new teamster must be found to keep the logs moving. It was March and soon the sun would destroy the ice haul roads. Any logs left in the woods at that time would remain until the following year. This would result in a loss of income for Northwest Timber, and would reflect directly on the management of Christian Halvorsen.

Mid-March saw the elements turn to the fury of a blizzard of such savagery that all work was stopped for two days. Christian Halvorsen grew taciturn as the snow fell like a vast curtain of white. It was driven by gale force winds that sifted it through every crack and crevice, forming little drifts of the stuff around doors and causing a constant flurry from the skylights in the bunkhouse.

The men, confined to the suffocating atmosphere of the bunkhouse grew irritable. Loud confrontations over imagined insults or cheating at cards threatened to become all out brawls. The bull cook ruled the bunkhouses, and his word was law. But in the two days of the blizzard, Edgar often needed the aid of Christian to settle disputes between burly lumberjacks intent on destroying each other. Invariably, the camp boss showed up to negotiate peace wearing his caulked boots and carrying a grub axe handle. His mediation was generally quick and successful, as the combatants viewed the rangy, muscular frame of the boss, and the sturdy hickory in his hand. Of course, there is always an exception to the rule, and such was the case on the afternoon of the second day of the storm.

Christian was sitting in his beat up rocker with his feet propped up on an empty nail keg, reading his copy of *Hamlet* for the ninth time. Edgar, the bull cook burst into his office.

"Boss, Bill Young and Mike Feeney are at it again, this time its going to be blood for sure!"

Christian laid his book down wearily and picked up the grub axe handle.

"Okay Edgar, let's go see what the problem is."

"I don't know if that'll do it," Edgar said, looking at the handle, "Bill has a gun, and he's threatening to shoot Mike."

"That bad, eh! What's it about?"

"Bill said Mike was cheating at cards."

"And he's gonna shoot a man over a damned game of cribbage?"

"They's not playing cribbage Boss, it's poker for money, and Bill stands to lose near a hundred dollars."

"Damned idiots, they know that's against the rules, I oughta fire them both. What's Sven doing, is he in it too?"

"Yeh, him and Gus too, but they's peaceable."

"Well get over there ahead of me so they can clean up the cards and money, or I'll have to fire the whole damned bunch. Tell them I'm on my way!"

Christian took time to pack some fresh tobacco into his pipe before stepping into the storm. Then he walked to the bunkhouse and threw open the door. Bill Young was standing with his back to the door, and turned to face Christian as he entered. Bill was shorter than Mike Feeney by almost a head. It was easy to see he would come off second best in a fight with the two hundred and fifty pound Irishman. Now, with this new threat, fear showed clearly on his face. Bill pointed the Derringer he held at Christian.

"I ain't got no fight with you Boss, so stay out of this. I'm going to kill me a cheatin, Irish varmint."

"You ain't going to kill anybody Bill, at least not over a card game. Let me have that piece of junk, and you can get out of this without going to jail."

Bill looked at Christian uncertainly, and in his moment of hesitation Mike stepped forward and placed a meaty fist at the base of Bill's skull with all the force his beefy body could muster. The smaller man went down as if he'd been hit with a canthook and lay unmoving on the floor.

Christian picked up the Derringer and slipped it into his pocket.

"Did you cheat him, Mike?"

"Hell, Chris! He'd of cheated me if'n he had the brains for it. All I did was slip an insurance card in here and there. I'd of let it go as a joke, if he hadn't pulled that pissant gun on me."

"And if he hadn't caught you, you'd have taken his year's wages. That's why we don't allow gambling in the outfit. You can pick up your pay and hit the tote road. I haven't got room for card sharps here."

Christian turned as if to go, but faced the group of men again.

"Sven! Being that you aren't all lily white, you can tell Bill that he can pack his duffel too. That is when he wakes up," he said, as he looked at the lumberjack on the floor, who was now beginning to stir. "And the next time you show a pack of cards and money at the same time, you can find another outfit."

Mike had been digesting what had just happened, and the darkness of his face said he didn't like it. He stepped over the prone man on the floor and stood nose to nose with Christian. The reek of whiskey drifted into the boss's nostrils, and he knew that Mike's thinking was probably issuing from a bottle of "Old Crow" rather than his usually rational brain.

"Look here, Mr. Bull of the Woods! It ain't fair to send me down the road, and not Sven and Gus. They was playin same as I."

"They were playing, Mike. You were cheating. That's why you're getting your paycheck."

"Well, hell! If'n you're going to fire me anyway, I might as well get some satisfaction!" He shook his fist in Christian's face.

Wordlessly, Christian turned and took a step toward the door, then whirled to meet the sucker punch he knew would be aimed at the back of his neck. He caught Mike's fist with his left forearm, deflecting it harmlessly. His own right found the middle of the big Irishman's face, flattening his nose like a ripe tomato. As Mike staggered backward with the force of the blow, the boss opened the door and stepped out into the windblown snow.

Outside, Christian sort of wished he hadn't left the grub axe handle in his office when he stoked his pipe. But he knew this one had to be without a weapon, if he were to keep the respect of the jacks. He reached for a big chunk of hard-drifted snow.

The Irishman stood for a moment, shaking his head like an enraged bull. As his shock befuddled brain cleared, he put a hand to his demolished nose, getting a palm-full of the streaming blood in the process. With a furious bellow he stamped through the doorway into the swirling darkness of the storm.

Mike was met by a semi-solid mass of coldness that blocked out his vision and made him momentarily helpless, as Christian slammed the hardened snow into his face. The next thing Mike was aware of was being hoisted into the air and spun rapidly around once, twice, thrice and then being flung hard on his back on the frozen walkway. Dizzily, fighting to regain his breath he struggled to his knees, groping for a hold on the shadow before him. Christian's knee struck hard into Mike's forehead. The impact destroyed the remaining coherence of his thought processes and he slumped silently into the snow.

Christian spoke to the men now gathered around him.

"Take him inside and fix him up. I want those two to hit the trail in the morning."

Then he turned and strode briskly to his office. He hated doing what he had just done, but he knew that he had reinforced the respect his men had for him. It would be a long time before it would be necessary to do it again.

Peter had watched his mentor with wide eyed admiration. He had committed each of Christian's actions to his memory, but he doubted that he would ever be able to fill the shoes of a camp boss. He was developing the mental toughness that it required. But he knew that his frame was too slight to take on all comers as Christian did, and that appeared to be a necessary factor in the job. No, there were other ways of becoming successful. The rich owners of the outfits certainly didn't have to be master brawlers. They amassed their fortunes by using their brains, that was the secret of their success. He would somehow learn their ways, and he would become rich like them. Someday soon, he would show all of those in Sweden who had doubted him. One day, he would make Julia wish that she had been true, he would make her banker look like a poor chore boy!

Chapter 6

Down the Wild River

The last days of hauling logs went swiftly. The road monkeys were now shoveling snow into the sleigh runner furrows, to maintain a slippery surface long enough to bring the last logs out of the forest. On the last night of the haul, Christian approached Peter with a sheet of paper on which there was a list of names.

"Pete, I'm rounding up river pigs to go down the river on the drive. Some of the jacks are going back to their farms and some don't have a hankering for ice water and wet beds. Sven and Gus are going, thought you might like to try your hand at riding logs."

Peter had hoped all along that he might be included in the spring log drive, the promise of adventure on the churning Mississippi appealed to his young senses. He broke into a broad grin.

"You bet I would, Boss. I've been thinking about it all winter."

"It's a miserable, cold, wet, dangerous job that isn't fit for a human being. But it pays fifty dollars a month Kid, still interested?"

"Sure, I hauled plenty of those logs, let them haul me for a while."

"Well, it's not quite that easy, but I figure you can handle it, you done everything else all right. Say Kid, what you figure on doing after we get to Minneapolis with the logs?"

Peter shrugged, "I don't know, I guess I'll have to find some kind of job. I think after I get enough money, I'll ask Sarah to marry me."

"Whoa there, Kid! Don't get the cart before the horse, there's plenty of time to think about tying that kind of knot. You aren't eighteen yet, are you?"

"No, Boss. But Sarah and I,...we've been together, and it isn't right this way."

"Look, Pete, just because you ride a horse doesn't mean you have to buy it. If you're serious about the Indian girl, there's plenty of time to marry her after you make a stake for yourself. A guy gets married young, he hasn't got a chance. Everything he earns goes into supporting a family, and he winds up dying with a pocketful of wishes and no money."

"But Chris," Peter said, reverting to his superior's given name, as he did when they were talking man talk. "You aren't married, and you don't have a stake either, do you?"

"You don't always see everything that's there, Kid. I don't let on about it because I don't want the loggers to know. I own twenty five percent of Northwest Timber, that's why you don't see company people out here. I am company, and I'd prefer it if you keep your jaw locked on it. The men wouldn't be the same if they knew, they'd always be crying for something or scared I'd fire them for farting in the wrong direction. I tell you, because it's different between you and me, Kid. I don't have a son, not saying I won't some time, cause I'm not too old to stud. But you're a good kid, and I want you to get started on the right track. I want you to be something besides a poverty stricken jackass of a logger."

Peter regarded the older man thoughtfully. "You're right Chris, one must put the horse first. I will become settled into a good job before I speak of marrying. But right now, I don't have any prospects after the log drive."

Christian poked some tobacco into his pipe and lit it. "I've got a friend who owns a sawmill in Minneapolis,...pretty big one. I went to logging timber years ago, he went to sawing it up. Turned out the big money was in the sawing. I'm not complaining, but his outfit is worth a dozen times the value of Northwest Timber. He doesn't have a son either, he might like having a smart young lad like you around."

"You think you might be able to get me a job with him?"

"Could be, if you keep shut about this marrying thing. He'd only want somebody who'd concentrate on the job, and not be all moonstruck over a woman. Anyway, we'll talk about it after the drive, when we're in Minneapolis."

Chris left to sign up other prospective river pigs for the drive. But he was thinking about Peter, whom he now considered as his protege. The lad could move upward in the lumber business, but not with a squaw for a wife, even if she was a half-breed. The society of Minneapolis would not accept her, hence the upper strata of business would not accept him.

Peter spent the evening thinking of the coming log drive, and the prospect of a good job at the end of it. Sarah would not be happy to see him go. But she would be glad he had gone when he had a good job with a big company, and she could join him in Minneapolis. She was smart and beautiful, and he would be very proud of her when he was successful. He could feel the closeness of it all. He would be rich and powerful, but for now he would not speak of marrying.

The March sun was sending the first trickles of melt water into the Mississippi. The ice below the rollways, with their forty foot high piles of logs, was melting back from the shore. Soon the ice would go out of the big river, and most of the logs would go with it. A small crew went further down the river to a backwater where the ice had already melted forty or fifty feet off the shoreline and began felling logs left there for a purpose. They skidded them with a team to the riverbank, where they were rolled into the water and chained together to form the wanigan. The wanigan was a huge raft that carried the cookshack and necessary supplies down the river with the log drive.

The rest of the remaining lumberjacks busied themselves dumping the piles of logs at the rollways into the river. Peter was given a peavey (a heavy wooden pole about four feet long with a sharp metal point on one end, and a swinging steel hook about a foot from the pointed end.) The point and the hook bit into a log, and the peavey was used as a lever to roll it.

The jacks removed all of the logs at the bottom of a pile, leaving only a main key log. Then the most experienced man went in on a floating log to remove the key. This time it was Sven. Peter watched as he moved his floating log close to the bottom of the huge pile. He put his peavey onto the log and twisted it. Then he pulled his peavey clear and pushed with it against the log pile at the same time.

As Sven's escape log floated into the current, the key log rolled into the water. Hundreds of logs on the rollway followed thundering their way into the river in a frightening, but magnificent maelstrom of rolling, tumbling, bouncing timber.

After the main body of logs splashed into the water, the real work began for the jacks. Every log remaining on the rollway had to be turned with peaveys, one man on each end until it rolled down the slope into the river. It was bone grinding, muscle stretching labor of the hardest kind. And when the sun dropped below the horizon, Peter was so tired he could barely eat. He fell into a deep and dreamless sleep the moment he hit his bunk.

As the trickles of snow-melt turned into little torrents, the river rose. The ice broke into huge chunks that went hurtling down the river, taking the first logs with them.

"There's no more Sundays, no holidays, only work days until we reach Minneapolis," Christian said to the crew.

"Those of you that want to get away from dry rolling these logs go with Sven. It's time we herded the bunch that's in the river. Those as don't like getting dunked in ice water stay here until the last log hits the river, then follow them down."

Peter and Gus went with Sven and a bunch of jacks that took pride in being cat-footed river pigs. After Peter picked up his bedroll and gear to stow on board the wanigan, he went to Christian.

"Boss, I know I won't get a chance to say goodbye to Sarah. I wondered if I might leave a letter here with the camp guard in case she comes here."

"Sure Kid, give it to me and I'll leave it with Lone Man when we all pull out of here." (Lone Man was the only Indian in the outfit. He was aptly named, because it was his job to guard the company property until the lumberjacks returned the next fall.)

Peter handed his letter to Christian and dashed after the other jacks who were already walking away down the bank of the river. Christian watched as they disappeared, then he looked thoughtfully at the letter in his hand.

"He's got no chance at all with a squaw wife." He said quietly, but with certainty, to himself. Then he packed his pipe, and with a single match lit both the pipe and the letter.

Peter had created a picture of himself riding down the river with pike in hand, while balancing precariously on a great pine log. It was more illusion than fact. He, along with the other river pigs, spent most of the time sitting on the river bank in the cold drizzle of April. They watched to see that the logs didn't jam up on boulders, or at a sharp bend in the river where the current tended to drive the logs aground.

Often they would have to pile into a bateau (a twenty foot flat-bottomed boat that was pointed on both ends) and row and pole out to where a bunch of logs were jamming up. It was not an easy proposition, when one considered the countless logs floating down the river, any one of which could crush or capsize the boat.

When they reached the jam, they would use peavies and pike poles to work the key log loose. Then they would paddle and pole as fast as they could to evade the rush of logs they had just freed. Back at the shore they would trek along the river bank clearing potential snags from the river, more often than not at least partially immersed in the icy water.

The days were worked from light to dark. Time out was taken to wolf down the hot food brought to them from the wanigan, which would be tied up against the shore at a convenient backwater. In good weather, the river pigs might sleep in a dry bedroll on the wanigan if there was room, or beside a crackling fire on the river bank. In days of heavy rain, they worked wet, ate wet and slept wet. It was the damp misery of working on the long log drive that reinforced Peter's decision to abandon the life of a logger when he reached Minneapolis. Christian's admonition, "Nobody ever made more than a measly living swinging an axe." was with him constantly now, and his resolve to better himself became a consuming desire within him.

Sarah walked down the trail to the logging camp with apprehension gnawing at her mind. Forest birds and animals flitted and scurried through the small brush and saplings where there had been a pine forest three years earlier, but she took little notice. It had been two weeks since Peter had last come to Wise Otter's cabin. She knew it was the time of the log drive, but surely he wouldn't have left without saying good-bye to her.

As she approached the logging camp it appeared to be deserted. The great sleds stood in a row, and no smoke rose from the cook house chimney. Sarah quickened her step, and half walked, half ran to the bunkhouse. She threw open the heavy door and was hit by an overpowering smell of staleness. The cavernous room was empty. A solitary pair of wool socks hung where they had been forgotten, on the slim pole near the ceiling that served as a drying rack. The place stank of old tobacco smoke and unclean bunks.

Sarah slammed the door shut and ran to Christian's office. A large padlock was fastened through the hasp on the plank door. A sick feeling of disappointment rose in her throat, as she fought back the tears that were coming to her eyes. He couldn't have left her without a word, Peter wouldn't do that. As she turned to walk away she started with surprise.

An Indian stood in the pathway, quietly regarding her. It was Lone Man, a tall, rangy, middle aged man who lived by himself a little way north of her village. He spoke to her in Chippewa.

"You are Sarah, granddaughter of Wise Otter. Do you look for Christian?"

Sarah regained her composure. "I didn't know they had gone. I look for the young man called Peter, he is a lumberjack."

Lone Man looked at her gravely.

"Yes, I know of him. He is gone down the river with the logs, maybe this many days." He held up both hands with fingers spread.

"Did he not leave any word for me? Perhaps a letter or a message?"

"No, he left nothing."

He reached down and picked up a stick, then continued.

"Young women who are the daughters of the Chippewa often give their hearts to the white men. Many times when these men go with the logs, they forget about the Chippewa women and go to their own." He broke the stick and flung it from him.

Sarah wanted to protest, to say that she and Peter were different, that she was almost as white as he, but anger suddenly gripped her. She turned and walked swiftly back the way she had come.

Peter sat on the river bank at a bend in the Mississippi a few miles below the village of Brainerd and just above the river's confluence with the Crow Wing. The sun was shining brightly, and he and Sven were idling on the shore of the great river, watching the steady flow of logs traversing the curve in the channel. It was wonderful to relax after two weeks of rafting logs through the series of lakes that made up the river's channel above Brainerd.

They had formed the logs into great rafts, as they were spilled into the lakes by the river's swift current. The rafts then had to be poled, rowed and half towed in the sluggish current of the lakes. It was nearly eight miles before the river resumed its swift travel in a narrow channel at Brainerd.

The work had been wet and tiring, and Peter had learned the true meaning of "river pig". He had earned the title there in the lakes of the Mississippi. He learned to jump from log to log, relying on the sharp calks on his boots for footing and a pike pole for balance. He had taken more than one dunking at first, and was forced to spend entire days in sodden clothing. Gradually, he had become 'cat footed', and was able to work for an entire day with no more of him getting wet than his boots and lower legs. Now the lakes had been crossed, and the logs would follow a swift river the rest of the way to Minneapolis.

"Sure is a pretty sight, all them logs just whipping around that bend," Peter said. "Don't know as how the boss needs anybody watching here."

"Wouldn't be all that sure of that," Sven returned. "There's some big boulders just below the surface on the near side, where the water foams up. In a year with lower water we've had a bad jam on them."

"My father always said, 'don't borrow trouble', Sven. You worry too much." Peter grinned and stretched luxuriously on the grass.

"Just the same, I'll be glad when we're gone from here. The Crow Wing pouring its water in here makes it damn tough to handle a boat, much less untangle a jam."

"Yeah, I guess so...Sven, do you think I should marry Sarah?"

"If you want to. Did you ask her?"

"Didn't have a chance to, we pulled out too fast. Christian says I should wait."

"Reckon he's right, you're still wet behind the ears."

"What's that mean?"

"It means you're still a greenhorn as far as life is concerned. If you wasn't, you'd of knowed what that means."

Peter's face reddened. "Shit, Sven! I can do damn near anything any man here can do. Just because I don't understand every smart-ass thing you say doesn't mean I'm a greenhorn!"

"Sure, and you can get a hard prick in five seconds. But I'll bet it's soft again in another five. You ain't a man yet, Pete. You're still part boy. There's lots of time to get yourself all tied up. Why don't you forget all this marrying shit for a few years? Sarah will wait, and if she don't, there's a lot of hot little things that would love to get their fingers in that curly hair of yours."

Sven reached out and tousled Peter's dark locks with his calloused hand.

Peter grinned self-consciously. "Yeah, maybe you guys are right, and it's not like I'm going away forever. I left a letter with Lone Man telling her to write to me at Northwest Timber in Minneapolis. I can get her to come there after I get a job."

Sven laughed. "Goddam Pete, you've got a simple mind. I thought you just agreed to forget getting married. Now here you are making plans to drag Sarah to Minneapolis with you."

"I love Sarah, and I kind of got used to being with her. But I'm not going to get married for a while."

"Sure, now you got hot pants, and can't get along without getting your wick dipped every week. Look, Kid, there's all kinds of women that specialize in taking care of problems like yours, in Minneapolis. How do you know that Sarah will have you anyway, if you haven't asked her?"

"I know she loves me, that's how!"

"Sure, and maybe she's bedding some good looking buck by now."

In exasperation Peter swung a hard right fist into his cousin's chest.

"Damn you Sven, I should kick your ass for that! You know Sarah's not that kind of woman. One day you'll find a woman of your own, and I'm going to make her out to be some kind of slut." He was about to say more, but Sven motioned for him to be quiet.

"Listen!"

A loud thumping , creaking, grinding sound was coming from the river just beyond their field of vision. The two men sprang to their feet and ran crashing through the brush that screened the lower part of the river bend. A few hundred feet further they broke out of the brush at the water's edge. Peter's eyes grew large, and his mouth opened.

"By Golly, look at that!"

Sven shook his head. "Goddamn, I was afraid of that. Now we're in for our share of hell on earth!"

Somewhere on the bend a heavily branched tree had been undercut by the current, and collapsed into the river. It had floated along with the logs that massed around it until it reached the point where the Crow Wing flowed into the Mississippi. There the current of the Crow Wing drove the tree onto a cluster of submerged boulders. The logs behind the tree came to an abrupt stop, and the logs following slid up over them. Their combined weight pushing the tree more securely down into the boulders. As more logs arrived, they piled up on the obstruction, twisting crosswise in the current until they too were pinned to the bottom in a ever growing mass.

"Sonofabitch!" Sven cursed. "We'll need help with that one. Go down and get the guys on the next bend. I'll go up to the Wanigan and get a bateau and some dynamite, and whoever is up there."

As Sven ran along the river trail slashed into the brush by several passings of river pigs, he was forming a plan for breaking the log jam. If it was a simple jam of logs, he could probably hook a cable to the key log and have a team of horses on the river bank pull it free. But with an uprooted tree forming the base of the jam, it would take dynamite. Ten horses couldn't pull that free! He would have to place a charge down under the trunk of the tree, now pressed down under several feet of fast flowing water. The charge would have to be large enough to completely destroy the tree. The trouble with that was, several thousand board feet of good timber would be destroyed too. Christian Halvorsen wouldn't like that idea, the damned guy acted like he had a share in the company! Where's that damned sand bar that the wanigan is anchored to?

Shit, this is the first bend of the river, the damned raft is a half mile further up! He ran faster and his lungs labored under the coating of pipe smoke he'd inhaled through the years. He slowed to a walk to ease the pounding in his chest and scanned the far shore for river pigs working the other bank. A large object with smoke curling up from it was moving slowly along the far shore. The wanigan! The assholes moved it to the other side! They'd never get it back here, the logs would drift to a stop before they could! Sven shook his head and continued running up the trail, he had to get far above the raft.

Several hundred yards further he stopped and pulled his sheath knife from his belt. He began hacking at a slim aspen sapling beside the trail. With the trunk partly severed, he threw his weight against it and snapped the remaining soft ,white wood. A few strokes of the heavy blade removed the branches, leaving him with a pole about twelve feet long. He slipped the knife back in its sheath, and without hesitation waded into the icy water of the river.

Sven gasped for breath as the depth of the water reached his crotch. He had done this a hundred times, but the shock was always new. He silently cursed the crew that had moved the raft, Christian Halvorsen for having ordered it, the icy raging river, and the logs it carried. A huge white pine log was bearing down on him as he struggled to keep his footing on the slimy stones of the river bed. He threw his arms over it and heaved his body up, swinging a leg over the scaly trunk like a rider mounting a running horse. A smaller log drifted near, and he placed his pole across it to steady himself as he rose to his feet. With his boot calks gripping the rough bark of the great log, he stood pole in hand, like a tight rope walker in some insane, watery circus.

Sven was in his element now. He was the master, the star performer, as he deftly guided his clumsy vessel further out into the stream. Ramming his pole against the stony river bottom, he forced the pine out into the deep water of the channel, and into the company of a drifting mass of timber. Carefully, but swiftly he jumped to one log and then another as though they were giant, moving stepping stones. It was no job for a novice, the water was swift and deep. One slip and he would be thrown in among the logs, to be crushed and drowned. But Sven didn't think of that. He thought only of the pole in his hands, the logs around him, and the nearing shore. The men on the wanigan had seen him. They poled the giant raft against the river bank, and threw a line around a stump jutting out over the water. Sven poled his last log into the shallow water near the wanigan and jumped lightly on to its deck.

Christian stood on the log deck, his stub pipe tightly clenched in the corner of his mouth. "What's up, Sven?"

"Logs are jamming bad below the bend, we need help and dynamite!"

"You need to blast? Can't you pick the key log out?"

Sven looked at Christian sourly. "Nope, damned tree is at the bottom of the pile, the whole river is nearly bridged by now. We got to blow that tree, its branches are jammed into the boulders down there."

Christian turned to the men now gathered behind him. "Get the blasting stuff in a bateau, and each of you grab a peavey or a pike, maybe we can still get around the jam before it closes off the whole river."

Six men grabbed oars and began bending their backs in unison, sending the boat swiftly down the river. Sven and Christian stood in the bow and stern with pike poles, deftly guiding floating logs away from the craft. As they reached the bend, the current slowed, and the water was rising on the river banks. A huge dam of logs was forming.

The center of the pile was now about ten feet high and climbing, as more logs arrived and were forced onto the pile by the rising river. A torrent of water was still pouring through a gap between the shore and the log jam. It was through this churning flume that the bateau now sped. The men at their oars worked frantically to keep the bateau straight with the current. As the surging water caromed off submerged boulders, it sent gushers into the air that soaked them and threatened to swamp the boat.

"Turn her toward the jam." Christian shouted above the roar of the water.

The men responded, and the boat slipped into the relative quiet water below the dam of logs.

"Pull her up close to the tree, there where those branches are sticking out, then hold her," Sven shouted, as he began assembling a bundle of dynamite sticks. "I'm going to ram the charge down under the trunk of that son-of-a-bitch."

"Keep the load small," Christian said. "No use busting up good timber to clear a measly tree out of the way."

"Better to bust up a few God damned logs than somebody's ass." Sven spat at Christian. He grabbed another handful of brown sticks and added them to the growing bundle.

"Maybe so, but I think that's more than enough to do the job. Plant her, and let's get out of here."

Sven looked at the charge skeptically, then started tying it to a small pole. He mumbled uncomplimentary comments about Christian's lineage, just loud enough so that the men nearest him could hear. The oarsmen hooted, and Christian colored.

"You got anything to say, do it on shore, you fucking, smart-ass Swede."

Sven grinned, satisfied that he had got to his Norwegian boss without insulting him to his face. He plunged the charge deep into the water, and tied the pole to a branch of the tree. He held the fuse to some glowing coals from the cook's stove, that he carried in a covered can for the purpose. The end of the fuse blackened and began spewing smoke.

"Let's get the hell out of here!" He hollered as he pushed the bateau away with his pike pole.

As the men reached shore, they were met by Peter and the river pigs from downstream. Now the group watched the log pile expectantly as Christian counted off the seconds, "30, 29, 28,…3, 2, 1. " He turned to Sven.

"The fuse went out. We'll have to go out and set it again."

"Hell no!" Sven said. "I gave it an extra minute. It should go just about… ."

His words were cut short by a huge geyser of water and flying debris, followed by a loud "whump!" A flurry of broken branches and splintered logs splashed into the river and floated away, but the jam held.

"Damn! Damn!" Sven swore, adding a string of expletives in Swedish which were not lost on the Norwegian boss.

"I knew that charge wasn't big enough to do the job, but you had to worry about a few stinking feet of lumber, you tight fisted herring choker! Now we'll have to blow it again, twice the risk and twice the cost!"

Christian colored, but he knew Sven was right, and as always he was fair.

"You're right, Sven. But cussing at each other won't help. The tree is busted up though. I think we can yank the key log out with a double team of horses and a cable. I'll tie the cable myself, being that it's a risky business."

"Shit! I don't need the boss to do my job!" Sven growled. "And I don't need horses and cable to get that key out. Hell! It'll take a couple of hours to get the nags over here, by then the jam'll be twenty feet high!"

"You're right about that, Sven," Christian said. "But do you think you can get that bunch of timber apart with a peavey? It'll be damned risky."

"Never seen a jam I couldn't bust yet. If you won't let me blow her apart, I'll take it apart a stick at a time." Sven held up a peavey. "Just give me some good oarsmen, and nobody as has a wife and kids,... just in case."

Christian knew that the braggy Swede sometimes let his pride get in the way of his judgment. Still, he had seen him break up some hellish jams.

"All right, those men that are good in a bateau and want to go, grab an oar!"

Peter jumped down to the boat with the other men, but Sven clamped a hand on his shoulder.

"You better stay here, Pete. I wouldn't want the boss to have to write to your mom if this goes wrong."

Peter twisted free of his cousin's grip and picked up an oar. "You said I'm not a man yet, guess I'll have to prove you wrong!"

Sven laughed and slapped Peter's back. "I guess you'll do that all right, but take care."

The bateau glided swiftly across the water which was now almost free of floating logs. The growing mass of the log jam creaked and grumbled with the strain of the thousands of tons of logs and water now piled up behind it. Peter looked up to the top of the growing pile of timber from the fragile hull of the bateau. He felt fear claw into his stomach and fought hard to stem the surge of panic that began to flow through him. He forced himself to concentrate on the oar in his hands and his cousin in the bow of the boat. Sven was standing, peavey in hand studying the structure of the gigantic puzzle before him.

"I figure that little pine is the key," he said. "But, we'll have to get three, maybe four of these others away from it before I can get it out." He hooked his peavey into a log and threw his weight on the handle. The pine moved slightly, then stopped. "I can't get enough leverage on it from here, I'll have to get on the pile."

"I don't think you should do that," Peter said. "What if the pile goes?"

"It won't, that's not the key," Sven said, as he jumped lightly to a log at the base of the jam.

Somewhere beneath the surface of the water a log slipped a few inches with the enormous pressure against it, then another moved, and another. The great pile shuddered, and the small key log snapped like a match stick. Sven turned to jump back into the bateau just as the log he was standing on twisted free of the mass. He was thrown into the water twenty feet from the boat as the jam began to move. Peter grabbed a pike pole and jumped to the bow of the bateau, reaching with it to the floundering man.

"Swim Cousin! Swim!" he screamed.

Sven saw Peter and the pole, and took a few frantic strokes toward it before the logs descended on him. The last Peter saw of his cousin in life, was the terror in his eyes, and his mouth frozen in a scream. Peter stood paralyzed in the front of the boat with the pike still extended. The other men pulled desperately on their oars, to avoid the rush of timber and water that was about to destroy them all. Somehow they fought their way down the river amid the racing logs and beached the boat on a small sand bar. Two of the men knelt and prayed quietly. The others stood silently and stared at the river and the floating logs. No one spoke.

Two days later the leading river pigs found Sven's body floating in a muddy little backwater. They wrapped him in his bedroll and a piece of canvas from the wanigan and carried him to a little ridge above the river. There all the men paid their last respects to the braggy, beloved Swede. Silently they took a last look at his bleached, bruised face before they tied the canvas shut.

Christian said some words over the brave Swede who had been a "damned good jack and a better man," and if he choked up a few times, not a man thought less of him for it. Then Peter began reciting in his trembling, young voice, "The Lord is my shepherd, I shall not want...." All the men that knew the words joined in, those who didn't bowed their heads. They buried Sven Thorson in a little clearing above the Mississippi, with a cross hewn from an oak tree to mark his grave.

That night Peter took pencil and paper and placed himself at the cook's table on the wanigan. In the dim light of a kerosene lantern, he wrote:

My dearest Mother, Father, Sisters and Brother,

I write to you tonight about a happening that brings great sadness to all of us. On this day we buried my dear cousin and good companion, Sven Thorson. He rests on a little knoll by the shore of the Mississippi River some twelve miles south of the village of Brainerd, Minnesota.

I was with him when he met his death in a terrible accident during the log run on the river. A huge log jam built up on a dead tree which came to rest amid some boulders in the stream. After vainly trying to blast the jam free, Sven bravely and foolishly tried to pick out the key log with a peavey. The key log broke while he was on the pile and he was thrown into the water. I tried to reach him with a pike pole, but the logs came down too fast. Sven was crushed beneath the mass of falling timber. I do not know if he was killed that moment, or if he was drowned in the flood. We men in the boat narrowly escaped with our lives, managing to make it to shore in the turmoil of logs and water. I held on to the faint hope that he might have made it to shore somewhere downstream. But that hope was dashed when we found his body today, two days after the accident.

We buried him as properly as we could, saying good words over him, and finishing with the twenty-third psalm. We made a mighty cross of oak and placed it at his head. It will stand for many years, so that should some member of his family wish to visit him, he can be found. I am sending his Bible and a few small things of his to his mother and father, so that they may have some remembrance of their son who died so far from them.

Sven was not just a cousin, but a best friend to me. He helped me get a job, and saved my life, as I wrote to you. He gave me much guidance and comforted me when I was sad or homesick. I will sorely miss him, and I will always carry with me the look of terror on his face as the timber and the river claimed him. Do not fear for his soul. A good man like Sven must surely be in heaven with the saints and Jesus. He will always abide with me in my memory and I know that one day I will see him again.

As for me, do not worry, the grief of losing Sven will pass. I have my friend Gustav, and my boss Christian who treats me as a son. There is also a young woman that I keep company with. Her name is Sarah. She is the daughter of a French trapper who was also taken by the river. Sarah is beautiful and kind, and is a teacher at a school near the logging camp. She is also a healer, the one that helped me when my hands and feet were frozen. When I have a good job in Minneapolis, I will ask her to marry me. Perhaps by then I will have enough money to send for Mother and Father to come and visit.

I have decided that I will not go logging again. I have seen enough of the hardship and loneliness of the wilderness. It would never again be like it was with Sven and Gustav and me, and I do not wish to end my days in a lonely grave as Sven did. Christian has a friend who owns a sawmill in Minneapolis, and he says he will try to get me a job with him. He says there is much need for the knowledge of accounting that I learned from Fry, while I worked with him after I froze my hands and feet. I have determined that one must work with his mind to be a success, since using the back only leads to a worn and broken body. You will see that I will become a man that will make you proud when I return to Huskvarna.

I must sleep now, if sleep will come. I will be back on the river tomorrow. The channel will be mostly straight and clear from here, the logs float swiftly and soon we will be in Minneapolis.

I give all my fondest love and miss you greatly. I will write again from Minneapolis.

Your son and brother,
Peter

In the second week of June the crew of Northwest Timber floated the huge string of logs into the holding pond of LeBlanc Lumber Company at Minneapolis. Christian Halvorsen now stood with his crew of weary river pigs on the pier of the sawmill.

"Listen up, you waterlogged bunch of jacks, I've got good news for you. The company has had a good season, and LeBlanc has loosened his purse strings enough to give us a decent advance on the timber we've brought in. That means that every mother's son here will get his pay in hard cash—no credit slips this year!"

The announcement was met with a loud cheer of approval from the clustered men. It meant that they would not have to take vouchers of credit to stores and bars to have them cashed. It would save them the ten to twenty percent of their pay that was usually charged for redeeming the vouchers.

Christian held up his hand. "Besides that, everyone that made the log run gets a five dollar gold piece as a bonus! Now line up in front of Fry and get your pay!"

Another cheer went up from the lumberjacks. They ran to line up in front of the packing box that Fry was using as a makeshift desk. Peter took his place at the end of the line so that he could talk to Christian, who was now shaking hands and slapping backs as the men received their pay. When Peter's turn came, Christian gripped his hand and placed his left hand on Peter's shoulder.

"Damn fine job you did, Kid! I never saw a greenhorn do so many different things so quick!" Then he spoke more quietly. "I'm giving you an extra gold piece, because of the extra work you put in with Fry. I figure none of the other men would have done it for nothing."

Peter was surprised and grateful. "I thank you very much, Boss. It's nice the company is so generous, I mean with the bonus for all the men."

Christian looked uncomfortable, he shifted his eyes away from Peter's.

"The company isn't generous, it never is. My partners wouldn't give the men a dime more than they have coming."

"Then where did the bonus come from, did you pay it yourself?"

"Naw! I'm not that generous either.... The money was Sven's. I figured the men might just as well get it. Otherwise the company would have kept it."

Peter looked at Christian oddly. "But shouldn't that money have gone to Sven's parents?"

Christian poked some tobacco into his pipe and lit it before answering.

"Look Kid, you need to know how business works if you're going to be a part of it. There's no way my partners would send that money to Sweden. Besides, there's no guarantee it would ever get to his folks if they did. Now let's forget about it and go see Charlie LeBlanc about a job for you."

Peter shrugged his shoulders and walked to the sawmill with Christian. The two gold pieces in his hand felt cold, as though they had come from Sven's grave.

CHAPTER 7

CHARLIE LEBLANC AND COMPANY

Charlie LeBlanc's office in the mill was situated on the second floor, in a section of the huge building that was reserved for supplies and bookkeeping. As Peter climbed the stairs he looked out over several hundred feet of snarling saws and planing mills. His eyes grew wide, and he stopped on the landing at the top of the stairs. "Golly!" was all he could say.

Christian grinned, "Ain't it something?"

"Golly!," Peter said again, as he looked down at the workmen stacking lumber on big carts and manhandling timber on the saws. "They look like a bunch of ants on a big anthill. How many men work here?"

"Maybe three, four hundred. I said it was big. You give Charlie LeBlanc a good impression, and you got a good future, Kid. Come on in."

As they stepped through the doorway, Peter entered a world new to him. The room was richly paneled in wood that was stained a dark reddish color. The floor was of hardwood polished to a satiny finish and heavy curtains hung at the windows. An officious looking man in a white shirt , tie and vest sat at a large wooden desk. Near him was a door on which "Charles LeBlanc" was spelled in large gold letters. As the man looked up from a ledger before him, his face lit with recognition.

"Mister Halvorsen, how good it is to see you! I trust you have had a good season."

"Yes, Ernest, we have." Christian gestured to Peter. "This is my assistant, Peter Hokanson."

The man rather disdainfully extended his hand to the youth before him, dressed in loggers clothing that were soggy and stank of river mud.

"Glad to meet you, I'm Ernest Carruthers, Mister LeBlanc's chief accountant." He got up from his desk, revealing a gangly tall frame with a slight pot belly. "I'll see if Mister LeBlanc is busy."

In an instant the door reopened and a short, black-mustached figure dressed in a pin striped blue suit appeared, he was smiling broadly. He gripped Christian's hand, shaking it as though he intended to separate it from the larger man's body.

"Christian, my good friend, it is so wonderful to see you! The bull returns from the woods, eh! You look as always, like one of the sturdy pines you bring me! And this," he clapped a hand on Peter's shoulder, "must be the lad you wrote to me about."

Christian smiled. “Yeah, this is Peter Hokanson. He’s kind of shy, but he’s a good lad. Peter, meet Charlie LeBlanc, the best friend a man could have.”

“Hokanson,...a Swede, eh! I hoped with all that curly black hair you’d be French like me. But never mind, Halvorsen is a Norwegian, you can’t be worse than that. But let’s go into my office where we can talk privately.” He cast a meaningful glance at Ernest who had emerged from the office behind LeBlanc and was now listening intently.

LeBlanc’s office drew a low whistle of admiration from Peter. It was huge, with more of the same reddish wood of the outer office. It had ornately carved panels with framed paintings on the walls, and stained glass windows that fairly glowed in the sunlight. There was a carpet on the floor and French provincial chairs surrounded a long table of the same style. The desk at which Charlie LeBlanc worked was a massive work in cherry wood richly carved and inlaid with gold. His chair was of the same wood, and was upholstered with a rich, redish brown leather.

“You like, eh!” Charlie’s face mirrored his pride. “Young man like you, you smart and work hard, maybe you have office like this someday too. But sit, be comfortable, we not formal here.”

Peter walked to a chair and sat down carefully, obviously ill at ease in the elegant surroundings. Christian sprawled on another chair and leaned comfortably on the table.

“The kid’s smart, Charlie, and nobody works harder,” Christian said. “He’s made the company a bundle this season, and him being just an ‘old country greenhorn’ when he started. But how about some of that expensive brandy you always have in that cupboard by your desk?”

"Sure, sure! I give you my money, I give you my brandy, maybe some day you surprise Charlie, you bring me something nice." Charlie laughed as he poured a healthy shot in a brandy snifter and handed it to Christian.

"Naw, that wouldn't be as much fun as cadgin your liquor. Besides, look around you, you can afford it, I can't. I'm just a poor stumble footed lumberjack with callouses on his hands, patches on his pants and empty pockets. After I pay my men, I ain't got enough left to keep body and soul together. I got to go to the bankers and sign over my soul so I can log again next year." Christian inhaled the aroma of the brandy, then took a sip as Charlie poured and handed a glass to Peter.

"You got many mortgages on that soul of yours, my friend. But you don't have to do that. I asked you many times to come in with me, but what you do, eh?...You say you got to be your own boss!...You know what you are my friend? You a damned, block-headed, pig-brained Norwegian that ain't ever going to have a pot to piss in....But you're my friend, and I love you like a brother, and besides that, I owe you. So any time Christian, any time at all, you say the word and you got an office next to mine." Charlie raised his glass in a salute to his friend, then tossed the brandy down.

Christian emptied his glass, then held it out for a refill. "Thanks Charlie, but I still got to walk the timber for a few years. But I'd appreciate it if you've got a spot for the kid, I don't want to see him tore up in a log jam like Sven, or get squashed by a tree, or have his legs broke."

"Yeah, I was damned sorry to hear about Sven—Fry told me when he came in yesterday. He was a cocky, braggy fart, but I liked him. He wasn't one of them bastards as will kiss your ass, then stab you in the back." He scowled and pointed to the door. "Like that one out there."

Christian raised his eyebrows. "Then maybe it's time you get some new blood in your outfit. Pete's reliable, and I can trust him at my back. I wouldn't bring him here, except I think he's got a better chance with you than with me. Think you can find a spot for him?"

"I guess we're not talking about board mill labor, are we?"

"No, not log turning or board carrying, the kid's too good for that. He's good with books. But he's not afraid to get a little dirt under his fingernails either. I'm just asking you to give him a chance to prove himself."

Charlie swirled the brandy in his glass and inhaled the vapors, his manner changed abruptly as he turned to Peter. The laughing face became serious, the mild brown eyes were suddenly alert and sharp.

"Tell me what you can do, Peter. Tell me why it would be worth my while to hire you."

Peter had been waiting for this moment, as the two older men visited. He had been summing up his skills that might be of use to Charles LeBlanc. Now he summoned up all the courage of his young spirit and answered with a calm deliberate manner.

"Mister LeBlanc, I can do anyting I am told to do, and what I don't know I will learn! I can drive a team or roll logs with any man, and I can swing an axe better than most. But I can also work on accounts and go out and purchase shrewdly for your company. I can figure the timber that the loggers send in to you, or go out in the woods and figure it at their camps. But mostly, you should hire me because I will never cheat you or lie to you. Your interests will be my interests, and I will never betray that."

Charles LeBlanc regarded Peter seriously. "Ma foi! This lad means what he says."

Christian drained the last of his brandy and reached for the bottle on Charlie's desk. "I told you that Charlie, but you frogs always got to get it from the horse's mouth. Got a cigar?"

Charles LeBlanc absently took a handful of cigars from the box on his desk, clipped one and stuck it in his mouth and handed the rest to Christian. He was still looking at Peter intently.

"Your family, they are in Sweden? Perhaps you have a girl there. Perhaps you will get homesick and go back to her?"

"My family is in Sweden, Mister LeBlanc, but I have nothing to go back for, surely not a girl. I came here to make my fortune, and I will do it, by golly!"

Christian had been waiting for Peter's answer, now he lit a cigar and nodded approvingly.

"The kid has his head on straight, Charlie. He knows that the family stuff has to wait until after he makes a place for himself."

The small Frenchman walked to his desk and sat down in the leather chair, he clasped his hands on the desktop.

"The man I need must be young and smart so that he will learn what I need him to know when I am older. Above all, he must be absolutely loyal to me. The romance thing,...ah yes,...a young man needs to sow his oats from time to time, eh? But a serious encounter, a home and family too early will take too much from him, and leave too little for me. I would not want such a man. I myself was thirty before I married, and my daughters are now nineteen and sixteen. Unfortunately, I have no sons. My wife could have no more children after our second daughter, and so I have no male heir."... He sighed...."But then, we all have our crosses to bear, and that is mine. Tell me Peter, does your father have sons besides you?"

"Yes sir, my older brother Johann, he works with my father in his wood shop."

"He is a lucky man—did you say wood shop? What kind of a wood shop?"

"He builds furniture, church pews, things like that. I learned much of the trade before I came to America."

Charles LeBlanc smiled approvingly. "Peter, I think I have a place for you, it pays twelve dollars a week to start. But of course you will have to find room and board. Will that be satisfactory?"

Peter hesitated—the brown eyes of Charlie LeBlanc narrowed to pin points of black.

"What! Is it not enough then?"

"No, it's not that,...I have a friend, Gus. Could you give him a job too? Maybe in the mill?"

"By Lucifer's unholy name! Damn me, if you haven't brought me a priceless jewel, Christian! The kid isn't on the payroll yet, an he's asking me for favors."

The Frenchman's face broke into an incredulous look and he started to laugh with such gusto that a button popped off the front of his jacket and bounced across the floor.

Christian took a long drag on the cigar he had cadged from Charlie.

"Yeah, I know what you're thinkin, Charlie. He did the same thing to me, upped the stakes on his wages before I'd hired him. I was glad I took him anyway, earned every cent of it, with interest to boot."

"That good, eh? Well, by damn Peter, if your boss sets such store by you, I should let him keep you, eh? But I won't, I'll give you a try and your friend too. That is if Christian doesn't object."

Peter glanced at Christian nervously. His face showed all the earnest feeling of a small boy.

"Golly Boss, I didn't mean to take Gus away from you. It's just that he's the only real friend I have in America,...besides you, I mean."

Christian waved the apology away with his cigar.

"Don't worry about it Pete. Actually, I'm lucky to get rid of you damned unruly Swedes all at once." He reached to shake Peter's hand. "Good luck Kid."

Charlie took the bottle of brandy and poured healthy slugs all the way around. He raised his glass.

"It's settled then. A toast gentlemen, to friendship, business and prosperity!"

Peter's introduction to the world of business had begun.

As they left Charlie's office Peter asked Carruthers if any mail had come for him. The accountant looked at Peter condescendingly.

"And why would mail for you come to the office of Charles LeBlanc?"

"Because I asked my..., someone to write to me here."

"Humph! We're not the public post office—anyway there's no mail for you. Since you are going to be employed here, you'd best hasten to get your own address. I won't be granting you special favors, even if Mister LeBlanc does."

Peter Bristled. "And how do you know Mister LeBlanc hired me?"

Carruthers reddened. "I make it a point to know everything that goes on in the company. It's useful in dealing with upstarts."

Peter was about to reply, but Christian motioned toward the door, so he turned on his heel and left. The accountant followed him with his eyes—the young Swede would bear watching.

"Let's get something to eat," Christian said. "I know a decent restaurant near here. They rent rooms on the second floor, maybe we can find you a place to stay at the same time."

Peter nodded his assent. "Chris, why do you think Sarah didn't write to me?"

"Dunno, it's hard to tell with women, maybe she's had a change of heart."

"But why would she do that? I mean,…the way we were and all, it just doesn't make sense."

"Well, maybe she got to thinking and she got cold feet. She sure as hell knows you were fixin to get serious. Maybe she doesn't want to come to the city."

"Why? We can have a good life here."

"Sure Pete, you can because you're white. But a smart girl like Sarah knows that half breed women don't fit in here. Maybe she's figured it out that she's better off up there near her people."

"Why wouldn't she fit in? Damn it Chris, you sound like you want me to leave Sarah! I love her, and I won't quit on her until she tells me she doesn't love me!"

The unusual vehemence with which Peter spoke made Christian pause as they walked. He threw the butt of his cigar into the dirt and stepped on it before he answered.

"It's all right Kid, I think Sarah is one hell of a woman, I just don't want either of you to get hurt. These big city people aren't like you and me. There's some as wouldn't associate with someone that has Indian blood, no matter how wonderful she is."

Peter looked as though his world was about to end. "If that's true,...if that's why she hasn't written,...I've got to go to her. It doesn't matter if I have to swing an axe for a living, I want Sarah with me."

Christian gripped the young Swede's shoulder hard. "Whoa there Kid! Don't go jumping off your log before the time is right. You just got a chance with Charlie LeBlanc that a lot of guys would sell their souls for. I've got a better idea."

"What's that?"

"After I take care of some business with my partners, I figure to go back up to the camp and do some timber cruising. There's some surveys I got to do before fall. Suppose I go see Sarah and get her to write to you?"

"Maybe,...but I guess I could write to her at the school."

"Yeah, but with the way the mail is up there, you couldn't be sure she'd get your letter. I tell you what, Pete, why don't you write her a letter and I'll deliver it to her. That way you'll be sure she gets it, and I can kind of convince her to write, if she has any doubts."

Peter's face lit up. "Golly Chris! Would you do that for me?"

"Sure Pete, that's what friends are for. Now let's go eat, and maybe we can find Gus and tell him about his new job too. You two are going to have a lot of fun together here in Minneapolis!"

In the last week of June, Christian Halvorsen stopped at the office of Charlie LeBlanc. After the two men had exchanged greetings, Charlie poured two generous brandies and offered Christian a cigar.

"So, my good friend, are you about to return to the timber?"

"Yeah, after the Fourth of July, gotta hell around a little first."

Charlie laughed. "By damn, still the ladies' man, eh? How come they never been able to put a branding hammer to that square Norwegian head of yours?"

"M—m—m, just lucky I guess. You know Charlie, I just might get serious one day, the nights are getting longer and my bunk is getting colder every day."

"Good, good, then maybe you come in with me, eh? Better hurry though, I think you got competition now."

"The kid? How's he doing?"

Charlie grinned. "I think you steered me right on him, my friend. I got him doing a little buying for me, just little stuff here and there. He got the merchants bitching because he squeezes them down to the last nickel. I like that boy,... but I don't think Ernest does. Pete makes him look bad."

"Never did like that Carruthers, seems like a devious bastard to me."

"You right about that, but he's a damned fine man with the books. I don't trust him either, but I need his business brains. Maybe everything goes good, one day I don't need him, eh?

"Could be Charlie, Pete's bright and he works hard. He'll make a good ramrod one day. But, I didn't come over just to talk about the kid. Wondered if maybe we could get a little poker game going one night. Wouldn't seem right if I didn't trim you a little while I'm in town."

Charlie laughed. "You damned right, if Charlie he's remember right, it was you big herring choker what got trimmed last time. Sure, we get some of the fellows together, we have a little friendly game, eh?"

"When should we do it? I can't tonight, there's this widow needs my attention. She's already sent her kids over to her sister's house." Christian winked at Charlie.

"That's good, maybe she going to hit you with that branding hammer. I tell you what, my friend, I have a little place out on Lake Calhoun. We having a little party on the Fourth,...food, fireworks, a little whiskey and like that. Why don't you come sometime the day before and we'll have a game that night. You can stay over for the party, eh?"

"That sounds damned good to me Charlie, only I don't know about staying over. I don't want to crowd you, and I kinda promised the widow I'd spend the Fourth with her."

"Hey, what we got here, something serious, eh-h? You don't worry about the crowding Chris, we got eight bedrooms. I'm bringing Peter out—let him meet a few people, you know. You can bunk with him, take the surrey into town in the morning, bring this widow out to the party. Sure, sure, bring her kids out too, we got nice place, room for the kids to play, eh?"

"Much obliged Charlie, I'll tell Iris and see if she'd like that. The game's a deal, so polish up your gold pieces. I want them nice and shiny when I pocket them. I got to go now, I'm meeting my banker in a bit."

"Is good, Chris, get lots of money for me to take from you,eh! Charlie feels lucky, I think Christian Halvorsen he going to lose big."

"Sure, Sure! I'll see you on the third, Charlie"

Peter and Gustav rented a room together at the restaurant and boarding house Christian had shown them. Now the friends were whiling away an evening at the bar.

"Pete, you like working for Charlie LeBlanc?"

"It's better'n anything I ever thought I'd get when the log run ended. Why, aren't you happy there?"

"Oh hell,…it ain't that I'm unhappy, it's just different things."

"Like what kind of things, Gus? I think if you've got a problem, Charlie will listen to you and try to set it straight."

"Well, for one thing, its the heat and the noise. It's not like it was in the woods, Pete. It was quiet there, cept for the wind blowing through the pines, and the sound of axes and men talking and cussing. And it was cold, so we had to work to keep warm, and nobody was standing over you like you were a damned slave. Here the damned steam engines make so much heat I 'bout sweat my balls off, and there's that God awful screaming from the saws all day. I don't like it—I'm thinking about chucking it, Pete."

"You've never been one for quitting something without good reason, Gus. The heat'll let up in a month or two, and you can plug your ears against the noise. I figure there's something else bothering you."

"Yeah there is, they've got me on a gang saw. It's run by a guinea by the name of Nick Pelliochi. He's a son of the devil himself. I think he hates my guts, rides my ass every minute of the day. Hell, Pete! I can't do enough to satisfy the bastard."

"Uh huh, I've seen him. He's always bragging about how much his crew puts out. It's not just him though, the foremen get a bonus for putting out more than their quota."

"Just the same, I'd like to kick Pelliochi's ass. Speak of the devil, here the fat-ass guinea comes."

A heavy set dark faced man had just entered, he scanned the bar, and headed for the two young Swedes. His face was lit in a smile that revealed several missing teeth.

"Hey, what we got here, a couple of Swedes drinkin' together? You gonna buy ol' Nick a beer, Gussie?"

"I'm damned near broke—buy your own beer, Nick. And if I wasn't broke, I wouldn't buy for you anyway."

"Whatsa matter Gussie, you tryin' to hurt Nick's feelin's?"

"You hurt my feelings all damned day, you stinking guinea, and call me Gus, I'm not a little boy."

Nick's face darkened. "You better watcha your mouth, Gussie. You just a little pissant Swede thatsa work like a little boy. Worse than dat, you work like a little girl."

Gus answered by jumping off his bar stool and delivering a hard punch to the Italian's face. Nick staggered back with a surprised look. A trickle of blood appeared at the side of a nostril. He wiped it away with his hand, his smile replaced by a thundercloud of anger.

"I'ma gonna kick your ass, Gussie."

Nick lunged forward, pinning the young Swede against the bar. He drove a pile driver fist into Gus's mid section, then pulled him into the open by his shirt front. Gus saw Nick's right fist come hurling at his jaw, but the pain in his stomach paralyzed him. His head snapped back with the blow, and he fell senseless to the floor.

"Come on, get up, I'ma not through with you yet." Nick kicked Gus hard in the ribs.

Peter stepped forward and pushed Nick away roughly. "Leave him alone, can't you see he's hurt?"

Nick turned his attention to this new adversary. "You wanna lesson too, boy? Okay, Nick gonna give it to you!"

He swung hard at Peter's face, but connected with nothing but air— instead he was rewarded with two sharp jabs to the jaw. Nick stepped back, then lunged at Peter, trying to pin him against the bar. Peter danced away, jabbing Nick twice as he did so.

The Italian was a picture of fury now, as he plodded in, catching Peter's jabs on his meaty left arm. He swung a haymaker right, catching Peter on the shoulder. It spun him back against the ring of men that had gathered to watch. Nick pressed the smaller man, seemingly impervious to the rain of sharp jabs that Peter delivered. He stayed always in the center of the ring of spectators, forcing Peter against the wall of bodies.

Fear had a grip on Peter, pumping adrenalin to his muscles. He hit Nick hard as he tried to stay out of the big man's reach, but Nick absorbed the blow like a sack of flour. Peter knew now that he couldn't put the tough

Italian down. What would Chris do? he thought as he ducked another vicious swing. He could see the Norwegian in his mind's eye, "Sometimes you just have to take your licking, Kid."

Nick's blow was aimed at the stomach, but it caught Peter in the chest, driving him up against the men behind him. The Italian grinned as he sent a haymaker right at Peter's head. The young Swede ducked, and the blow only grazed his ear.

"Gott damn!" A huge German behind Peter swore as he rubbed his chest.

Nick's eyes widened in surprise as a monstrous fist descended on the top of his head like a post maul on a post. His eyes rolled up, and he sagged to the floor.

"Schweinhundt! Vy don' choo leave dem boys alone?" The German spit a chew of tobacco juice beside Nick and walked back to the bar, rubbing his calloused hand.

Gus was sitting up rubbing his jaw. "I think the bastard broke my jaw. He sure can punch." He took the hand that Peter extended to him. "Where'd he go?"

Peter pointed to the prone form, just starting to stir.

Gus looked at Peter in astonishment. "You did that?"

Peter shook his head and grinned. "Naw, he would have killed me. It was Adolph, the German, with one blow!"

"We aughta piss on him." Gus said, still feeling his jaw.

"Naw," Peter returned, "we know he can whip us, let's help him up."

The two Swedes each grabbed a hairy wrist and hoisted the still wobbly Italian to his feet.

"Mama Mia! " Nick said. "What in our holy mother's name hit me?"

"Adolph, the German," Peter said. "You hit him by accident when you swung at me."

"Damn me, I'll remember not to maka him mad. You boys ain't got no size to you, but you spunky little bastards. Nick, he'sa like dat, what you say we have a beer on Nick Pelliochi?"

From that day, Gus no longer had problems with his foreman. To the contrary, he became one of the Italian's favorites, though Nick never did stop calling him Gussie. Peter learned that sometimes a man must fight, even though he will be beaten. He now knew he didn't have to win to gain respect, just standing up for himself was enough.

Chapter 8

A Love Lost

On the third of July, Peter quit work early at Charlie's command, and drove his team of matched Morgan's to Charlie's "cottage" on Lake Calhoun. The house was much more than a cottage. It was a two and a half story mansion set well back from the lake, and it sported a large stable, a boat dock and spacious grounds. Peter brought the team and surrey down to the stable, and gave them to the stable hands who were busily brushing down the teams of early guests. Charlie, who was coming with business friends, had not yet arrived. So, Peter walked down to the dock, where a sailboat and rowboat were moored. A hedge of lilacs screened the shore of the lake for about fifty feet, and extended to the pathway from both sides. As he passed the lilacs, a feminine voice greeted him.

"Hi there!"

A young woman seated in a wicker lawn chair waved a book at him.

"I said, 'Hi there.'"

"I'm sorry, I didn't see you, hello."

"I know, that's why we have the hedge, so we can have privacy."

Peter blushed. "Golly, I'm sorry, I didn't mean to intrude."

"It's all right, it's not like I'm nude sun bathing or something. I haven't seen you around—who are you?"

"I'm Peter, what's your name?"

"Kathryn,…everybody calls me Kat. Charlie's my dad. I bet you're the new man that Dad hired. He talks about you a lot."

"I hope it's good—my friends call me Pete."

"Of course it's good, silly, otherwise you wouldn't be here. Dad doesn't bring the ordinary help home. He likes you a lot, he says you're smart and ambitious. He didn't tell me that you're cute too."

Peter blushed again. "Golly, are you always like that?"

"Like what? Oh, you mean, do I always say what I 'm thinking? Sure, everybody should, that is if it's good. If I'm thinking something mean, I don't usually say it."

"Well, I think you're pretty. And you're friendly. Most girls act like they're afraid to talk to a man."

"You mean like my sister Lucy. She acts so stuck up, she'd never talk to a man unless she was introduced first."

"She's your older sister, right?"

"How'd you know?"

"Your father said he has two daughters, one nineteen and one sixteen. You have to be the younger one."

Kathryn pouted a little. "Does it show?...How old are you?...I guess eighteen, and that's just right."

"Sure, I'm eighteen. But what's it right for?"

"My dad is giving Lucy a birthday party down at his club next month. And you're just the right age to be my escort."

Peter was dumbfounded. "Well,...golly, I don't know,"

"What's the matter, Peter. Don't you like me?"

"Well, I've barely met you,...and I've never had a girl ask me out before. The man is supposed to ask the woman."

Kathryn flared. "That's dumb! What's a girl supposed to do if she likes a boy, drop her hanky and act like this?" She adopted a languishing expression.

"Golly, I guess I never thought of it that way. I suppose since I work for your father, I could escort you. That is, if your father doesn't object."

"He won't if I ask him. Besides, we should be nice to you, since you're not from around here. I can tell by your accent. You're Swedish, aren't you?"

"You're right, I was seventeen when I came to America, that was last November."

"You came to America alone? Didn't you have anyone with you? Weren't you horribly afraid?"

"Sure, I was afraid and lonely, but I had my cousin Sven here. And I made a good friend, Gus."

"Your cousin, what does he do? Does he work for Northwest Timber?"

"He did, but he got killed by a log jam a couple of months ago. I helped bury him."

Kathryn was horrified. "Oh, how terrible for you, to be alone in this big country without a single relative!"

Peter felt a choking in his throat at the thought of Sven's face as the logs caught him. He brushed the thought away.

"Let's talk about something else. What are you reading?"

"*Tom Sawyer,* it's about these boys that live way down south, near the Mississippi River. They do all kinds of interesting, adventurous things. It makes me wish I were a boy."

Peter laughed. "Why would a pretty girl like you want to be a boy?"

"Because boys can do all the wonderful things. They can be loggers, and railroad engineers, and soldiers, and cowboys. Besides, they can wear trousers, while I have to wear this." She wrinkled her nose and looked down at the white skirt and sailor collared shirtwaist she wore.

Peter laughed again. "But you do interesting things. You sail, ride horses, go fishing and drive your father wild." He counted off on his fingers.

Kathryn laughed, and Peter thought he had never heard a more melodious sound. "How do you know all that, smartie?"

"Well, the sailboat is right here and I saw a sidesaddle at the stable. And there are some big fish heads nailed on the stable wall, with Kat written under one of them. I just guessed you drive your father wild, because you want to do everything."

"You're right, of course—Peter, do you know how to row a boat?"

"Sure Kat, I used to row all the time in Sweden. We'd put a big bait out behind the boat and fish for pike."

"Wonderful! Let's do it!"

"You mean right now?"

"Of course! When you want to do something you should do it right away. Otherwise you lose the magic. You row, and I'll put out the fish line." She dropped her book, and taking Peter in tow, ran out on the dock.

Peter worked the oars with strong, swift strokes out to where the edges of the weed banks and the deep water met. The feel of the wood in his hands and the slap of wavelets against the hull were exhilarating. Sun, water, a gentle breeze and a pretty girl as a companion—he thought he had not felt this happy since he left Sweden.

He watched Kathryn as she fed the heavy bucktail lure into the water. She had sandy gold hair pulled back behind her head and tied with a white ribbon, her oval face and turned up nose were tanned, her eyes a bright blue. He thought of how much fun she would be to know, then guiltily he remembered Sarah.

As if sensing his thoughts Kathryn spoke. "Peter, do you have a girl?"

He avoided a direct, truthful answer. "I had a girl in Sweden, she married someone else."

"Why?"

"Because I came to America, and she didn't want to."

"I think I would have come if I loved you, and you asked me to."

"That's nice, but it couldn't happen."

"Why? Do you think I'm so ugly?"

"No, I think you're pretty. But you're too young to think of that."

Kathryn looked at him sulkily. "You think I'm a child. I'm not! And besides, you're only eighteen yourself. You're just a boy, not a real man!"

Peter dropped the oars and the boat drifted to a stop. "Golly!…I just meant that we both are too young to think of getting married. And we don't even know each other. We shouldn't even be talking about things like that."

Kathryn pouted. "Now look what you've done, my line is all tangled up in the weeds because you stopped rowing!" She pulled it out of the water and threw it in a pile on the floor. "Take me back to the dock. I don't want to fish after all!"

At the shore Kathryn jumped out of the boat and stormed up the path to the house. Peter picked up her book and followed reluctantly. At the porch, he met Charlie and he was grinning broadly. "I see that you have already met Kat. Pay her no mind, Pete. Charlie, he's spoil her bad, and she has too much will to be good for a woman. But then, she's Charlie's little girl, what else can I do, eh? Come, you meet the rest of the family."

That night the men gathered together in Charlie's den to play cards. Christian, Charlie, and some other businessmen sat at a high stakes table. Peter and a few younger men played for nickels and dimes at another table. Peter noted the pecking order involved, and told himself that soon he would be at the other table. Already he had met a banker, a railroad man, and a manufacturer of machinery. Peter memorized the names of each, and what he did. Later, he wrote the names in a little notebook that he would keep for his entire career. Now he worked to ingratiate himself with these lesser men, who like himself were working their way up the ladder of business.

In the early hours of the morning, as Christian and Peter were readying themselves for sleep, Peter gave Christian an envelope.

"It is my letter to Sarah." he said. "Please give it to her as soon as you get back to the camp."

Christian looked at him soberly. "Sure Pete, as soon as I get there. And I'll talk to her too,...make her understand what your situation is. It'll all work out for the best."

"Thanks Chris, I'm glad I have you for a friend." That night Peter went to sleep with visions of the dark haired Sarah in his mind. But oddly, he dreamed of being with a blue-eyed blonde behind a lilac hedge.

Christian awoke the day after the party with a splitting headache. The celebration had not gone well for him. He lost heavily at cards, to the point where his share of the logging company was in peril. He had taken Iris to the party, but the 'less than wealthy' woman had not been well received by the wives of the business men. Iris had felt hurt and out of place, so Christian had taken her home early, then retired to his own room with a bottle of whiskey.

The only consolation about the whole affair was that Peter had met Lucille, the quiet, willowy, brunette daughter of Charlie LeBlanc. The two seemed to get along well. Peter had even danced a polka or two with her on the outdoor floor Charlie had erected for the party. But it seemed to Christian that Peter had been more interested in the tomboy younger daughter. Not that it mattered, maybe one or the other of them would make him forget the Indian girl.

Though Christian didn't realize it, his attitude toward Peter had become paternally protective. Now at middle age, he had no sons, and was unlikely to have any. In his mind he had adopted the young immigrant, and wanted him to succeed in business more fully than he himself had. He was willing to follow any course of action that would insure this. He took Peter's letter to Sarah from his suit pocket and looked at it thoughtfully. He had promised Peter he would deliver it to Sarah, but what would be its consequences to the young man? He opened the envelope and removed its contents. It read:

My very dearest Sarah,

It has been too long since I have talked to you and held you in my arms. I love you deeply, and wonder why you have not written to me as I asked you to do, in the letter I left with Lone Man.

I am in Minneapolis, and working at the job Chris got for me with the LeBlanc Lumber Company. I have not written to you since I arrived because Chris feared my letter might not reach you. He has agreed to carry my letter to you personally, so that I might be sure you receive it. He has been a true friend to me since I came to this country, and I think it would have been very hard for me without him. I now have a post office box of my own, so you can write to me at post office box 473, Minneapolis, Minnesota.

In my worry over not hearing from you, I talked to Chris. He thought that you might not like to live here, and so may not want to see me anymore. I implore you not to feel that way, if it is so. I love you, and I want to be with you. I will do anything within my power to make you happy if you will one day marry me.

I am working hard to make something of myself, so that if you will marry me you will be a proud wife. But, if it is in your heart that you cannot live in the city, I will come back to you and be a lumberjack, or we can buy a farm as I once dreamed of doing. I know that if I stay here I will become rich and powerful, but it will be nothing if I lose you. My happiness is with you, and that is where I will be.

Please write to me as soon as you receive this letter. I cannot wait to here from you, my dearest Sarah.

With all of my warmest love,Peter

Christian walked to his bureau and removed a new envelope. He sealed the letter inside and placed it in his pocket. Late that day he would be in Grand Rapids.

The next morning Christian was driving a buggy along the haul road to the logging camp. The fringe of little cords on the horse's fly blanket made swishing sounds as he trotted. The sound was pleasing—Christian was glad to be in the open again. The only thing that dampened his spirit was his need to talk to Sarah. But what must be done, must be done. There was no point in postponing it, and having it hanging over his head. He wouldn't stop at the camp, but would go right on through to the Indian school.

Father Goebel was stripped of his cassock, and was working in his garden, when Christian arrived at the little clearing that housed the church, school and parish house. The slightly built priest was perspiring profusely despite the coolness of the early hour. He put down his hoe and held out his hand as Christian stepped down from the buggy.

"Christian Halvorsen! What a surprise! You'll forgive my appearance, I hope. I was doing a little hoeing before the black flies come out."

"Of course, Father. It's nice to see a priest doing something besides tending to his spiritual duties. It makes them seem more human. We tend to forget that priests are mortal like the rest of us."

Father Goebel laughed. "Well put, my friend. Sometimes I think you Protestants have a better insight on men of the cloth than my parishioners. What brings you here on this fine morning? I trust it isn't the need for spiritual guidance."

Christian smiled. "Well Father, I guess I'm probably in need of guidance. But no, that's not what brings me here. I was hoping that your teacher, Sarah, was here. I need to talk to her."

"Sarah? No, she's off for the summer months. You'll probably find her at her grandfather's place. Is something wrong?"

"Not really, I'm just delivering a message for one of my lumberjacks."

Father Goebel's face clouded. "Oh yes, the young Swede, he came to Mass with Sarah a few times, then he disappeared. Sarah seemed to have something bothering her after that. She seemed to withdraw, not at all like herself."

"Yeah, the road of love isn't always smooth, is it? He went on the log run and she probably just misses him. Anyway, I better go see her. Why don't you come over to the camp some night, we'll play some chess."

"That would be nice, Christian, I sometimes long for someone to talk to who isn't either ill or in trouble."

Wise Otter, Sarah's grandfather, was sitting outside his cabin on a chair made of willow wands as Christian approached. Christian raised his hand in greeting, then stepped down. The two warriors clasped hands, then Christian spoke in French.

"It is good to see my friend, Wise Otter. Are you and those of your lodge well?"

"Wise Otter welcomes you, my friend. We are well—do the spirits smile on you?"

"They do, will Wise Otter share a pipe with me?" Christian brought a new sack of tobacco out of his pocket.

"I have brought a tobacco we have not shared before."

Wise Otter nodded. "My daughter will bring us tea." He spoke a few words loudly in Chippewa, then continued:

"We have not spoken since the moon of snows. What brings my friend to the lodge of Wise Otter?"

Christian carefully packed a long stemmed pipe with tobacco, lit it and passed it to the old Indian before answering.

"I bring words for your granddaughter, from the young lumberjack, Peter. Is she still of your lodge?"

The old man's eyes squinted slightly, then his face became impassive.

"Yes, she is down by the stream, she grieves for the young brave. She thought that the great river had taken his spirit, as it took her father's."

"The great river took his cousin's spirit, but Peter lives in the great village, Minneapolis."

Star Flower came out of the cabin and gave each of the men a cup of tea, then retreated back inside.

"Yes," Wise Otter ruminated, "I have heard of that great village. It is said that it reaches farther than the eye can see. One day before the great spirit closes my eyes I would like to go there—Does the young brave return?"

The one person Christian could never lie to was the old medicine man. He sipped the tea slowly as he thought of his answer.

"He has promised his arms to another chief, he must work for another tribe. He wishes to bring your granddaughter to them. But, I fear they will not take her into their lodges."

Wise Otter drew heavily on the pipe, then exhaled the smoke slowly. "It is a thing I have seen before, it is an evil thing and it will do evil to Sarah. But she carries his child, she should be in his lodge."

The words took the speech from Christian—now it was his turn to draw deeply on the pipe. He had been totally unprepared for what Wise Otter had just told him. A half-breed wife and a young child would destroy Peter's chances of success. He didn't know what to tell this old warrior.

"Yes, it is an evil thing, my friend. The young sometimes sow seed before the time is right. And we, the elders must decide what to do. What think you, Wise Otter? Would you send your granddaughter to a lodge where she will be despised, or would you have the young brave break his word to his chief?"

Wise Otter sat silent for several minutes, then he spoke slowly and gravely.

"As an elder of your own tribe, you know that I would ask for neither. Yet, my granddaughter grieves, and the child will be born. There is no brave in the lodge to provide for him. Sarah has none to hold her when her time comes, and I am too old. Soon the Great Spirit will take me to the happy hunting ground. What will happen to the child then?"

It was what Christian had hoped for. The old Indian was wise, and in that wisdom he had provided an answer.

"Wise Otter speaks truth, and his wisdom provides a way. Sarah's child shall be as a child of my lodge. On every moon I will give Sarah that with which to care for the child and herself. But she must not go to Peter, or tell him of the child. Do you agree, Wise Otter?"

Wise Otter nodded and offered Christian his hand. "It shall be as you have spoken. Now go, my friend, and tell Sarah of these things. My heart is heavy for her, and I cannot."

Christian found Sarah in a little rocky glade by the stream the Indians called "Singing Water". She looked at him with surprise, and jumped up from the pine stump she had been sitting on.

"Christian! How wonderful! I had not expected to see anyone from the logging camp so soon." She ran to Christian and threw her arms around him. "Peter,…is he all right?"

Christian took Sarah in his arms and hugged her, then sat down on the stump, motioning for her to join him.

"Sure Sarah, he's doing real good, he wanted me to come and see you. He sent this letter for you."

He handed her the envelope, and watched as she tore it open with shaking hands. He packed his pipe and watched happiness spread across her face as she read. Sometimes, he thought, this whole world stinks. She loves him and he loves her, but it takes more than that, much more.

"It's wonderful!" Sarah said. "He says he wants me to marry him, he wants me with him!" Then she looked troubled. "But he said he left a letter with Lone Man for me. I saw Lone Man, and he said he didn't have anything for me."

Christian shrugged, "Maybe he didn't want you to get it. Did Lone Man say anything else to you?"

"Yes, he said something about Chippewa girls giving their hearts to white men, then having them leave. He seemed angry, he broke a stick and threw it away....He didn't want me to have the letter! He didn't give it to me!"

"It would appear that way."

"But Peter said something else, he said you thought I might not want to live in the city with him. That maybe I didn't write because of that. Why would you think that?"

"I didn't know how you and Peter were, Sarah. And I didn't know about this letter thing. I thought you probably got wise by yourself."

"What do you mean?"

Christian looked into Sarah's eyes earnestly. "Peter's got a new job with a big sawmill. His boss doesn't want him to be fooling around with a woman now. He wants him to be minding his job without any distractions until he gets established. He's got a chance to be something, Sarah, a chance that doesn't come often. If you go there now it'll wreck his chances."

Sarah's face clouded with disappointment. "He didn't say anything about that. He just said he wants to be with me."

"Of course he wouldn't, Pete's young and in love, he's not looking ahead. You and I have to think of what's best for him if we care about him."

"I suppose you're right, I'll wait until he's ready. I love Peter, and I don't want to hurt him."

"It's not just that, Sarah."

"What do you mean?"

"I took a woman to a party on the Fourth, she is white but she isn't rich. Those women would hardly say hello to her. You're half Indian, how do you think they'll react when Peter brings you and an illegitimate child around?"

Sarah hung her head, tears starting in her eyes. "Is it really so bad?"

"It's rotten, but that's the way it is. We might as well face it, even though it hurts like hell." Christian put his arm around the shoulders of the girl, who had begun crying quietly.

"But I love Peter, what can I do?"

"It's hard, I know. But if you really love him, you're going to have to let him go,...for his sake. You don't want him to be a lumberjack or a dirt grubbing farmer all his life, do you?"

"No,...but the baby is coming,...what would I do? I can't support myself, much less a child too."

Christian held Sarah closer. "Don't worry about that, I'll take care of you and the baby. After a while, you'll find another man, and you can get married. And your child will never lack for anything, I promise that."

"I don't want another man, Chris. I love Peter, isn't there some way,... —why do people have to be so cruel?"

"I don't know, but it's the way it is. Peter can't have both you and a career. I think you should do the right thing before you both get hurt worse than you are already."

"What,...what do you want me to do?"

"Write him a letter telling him there's somebody else, that you don't want to see him any more. It's the only thing that will give Peter a chance in life."

"I can't do that, I can't lie to him like that. We're going to have a baby, the baby needs to have a father. I don't understand how you could even suggest such a thing."

"I wouldn't if I could see another way. But, if Peter thinks there's a chance of being with you, he'll throw away his job with Charlie LeBlanc if you don't go to him. Then later, when he's drudging in the timber every day, he'll start hating you because you came between him and what he really wants to do. Men are like that, Sarah."

Sarah buried her face in her arms, her body convulsing with sobs. "All right, Chris, I'll write him a letter. I'll tell him we can't see each other anymore. But I won't tell him there's another man!"

Chapter 9

Kathryn and Lucille

Peter worked hard and long on the days after Christian's departure for the logging camp. Ernest Carruthers was his immediate superior, and the chief accountant loaded Peter with work far in excess of that required of his more subservient peers. Though Carruthers's intent was to require such excessive performance from the young Swede that he would quit his position, the opposite was true.

Peter buried himself in his work, for it gave him respite from thinking of Sarah. A letter from her would surely come soon. Peter agonized over what it would contain. He had been confident of Sarah's love. But now after the many weeks of separation without word from her, the first ugly seedlings of doubt were emerging from the fertile soil of their love. He could not help but remember how the infrequent letters from Julia had preceded the letter from her mother which severed their relationship.

So, Peter worked late into the evening every day, and as he worked, he learned. Contrary to Carruthers' hopes that Peter would abandon his position, he was becoming more secure. Charlie Leblanc observed Peter's industrious attitude, and smiled with approval.

A little better than a week after Christian had left, Peter returned to his room late in the evening. Gus was smiling as he waved an envelope in the air. "She wrote, Pete. It's from Sarah!"

Peter grabbed the envelope and retreated to a window where the last rays of the summer sun were filtering in. As Peter read, Gus thought he could see his friend's shoulders sag. When he turned from the window, Peter's face showed a tired forlornness Gus had never seen in his friend before.

"What's the matter, Pete?"

Peter didn't answer, but handed the single sheet of paper he was holding to Gus, then he returned to stare out of the window.

Gus looked at the paper—the few lines written on it might as well have been in Latin.

"You know I don't read English, Pete. What'd she write?"

Peter turned to Gus, his face a mask of pain.

"She says we're through. She says it would be better if we don't see each other anymore. She says not to write, she wishes me a good life."

His face contorted with anguish, and tears he could no longer contain ran freely.

"Damn it! Gus...Why do they always wish you good, when they've just hurt you so bad?!"

"I dunno," Gus said. "I think it's so you won't be so mad at them."

"But I am mad! I'm damned mad! I love Sarah, and I thought she loved me. First she doesn't write to me. Then when I get Christian to talk to her for me, she says she doesn't want to see me anymore. She's a damned bitch, that's what she is!"

Gus was embarrassed. "I don't think you mean that, Pete. Sarah healed you when you almost died of frostbite. She helped you with your writing and figuring, otherwise you wouldn't have your job. She loved you when Julia quit you. She's no bitch, she's a nice woman. She just changed her mind... women do that. It's in them, just like having babies."

"But why?...I would have loved her and taken care of her til I died. No man can do more than that!"

"I don't think that's it at all, Pete. There's more to it than that. Maybe she has somebody else. Maybe she's afraid to tell you."

Peter sat down and covered his eyes with his hands.

"You know Gus, it's the same thing that Julia did to me. I really loved her, and she left me for somebody else. Women pick and choose by what will get them the most, or what's the most convenient for them."

"I guess that's partly true, but that's their right. I mean...we expect them to choose us because we offer them something that we think is just great. So we shouldn't be mad because they choose something they think is better."

Peter thought about his friend's statement for a few minutes.

"If that's so, then we should do the same thing, Gus. From now on I'm going to look at women that have something to offer besides making love."

"You mean, like Charlie's daughters?"

"Could be Gus, women like them anyway. I couldn't do worse than I've done so far, could I?"

Gus shrugged. "I guess not, but if I were you, I'd stay away from women until the hurting is gone."

"Yeah, right now I just want to forget all about them."

The next weeks passed swiftly for Peter. He spent virtually every waking hour at work, taking only a few hours to eat and rest. The fact did not escape Charlie LeBlanc. On the third Monday of August he called Peter into his office. Charlie offered Peter a cup of tea since he had a strict rule against employees drinking spirits during working hours.

"Sit down, Pete.…You working too hard, you need a little rest an fun. Charlie got a favor to ask of you, that maybe give you both."

"Yes Sir, anything at all."

"Pete, you no call Charlie 'Sir' when he's ask you for favor. You call me 'Charlie', eh? When you ask Charlie for favor, then you call him 'Sir'. Okay?"

"Sure Charlie, what do you need?"

Charlie frowned. "It's funny thing to ask—Charlie he's wish he didn't have to—but he promised. Next Friday I having a birthday party for Lucille, she's gonna be twenty years old. Everybody's dress up and we all go down to my club. The girls, they all have somebody to take them. You know,…so they got somebody to dance with an stuff. Except Kat,…she don't have nobody.

Charlie say, "Kat, you too young, you don' need no escort, you go with papa and mama, eh? " Charlie drew on a cigar and blew the smoke at the ceiling.

"You met Kat, you know how she is, Pete. She got all huffed up and say she's not a little girl. Charlie, he's get mad an say she do as he says. Next thing she's crying, an Charlie can't stand that. Pete, she's want you to take her to the party."

Peter laughed, "I know."

"What you mean, you know?"

"She told me when I met her."

Charlie grinned and shook his head. "That's my Kat, she's do those things to me all the time. But what can I do? She's Charlie's little girl!.... So then, you'll take her, Pete?"

"Sure Charlie, I like Kat, even if her fuse is a little short."

"That's good, I tell her." Charlie pointed a finger at Peter. "But no funny stuff though, she's too young. You just take her to the party, you dance with her, make her have a good time, that's all....Eh?"

"Sure Charlie, I wouldn't think of anything else, she's just a kid."

"That's good, you take my little buggy with the sorrel. An here, you get something to wear so you look nice, eh!" Charlie pressed a gold piece into Peter's palm.

Kathryn was in a quandary. "Mom, my hair looks awful, it's all frizzy! And this dress doesn't fit right, it's all loose on top. Peter's going to think I'm a little girl."

Elizabeth, her mother, paused in her work on the light blue gown's hem.

"Kat, your hair looks just fine, Peter will love it. And you can pad the top of your dress with a little cotton. Glory be, a person would think it was your wedding instead of your sister's birthday."

"But Mom! You don't understand, I practically forced Peter to take me. I want him to be proud of me."

"Peter's a nice young man, I'm sure he'll be very proud of you. And after all, he's very fortunate to be invited at all. He is one of your father's employees. My lands! Charlie usually keeps a very strict separation between business and family. I really don't understand how Peter just came out of nowhere, and already is your father's favorite."

Lucille turned to her mother as she primped her own head of glorious brunette hair.

"It's because Peter is smart and ambitious, and he always treats Father with respect. Besides, Christian Halvorsen brought him, and he and father have been friends forever."

"Yes," her mother agreed, "Charlie has always felt indebted to Christian, because he saved Charlie's life when they were both young."

"Wasn't that something about a fight, Mom?" Kathryn had heard the story before. But she had spent many hours on Christian's knee as she grew up, and she regarded the big Norwegian as a favorite uncle.

"Yes, Charlie got in a fight with another lumberjack. They had both been drinking, and when Charlie got the better of the other man, he pulled out a gun. He would have shot your father, but Christian broke his arm, then knocked down two of the lumberjack's friends when they entered the fight. Christian has been Charlie's best friend ever since."

"I wonder if Peter would fight for a friend like that." Kathryn said.

"Your father told me, he did just that, before the party on the Fourth. He stood up for his friend, Gustav. It was with one of the foremen, I think."

"Oh really?! Did he win?!"

"It didn't end that way, the man was bigger and tougher than Peter. He would have beaten Peter, if a big German laborer hadn't ended the fight."

"Oh -h—h! I wish he would have beaten the guy up like Christian did."

"Oh Kat! Sometimes you're such a child," Lucille said. "There's more to a man than just being able to beat another man in a brawl. Peter is kind and sensitive, and he's good looking, but he doesn't go around strutting like a rooster. And, he knows what he wants—he's going to be an important man one day."

"How do you know so much about him, smartie? You only met him once, at the Fourth of July party."

"I talked to him a long while when you were dancing with all of the other guys. He told me all about Sweden, and the girl there that threw him over for another man. I could see the hurt in him then, he's a gentle man, I like him."

Kathryn bristled. "Well, you just stay away from him with those long fingers of yours. He's my escort, and you've got Stephen and a half dozen other guys chasing you anyway."

"Well, you wouldn't have to worry so much if you weren't such a tomboy, and didn't have such a temper. Peter thinks you're strange already."

"Did he say that?! Did he say I'm strange?!"

"He didn't exactly say it that way, just that you were different than any other girl he knows. He wondered if you always got mad so easily."

"Pooh on you, Lucy! Peter thinks I'm pretty, and he says I'm friendlier than other girls, he likes me a lot. So there!"

"Girls!" Elizabeth said sharply. "You sound like a pair of brazen hussies squabbling over a man. Remember this is just a party, and Peter is only Kathryn's escort. When the time is right for a serious involvement, it would pay you both well to remember that you must marry within your station in life, not below it. Young men like Stephen will enhance your position in life. A lumberjack will not, no matter how nice he is."

"But, Dad was a lumberjack once," Kathryn protested. "He's always telling stories about it."

"Yes, but that was a long time ago, and he and I rose above it. You must consider your place in society now."

The strong willed Kathryn stuck her lower lip out in a pout, but said nothing. Lucille only smiled.

"Golly! You're beautiful!" Was all Peter could say as Kathryn swept down the long staircase of the LeBlanc mansion. Her father, who had been chatting with Peter, smiled proudly.

"She is,...my little girl. She gonna be a real beauty, a real heart breaker. You make fine looking couple, you and her. Maybe some day something come of that, who knows, eh?"

"Golly!" Peter said as he took Kathryn's hand. "You'll be the prettiest girl at the party."

"Don't let Lucy hear that, she'll be jealous. She's been working all day to look like a princess." Kathryn smiled happily. "And my, aren't you handsome. I just love a man all dressed up with a suit and tie, it makes them look so dignified, like one of those southern gentlemen."

"Kat, she's read too much," Charlie laughed. "She's think all southern people live on big plantations. She don't know everything down there is changed since the war. But never mind, you two go on down to the club. We'll be coming soon's I get Liz pried loose from her mirror."

The little sorrel trotted briskly, and Peter had to rein him in to avoid having dirt thrown up on Kathryn and himself. At a comfortable walk, the ride was smooth, the evening air warm, and conversation possible.

"Peter, do you think I'm a tomboy? Lucy says I'm a tomboy, and that I have a bad temper."

Peter laughed. "No, I don't think you're a tomboy at all. I like girls that do things, like guys."

"And,...my temper, do you think it's that bad?"

"You're spicy, that's all. I think that's good, if it's not too much."

"I know it's too much sometimes, I promise I'll be good tonight."

"Good, then we'll have fun all night. Is Lucy coming with your parents?"

"No, she's coming with Stephen."

"Stephen who?"

"Stephen Crane, he's the banker's son, you met him out at the lake."

Peter searched his memory—there was a slight, unassuming, dark haired young man in the card game. "Yes, I remember him, is it serious?"

"Mother would like it to be. But I don't think Lucy is, she likes a stronger man. Stephen is sweet, and his father has a lot of money. But he's so quiet, it's almost like he isn't there sometimes."

Peter thought of the slender, haughty beauty that was Lucille with the introverted Stephen. The incongruous nature of the pair made him smile.

"Are you thinking of something funny, Peter? You're smiling."

"No," he fibbed, "I guess it's just because I'm so happy."

"I'm glad, because I am too." Kathryn leaned over and kissed Peter's cheek. "This is going to be a wonderful night!"

Kathryn proved to be an able and vigorous partner in a series of waltzes and polkas. When they left the dance floor both were perspiring heavily and laughing exuberantly. Peter could not remember when he had felt so care free.

When they returned to the table set up for family members, Charlie poured a light colored bubbly liquid into the glasses of his guests. He raised his glass.

"Family and friends, let us drink a toast to the firstborn of my family on her twentieth birthday. To the lovely and gentle Lucille, drink everybody, to her health and happiness."

Peter tipped his glass with the others, and sneezed. To his embarrassment, the rest of the party broke into hoots of merriment. He blushed and apologized.

"It tickles the nose, I didn't expect it."

"It's champagne," Charlie laughed. "Charlie, he have it shipped from France. It makes a happy time happier, but too much will make you very sad in the morning. Now, I have persuaded the orchestra to give us another treat from France. They will play a quadrille, everybody dance!"

"Oh wonderful!" Kathryn said. "I love to do the quadrille, come on Peter!"

"But I don't know how to do it," Peter said. "I would feel embarrassed in front of all these people."

"You can learn. I'll teach you. Don't be an old pooh, Peter."

"Why don't you dance it with Stephen?" Lucille asked. "I'd rather rest, and Stephen does it beautifully."

In obedience to Lucille, Stephen rose from the table and offered Kathryn his hand. Kathryn gave her sister a look that bordered on hostility, then took Stephen's arm, and smiling at him sweetly entered the dance floor.

"Thanks, Lucille, I'd had enough dancing for a while. But Kat can be insistent and a little difficult at times. It's hard to tell her no."

"That's because Father spoils her so badly. She's just like him, and so he gives her almost everything she wants. I think, inwardly he wishes she were a boy."

"You mean because he has no sons?"

"Yes, and I think that's why he has taken to you so remarkably. You are everything he wanted in a son."

"That makes me feel a little strange. I don't want to succeed because he likes me. I want to succeed on my own merit."

"Don't worry about that." Lucille patted his hand and and gave him an enigmatic smile.

"You will earn your own place, Father knows that, and so do I. Your independent nature is one of the things I find to be attractive in you."

Her hand had lingered on his for a moment, and the touch along with her mysterious smile sent little prickles along Peter's spine. He had thought Lucille to be a beautiful young woman, but somewhat haughty and distant, certainly beyond the reach of a poor lumberjack. Now he looked into her eyes and saw something that he couldn't identify. Was it invitation, or just friendliness? He averted his gaze.

"Have you been going with Stephen long?"

"We've seen each other for a little over a year, off and on. Stephen is a very sweet young man, we are very good…friends."

"I thought you were more than that."

"One should never judge by what others say. Mother would like me to marry Stephen. She looks at it as another step up the social ladder. His father has a great deal of money. And to Mother, money is very important, and for that reason those who have it are important."

"And your father, does he feel the same?"

"No, Father has more depth to his character than mother. At heart, he's still a lumberjack, and will always be one. By hard work and shrewd dealing he has acquired money and power. But it is the act of getting, not what he has that's important to him. I see the same thing in you, and that's why you and father get along so well."

"You are very understanding of human nature, I admire that in a woman. My mother told me when I looked at pretty girls, 'Beauty does not always carry understanding on its back.' She was right. I find you beautiful, but more important, you can think."

"Thank you, Peter, I find you handsome and thoughtful, and very much a man. "

He didn't know why, but the compliment caused Peter to flush.

"I don't know if it's the champagne, but I am very warm and it's so noisy in here, would you like to go out on the porch?"

Lucille gave him another enigmatic smile. "Yes, I would, Peter."

As they left the table together Kathryn glanced at them from the dance floor. She frowned slightly, then squeezed Stephen's hand and smiled at him sweetly.

The porch was a spacious addition to the outside of the club building and overlooked the Mississippi River. It was screened to keep the swarms of mosquitoes, that spawned in the vegetation below, at bay. A sprinkling of wicker furniture was provided for those members who wished to escape the heat of the ballroom, and enjoy the cooling breezes wafting up from the water. At the moment it was deserted, except for a couple in a far corner who were oblivious to the entrance of Peter and Lucille.

A summer moon cast its pale light on Lucille's face, complimenting her opaline skin and the shadowy darkness of her hair. Peter felt the nearness of her slender figure as they stood at the railing listening to the symphony of sound sent up to them by the creatures of the night. He felt the primitive feelings awake in him, feelings that had been subdued since he left the logging camp, and Sarah.

He tried to brush aside his instincts and started to speak, but Lucille put a single finger across his lips and slipped into his arms. He felt her delicate fingers insert themselves in the curly hair at the back of his neck, pulling his head down to meet her own. His arms became as creatures with their own mind, refusing to obey the caution within his will. For long moments nothing existed , save the passion of their lips and bodies joined together. Then, they were brought crashing back to reality by a soft masculine cough. They separated instantly, confused and embarrassed by the untimely arrival of Kathryn and Stephen.

"You skunk!...You no good, rotten skunk!" Kathryn screamed at Peter. "With my own sister! You're worse than a skunk, you're a jackass, a big horny old jackass! And you!...She turned to Lucille. "You're a whorey slut. You've got your own man, why do you have to take mine?" She broke into a loud and watery fit of crying.

Stephen, who had been regarding Peter with nervous indignation, tried to solace Kathryn, and stifle the outburst that was causing a few curious heads to poke through the doorway of the ballroom. Finally, having partially succeeded, he said, "I'll take you home, Kat." Turning to Lucille, he asked, "Does this mean we're through, Lucy?"

Lucille, who had gathered her composure answered matter of factly. "No, Stephen,...we never were."

With a countenance filled with virtuous outrage, Stephen turned to Peter. "You, sir, are less than a gentlemen!" Then, hustling Kathryn along, he stormed through the crowd.

Lucille gave a great sigh. "I guess, since there's no place else to go, you might as well take me home too, Peter. The party's over, I think."

The next day an uneasy Peter went to the office to catch up on his work. Since it was Saturday, it was unlikely that Carruthers and the other clerks would be there. The incident at the party had left Peter unnerved and he felt a need to work alone and sort out the confusion in his mind. He had made a bad error in judgment, an error that could cost him his position in the company, and possibly in any other company in the tight-knit industrial society of Minneapolis. A deep foreboding permeated his mind as he tried to concentrate on the figures in the ledger before him. He didn't hear the door open behind him, so intense were his musings. Then a familiar voice roused him from his reverie.

"Is a good thing to work when a man is troubled, eh?"

Peter turned, his mouth hanging open in trepidation.

"Oh! Mister LeBlanc, I didn't hear you." He jumped up from his chair, knocking the ledger on the floor as he did so.

"What the matter, Pete? You look like you see a ghost, sit down—take it easy. You and Charlie, we gonna talk a little."

Peter retrieved the ledger from the floor and sat down uneasily. Charlie sat down on Peter's desk and lit a cigar.

"We made a mess of things, eh? My wife, she so mad at me she don't sleep with me last night. The girls, they mad at each other, things so cold aroun' the house it's more like winter than summer. Charlie, he have to get out, he figure you be here."

Peter started to apologize. "I'm sorry that I made so much trouble, Mister LeBlanc, I…"

Charlie held up his hand. "Your apology is okay by me, but you not to blame alone. Charlie, he made you take Kat to the party, he shouldn't do that. The girls, they act like little witches some times, eh? "

"But, you said I shouldn't do any funny stuff, and I let you down. Golly, I feel miserable. I'm awful ashamed, Mister LeBlanc."

"That's good when you know you made mistake, that's set a man aside from a lout , that's good. But I not like you to call me 'Mister LeBlanc' when we talk like this. Call me 'Charlie', we in this soup together. Charlie, he tell you no funny stuff with Kat. And you didn't do that, eh? You think Charlie he not know Lucy set her cap for you?"

"But it was my fault for not controlling myself, Charlie. It's just that she's so awful pretty, and she smelled so good, and... "

"An she was willing, eh? You think Charlie he don't know how that feels, Pete? The thing is, everybody mad at everybody else. We got to let things cool down, Pete. An Charlie he want you to keep your mind on your work. So, it better you stay away from the house for a while. Otherwise, my wife she gonna shoot you, or shoot me, okay?"

"Sure Charlie, I'll never go near Lucille again."

"Charlie he didn't say that, you just let things cool down for a while, Pete. Charlie gonna keep you so busy you don't have time for any woman."

"What do you mean Charlie? Things are starting to slow down here."

"You remember when you told Charlie about your papa's business? I hired you because you know something about making furniture. Is nobody else here know nothing 'bout furniture, except dumping their asses on top of it."

"Sure Charlie, I know something about making furniture, but this is a lumber business."

"Pete, you still a little dumb. Charlie he has a lumber business, but he can't buy more logs than we getting already. So what he do to make more money, eh?"

Peter's eyes widened. "I see, we make furniture from the hardwood lumber we're sawing now."

Charlie laughed. "Now you thinking like a business man. I been sawing hardwood an aging it for furniture for ten years. Now there's a fella, he's old, wants to sell his factory. Charlie gonna buy that factory—Pete he gonna run it. What you say, you think you able to do it?"

Peter looked Charlie straight in the eye. "You bet I can, but why me? There's got to be people right there that know more about the business than I do."

Charlie puffed on his cigar. "Sure, there's all the people there that it takes to run ithe place. But you gotta think like a business man, Pete. Those people, they Perkins's men. They gonna do things like he been doing, only not so good. Charlie he needs a man that gonna do it his way, that ain't gonna sit back an take it easy. Somebody ambitious, an loyal, that's make the business bigger an better, eh?"

"Sure Charlie, I see what you mean. But I'm young—will they work for me?"

"They gonna give you hard time at first, Pete. But you show them you know what you're doing—you fire one or two that make trouble—you be the boss pretty soon. You need to know something, you telephone, is like Charlie's sitting next to you, eh?"

Chapter 10

Bossman Pete

Perkins Woodworks was a dingy frame building located six blocks west of the LeBlanc sawmill. As Peter viewed the structure, he saw it as a challenge, a challenge that would begin a long and illustrious career in the world of business.

He resisted the impulse to go straight into the office of Theodore Perkins and introduce himself. He wanted to see the company as it really was, as it operated from day to day. He walked along the front of the building to the yard, an area where long, slope-roofed buildings filled with drying lumber stood.

As he strode down the aisle between two of the buildings, he was appalled at the careless disarray. Good lumber lay crisscrossed and warping in the sun everywhere. Stacks of oak and maple that should have long been under cover stood in tilting piles where they had been slipped off of delivery wagons. Near the center of the yard, a huge pile of sawdust and wood scraps inched its way toward the building, as cleaning people took the shortest possible route in removing detritus from the work floor.

This would have to be cleaned up immediately, Peter thought. Was old Perkins running with such a short crew he couldn't keep his yard in order? In his mind, he could see the disaster a single spark could cause. He shuddered as he saw the smoke billowing from an old steam engine laboring at the shaft that drove the machines inside the building.

He was about to walk to an old warehouse that stood with an eastward tilt, like a drunk leaning against a lamp post, when he heard voices behind one of the stacks of lumber. He walked quietly to the source of the voices, where he found two men sitting on large wooden blocks, playing cards. The men looked up in surprise, but made no attempt to dispose of the cards.

"Hey! Whatcha doing here, kid?" The grimy one with decayed teeth said.

"This is private property, if you're lookin for work, get your ass over to the office. Otherwise get outa here."

Peter looked at them impassively. "Do you men work here?"

"Yeah, we work here. What the hell is it to you, kid?" The fat one with the bald head grunted.

Peter shrugged his shoulders and walked away. The two men laughed at him and continued their game.

"Shittin snotty nosed kid," the grimy one said.

One look inside the warehouse was enough to satisfy Peter that it was as shoddily run as the yard. An old, bent man and a sandy haired boy of about fifteen were listlessly crating rocking chairs for shipment. The old man was animatedly telling the boy about some past war experience, occasionally stopping to drive a nail in the crate before him. The boy made no movement except to pick up a slat and hold it to the crate when the previous one was nailed. Neither paid the least attention to Peter's presence and Peter saw no need for speech. He walked to the open door of the factory, where another boy was pushing a wheelbarrow of sawdust toward the pile. He settled the load to the ground as Peter approached.

"You lost?" he asked. "Clarence don't like no strangers wandering around."

"Who's Clarence."

"He's the foreman, grumpy old fart."

"Is Perkins here?"

"Naw, he ain't been here fer days. There's somebody else takin' over, so old Ted don't come in much anymore."

"So who runs the place when he's gone?"

"Clarence, and George the bookkeeper. Say, you sure are a nosy sucker. Who are you, anyway?"

"Your new boss," Peter said, and walked into the building, leaving the boy agape.

Peter thought he had never been in a dirtier place in his life. A cloud of dust filled the air and settled on every horizontal surface to a thickness of several inches. Men worked at various machines and workbenches shrouded in gloom, despite the brightness of the day. The only real light in the place was that which filtered in at the open doors, and at the bottoms of the huge windows that had been opened to allow the entry of fresh air. The large panes of glass were opaque with a thick coating of grime. As he stood looking about, a rough voice issued from the gloom.

"You there, what are you looking for?"

Peter turned to confront a tall, grizzled man who was peering at him through dust laden spectacles.

"Are you the foreman, are you Clarence?"

The man looked at him disapprovingly. "Yeah, I'm the foreman. If you're looking for a job, go to the office. Won't do you any good though, we've got more than enough help."

"Thanks, but I've already got a job. I'd like to talk to you and George."

"A salesman! You're a salesman, aren't you? Don't matter, we don't need anything, and we're busy. So trot your hind end out the way you came, and if you come again, go to the office. Not that it'll do you any good."

"Sorry Clarence, I'm staying. My name is Peter Hokanson—Charlie LeBlanc called about me."

The foreman's face became ashen. "You're Hokanson?!"

"*Mister* Hokanson, to you, Clarence. Now, let's go to the office. I want to talk to you."

George Riebeck looked up from a pile of papers on his grimy desk. A single incandescent bulb glowed feebly overhead, receiving little help from the failing transparency of the windows. He was a small man, with a look that reminded Peter of the rats on the immigrant ship. His eyes appeared huge as they focused on Peter through the thick lenses of his spectacles. He applied a large handkerchief to his pointed nose and blew loudly before acknowledging Peter's presence.

"Damned dust! Clogs my sinuses every day. Makes life a misery, a pure misery!—Who do we have here?" He addressed his query to Clarence, who looked nervously at Peter.

"George, this is 'Mister' Peter Hokanson. Mister Hokanson, this is George Riebeck , and I'm Clarence Olson."

George's face lacked recognition for a moment, then as though a huge hand had pushed him, he leaped to his feet , his expression now incredulous.

"Of course! Please forgive me, I wasn't expecting you to come alone, and through the plant." Almost as an afterthought he extended his hand.

Peter ignored the offering, and walked to an inner office instead. He opened the door and viewed the musty interior which stank of cigar smoke. A sagging leather chair set behind a scarred desk, he sat down in it and motioned for the two dumbfounded men to sit on a pair of straight backed, wooden chairs against one wall.

He stared at them for long moments, as though he were a schoolmaster about to chide a pair of neglectful students. The hardness in his eyes belied the youthfulness of his face—the two squirmed uneasily.

"Clarence," Peter began, "are you responsible for all the work that is done in all areas of this factory?"

"Well yes, that and the warehouse and yard."

"Then, might I ask, why are you doing it so poorly?"

"What do you mean? I've always got the orders out on time."

"I mean,…the whole place is a stinking mess, the yard, the warehouse and the plant. You're wasting good lumber in the yard, the warehouse is a mess, and this plant is a cruddy, dark firetrap."

The foreman colored and his eyes grew dark behind his dusty spectacles. It was obvious that he was not used to being called to account, and certainly not by a kid young enough to be his son.

"It's old Ted, he wouldn't give me help to clean up the place. I know it looks like hell, but it isn't my doing."

"Why don't you use the help you already have?"

"Now listen here, K...Mister Hokanson, those men all have work already, no man can do two jobs at the same time."

"You're right on that, Clarence, but they're not even doing one. You told me less than five minutes ago that you had more than enough help—The two men out in the yard, what are they supposed to be doing?"

"Stacking lumber in the sheds, and moving it into the planer. They've always got it in when we need it."

"That's nice, and they're allowed to play cards in between?"

"You mean... !"

"Clarence, those men were playing cards when I walked through the yard. And the old guy in the warehouse was telling war stories and the kid was listening."

Clarence's face was dark red now, a picture of indignation. "I had no idea that was going on! If I had, I would have fired them both!"

"That's just the point, it is your job to know what is going on,...and you're not doing it, are you? As for firing those two men in the yard, don't do it,... yet! You and I are going to make workers out of them, we're going to make workers out of all the men in this company!"

"How in the hell are we going to do that, on the measly wages old Ted paid them?"

"Are you saying I should raise wages?"

The foreman took off his spectacles and looked at Peter belligerently.

"Well, it'd be a start."

"Wrong,... no man ever did better work for higher wages. We'd just be paying them more for loafing. A man does good work because he has pride in what he does. When he does good work and enough of it, we talk about pay."

"So you tell me, 'Mister Hokanson'—how do we get them to do that?"

"I will tell you, Clarence. First, we clean up this shit hole! I want every man jack here to start cleaning,...now! And they don't stop until I can see the machines bright and shiny, and the light streaming through the windows!

And you can tell the two card sharps in the yard that if they want their jobs they better start stacking lumber like the devil himself was their foreman. I want the warehouse clean and neat, and I don't want to hear any more war stories out there."

Peter turned to George. "You do all the record keeping?"

George puffed up with pride. "Yes sir, all the accounts payable and receivable. The payroll, the ordering and most of the selling, just about everything!"

"What'd Perkins do, sign the checks?"

"Not even that, old Ted was old fashioned, he paid everything in cash, or rather, I did." George beamed.

"Sounds like you had an awful big job, maybe that's why this place is such a stinking boar's nest."

"Well, I guess so, old Ted didn't care much."

"But I do, George. When we get through here, I want you to do the same thing the men in the plant are doing, you understand?"

George was crestfallen. "Yes sir, is that all?"

"No, it's not. Starting today, we pay everything by check. And I sign all the checks until I'm satisfied with the operation of this place. Tomorrow I want all the books available to me, particularly the payables and receivables. And as soon as I'm through with them, I'll be taking over sales and purchasing. Are there any questions?"

"Yes there is, are you demoting me when you've just come in the door? I've been doing the sales and buying for a long time."

"No George, I'm going to give you some help. We are going to be very busy. Now let's get going!"

When the two men had left, Peter picked up the telephone and asked to be connected with LeBlanc Lumber. "Hello Charlie, this is Pete.—Yeah, I'm getting started. The place is a mess, it's like the men are trying to work in a rathole.—Yeah, they're cleaning it up now, I need to borrow your sawdust wagon.—For a couple of days, at least. Thanks.

Peter sat for while, writing a list of things to be done in the out-of-date factory. Then he walked through the door of the work floor. There was a bustle of activity, and the air was thick with flying dust as the men broomed down the ancient accumulation that covered everything. A middle aged man was busily cleaning a row of lathes near Peter. The man turned and grinned as Peter approached.

"They say a new broom sweeps clean, and I guess that's true alright. And long overdue, I'd say."

Peter held out his hand. "I'm Pete Hokanson, I'll be running this outfit for Charlie LeBlanc."

"Curtis Miller here. Glad to meet you, Boss. It's high time we got some young blood around here. I'm more than glad to see it."

Peter grinned. "I hope there's more that feel the way you do, or I'm going to have it awful tough."

"There's a few that might try to make it rough on you because you're new, and young. But most of the guys are tired of things being the way they were. It's real hard to work in this dirty old hole."

"Didn't Perkins care?"

"He used to. That was before his kid got killed when the boiler blew. Ted Junior was a strapping young fellow, strong and bright. The old man figured to hand over the factory to him. That was about ten years ago, old Ted just went downhill ever since. He just didn't care anymore, I guess."

"What about Olson, couldn't he keep things going right? There's no excuse for this, to my way of thinking." He pointed to the piles of grimy sawdust at their feet.

Curtis looked at Peter carefully, his voice was cautious when he spoke.

"That's another story, and I need my job. Clarence and I don't get along none too good as it is."

"It's okay Curtis, what you say to me stays with me. What's the story with Olson?"

Curtis was hesitant. "Well, I guess you got a right to know everything, since you have to run this old junk pile. Clarence was Ted's foreman a long time ago when I was just a kid. And he was a real company man, a pusher from the word go. I mean, there wasn't a speck of mouse shit that Clarence didn't notice.

Then, as Ted Junior started growing up, the old man got to giving him some of Clarence's authority. That didn't sit too good with Clarence, and finally he let old Ted know about it. The old man must've figured that his kid could handle Clarence's job so he put Clarence back on the finishing line doing final inspection of the furniture, and give young Ted the foreman's spot."

"Why didn't Clarence quit?"

"Well, shit! Ted made it look like a promotion, called Clarence the 'Chief Inspector', so it wouldn't look like he was getting kicked down the shit hole. But they both knew he was, and Clarence let it ride because he had a family and needed a paycheck like everybody else.

"And then Ted's son got killed, and the old man put Clarence back in control, right?"

"You got it right. Only it was never the same again, neither one of them cared anymore. And here we are. And I can't say I envy your job."

Peter regarded Curtis thoughtfully. "You believe in laying it on the line, don't you?"

"It's the only way to be, Boss."

"And you've been here since you were a kid?"

"Yep, about thirty years."

"So you know the business."

"Look Boss, I don't believe in bragging, but I've done every job in this old shit hole, from the yard to the finish line."

"And Clarence, how old is he?"

A few years younger than old Ted, I guess. I think he's about ready to hang it up. When young Ted was killed, the old man gave Clarence a small share in the company so he'd take over again. So now with LeBlanc buying it, he's got some money. I wouldn't be surprised if he quits on you. He hates young men since Ted Junior took his job."

"And you, Curtis? How do you feel about working for a kid?" Peter grinned.

"I think it's not the age that counts, so much as it is having an instinct for business, and for people. If you can do the job, I'll be glad to call you 'Boss'. If you can't, I'm not so old I can't get another job."

Peter laughed. "You lay it on the line all right, I think we're going to get along just fine."

At seven the next day, when Peter arrived at the office, Clarence Olson was already there. He was not dressed in work clothes, and his attitude was openly hostile.

"Just came in to tell you I won't be working here anymore. I've had my belly full of working for smart-ass kids. I guess you'll have to get the orders out by yourself."

Peter felt the hair raise on the back of his neck, but forced back the anger.

"I guess I'll have to do just that. Good-bye, Clarence, enjoy your retirement." He turned on his heel and entered his office, leaving the man without the fight he so badly wanted.

By eight o'clock Curtis Miller was the new foreman of LeBlanc Woodworking, and Peter was sitting at his desk studying the ledgers of the company. He skimmed through the most recent entries in the receivables ledger. Then frowning, he paged backward, reading the columns carefully.

"George!" he hollered. "Come in here!"

The bookkeeper scurried into the office. "Yes Sir, what do you need?"

"These sales accounts, some of them go back for almost a year with no payment entered."

"Yes sir, Mister Hokanson, a few of them are a bit behind."

"What's being done about it?"

"Well Sir, old Ted goes around to collect once in a while."

"When did he last do that?"

"I can't rightly say, Mister Hokanson, not lately though."

"And we're still shipping furniture to all of these?"

"Yes Sir, old Ted didn't want to lose any customers."

Peter shook his head and sighed. "Okay George, we'll talk about this later. You can go back to your work."

Peter closed the ledger, this would require immediate action. He would have to get someone to go out on collections, someone with guts, that he could trust. Gus,—the brassy young Swede didn't lack courage, and he was smart enough. Gus was a talker and he got along with people. But he didn't read and write in English. He could read numbers though, that was the same. Maybe he could learn the English, and Peter could duplicate the bills in Swedish until he did. It would be cumbersome, but it might work. He'd have a talk with Gus.

He opened the payable ledger and paged through recent months. All the entries were completed in George's precise hand, most of them going to LeBlanc Lumber. Perkins had been a good customer to Charlie. He was prompt in paying his bills, even though he was remiss in collecting. Peter wondered how he had been able to keep the company running. Perhaps the key was in the wages he paid.

Peter was about to close the ledger when one of the most recent entries caught his eye. It was for July twentieth and read: "Two thousand board feet, no. 1 oak lumber…$100.00." Peter looked at it thoughtfully, then studied the other recent entries for LeBlanc Lumber. His face became grim—he slapped the ledger shut and put it under his arm.

"I'm going over to see Charlie LeBlanc." He told George as he hurried out the door.

Charlie looked up from a stack of papers on his desk. "Hey Pete! Charlie was thinking about coming over to see how you doing, you beat me to it. You got things running already, eh?"

Peter gripped the Frenchman's outstretched hand. "Just barely started, Charlie.. Got a new foreman, and maybe I'm going to have a new bookkeeper. You too, I think."

Charlie's face clouded. "What you mean, Pete?"

"Would you ask Carruthers for the receivable ledger Charlie?"

Charlie left his desk and went into the accountant's office. A moment later he returned with a large book, followed by Carruthers.

"What do you need, Mister Hokanson? I'll find it for you." The accountant said, eyeing Peter suspiciously.

"Thanks, but it's just routine," Peter said. "We won't need your help. And close the door behind you, please."

After Carruthers had left, Peter opened both ledgers to July, and began studying them carefully. His face became increasingly grim.

"You look like you just found a dead skunk in your picnic basket," Charlie said. "How about you tell Charlie what you looking for, eh?"

"Here, look at Perkin's ledger for the twentieth of July!"

"It say Perkins pay me a hundred dollar for two tousan feet of oak."

"Now look at your ledger!"

"It say Perkins pay me seventy five dollar for one tousan, five hundred feet of oak." Charlie looked at Peter. "Is maybe a mistake, I ask Carruthers."

"Not yet," Peter said, "look at these other entries. One thousand feet of maple on the twenty fourth in Perkin's ledger, eight hundred in yours. It's the same thing all the way back."

Charlie looked through the figures, becoming more angry as he read.

"Those sons of bitches! !," he exploded, "they been taking Perkins' money all along."

"Or maybe yours, maybe both."

"What you mean, Pete?"

"What if Carruthers was actually shipping the amount Perkins shows? It would be easy for him to work up a phony invoice. And since Perkins always paid in cash, he could pocket the difference.

Or maybe he was shipping short loads and Perkins's delivery and receiving men were in on it. Or, they could be shipping full loads and stealing part of it and stashing it somewhere."

"Yeah, I see what you say." Charlie was flushed with anger. "But how we gonna know how many skunks we got in the picnic basket? I gonna go and knock Carruthers on his ass, he'll tell me, by God!!"

"No Charlie, he'd just say his figure is right, and George over at Perkins was doing the stealing."

"I see what you say, but how we gonna know who doing the stealing?"

Peter thought for a few minutes. "You send an invoice with your driver?"

"Two of them, they get one, we get one."

"And yours is signed?"

"Yeah, by Perkins' yard man. So what?"

"Can I have a few of them?"

"Yeah, Charlie get you some. What you gonna do with them?"

"I've got an idea, Charlie. Just don't say anything to anybody yet."

At the furniture factory, Peter found the invoices he was looking for. The amounts on them matched the figures in George's ledger. It didn't surprise him, but it proved nothing. Each was signed with a crude signature, "Harry Brett".

He walked out to the yard, where the two yard men were busily stacking lumber. "Who's Harry Brett?"

The bald headed one turned and looked at Peter sheepishly. "I'm Harry,…about yesterday…I'm awful sorry, we didn't know who you were, Mister Hokanson."

"I'm willing to let it pass, this time, Harry. But next time I see either of you loafing, you'll be making tracks down the street.—But that's not what I'm here about. Is this your signature, Harry?" Peter handed the fidgeting man an invoice.

"Yeah, it's mine all right, why?"

"Was that load the full amount?"

"Sure, it's that stack there. See that board with the invoice number on it?"

Peter counted the boards in the stack and figured the board feet in his head, it tallied. The delivery was straight, and so, it would appear, was George. Leaving the yard men scratched their heads, he walked back to LeBlanc Lumber. He found Charlie chewing on the stump of a cigar, an empty brandy glass in front of him.

"Well, out with it Pete! What you find out?"

"This load tallied with George's book." He held up an invoice. "But it doesn't match Carruthers's invoice, and the signature is different."

"The stinking son of a bitch," Charlie muttered. "All this time that bastard been stealing from Charlie—I'm gonna kill him."

"But Carruthers didn't sign it either, I know his writing, it's not his."

Charlie grabbed the pair of invoices Peter held. "Dammit, you right, Pete. What the hell is going on?"

"Maybe it's time we ask Carruthers?"

"You right, Pete, I gonna strangle it out of him!" Charlie stormed into the accounting room. "Ernest! Charlie wants to talk to you!...Where is that bastard anyway?!"

A junior clerk looked up from his papers. "Why, he left right after Mister Hokanson a while ago, said he had to do some business. Can I help you, Mister LeBlanc?"

Charlie was furious. "Maybe you can tell me who the hell signed this invoice!"

The clerk looked at it carefully. "The writing looks familiar, but we don't have a Harry Brett here."

"I know that you dumb ass, I want to know who the hell forged that signature!"

The clerk cringed. "Yes Sir, it looks familiar, but no clerk would write that poorly. Wait a minute, I think I might know. Billy, come over here!

A young boy who was sweeping the floor put his broom aside and hurried over. "Yes, Mister Aikins?"

"Mister LeBlanc wants to talk to you."

The boy looked at Charlie apprehensively. "Yes Sir?"

Charlie glared at the boy who was beginning to tremble with fear. "Billy, did you write that name on this invoice?"

"Yes Sir,...Mister Carruthers told me to do it. He said that Perkins's dock man forgot to sign like he often did, and he didn't want to make trouble for the man."

"May the blessed mother save us! How many times did you do it, Billy?"

"Lots of times, Mister LeBlanc. Was it wrong? I wouldn't have done it if I knew it was wrong."

Charlie's face softened. "Wrong enough to get you in jail if you not just a dumb kid. Now go back to your sweeping, an you not do it again." He turned to Peter. "What wè gonna do now, Pete?"

"Does Carruthers have a house?"

"No, just a room, he's a bachelor. You think he's there?"

Peter shook his head. "The railroad station! He knows we're onto something and he's going to run."

Charlie grabbed Peter's arm. "Come on, Charlie got the blacks on the surrey today. We gonna catch that bastard!"

Peter hung onto the surrey seat with clenched fingers as Charlie whipped the two Morgan's into a gallop. They raced through the streets, startling more sedate horses into rearing panic, evoking curses from the struggling drivers. Once or twice they forced frightened pedestrians to run from the street to save themselves from the charging team.

Then they were there, at the very station where Peter had first put his feet on the soil of Minnesota.

A locomotive set on the rails making hissing sounds as dock men loaded freight on one of the cars. Charlie pulled the Morgans to a sliding stop and leaped off the carriage. He took only a moment to wrap a hitch rope around the rail before dashing into the station. Peter followed behind, barely able to keep pace with the Frenchman. The depot was empty, except for the ticket agent.

"Did a man buy a ticket?" Peter yelled at the agent.

"Yep, but you better hustle if you wanna catch him, train's 'bout ready to leave."

They ran through the door as the eastbound locomotive started making its first chuffing sounds, and the long drive rods slowly started turning the wheels, bringing the train into a creaking life. Charlie and Peter dashed through the door of the last coach, past the startled conductor.

"Stop this damned train!" Charlie yelled as he ran up the aisle.

"But I can't without reason,...The flustered man found no time for further words as Charlie and Peter dashed into the next car.

Ernest Carruthers was sitting in the first passenger car of the string of three, nervously peering out of the window as he waited for the train to leave. He hadn't had time to pack his few belongings, but he carried a small valise that was very heavy, despite its size. He was holding the bag on his lap, clutched to him, when he saw Charlie and Peter on the station platform. In terror he dashed from the train just as his pursuers entered the last car. He was running across the street as fast as his spindly legs could carry him when Peter saw him through a window.

The young Swede leaped from the car and gave chase to the lanky accountant as he struggled to make an escape. The heavy bag hindered Ernest, but he could no more drop it than he could give up his life. They ran down the street toward the restaurant where Peter had stopped to eat when he arrived in the city. The young man was gaining rapidly, the tall paunchy one was puffing hard, his breath coming in great gasps. Ernest could not give up and he could not escape the swiftness of the youth.

In panic he stopped and turned, his hand found a coat pocket and the handgrip of a small revolver. He was in the act of drawing it when Peter's body hit him. Ernest felt the hard muscled shoulder in his midsection driving the air from his lungs. Then he was flying to the paving stones with his arms flapping like gaunt wings. The valise crashed heavily to the street and the gun went clattering and skipping across the cobbled surface. Peter was sitting astride Ernest with his fist cocked when Charlie reached them.

Despite his anger, Charlie broke out in laughter at the sight of Peter astride Ernest's paunch. As he would later say, "Peter looked like a lumberjack sitting on an anthill."

"What the hell are you laughing at, Charlie?" Peter asked angrily. "The bastard tried to shoot me!"

"Charlie, he laughing at you riding that poor son-of-a-bitch. I think you can put your fist down. Looks to me like Ernest he got the fight knocked out of him."

After they had turned the submissive Ernest over to a policeman who had been lounging at the front of the restaurant, the two went to the police station and made statements. Charlie filed charges against Ernest, then returned to his office with Peter. He broke out his brandy bottle and cigars.

"We make exception to the rule one time, eh?," he said, as he filled a glass and handed it to Peter. "Now, let's see what that bastard stole from Charlie."

They dumped the contents of the valise in a heap on Charlie's desk and both men stared in amazement.

"Whooee! I never saw that much money in my life." Peter exclaimed.

"Son of a bitch coulda retired a long time ago if he wasn't so damned greedy!," Charlie snorted. "Let's count it, you count the paper, Charlie, he count the gold and silver."

The total came to eight thousand, two hundred and eighty dollars.

"Wonder how much of this he earned," Peter said.

"Don't matter, where he's goin he don't need money, eh?"

"Yeah, I guess so, still it's a shame he's going to lose his too."

"Pete, you too damned, soft hearted to be good. He took Charlie's money, now Charlie gonna take his. But you know, Charlie he not find out if you not so smart."

"It's okay Boss, it was my job to notice."

"Sure, but most men wouldn't notice, or they wouldn't give a damn. And you almost got shot trying to save Charlie's money. Charlie gonna make that right."

"I know you will, Charlie. You've been awful good to me."

"I don't mean sometime, Pete—Charlie he do it now. You gonna get fifteendollars a week, starting now."

"Golly, thanks Charlie."

"An, you gonna get half of what you save Charlie!" He pushed stacks of paper money and gold coins at Peter. Four tousan, one hunerd and forty dollars. What you say, eh?"

Peter was speechless, he had worked hard and saved twenty dollars since he started working for Charlie, along with the money he had saved from his logging work, he had almost two hundred dollars. Now, in a moment he had twenty times that. "Golly!...Golly!"

"What you gonna do with it, Pete? You can buy a fancy house with that." Charlie's grin showed he was enjoying the moment.

Peter appraised the pile of coins thoughtfully. "I wonder if I could buy into the factory with it?"

Charlie laughed. "That's what Charlie he hope you say. You gonna be helluva businessman, Pete. Charlie he do better than that if you want. The place worth bout twenty tousan dollar. I lend you enough so you buy half, Charlie an you, we partners."

The deal was made that day. Peter made the transition from employee to a partner in business before his nineteenth birthday.

With Charlie Leblanc as his mentor Peter rapidly became an able plant manager and businessman. Curtis Miller breathed new life into the manufacturing operation. Under his able leadership, the men developed a new sense of responsibility and pride. Production rose sharply enough to require a full time salesman.

Gus Svenson, who with the help of a tutor, had become English literate, filled the position. He joined it effectively with his work on collections, bringing a new financial strength to the company. George Riebeck, contrary to

Peter's first impression, proved to be an able accountant and business consultant. Peter made him responsible for the company finances, and to George's great joy, authorized him to sign company checks.

In two years of hard work, and with incredible luck, the greenhorn lumberjack became a respected businessman. The furniture plant was flourishing, and Peter was able to pay off the loan made to him by Charlie LeBlanc.

As Charlie had predicted, Peter was far too busy to think of romance, and so the old sores healed. Julia was a distant memory, Sarah he thought about occasionally and Lucille was someone Charlie mentioned, but Peter was reluctant to pursue. Still, he was a young man, and Lucille was a beautiful young woman who was courted by a growing number of suitors. To say he had forgotten her would be false. And Charlie certainly did not put any obstacles between his daughter and Peter.

Chapter 11

A Woman's Love

It was the first of September 1899. Peter was thinking about all that had happened since he had arrived in America less than four years ago. The office he now sat in was comfortable, not as resplendent as Charlie LeBlanc's, but a far cry from the stinking log barrack that had been his home that first winter. He and Gus had given up the room they shared above the restaurant and rented a small house together. That wouldn't last long, he mused.

Gus had done well as a salesman, and he was now engaged to the daughter of one of his customers in the city. The wedding would be next June, and Gus was thinking about buying the house they now lived in. Maybe it was time for him to think of doing the same. He was established now, as Charlie had wanted, and the relationship between the two men was good. Charlie mentioned his daughters more often, almost pointedly, it seemed.

Peter had seen both of the young women on occasions, such as the Christmas parties at Charlie's mansion and the annual Fourth of July celebrations at the lake.

Lucille had always been pleasant but not forward like she had been the night of her birthday party. She had a number of suitors, but as far as Peter knew, no serious one, a fact that made her mother increasingly nervous. When Peter danced with her, he always became excited and invariably went home to spend a restless night thinking about her. She was fun to be with, in a comfortable way, though she definitely had a strong sensuality that made Peter want more of her.

Kat was a different matter, now nineteen, she had blossomed into a vivacious beauty, who never missed an opportunity to tease Peter. At gatherings, she made a point of bringing her current date over to introduce him, then proceeding to flirt with Peter outrageously. Peter was never quite able to figure Kat out, she was devastatingly attractive but he wondered if being married to her wouldn't be an endless torture of the type she made her dates suffer. Being married to Lucy would probably be comfortably tranquil. Being married to Kat would be crazily exciting.

Even Charlie's wife Elizabeth had taken to talking with Peter, and smiled at him approvingly when she introduced him to friends. Since Peter had become a partner in the furniture factory she regarded him as socially and financially acceptable, and therefore an eligible bachelor. His dark good looks and pleasant manner also gave him points with Elizabeth, because to her, social grace was nearly as important as position and power.

Yes, Peter thought to himself, it would be a good time to acquire a home and family. In the future, he would want sons to follow him into his business ventures. To have that, he must marry soon. Peter was not aware of the fact that for the first time he was not falling helplessly in love, but was planning it as a career strategy. Though he had always been ambitious, in the last three years that ambition had become the single driving factor in his being. Success was everything, the acquisition of money and power stood above all other needs.

On the fifteenth of September he would celebrate his twenty-first birthday. A party at the club was in order. Yes, he would arrange one and ask Lucille to accompany him. For a night he would be reigning prince, and if she accepted his invitation, Lucille would be his princess.

Lucille had indeed accepted Peter's invitation, and now they were dancing the first waltz alone on the floor, in honor of Peter's twenty-first birthday. It was a milestone in his life, at twenty one he was recognized fully as a man, and the applause of the spectators as he and Lucille glided gracefully around the floor was intoxicating to his spirit. Lucille was truly his princess tonight, dazzling in a light blue gown that was pulled tightly about her waist. Her hair was not pulled back like that of many of the women, but flowed like a soft dark mantle about her shoulders, a delicate tiara of baby's breath and tiny blue flowers crowned her head. Peter looked at her in awe, and almost said "Golly!", but decided that tonight that childish exclamation was not appropriate. Instead he smiled and held her a little closer.

Lucille eased away from him enough to be able to look into his eyes.

"Happy birthday, Peter. It is, isn't it?"

"Fantastic! The best one of my life."

"I'm glad, I've been waiting for this you know."

"You have? You knew this would happen?"

"Of course, this or something like this."

"How'd you know that?"

"By the last time we were here, by the way you held me then."

"But I haven't asked you out, it's been so long—you knew I'd ask you?"

"Of course, you're so much like Father, I knew there were things you had to do first. That's why I haven't married anyone, I had to see if I was right, and I was."

The music ended, and Peter led Lucille off the floor and back to the screen porch, where they stood holding hands.

"You mean, you turned down other men because I might ask you?"

The enigmatic smile was in her eyes again. "Don't you want to, Peter?"

He flushed and could feel the warmth climbing in his face. "Yes,…I do, I just wasn't ready to ask you."

"Why?"

"Because,…I thought you'd want to know me better, I thought you might say no."

"But I do know you, I've known you for years."

"That isn't what I mean, you don't know all about me."

"Peter, the only way you get to know somebody that way is to live with them. Do you want to live with me first?"

"No,…I mean, I don't want it to be that way with us. I want to marry you."

"Is that a proposal, Peter?"

Peter took Lucille in his arms then, it wasn't the way he would have planned it, but it was what he planned.

"Yes Lucy, will you marry me?"

The enigmatic smile faded from her eyes, her face became calm and loving.

"Yes, Peter Hokanson, yes, I will marry you."

They kissed then in an embrace that spoke of years of waiting. Not searching as before, but freely giving, sealing a question asked, a promise given. They held their embrace, oblivious to everything until an autumn wind arose and spatters of chilling rain were blown through the screening of the porch. They drew back then, and Peter drew a line down Lucille's nose with the droplets of rain clinging there.

"I think we should go and tell your mother and father."

That night, the champagne flowed freely, for Charlie LeBlanc could not contain the good news, but insisted on announcing it immediately. Taking his daughter in one arm and Peter in the other, he led them to the bandstand, where he silenced the music with an upraised hand.

"My friends! My friends, listen to Charlie! Charlie he has wonderful news!"

All became silent as the celebrants looked at Charlie expectantly. He squeezed the young people to him, his face glowing.

"My daughter Lucille and my young partner Pete, they gonna get married! Those who know Charlie good, know how happy that's make him. Everybody get a glass of wine, we gonna toast this fine young couple!"

Amid the cheering and flurry of people Peter noticed Kat and her date leave the party. Her mother had a troubled look on her face which she quickly changed to a smile when her eyes met Peter's.

Late that night, when Peter took Lucille home, the rain had stopped and a warm breeze was blowing from the south.

"Can we walk in the garden, Peter?" Lucille asked. "It's so nice I don't want to go inside just yet."

They walked along the rose lined pathway, and up to the gazebo which stood alone on a small hill behind the mansion.

"It's so beautiful up here," Lucille said. "Father built it when I was a little girl. I came up here with my dolls all the time and I'd pretend I was a mother and this was my house. Only I never had a little boy around to play the father. So I'd pretend that this big rag doll I had was the father. I called him Mushy, because he was so soft and floppy. Did you ever play father, Peter?"

Peter laughed. "No, my sisters always chased me away when they were playing with dolls, because I always pulled their dresses up, the doll's I mean."

"Do you miss your family? I think about that sometimes, it must be hard, being without your family."

"Yes, I do, especially at Christmas. The first Christmas I was here we went hunting because we were all so lonely. I got lost and almost froze to death." He chuckled. "But I wasn't lonely anymore."

"Oh, how terrible! Was that with Gus?"

"Yes, and Sven, it's one of the things I remember Sven for. He saved my life, but I couldn't save his."

"But that wasn't your fault, nobody could have."

"I know, but he was my only relative here, and I miss him."

"You know what, Peter? You're going to have lots of relatives here, all the sons and daughters we're going to have."

Peter smiled. "Good, when do we get started?"

The enigmatic smile crept back into Lucille's eyes. "When would you like to?"

"I'd like to right now, but don't you think we should wait til we're married?"

"I guess so, can we be married soon?"

"How soon?"

"How about Christmas? Then you won't be lonely."

"Christmas? That's only three months away! We haven't got a place to live or anything."

"We could live here, there's acres of room."

Peter thought of Kat, and her voluptuous body and ways. "I don't think that would be a good idea."

"But why? We could have almost the whole second floor to ourselves, Kat only needs one room."

"I just don't think it would be a good idea."

"If you're worrying about my mother and father, don't. Father loves you like a son, and Mother is a real sweetheart when you get to know her."

"I'm not worried about them at all, Lucy. I just think newly married people should have their own place."

"I'll bet your parents didn't when they married, did they?"

"Well no, but that was different, there wasn't anything, and they didn't have any money."

"Peter, I don't understand, it would be just until we can get the house we want. Next summer we can have one built. Please,...I know Father and Mother will be thrilled to have us. We can get married the Saturday after Christmas and have a wedding dance at the club.

Everything will be festive, and maybe there'll be a nice snow so we can go to the church in a sleigh. Oh it would be so wonderful!"

In the end, Lucille got her way despite Peter's reservations. The endless round of planning began. For Peter, as with most men, the planning would be simple, Gustav would be his best man and that was that. Since he had no relatives and very few close friends in Minneapolis, he saw no need for a large wedding. Lucille and her mother had other ideas, the LeBlanc position in society demanded a large wedding and a gala reception afterward.

Lucille complained to Peter that she wanted several bridesmaids, and that therefore he must have groomsmen as their escorts. Finally, he was able to convince Christian that he must come down from the logging camp for the event. He then chose Andre LeBlanc, a cousin of Lucille's, as a third member of his party. His part of the planning completed, he immersed himself in his work, surfacing only to spend time with Lucille in the evenings.

Elizabeth had been cool to the idea of the young couple living in the mansion. But she warmed to the idea when Kathryn gave Lucille her support.

"It will be fun, Mama!," she said. "I've never had a brother, and now I will have one, and Daddy will have a son. We'll be a big happy family! And besides, this big old house will seem so empty with just the three of us."

If Kathryn held any animosity toward her sister for taking Peter, she gave no sign of it. So the matter was settled, and the second floor of the mansion was prepared for the young couple's occupancy.

As the weeks passed, the three women were happily working on wedding plans. The pastor was consulted and the forthcoming marriage was announced. Invitations were sent out, and the club ballroom was reserved for the reception. Decorations were planned and food and drink ordered. All of the women in the party spent hours with the seamstress that Elizabeth had chosen to make the gowns. As the date approached, the women became irritable, and Charlie and Peter took to playing billiards at the club to escape the frenzied activity.

On one such evening, Peter was sipping a brandy as Charlie made the break on a game of eight ball.

"Did you have to go through all this when you got married, Charlie?"

"Naw! And a damned good thing, otherwise I'd probably be up in the woods with Christian. It wasn't so civilized then, now the women got to decorate everything. You know what Liz tole Charlie yesterday? She's want the stable man to braid white ribbons in the horses' manes and tails! My black Morgans with ribbons in their hair! ! Damn me, my friends gonna laugh me out of town!"

Peter choked on his brandy,and sprayed it across the billiard table.

"You're going to do it then?" he asked, laughing as he wiped up the liquor with his handkerchief.

Charlie shrugged. "You can't argue with Liz when she makes up her mind about something. You gonna find out, Lucy she's the same way!"

"I know, I didn't want to move in with you and Liz either. I lost that one."

Charlie leaned on his cue as Peter expertly banked a ball into a side pocket.

"You know Pete, Charlie wondered about that. You think you gonna be uneasy with Kat around, eh?"

Peter nodded. "I did, but she seems to be taking it okay."

"Uh-huh, but you never know bout Kat. Charlie he her old man, an he don understand her. Lately she been running around with this musician, he used to play a horn, I think it was a trumpet, here at the club. That's where she met him, and Charlie he damns his ass that he ever took Kat down here. She got to liking this guy, a real brassy, cute dressing asshole. Charlie he can't stand the smart talkin bastard, he thinks this guy just after money an something else.

Anyway, Kat an me got to fighting over him. First time anything really come between us. Charlie he thinks there gonna be trouble over it. It's not like with you and Lucy. I like having you there an we gonna have fun. But watch out for Kat, she don give up easy once she set her mind bout something, an she don like losing."

"You think she might make trouble between Lucy and me?"

"Maybe, maybe not. But she can't make trouble if you don let her,eh?"

Charlie looked at Peter seriously, and his expression revealed his concern.

It was the Sunday two weeks before Christmas, and Christian was sitting in the cabin of Wise Otter with a small, curly-headed, little boy on his knee. The little boy, now three years old was happily playing with Christian's pocket watch. Christian's face was sad as he listened to the gaunt figure lying in the bed beside him. The old man's French came slowly and so quietly that Christian had to lean forward to hear.

"We have been friends for many moons, Christian. We have been as two warriors sworn by the blood oath. I have seen the sun rise on many days of good, and I have seen it set on days of evil. Now it is time for Wise Otter to go to the land where there are always deer to hunt and the wild rice hangs from the stem in great fullness. I go to be with my son, White Buck who waits for me, and with my other children and Quiet One who bore them."

A deep wracking cough convulsed his withered frame. When he was quieted, Sarah wiped flecks of blood from the sides of the old man's mouth. He drew a labored breath and continued to speak in rasping sighs.

"You have walked with honor, my old friend. You have seen that this little one has lacked nothing, and have come to us bearing gifts for many moons, both in the time of snow and the time of growing things."

"It is as one man should do for another, and for those who cannot hunt for themselves," Christian said. "And I will do so until this one grows tall and strong."

"It is good," Wise Otter said. "But my heart is sore in my breast, that Sarah is without a man. She is young, and she should share her bed with a man."

"I think so too, old friend, but I don't know where to look for such a man. Sarah must find him, if that is her desire."

"In the old days," Wise Otter whispered, "we would sometimes arrange a careful match for such as she." The old man feebly moved his hand toward Sarah, and then to the boy.

"You are still strong Christian, and the boy knows you as a father. It would fill my spirit with joy if you would take Sarah and the boy to your lodge."

Sarah gasped. "Grandfather, you cannot ask for such a thing!"

"I must, my granddaughter—Christian lies alone, as you do. Would you refuse him as a husband because he does not walk in the youth of his days? Would you deny the boy a father who is strong and kind?" His eyes flickered, then came to rest on Christian's.

"Would you refuse Sarah as your woman, Christian? Is she not pleasing in body and spirit?"

Christian breathed a deep sigh. "In the summer moons, I sometimes thought of asking Sarah to bring the boy to my lodge, Wise Otter. I would do so now, for my heart reaches out to them. But, in the land of the white-man, it is always for a woman to say with what man she shares her bed."

Wise Otter closed his eyes, and those near him would have thought his spirit had passed from him, were it not for the shallow breaths which came in wheezing sighs. After a few moments he had gathered enough strength to speak.

"My granddaughter, speak the thoughts of your heart."

Sarah was astonished by her grandfather's request, and by Christian's answer to it. Now she closed her eyes to blot out the two men as she searched for an answer. Christian had always been kind to her, and like a father to her son. Still, she had never thought of him as a possible husband, but rather as a favorite uncle.

In the summer they had sometimes walked hand in hand down the forest paths, with Christian carrying the boy on his shoulders. That must be what Christian was referring to. It had been pleasant, but she had never thought of it in a romantic sense. She loved Christian, but not as a lover or husband.

It was a terrible situation, she wanted her grandfather to die in peace, but could she promise herself to a man because of it? She felt something being placed into her hand, and opened her eyes. It was a letter. Sarah opened the rumpled page and read:

Dear Christian,

Lucille and I were greatly pleased that you will attend our wedding, and that you will stand up for me in the wedding party.

Preparations are nearly completed, and we look forward to seeing you. We expect you will arrive early enough to share Christmas with us.

I am marrying the most beautiful woman in the world, and I am very happy.

Your friend ,

Peter

Sarah's face paled, and she forced back tears that were pressing insistently at her eyelids. She looked up at Christian—his face showed the compassion and love of the man. Kindly, she took her grandfather's frail hands in her own.

"I will be proud to be Christian's wife, if he will have me, Grandfather."

The frail hands pressed hers, the tired eyes opened. "It is good," the faint voice whispered. Then the old warrior closed his eyes and took his place in eternity.

Christian rose from his chair, and holding the boy on one arm, he drew Sarah to him. Star Flower gently closed her father's mouth, then she crossed to a shelf near the chair he always used, and returned.with an old pipe made of pipe stone and sumac wood and placed it in the old warrior's hands, pressing his fingers firmly over it. Then she began a chant that was difficult for Christian to understand, even though he understood some of the Chippewa language. Sarah clung to Christian, her face buried against his neck, she was crying with deep convulsive sobs.

"She is telling the spirit world that a warrior comes to them." She told him through her tears. "She calls to White Buck to receive his father, and tells Quiet One and Blue Waters to prepare a bed for him."

Star Flower washed her father and dressed him in his fringed warrior's shirt trimmed with colored porcupine quills and egret feathers and put the beaded band with eagle feathers on his head. Then she, with Sarah, placed him on his best blanket with his knife and war club from the days of his youth. They wrapped it tight, after Christian had smoked a pipe in his honor and shook the ashes over his body. Then they sewed him into a piece of canvas that Christian brought from the logging camp and placed him high in a tree to freeze until the burial mounds again were soft, and the burial ceremony could be completed.

Afterward, Christian sat with Sarah on her bed where the boy was sleeping. He placed his hard muscled arm around her slender shoulders and began to speak, slowly, unsurely. "It was a hard thing we did to you…me and Wise Otter. I wanted him to die peaceful, or I wouldn't of pressed you with that letter. I guess,…what I'm feeling,…is that I've come to love you over these last couple years. But, if you don't care about me, I won't hold you to what you told the old man. I'm awful sorry for you're pain, Sarah. And, I'll do whatever I can to help."

Sarah put her hand on the big Norwegian's weathered face. " I believe in you Christian, and I'll be a good wife to you. Maybe I don't love you quite the same as I loved Peter, but I've loved you in a different way for a long time. You're here for me, like a big solid rock that I can depend on, and you've been a father to little Christian. Yes, I'll marry you, and be the better for it."

He took her in his arms then, and when he kissed her, she kissed him and took comfort in his embrace.

"Do you want to be married by Father Goebel?" Christian asked.

"It would be nice, but you'd have to become a Catholic first. You're a Lutheran, aren't you?"

"I was, but I haven't seen the inside of a church since my mother died."

"When was that?"

"Let's see, it w-a-as the summer of eighty."

"Christian Halvorsen, you're teasing me!" A tentative smile brushed some of the sadness from her face."That's nineteen years!"

"No! I'm not teasing you." A boyish grin crackled across his face. "I went to my mother's funeral. That's the last time time I went to church."

"Haven't you even been to weddings and such?"

"Just my friend Charlie's, and he was married by a courthouse clerk. Shit, I spent most of my life up in the woods, one place or another. I'd listen to a traveling preacher now an again, but that's not the same as going to church."

"Then you wouldn't mind converting?"

"No-o-o, I don't think so. What'd I have to do?"

"Well, you'd have to go to instruction."

Christian scrinched up his face. "I would?"

Sarah laughed, and the sadness was all swept from her face. "And you'd have to go to confession."

Christian looked at her suspiciously. "What's that?"

"You tell the priest about your sins, and ask for forgiveness."

"What!! You mean I gotta tell Goebel about all the things I done wrong?"

"Well, maybe not all of them."

"Damn good thing, otherwise it would take hours. What else?"

"You have to go to Mass every Sunday, and on Holy Days."

"Humph, if I gotta go to church that much I might as well be a priest."

Sarah laughed. "Then you wouldn't be able to marry me."

Christian gave a sigh of resignation. "Oh yeah, I forgot about that. How long would all of this take?"

"I think we could be married in the spring."

"That long, huh? Do you think it could be before the log run?"

"Maybe, Easter is in the first week of April."

"What's that got to do with it?"

"That's the end of Lent, Father Goebel won't marry us until after Lent."

"Damn, that's cutting it close, Honey. The river may be breaking up before then."

"I'll pray for a late spring."

"You do that Sarah. There's one other thing, I got to go to Minneapolis, I promised Peter."

Sarah's expression saddened. "I know, but do you have to go before Christmas? With grandfather gone, it's going to be awful without you. Little Christian needs his dad at Christmas."

"Yeah, it's funny how I think of the kid like he was my own. You know, we're like a family already. Shit yes, I can go to Minneapolis after Christmas."

Peter was married to Lucille on the Saturday after Christmas 1899, with Christian as a grooms man, in a huge church wedding.

Sarah married Christian in the little Indian chapel before a handful of family and friends. It was just before the log run in 1900, which was held up by a late spring thaw.

CHAPTER 12

FAMILY CONCERNS

It was February, the most dreary and desolate month of the long Minnesota winter. Peter and Charlie were sitting in the comfortable lounge of the club that late Friday afternoon. A sprinkling of businessmen were talking in little clumps. Business was slow at this time of the year, a situation which Charlie was addressing.

"The lumber business is starting to go downhill Pete, guys like Christian are chasing the timber further north every year. An now they got to haul the timber in on the railroad, cause there ain't much close to the rivers anymore. Good timber is gonna get more expensive every year, an they opening up the big stands out west. Maybe twenty years an logging gonna be over in Minnesota, eh? We gotta find someplace else to invest."

"Yeah," Peter said dryly. "The mill business is getting slower, I know. Thank God the furniture factory is booming. People that were settlers twenty years ago have money now, they're buying like crazy. I think we should build a new factory."

"We do that," Charlie concurred. "We tear down some of them old storage sheds an build a new factory, two, three floors high."

"Yeah, and we'll put in all new electric machines, the old steam engine is obsolete."

"Okay, we gonna do that. We can always sell furniture. But that's a spit in the bucket, Pete. Charlie need something big, something ain't gonna peter out in a few years, eh?"

"Sell the mill."

"Why should Charlie sell the mill, when it's still making money?"

"That's why Charlie, you can still get a decent price. When the timber runs out, it won't be worth anything. It's funny, here we are talking about the timber running out. A few years ago somebody said it would, and I couldn't believe it."

"Yeah, I know, but it's gonna happen. So, we sell the mill, what we do then, eh?"

"Put the money into something that won't run out, like you said."

"An, what's that?"

"Wheat, they're shipping wheat in from North Dakota, more every year. The mills that are here can't handle it. And there's more to come, lots more."

Charlie puffed on his cigar as he turned the idea over in his head.

"You got a good head on your shoulder's Pete. We build a flour mill, and an elevator to ship what we can't handle down the river. They ain't ever gonna quit growing wheat, an people always gonna eat bread an noodles, eh?"

"Sure, and you'll make money on every bushel that comes through, no matter if you mill it or not."

Charlie grinned. "I like that, Charlie gonna cut you in for a share if you help me set it up. But who we gonna sell the sawmill to?"

"How about Christian?"

"Naw, he ain't got the money."

"His partners might."

Charlie looked doubtful. "Those boys know the timber is gonna run out, they wouldn't give us a decent price. It's got to be somebody that don know that end of it. Somebody that's got money an a interest in the lumber. Charlie, he know who! I got a big customer in Chicago. He always crying bout I charge him too much for my lumber. Charlie he tell him he's thinking bout quitting cause he ain't got nobody to take over. He's greedy bastard, he gonna try to get the mill." Charlie smiled. "An I gonna let him, eh? But first we gonna saw enough lumber for the new factory, the mill, and the elevators."

The two men sat quietly for a few minutes, then Charlie spoke.

"Charlie and Kat had another fight, was pretty bad, Pete."

"Was it about Girard Rousseau?"

Charlie nodded gloomily. "Kat wants to marry that lousy tinhorn."

"And you called him that?"

Charlie clamped his jaw tight on his cigar and nodded again.

"Kat got mad and said she'd marry him no matter what you thought of him, didn't she?"

"What, you some kind of mind reader, Pete?"

"Naw, I know Kat. You oughta too, Charlie. She's never had you say no before, and she doesn't like it."

Charlie sighed. "You right as usual. What's Charlie gonna do, Pete?"

"Are you still talking?"

Charlie shook his head dismally. "Charlie said he'd see the lousy horn blower dead before he'd let him marry Kat. She got mad and went stomping out of the house."

"Well, maybe she'll cool down, Charlie. I think you'd better get ready to welcome another son-in-law though, if that's what Kat wants."

Saturday morning was bright and warm, a wind had come in from the south during the night, and the temperature climbed to 32 degrees. Lucille and Elizabeth decided to go shopping and asked Peter if he would like to accompany them. He deferred, saying he would rather work on a preliminary plan for the new furniture factory. Charlie went to the club to meet with the owner of an existing flour mill. The two men were enthusiastic about the new ventures, and were losing no time in getting started.

Peter was sitting with pencil and paper at a table in the room that served as a living room for he and Lucille. He was intent on a sketch he was making when he heard the door close behind him. It was Kathryn, dressed in a satin dressing gown and slippers.

"Oh! Peter, I didn't know you were here. I wondered if Lucy might have a headache powder."

"I don't know, but I'll look in the cabinet where she keeps remedies. Are you ill, Kat?"

"No," she said, smiling ruefully. "A bit too much champagne last night."

Peter laughed. "In the logging camp we'd chew willow bark when that happened. Of course we didn't have champagne, just cheap whiskey when we went to Grand Rapids."

He walked into the bedroom with Kathryn, and began looking through a cabinet filled with little wooden boxes, bottles and tins. "Here's one that says 'powder of salicin', " he said. "Is that it?"

Kathryn nodded. "Lucy's given it to me before. Do you have a glass of water?"

"Sure, Kat." He poured a glass of water from the pitcher on the wash stand and handed it to her along with the powder.

Kathryn sprinkled a bit of the powder into the water and drank, making a face at the bitterness of the solution.

I think I'd rather chew willow twigs," she said, as she handed the powder and glass back to Peter. "Do you mind if I rest a bit?"

Without waiting for an answer, she dropped herself on the bed. "Oh-h-h this feels so-o-o nice," she said. "I think I'm beginning to feel better already."

Peter turned from the cabinet, after he returned the powder—Kathryn was stretched out on the bed, with one long, shapely leg bent so that her knee was pointed at the ceiling. Her dressing gown had fallen away, exposing it to the hip. Peter was suddenly acutely aware that the gown was Kathryn's only garment. Embarrassed, he stood there dumbly.

"I think I may have a fever, come and feel my forehead." Kathryn patted the bed beside her.

Peter obeyed quietly, taking a seat beside her stiffly, as though he were sitting on a church pew at a funeral. Kathryn took his hand and guided it to her forehead, causing the unbuttoned top of her dressing gown to gap open as she did so. A portion of a full, white breast lay exposed to Peter's eyes. The muscles of his chest tightened sending a message to every part of his body. He sat there transfixed, an erotic sensation creeping through him despite his will. He pulled his hand away from the smoothness of her brow.

"You feel normal," he said, his voice coming out with a huskiness that drew a giggle from Kathryn. She smiled at him in a way that made his blood run hot, her eyes taunting him, her mouth moving sensually, forming a kiss and wafting it to him.

He was fascinated by her, like a bird watching the weaving nearness of a snake, waiting until it is too late to escape destruction. She reached upward, leaving the robe fall open as she locked her fingers in the shaggy curls at the back of his head, then drew him down to meet her lips. Peter was lost, his proper intentions flying from him before the fiery passion that was Kathryn. Her mouth on his demandingly, her tongue insistent in its exploration gave him no choice but to submit, then to merge his own mounting desire with hers. His hand searched for and found her breast and caressed it momentarily, then moved slowly down the flatness of her stomach.

Kathryn bit, hard, and Peter wrenched up and away from her in confusion—a trickle of blood found its way down his chin from his torn lip.

"God damn! What the hell did you do that for, Kat?"

"Because you're a fucking, horny Jackass, Pete! Because you threw me over for my sister, you bastard! I just wanted you to know what you threw away!"

Before Peter could gather his wits about him, she pulled her robe about her and ran from the room. Peter wanted to run after her, to stop her, to hold her, but he didn't, instead he went to the wash basin to nurse his bleeding lip. Later, he lamely explained to Lucille that he had bumped his lip on an open cabinet door, and his wife let it go at that. She didn't press the issue because Peter was in a vile, snappish mood, which happened some times. She had learned to leave him alone until his mood improved.

For the rest of the day, no one saw Kathryn, a circumstance that was not uncommon with the headstrong young woman. The next day, when Kathryn failed to appear in time for church, Elizabeth went to her room and discovered her daughter's absence. Much of her clothing was gone, and a note lay on her unused bed. The note was painfully direct, and moved Elizabeth to a tearful paroxysm that caused Charlie to be concerned for her mental welfare. When his wife's convulsed screaming subsided, and she seemed to be somewhat in control of her emotions Charlie read the note.

Dear Daddy and Mama,

I am going to Chicago with Girard. We will be married as soon as possible. Don't worry about me, I am with a man who loves me truly. I will write as soon as we are married and more or less settled down.

Love you both, and Lucy too.
Kat

"She's run away with that worthless horn blower!" Charlie shouted. "A two bit musician who plays in saloons and bawdy houses! My little girl,... she's gone with a bum like that!"

"It's all your fault," Elizabeth moaned. "She met him at your club. And you wouldn't let her bring him home, because you didn't like him. So now, she's run off with him. O-o-h! We'll never see her again, I just know it. Why did you have to be such a stubborn brute?"

"What the hell you saying, Woman?!" Charlie continued to shout. "Who was it was preaching to Kat about keeping to her station? Bah! The only station she gonna keep to is a railroad station! She couldn't stand your nagging alla time, that's why Kat left, so she could have a life for herself."

"Well, somebody had to tell her what was expected of her! She would have paid more attention to me, if you hadn't spoiled her so bad. You did it since she was a little girl. Every time I told her she couldn't have something, you'd give it to her anyway."

Charlie let out a great sigh. "I know, Liz, Charlie he was that way with Kat. But he couldn't help it, she has a way of twisting him around her little finger. But this make Charlie feel bad, like you do. Charlie he wanted something better for his little girl then following a two-bit band around, an sleeping with a horn blower that ain't gonna ever amount to nothing."

Elizabeth, was somewhat mollified by Charlie's acquiescence, but she broke into another fit of tears. "But what are we going to do, Charlie? You've got to go and bring her back! If she's going to marry Girard, at least we can give them a decent wedding."

Lucy, who had been watching the episode quietly, now spoke. "Father, Mother, Kat is grown up now. She can do what she wants, and I think she really wants to get away from here."

She glanced at Peter who was standing quietly with his hand over his mouth to cover his swollen lip.

"I think it's unpleasant for her to be so close to Peter, even though she was in our wedding and all. You can't bring her back if she doesn't want to come. Besides, Chicago is a big city, how would you find her if you did go?"

Elizabeth had been given a new target to vent her frustration on. She turned on Peter.

"You're the one that made Kat leave. You led her on, then you broke her heart. And even if you did it to marry Lucy, I just can't forgive you that. God will punish you some day for carrying on like...like an alley cat!"

Charlie held up his hand to silence her. "Close your mouth, Woman! You gonna have us all fighting like a bunch of street dogs. Kat, she Charlie's little girl—but where love is concerned, Pete he done nothing wrong. Kat, she chased Pete, he didn't chase her, eh? So, don go saying it's Pete's fault Kat's gone. It hurts like hell, but I think Lucy she's right. We gotta let Kat do what she wants to do, even if she gonna get hurt."

In the days that followed, Charlie and Peter threw themselves into their work, planning the new factory and flour mill. But there was a melancholy in Charlie that Peter had never seen before. Sometimes in their planning sessions Peter would have to stop and repeat himself when making a point. Charlie's eyes would have strayed from the plans before him to some distant, private place. Peter's heart went out to his mentor, feeling a twinge of irrational guilt for the pain he bore. If he had chosen Kat, he thought, Charlie and everyone else would be happy—but would he? His mind formed a picture of Kat on the bed, and he forced it away—what was done, was done. He had married Lucille because he had wanted it, and he bore no responsibility for Kat's actions.

One day in March, Charlie came to Peter's office. He looked grim. "I got a letter from Missis Rousseau." He said, spitting out the words with distaste. "She just got married a week ago."

Peter looked at him uncertainly. "Are you and Elizabeth going to visit them?"

Charlie exhaled heavily. "Nothing would make Charlie happier."

"Then why don't you go? I can take care of things for you."

"Because I can't. They're moving to Kansas City. He got a job there." For the first time that Peter could remember, he saw an utterly hopeless sorrow in the bluff Frenchman's eyes. "I lost my little girl, Pete. I lost my little Kat. Charlie he ain't ever gonna see her again."

For the first time ever, Peter put his hand on the older man's shoulder to console him. "No you haven't Charlie. Kat loves you. She'll be back, maybe not real soon, but she'll be back."

"You think so? Charlie he's thinking Kat left because he didn't like this Rousseau. Maybe if Charlie wasn't so pig-headed, Kat would still be here, eh?"

"I guess we could all blame ourselves, Charlie. But the fact is that Kat left because she's Kat. She's impulsive, and she has to do what she has to do, right away. Otherwise she'll lose the magic."

"What you mean, Pete?"

"It's something she told me when we first met. She said that when you want to do something, you should do it right away, otherwise you'll lose the magic."

Charlie smiled wanly. "That's Charlie's little Kat, even as a little girl she had to do everything as soon as she thought of it. I think, maybe you right, Pete. One day Kat gonna think bout coming home to Charlie."

One morning in March Peter woke up to the sound of Lucille vomiting. He jumped out of bed and went to her, his face drawn with concern.

"What's the matter, Lucy, have you the stomach misery?"

"It will pass, Dear. It always does."

"You mean you've been like this before?"

"Yes, a few times."

He looked at her pasty complexionand worry lines formed on his face.

"You'd better see a doctor right away. I'll take you myself."

"There's really no need for that. Aaron can take me, he's not that busy in the stable anyway. Besides, it's not life threatening." She gave him her enigmatic smile.

Peter was puzzled. "You're sure, Lucy? You don't look so good."

"I'm sure, you just go to work."

Later, at Charlie's office, Peter told of Lucille's recurring illness. "I'm really worried, Charlie. Lucy's never been sick before."

Charlie started laughing. "You don worry bout it, Pete. Lucy she gonna be all right, it just gonna take a little time."

"But how can you know, Charlie? She was vomiting like she had too much wine, only she didn't have anything."

"You know Pete, sometimes for a smart young man, you awful dumb. But you ask Lucy, she gonna tell you everything is okay."

Peter returned to his own office, but despite Charlie's reassurance, he worried all day. That afternoon when he returned home, he rushed to Lucy who was sitting in her favorite chair crocheting. She didn't look in the least ill, but rather had a sort of rosy glow to her complexion.

"You look like you're feeling better," he said. "Charlie said you'd be all right. But I still can't understand how he knew."

Lucille looked at him lovingly. "My precious darling, you are such a dear. But you are so naive it makes me want to hug you like a child."

"I don't understand—Charlie said I was dumb. And now you say I'm naive, just because I worried about you being sick."

"Come here, my precious baby, and I'll explain to you."

Peter knelt beside her chair, and Lucille hugged him tight, his head pressed into her bosom.

"You see Peter, lots of women get sick in the morning when they're the way I am. It's just part of it."

Peter's face lit up. "You mean…."

"Yes Peter, we're going to have a baby."

"Oh golly! Oh golly! Oh golly!"

Lucille laughed. "Is that all you can say, Peter?"

"Yes! I mean golly, I'm so excited I don't know what to say, except I love you Lucy!"

"Don't you want to know when?"

"You mean you know?"

"Yes, my darling, at least close."

"Well, tell me!"

"In October, my darling. You're going to be a father in October."

The 'driving effect' on Peter was instantaneous. He pushed himself and those about him with renewed vigor. He was going to have a son to follow him in his business, and it must be one of the greatest businesses in Minneapolis, in America. The thought that his baby might be a girl was dismissed from his mind—he would have a son.

The effect of Lucille's pregnancy was not limited to Peter. Charlie was smiling again. The prospect of a grandchild gave him new energy and purpose. His melancholia over Kathryn's absence diminished. He now viewed her departure as one of life's disappointments, rather than a tragedy. He had been blessed with two daughters, but no sons. Now he was eagerly expectant of the arrival of a grandson to carry on his blood, if not his name.

Elizabeth, in her happiness at Lucille's pregnancy, brought forward a concern.

"Building a house will be far too much for her to contend with in her condition," she said. "It will be far better to wait another year. The baby must be born here, where I can help Lucy."

Charlie echoed her concern. "We got lots of room—Charlie he be happy to hear a baby cry again. You got lots of time to build a house Pete. We building a factory and mill this year. You build a house next year, eh?"

Peter was skeptical, he wanted a home of their own. But, when Lucille said, "I really would like to have the baby here Peter,-—please," he put aside his reservations and agreed.

With the passage of the summer months, Peter spent every daylight hour at work, as he and Charlie drove the factory and mill skyward. As the skeletons of the buildings rose, Lucille's figure distended, a coincidence not lost to Charlie.

"It looks like you and Lucy gonna finish your projects bout the same time, eh?," Charlie Laughed. "Which one you the most excited about, Pete?"

"That's easy, Charlie. The factory is for my son, so he's the most important."

"You pretty sure it's gonna be a boy, eh? What if it's a girl?"

"It'll be a boy, Charlie. But if it's a girl, we'll celebrate just as much, and our second baby will be a boy."

Charlie laughed. "I got to say one thing for you Pete, you one confident young man."

In the second week of October, Peter was moving machinery into the new factory. He was supervising the placement of some new lathes when Aaron, the stable man came running into the plant.

"Mister Hokanson, you come home quick, your baby's coming."

Peter dashed for his carriage, and laid the whip to the sorrel—minutes later he was at the mansion. He ran into the hall, almost colliding with his mother-in-law.

"Is he here yet?," he asked her breathlessly.

"Is who here?"

"My son, is my son born yet?"

"Oh Peter! Calm down, Lucy's water just broke, it'll be a long time yet."

"But Aaron said I should come quick."

"You men! I swear Aaron's just as excited as you are, and he has five of his own. Why don't you go out to the kitchen and have some cookies and tea. I made some for the three of you, Charlie and Aaron will be along shortly, and they'll be just as nervous as you are."

"But, is the doctor here? She'll need a doctor, won't she?"

"Oh Peter! Cora Schmidt is here, she delivered Lucille, and she'll do just fine with Lucy's baby. Now quit fretting and leave us women about our business."

When Charlie and Aaron came they questioned Peter in unison.

"Is the baby here yet?"

"No, Liz said it'll be a long time yet—have some cookies."

The eating of cookies and tea took the three men ten minutes at the most. Peter began pacing the floor. Charlie and Aaron exchanged glances, and Charlie walked to a cupboard door and returned with a deck of cards.

"You gonna drive us all crazy in a little while with your walking back and forth. Let's play a little poker to pass the time, eh? We play for fun tonight, we play for pennies, eh?" He chuckled at the look of relief on the stable man's face.

The three men played quietly for some time. Fortunately for Peter, the play was for fun. He blundered again and again, and the piles of pennies in front of the older men grew. He was about to ask what was taking so long (for the fifteenth time), when there was a muffled scream from the second floor. The three men jumped to their feet—Peter jostled the table and sent cards and pennies showering to the floor.

"It's Lucy!," he exclaimed, and headed for the stairs.

Charlie took him by the arm, and led him back to the cupboard.

"The baby, he is coming," he said. "Have some more tea."

Lucille screamed several more times, then was silent. Peter looked at Charlie, his face worried. Then a thin wailing sound drifted down the stairs.

"He's here, your boy is here!," Charlie said too loudly.

Peter broke into a huge grin. "I'm going up to see him and Lucy!"

"No, wait," Charlie restrained him, "they'll call you."

Just then Lucille screamed again, not as loud as before, but a scream. The three men listened intently, the scream was repeated several more times.

"Something's wrong!," Peter shouted. "I'm going to her!"

"No," Charlie said, "they gonna tell you to get a doctor if something gone wrong. You wait a little yet."

Peter looked up the stairway and began pacing furiously. Then an angry wail stopped him— his face held a look of astonishment.

"That one gotta be a boy!" Charlie grinned.

A few minutes later the matronly figure of Cora Schmidt appeared at the top of the stairs. She was smiling broadly as she spoke.

"Would you like to come up and see your sons, Mister Hokanson?"

Peter dashed for the stairs, taking them three at a time, nearly running down the elderly Cora as she waddled back to Lucille's bedroom. He halted beside the bed where a flushed and perspiration bedraggled Lucille lay. There was a ruddy faced baby in each of her arms.

"Golly! Golly!" Peter said, bringing a wan smile to the face of his wife.

"Is that all you can say, My Husband?" she said in a tired but content voice.

By way of answer, he knelt beside her bed and covered her face with kisses.

Charlie had arrived, and Aaron behind him. Charlie knelt on the other side of the bed and kissed Lucille's forehead tenderly. Then he took Peter's hand and shook it vigorously.

"By the blessings of the Saints, you and Lucy done better than Charlie ever dreamed. You got two sons, one for the factory and one for the mill. We gotta celebrate! Open it, Aaron."

Aaron twisted the cork out of the bottle he was carrying, and the aroma of brandy drifted through the air. He gave the bottle to Charlie, who held it high.

"To my daughter and her fine sons, may they all live in health and happiness."

He put the bottle to his lips, and his pride and happiness were measured by the bubbles that swirled up into the amber fluid. He passed the bottle to Peter who raised it toward Lucille and his sons.

"To my lovely wife, and the mother of my sons, I love you."

He took several strong swallows then passed it to Aaron. The graying stable man took the bottle hesitantly, then raised it in turn to all present, from mother to father, grandfather and grandmother and even Cora, the midwife.

"I say long life and happiness to everyone on this fine day. May the boys grow big and strong, and may the rafters of this house ring with their shouts and laughter!"

He tipped the bottle and took several swallows of the brandy, then unaccustomed to such good liquor, he took several more for good measure. Everyone laughed and clapped their hands at Aaron's unusual eloquence. The commotion brought startled cries from the infants, and a pained, short laugh from Lucille. Cora immediately shooed the men from the room, threatening them with dire consequences if they did not leave the mother and babies to rest, immediately.

After much debate, names for the babies were decided . While Lucille wanted to use biblical names such as James and John, Peter did not.

"I want them to be named after the four best friends I have had in the world." he said.

Finally Lucille yielded, and the boys were christened "Sven Gustav" and "Charles Christian". In the months that followed, the babies grew strong and healthy. They were not identical and had begun to show their differences already. Sven was a quiet baby, content to lie in his cradle, smiling at the least attention. Charles was more robust, constantly demanding attention with loud cries.

Lucille, though considerably thinner from the demands of two babies at her breast, glowed with happiness.

With the redoubled efforts of the proud father and grandfather, the new factory was spewing out a constant stream of furniture. Soon a second shift was required, to fill the orders sent in by Gustav, who now traveled as far as

Chicago and Kansas City on his sales trips. Charlie's salesmen were riding the trains east to the coast and west to California to tap the growing market for flour and grain products there, as his new, efficient mill consumed carloads of wheat from the Dakotas. The year was to finish as a complete success for all.

Charlie's happiness was diminished only by the absence of Kat, who had not written since she left for Kansas City. Despite the happiness the twins brought to him, Charlie sorely missed her. Once in August, when he was in Kansas City selling furniture, Gus had seen Kat in a saloon where Girard was playing with a band. She had talked with Gus, and sent her love to her family in Minneapolis, but that was all. Charlie wanted to go to her and visit, but she had given no indication that she wanted him to, not even an address. So he buried the thought in work— one day she would return.

Chapter 13

A Blessing and Bitterness

Kathryn was sitting alone, looking out of a window of her room overlooking Basin Street in New Orleans. She was sad and lonely, and the weather was murky, with a drizzling rain that further depressed her spirits. It was just a few days from Christmas, and Kathryn was thinking of how it would be at home in Minneapolis.

It would be cold now, and there should be snow on the ground. Her mother and Lucy would be baking cookies and all sorts of goodies for their Christmas festivities. There would be a big tree standing in the high-ceilinged living room of the mansion. It would be decorated with glass balls of different colors and strings of popcorn and chains of colored paper would be wrapped around it. And there would be dozens of candles clipped to the branches. They would only be lit for a few minutes at midnight on

Christmas Eve—then only with Charlie standing by with a bucket of water in the event the tree should catch fire.

Kat smiled at the memory of how she had always been allowed to place the little glass birds on the tree. She had loved those birds with their silky brush tails. She had only been able to reach the lower branches of the tall balsam. So Charlie would take her in his arms and hold her high up, because she insisted the birds liked to sit in the higher branches.

She looked about her now—there was no tree. Balsams didn't grow in Louisiana. And even if they did, she couldn't afford one. She had managed to find a holly tree that no one seemed to care about. She cut a large branch and put it in an old whiskey jug to give a little Christmas cheer to the otherwise dingy room. Henry, the ancient Negro who cared for the building, brought her a sprig of mistletoe and she'd hung it from a candle holder on the wall over a battered table.

It would have to do, she thought—there would be no turkey setting in golden glory on their table, just a chicken if they were lucky. And there would be no presents, none at all.

There would just be Girard and her. They would go to Mass at the little church a block away on Christmas Eve, and they would have a little dinner on Christmas Day, and that would be Christmas. She wished that she had a fairy godmother who could wave a twinkling wand and transport her back to Minneapolis and her father's mansion, just for a day, just for Christmas Day. But she didn't, so she sat looking out the window, reminiscing about the events that had led her here.

Things had been hard for Girard and Kathryn in Kansas City. The job Girard was promised, with a well known band, had not fully materialized. Playing only a few nights a week, he was barely able to put food on the table, and he was forced to take a day job in one of the city's slaughtering plants. Kathryn had wanted to work, but the young Frenchman's pride was fierce.

"I will provide for us," Girard said. "A man who cannot provide for his wife should not have one!"

The weeks had passed, with Girard often working through the day butchering cattle, and on into the early hours of the morning, playing the trumpet. On Saturdays and Sundays he would sleep through most of the day, waking only when the exhaustion of his body was alleviated. Without telling her husband, Kathryn found a job at a store, where she worked on the account books a few hours a day. She was, in that way, able to set some money aside for a sudden need, without hurting Girard's pride.

In September, Girard heard that "ragtime" was growing in popularity in Saint Louis, and chances were good that a trumpet player would be able to find steady work with one of the many bands there.

"If only we had enough money for train fare and room rent," he said, "I'd have a chance to get into a real 'big time' band."

Kathryn got out the "emergency money" she had saved and showed it to Girard.

"We shall go to Saint Louis, Darling," she said. "You will have your chance."

"But, where did you get this—not from your father?" He had asked. The resentment he bore against Charlie had been strong in his voice.

"No, not from Daddy, I saved it from the money you gave me."

Girard had not sensed the truth, despite the fact that his taste for liquor and laughter had grown stronger and left little money for the necessities of life. He had taken her in his arms then, and made love to her with the gentle passion that had first won her.

They had gone to Saint Louis, settling in a room above one of the better night clubs there. Girard found a place with one of the larger bands, and things were better. He was playing five nights a week and on Saturday afternoon. Since he was at home during the day, Girard expected Kathryn to be also.

She chafed at the inactivity and begged him to let her find a job of some kind—she was tired of spending all of her time cooped up in the two little rooms they rented. Faced with Kathryn's mounting ill humor, Girard relented and let her take an afternoon job caring for the ill in a small hospital. She had truly liked the work, and her bubbly, direct personality soon made her a favorite with the staff. Best of all, it let her be with people, to feel needed and appreciated.

She thought of writing home, now that all was going well, but every time she took a pen in her hand, she would write, "Dear Daddy," and somehow nothing more would come. She knew how badly her departure had hurt Charlie, but she couldn't bring herself to say she was sorry. It was not because she was too proud. It was because, in doing so she would have to admit to herself that she had made a mistake. That was something she wasn't ready to do. So she suffered on in her self imposed exile, separated from family and loved ones, adrift in a dark sea of aloneness.

In November Girard had come home one morning with news. "The band is going to New Orleans," he said with a broad smile, "and we are going along."

Kathryn was stunned. "But we're doing so well here, Sweetheart. Can't you get a job with another band?"

"No, Beautiful. Jazz is the new thing, and New Orleans is where it's at. You can't have jazz without brass, and that's what I do. I'll become famous there—it's our biggest chance yet."

Kathryn knew it was useless to argue. Once again she took the money she had saved, and bought tickets on a steamboat returning down the river to New Orleans.

Unfortunately, things had not gone well in New Orleans—the band had trouble getting engagements. They had not yet adapted to the improvisation of New Orleans jazz, and they were ill prepared to compete with more established bands. After a month of one night stands and periods with no appearance at all, the band decided to return to Saint Louis where they were known and appreciated.

Girard refused to return—he adamantly stated that New Orleans was where he would acquire fame and fortune, and he wasn't about to leave. So they had stayed, and Girard had been able to get a job with a small Negro band whose lead trumpet player had been knifed in a brawl in one of the seedier night places.

"It will work out." Girard had said. "Things will be a bit lean for a while, but it's the start I need. We'll be living high soon, you'll see."

Things may work out, Kat thought. But right now she was more lonely than she'd ever been. And there were complications, she rested her hand on her swelling abdomen. God, how she wished she were back home now, especially now. She cradled her face in her arms and cried.

The year 1901 was a year of prosperity for Peter and Charlie. The furniture business prospered, and Peter moved Curtis Miller into the position of general manager of the factory, freeing Peter to plan other investments. Gus was now sales manager, supervising three travelling salesmen. The flour mill was being enlarged, and Charlie's sawmill cut lumber for another elevator to handle the torrent of wheat and corn flowing in from the Dakotas.

At last, Peter and Lucille were building their own home. The large two story structure was set on a portion of the acreage that housed Charlie's mansion. Peter had wanted to build on land he had found a mile to the south of the LeBlanc house, but Lucille had insisted on the site next to her mother. It was a small thing really, and the twins would certainly benefit from the nearness to their grandparents.

In the fall, Lucille became pregnant again, adding impetus to the completion of the new house. In November they moved into their new home, and Peter was greatly pleased with his wife's increased domesticity. She had kept their portion of Charlie's house well, but now she was filled with energy, constantly cleaning, cooking and caring for her two boys. Peter was content with his home and family. He had done very well since his arrival from Sweden six years ago. Much of his success was due to the friendships of Christian Halvorsen and Charlie LeBlanc, but he had taken the opportunities extended to him, and with his shrewd dealing and ambition had become a success.

Peter's letters to and from his family in Sweden had become less frequent through the years, though he made a point of writing to them before every Christmas. Now that he was successful, he longed to return for a visit.

It was true that he wanted to return as a conqueror of the new world, as he had vowed to do when he was a simple lumberjack. But there was also the genuine wish to see his mother, father and siblings again. He missed them, as one always misses his kin, his roots in life. When Lucille has her baby, and it is old enough to travel, we will go, he thought.

His father would be proud that the son he had despaired of becoming a cabinet maker, was now the owner of a furniture factory, the likes of which he had never seen. If all went well, perhaps he could even convince his parents to return with them for a visit in America. The thought excited him, and he built a private dream of how he would show his father the new factory. He would be amazed at its rows of electrically powered machines spitting out not a few, but dozens of pieces of fine furniture every day. His dream became almost a reality to him.

Peter was totally unprepared for the letter that came to him in the second week of March, 1902. It was from his sister Ingrid:

Dear Brother Peter,

I hope you and your family are well,especially your young sons, Sven and Charles. I long to see them and you, and wish that we may be reunited soon.

I have the very saddest of tidings that I must bring to you, though it causes my heart to weep within me. Our dear father passed away suddenly, and is buried at the old cemetery where his father rests.

He complained to Mother of an ill feeling in his chest one morning, but he went to work despite it. He was only at the shop a little while when he fell to the floor as though he were having a convulsion. Johann tried to give him a little liquor to revive him, but it was no good. Father died in Johann's arms within the hour. It was on the twentieth day of February, and he was buried on the twenty-second.

Mother cries too much, and she longs to see you, because you have always been her favorite child. Losing you to America was a great hardship for her. And now that her husband of so many years is gone, I fear for her.

Johann continues the work at the wood shop, as was the decision of us children in your absence. He has not yet married, and I fear he never will, for he drinks too much. Now that Father is gone, I fear it will get worse because he and Father were very close. Johann is a good craftsman, but he has no head for business. I wonder if the business will continue to prosper without Father.

I send fondest love to you and yours from all of your kin here in Sweden. May our Lord walk with you, and sustain you in your grief.

Your loving sister,
Ingrid

When he had finished reading, Peter silently handed the letter to Lucille, then went to a window and stood looking out at the city surrounding him. His dream had been shattered, he was unable to accept his father's death as real. A scrap of paper could not convey such a thing, his father still stood beside him in the little wood shop, and

Peter was asking him, "Father, is the president of the United States a Swede?"

He felt a hand on his arm and turned to be embraced by his wife. He drew her to him, and pressed his face against the sweet softness of her hair. Then he wept for his father and mother and his family so far away, and for the young man whose dreams had led him alone to America.

As the weeks passed, the birth of Lucille's baby approached, it would be in the third week in May. Peter had reconciled himself to the death of his father, and still planned to go to Sweden to see his mother, brother and sisters. In a few months the baby would be old enough to travel and they would go. Lucille was growing excited at the prospect of going to Sweden to see all the people and things Peter had told her of. The two of them spent hours planning the trip, going over the details again and again until they were about to burst with the anticipation of it.

On the second Sunday of April, the sun was shining brightly and the weather was balmy warm, as only the first days of spring following the harsh Minnesota winter can be. The early buds of the maple trees lining the street in front of the house were beginning to swell, and the crocuses near Charlie's gazebo were pushing their purple and yellow heads skyward.

"Oh! It's such a beautiful day, let's go for a walk Peter, let's do!" Lucy exclaimed.

Peter smiled at her, her face was flushed with anticipation. "Sure Sweetheart, the air and exercise will do us both good."

They strolled happily in the sunshine down the cobblestone walk that separated the imposing homes in the area from the muddy street. Peter was content, though the world he had dreamed of as a boy had not materialized. There was no vast farm with herds of fat cattle and flocks of sheep, with hired hands running to and fro tending them. But he was successful just the same, he was building an empire beyond his own expectations.

A carriage passed them, its horses splashing noisily through the puddles that pocked the street. Peter waved to the people in the carriage, and shielded Lucille from the spattering of muddy water that fell about them.

"Next spring that won't happen," he said. "Charlie told me that the street will be paved this summer."

"How wonderful," Lucille said, "we'll be able to walk without having to bathe afterward. She crinkled up her face in disgust as they approached a muddy cross street.

"Maybe we should go back, I don't want you to exert yourself too much in your condition."

"Nonsense! I'm just as able as ever, just a little clumsier. I had to take care of the twins when we built the house, and I did just fine. Just because I look like a big old cow doesn't mean I'm an invalid!"

She let go of Peter's arm and strode determinedly across the street. Half way across, her ankle twisted on a slippery stone. Lucille pitched heavily to the muddy ground.

Peter was beside her in an instant. He took her in his arms and lifted her from the smelly mud. "Lucy! Are you alright?"

Lucille grimaced. "I think I'm all right, just shook up a little. The ground is hard, even if I fell in the mud. Serves me right for being such a smartie, I guess."

Peter's face was grave with concern. "Shall I get the carriage? You can rest on the grass until I get back. No! I won't leave you here. I can carry you back."

Lucille managed a smile. "You can't carry me that far, I must weigh a ton. Just put me down, and we'll rest a bit."

Peter eased Lucille to her feet and stood there with his arm around her until she was ready to walk again. They returned to the house much more slowly than they had come. Despite her avowal that she was unhurt, Lucille moved more heavily than she had, and Peter thought he saw her clench her teeth once or twice. When they got back, Peter wanted Lucille to lie down, but she would have none of it.

"It's Sunday, and I'm going to make us a nice dinner. I got a chicken yesterday, I'll roast it and bake some potatoes at the same time. Be a sweetheart and fire up the range, and I'll get the stuffing ready."

Obediently, Peter went to the woodbox and picked out a few pieces of kindling. He was about to open the fire-door of the big, chrome trimmed range, when he heard a muffled cry from Lucille. He turned just as she dropped a large crockery mixing bowl, which hit the floor with a dull thud, and broke into a scattering of clay shards. She bent forward, grasping the edge of the heavy oak table with both hands.

Peter threw the kindling back in the box and leaped to Lucille's side—he gathered her into his arms. "Lucy! What's wrong?"

"Help me to the bed....I think it's the baby."

Peter picked his bulky wife up and carried her to their bedroom. He placed her gently on the bed just as her body tightened with another surge of pain.

"I think you'd better get Doctor Gordon," Lucille said. "I think the baby is coming early."

Peter ran to the telephone in the hall and gave its crank the two short and one long twist of Charlie's number, then fidgeted impatiently while he waited for an answer.

"Allo, dis is Charlie."

"Charlie, it's Pete, something awful's happened! Lucy fell, and she thinks the baby is coming! Get Doctor Gordon right away!"

"My God! Charlie he's harness the sorrel an get him right away! You stay with Lucy, Liz gonna be right over!"

Peter ran back to his wife's side. "Charlie's going for the doctor, is it any better?"

She looked at him without answering the question. "She's going to be all right isn't she? I couldn't bear it if she wasn't."

Peter squeezed her hand in his. "She's going to be all right." But inwardly he was frightened, for the baby, and for Lucy. She had set her mind on this baby being a girl. If it was a boy, Lucy would smile and love him, and say, "The next one will be a girl.". But if it was a girl, and something had happened to her!

He sat beside Lucille, gently stroking her forehead and whispering reassurances until Elizabeth came hurrying in. Then he paced nervously, while the older woman fluttered about her daughter, until he heard the sound of Charlie's carriage on the path to the stable. He hurried to the front door to excitedly usher Doctor Gordon in, and would have followed him back to Lucille's bedside, but Elizabeth shooed him away.

"Go sit with Charlie, he's going to be a bundle of nerves. You can't do anything here except to get in the doctor's way."

Obediently Peter went to the kitchen and began building a fire in the range. He wasn't hungry, but a pot of coffee would be a good thing. The door opened and Charlie entered, his face flushed with exertion and concern.

"How is Lucy? Do you know anything yet, Pete?"

Peter shook his head as he filled a coffee pot with water and put it on the range.

"The doctor is with her now, it's only been a few minutes."

"Do you have any brandy? Charlie needs a shot."

"In the corner cupboard, get me one too."

"What happened to Lucy?" Charlie filled a shot glass and tipped it down before filling one for Peter.

"We were out walking, she slipped on the muddy street and fell."

"Couldn't you catch her?"

Peter shook his head. "I didn't want her to cross the street, so she went ahead by herself."

Charlie poured himself another shot. "Hmph!...She's stubborn just like her mother."

"She's that all right, but I should have been with her. I'm worried about her. What if she loses the baby?"

"Don't buy trouble Pete, it'll find you by itself. Lucy's close to her time. If the baby comes, it'll maybe be okay anyway. If you know how, you might say a prayer though."

Peter nodded. "I've been doing that. What's taking so long?"

"It's only been a few minutes, you just told Charlie that."

"I know,...I'm going in to see, anyway!" He turned toward the bedroom and nearly collided with Elizabeth. Both he and Charlie stood still, waiting for her to speak.

Elizabeth's face was calm, but serious.

"Doctor Gordon thinks the baby is coming, but it will be slow. He'd prefer to have her at the hospital, but he's afraid the ride there might endanger her and the baby more. But then, he'd have better facilities if there is a serious problem. He wants you to decide, Peter."

Peter's face paled. "Then Lucy and the baby are in danger? I have to talk to the doctor."

He pushed past Elizabeth and went to the bedroom, with Charlie close behind. As he entered, Doctor Gordon was sitting beside Lucy, taking her pulse. On seeing Peter, he rose and pointed to the door—he followed Peter into the hall.

"What's the matter with Lucy, Doctor? She seems so still. Is she going to die?"

Doctor Gordon gave him a whisper of a smile. "She's just resting now, son. And don't you go getting upset. She's a strong woman and there's no need to worry too much yet."

"But Elizabeth said you'd like to have her at the hospital, is it that bad?"

"No, these things happen often. It's just that there is a little bleeding and I'd like her at the hospital as a precaution, that's all. But, we have to remember that the streets are rough between here and there, and it's about fifteen blocks. All that bouncing around could aggravate the situation. You'll have to make the decision if you want to move her."

"And if we don't, what then?"

"Then, there are some things I'll need. Somebody will have to go for them. And I'd like Mrs. Schmidt to assist me, she's an old hand and steady as a rock."

Peter placed his hand under his chin in deep concentration. "Doctor."

"Yes?"

"Since we're deciding about Lucy and her baby, shouldn't we ask her?"

Doctor Gordon's expression was disapproving. "Sometimes in cases like this, people can't always decide what's best for them."

"But if it were me, I'd want to decide for myself!"

"Very well, but if she gets emotional, you'll have to decide. I don't want her getting excited."

Peter turned back to the door. "I want to talk to Lucy alone, everybody else stay here!"

He closed the door behind him and sat down beside his wife, taking her hands in his.

"Lucy, Doctor Gordon would like to move you to the hospital for safety. But he's also afraid the ride may do you harm. I couldn't decide what to do without asking you."

She smiled at him wanly. "Thank you, Darling. I'm safe enough here. If anything happens to me or the baby, I want it to be here, in my home. And I want you with me this time, I want you holding my hand. Now kiss me, you wonderful Swede."

He bent over and kissed her tenderly, then went to tell the others of Lucy's decision.

Through the rest of the day, and late into the night Peter sat with his wife. At four in the morning, a little girl was born. Cora Schmidt washed the baby and placed it at her mother's breast. Lucy was pale and exhausted but she smiled happily at the tiny face.

"You see Peter, I did get my little girl, just as I said."

"That you did, my sweetheart. And a beautiful little girl she is."

He bent and kissed her on the forehead. "Now you must rest, to get your strength back."

As she closed her eyes, Peter looked up to see Doctor Gordon at the door, motioning for him to come. In the hall, the doctor placed his hand on Peter's shoulder, his voice was somber.

"The child is small, but strong Peter, she will be fine. But with your wife...there is some cause for concern. She is hemorrhaging. I've done all I can to stop the flow, and she is young and strong, but her condition is grave."

Peter's face went white with shock. "Do you mean that Lucy might die? After all this, the baby is healthy, but Lucy might die?"

A slight nod of Gordon's head affirmed his question. "All we can do now is pray, go sit with her Peter, and pray."

Peter went back to Lucy, she was dozing and he sat down quietly. How beautiful she is in sleep, he thought. But then he tensed, could she be gone? No, her breast was moving gently with her breath. She is so beautiful, he thought, she has to be all right—but she is too pale, she was always fair, but she is so white. God, my God, you can't take her from me now—we have just begun our life together, the boys and the baby girl need her,...I need her. Please God,...save her for us.

He sat with her through the hours, through the comings and goings of the doctor, always with the same grave look. Charlie and Elizabeth sat with him, and old Cora Schmidt brought him coffee that he left standing on the bed table. He prayed as he had never prayed in the loneliness of the woods or over the body of Sven beside the raging Mississippi. The sun filtered in through the curtains that Lucy had hung on the bedroom windows and then, Lucy's eyes flickered open. "Peter, are you here?" Her voice was small as though it came from a great distance.

"Yes, Lucy, I'm here."

"Is our baby all right?"

Peter's heart sank, the baby was sleeping peacefully in her mother's arm.

"Yes, she's fine, and you will be too."

She smiled the faintest smile. "Kiss me Peter."

He bent to kiss her tenderly.

"I love you, you wonderful Swede." She barely breathed the words, then the gentle rising of her breast stopped.

Cora Schmidt stepped forward and gently lifted the little girl from her mother's arm and wrapped her tenderly in a pink blanket. Peter fell forward on his wife's body and wept from the depths of his soul.

Late in the afternoon, Peter was sitting disconsolately with Charlie and Elizabeth in the parlor of their mansion. Cora Schmidt had found a wet nurse for the baby, a stout German woman whose own baby had died. An ambulance had come for Lucille's body and delivered it to the undertaker. This caused Elizabeth considerable grief.

"I and her sister should be dressing her for the funeral," she said, dabbing a handkerchief at her red eyes. "I feel so bad having strange hands touching her. Had I died when I was young, mother and Eunice would have dressed me."

Charlie looked at her tiredly, his own grief had destroyed the compassion he would normally extend to his grieving wife.

"Your sister would have been glad to bury you, alive or dead. Don't talk about that old hen in the same breath with Lucy! Anyway, they had to do it back then. Wash em up, comb their hair, dress em in their Sunday best and pop em in the ground before they got ripe. These are modern times, thank God we don't have to tend our dead anymore. It'll be bad enough just having her here for the wake."

Elizabeth sniffled, then broke down, crying pitifully. "I'm glad the wake is going to be here,…I can look at my little girl for…for one more night…before they put her away…forever."

She composed herself a little, dabbing her eyes with the sodden handkerchief again. "Anyway, it'll be a comfort with all our friends coming and praying for her."

Peter bolted from his chair and stood looking out of a window at the sun as it neared the horizon. His eyes were fixed in a stare that seemed to be looking for something beyond the red sunset. Then his face changed, and he turned to Charlie and Elizabeth, and all of the anger and hurts of his young life burned in his eyes.

"Why do we have to do it?! Why do we have to stand around with tears in our eyes, telling everybody how she died, while they gawk at her dead body and say how nice she looks?! She won't look nice! She'll look dead, with that waxy, wilted look dead people always have!" He ignored the storm of tears that washed his grief contorted face. "And, why do they have to pray for her anyway?! Lucy was a good woman and a good mother, and a wonderful wife. Why does anybody have to pray for her? It's us that need the praying, if there's anybody to listen."

Elizabeth stopped dabbing her eyes and her mouth dropped open. "Why Peter you mustn't talk so. God will surely punish those who deny him."

Peter's eyes fixed on her her, and his features were rigid with anger.

"Why? I prayed for Lucille, and she died. I prayed for Sven, and we found him floating in a pond. I've never had my prayers answered, why should I believe that there is a God who listens? Were those punishments for something I did or something they did?"

Elizabeth was horrified. "You are judging the Almighty, it is not for us poor mortals to understand his plans for us. We must accept what happens in life, and pray for guidance."

Charlie cleared his throat. "The way Charlie sees it, Pete, God puts us into the world with all of its pain, and says; 'Live your life here as best you can. It won't always be easy, but it'll never be harder than you can handle. And when it's all over for you, we'll see how you've done'. If we blamed everything bad that happened on God, there wouldn't be a believer on the earth. If God took Lucy from us, that's bad—but then, he gave us a little girl in return, and that's good. It's hard for us now, but we'll all live on, an we got to take the evil days with the good ones."

"Maybe you're right, Charlie. But right now it seems like my world has ended. I don't know how I'm going to live without Lucy."

"Charlie, he understand. You lose a wife, I lose a daughter, and I don know where the other one is."

Peter said nothing more, but he extended his arms to Lucy's grieving parents and drew them to him, each held the others close, seeking a respite for their grief.

The wake was not as distastefull as Peter had expected. Friends and neighbors came in droves, many bearing a favorite food dish for the family and mourners. Yet, while he was polite, Peter left the explanations to Elizabeth. She would tell the story of Lucille's untimely passing and cry with a friend, then compose herself only to do it again. This continued, with Peter biting his lip to hold back the tears until his friend Gustav and his wife came.

Peter walked with them to stand beside Lucy's casket and began to tell them how she had died. But now he could contain his grief no longer, he held the friend who had welcomed him to America close, and wept in the comfort of their friendship. When he had regained himself, much of his pain had been washed from him.

Peter was beginning to understand the wisdom of the old custom of the wake. The prayers were really not for Lucy at all, but for those left behind, that they might sever their relationship with her and pick up the remaining threads of their lives. He looked at her pale face and remembered the first time he had held her in his arms. He would always love her and cherish the time they had together. But now he must continue on, he had two sons and a daughter that she had given to him.

Lucille was buried the next day in a little cemetery, beneath an ancient elm. Charlie LeBlanc held his grandson Sven in his arms, Peter held little Charles. Each of the little boys played with a solitary rose, to be placed on their mother's casket.

On the first Sunday of May, little Lucille Kathryn Hokanson was baptized. She was held proudly by her grandmother, Elizabeth Leblanc. Mr. and Mrs. Gustav Svenson were the Godparents.

Chapter 14

Reunion

The weeks that followed Lucille's death passed listlessly. Elizabeth took charge of her little grandsons, and Peter at her urging, stayed on at the mansion. He had returned only once to his house. The building was barren without Lucille, it was no longer a home ringing with children's laughter and warm with the aromas from Lucy's kitchen. So he returned to the mansion, bringing his clothing and the wedding portrait of him and Lucille with him.

Every day he went to the house of Ursala, the German woman, to see his daughter. The baby was growing well and smiled a little smile when he tickled her chin with his forefinger. She was his remembrance of Lucille, and she would become the most precious person in his life.

One day in June, Peter and Charlie were at the club talking of business. They both had thrown themselves into work as a healing power. But still, Peter bore a look of sadness, a lack of enthusiasm, that was unlike him. Charlie assessed the young man sitting at the bar with him, then he tipped his brandy down and looked into Peter's eyes.

"Pete, Charlie no like seeing you like you are. He thinks you need a change."

Peter sighed heavily. "I'm okay, Charlie. I just can't seem to get back into the business."

"That's what Charlie means, when you take a vacation, eh?"

"A vacation?"

"Yeah! You know, a holiday from the business!"

"Well, I guess only when Lucy and I got married."

"That's no holiday, that's a honeymoon. When you come to this country?"

"In November of eighteen-ninety five."

"An it's nineteen-two, it's almost seven years you been working without a holiday, eh? You needa get away, Pete. "

"Yeah, I guess you're right, Charlie. Maybe I should take a few days off and do some fishing."

"Fishing! Who you gonna go fishing with? I tell you who,...nobody! You gonna go out in a stinking little row-boat an sit an think about Lucy and how you miss her! Then when you got your belly good and full of misery, you'll come crawling back, worse then you are now!"

Pete flushed at the sting of Charlie's perceptive statement. "Okay Charlie, what should I do, hole up in Sadie's whorehouse? Or maybe go to New York for a few weeks?"

"Maybe you should go to New York, but you not stop there. Your mama, she's still alive. Charlie, he think you should go see your family in the old country. You go now, while Charlie can mind the factory for you. It take you away from your misery, an maybe when you come back things not look so bad anymore."

Peter brightened a little. "Maybe you're right, Charlie. Lucy and I had planned on going as soon as little Lucy was big enough to travel. We wanted Mother to see her grandchildren. Only, now I could only take the boys."

Charlie shook his head. "I don think you should take them, it gonna be too much for you. Charlie think you go get some pictures taken, give them to your mama. Besides, the boys keep me and Liz from thinking bout Lucy...an Kat. We need them here as much as you needa get away."

"I guess I could do that all right. But Mother will be disappointed."

"She gonna understand, Pete. An maybe you all go when they a little bigger."

It was decided—Peter began preparations for his return to Sweden. On the second week of August, Charlie, Liz and the boys saw Peter to the train headed east. When he boarded, a sense of anticipation grew within him, raising his spirits despite the sadness of leaving his American family.

As the train moved out of the station, Peter looked about him. The train was new, faster and more comfortable then the old one that had brought him to Minneapolis. On this trip he could afford to eat in the dining car, and sleep in one of several "Pullman sleepers". He remembered well how he had hunkered up on a hard bench trying to sleep when he came. His food had been a little bread and cheese, or maybe a sausage or a smoked fish. The seventeen year old lad had lived on dreams then.

Now, nearly twenty four, he was returning to his homeland, already a success beyond his dreams. Fate had dealt him some hard blows. The unfaithfulness of Julia, the death of Sven and the loss of Sarah had all cut deeply into his soul. He had overcome those times of grief, and in time he would overcome the loss of Lucy. The pain was still intense, but it would lessen. There was still much for him to do, an empire for him to build with Charles and Sven, and little Lucy.

As the eager new locomotive drew its load of cars swiftly across the nation, Peter marvelled at how the cities and towns had exploded in the few years since his arrival. Everywhere there were new houses, stores and factories. Peter wondered how many of the logs he had cut and guided down the Mississippi had found their way to these new buildings.

The farmland had changed too, in seven years. There were few 'walking plows' turning the stubble left after grain harvest. Instead, he saw farmers riding plows pulled by three, four or more horses, that turned as many as three furrows at once. Here and there he saw a machine that was pulled behind a hay wagon, loading a continuous windrow of hay as a team of horses drew it along. Peter stared in amazement. Would they have such wonders in Sweden? He doubted it, much of the land there was poor and rocky, and the farms were too small to pay for such equipment.

The miles flew by swiftly. This train did not stop at every little town, but only at the larger towns, and at switchyards to pick up and drop cars. Otherwise, it fairly flew down the rails. In Chicago Peter boarded a different train much like the first, which reached New York City on the second day. The next day he would board a Swedish steam ship, "The Gravarne" and begin a trip across the

Atlantic for the second time. This time it would not be in cramped immigrants' quarters, but in a first class cabin with all the luxury of the time.

The Gravarne cruised at nearly twenty knots and the weather was clear and friendly to the shipload of tourists and business people. The ship put into port at Liverpool, England on the seventh day at sea. The next afternoon it again put to sea, reaching the Swedish coast on the morning of the second day.

Peter felt a tightening in his throat as he stood at the bow rail watching Goteborg materialize out of the early morning mist. He had not allowed himself to miss his homeland since his first seige of homesickness. But now, as a pair of tugboats took charge of the Gravarne, he was overcome by the desire to see all he had left behind. As the wharfs glided slowly by, it was as though he had left yesterday. He was a young lad again, going to meet his destiny.

The tumult of emotions he felt rise within him tore at his soul, demanding joy and sorrow at once. How grand it was, the old harbor. And God, how he wished Lucy were beside him with the children to see it all! Refusing to obey the tight clenching of his jaws, tears squeezed from the corners of his eyes. The familiar scene renewed old memories and heightened the pain of those not yet past.

As the ship settled into place at the dock, Peter scanned the crowd gathered there. There!...is that Johann with the whiskered face? And beside him holding the children, Ingrid and her husband, Wilhelm? Those young women, one holding a baby...were they his little sisters? Mary and Edith had been pigtail braided children when he left. He strained to see his mother's straight, slender form. Instead he saw a frail looking, bent figure. But she was looking up at him, waving. It is her—she looks so small and gray!

Then they lowered the stair to the dock and Peter was walking swiftly, almost running in the tide of passengers surging forward to meet loved ones. On the dock he pushed his way through the crowd and caught his mother in his arms. Amid his siblings laughing with tears in their eyes, he kissed her pale cheeks and said, "I am home, Mother! Peter is home!"

The reunion with his family was more emotional than Peter had imagined. There were new family members, both born and wed that Peter had never met. Ingrid now had three children swarming about her, Mary had a husband and a baby of her own, and Edith was planning a spring wedding. His brother Johann was still single, caring for his mother, and showed no signs of committing himself to marriage. His mother had aged terribly since Peter left, but she picked up in body and spirit as the days passed. She bustled about her kitchen with a vigor that had been long gone, according to Johann's observation.

Peter suddenly had a family of his own kin. It made him feel as though he were another person, someone distant and foreign from the Peter who lived in the city of lumber and flour mills. As he recounted some of his adventures to his family grouped about him, it was as though he were telling stories of someone else, a character in a book he had read.

On the second day he was home, Ingrid offered to go with him to their father's grave. Peter nodded assent.

"Can we go alone? It is something I would like to do with just you. I feel yet that Father should come walking through the kitchen door, Ingrid. A person cannot say good-bye across the thousands of miles."

"Yes, I thought so. Mother will stay in her kitchen, she is cooking a fat goose for supper. The rest have things they must do."

"Good, can we walk? I would like to walk down the old streets."

"Then come."

She led him out and onto the cobbled street. The great trees that entwined their branches overhead were beginning to drop their leaves, making a carpet of yellow, brown and red splotches beneath their feet.

"Do you remember how often we ran down this street to play in the pond, or skate in the winter?" Ingrid asked.

"Like it was yesterday. Often when I was in the logging camp, I thought about our skating parties. It is a part of me I'll never lose."

"Do you have a pond in Minneapolis?"

"We have lakes, many of them. It is not that much different than here. I guess that's why so many Scandinavians settled there."

"Peter,...do you ever think of coming back, to stay?"

"Do you ever think of coming to join me?"

"No, not anymore. I guess we're grown up now, we've got different lives. If you were my husband, instead of my brother, I would go."

"Wilhelm wouldn't go?"

"No, he's not adventurous, he's more like..."

"It's all right, Ingrid. You were going to say 'Julia'. That's long over, it doesn't pain me anymore."

They walked arm in arm in comfortable silence the rest of the way to the cemetery. Ingrid led him up the little path between the rows of ancient monuments to an area sheltered by birch trees. A single, blue granite stone stood out from the rest, the grass on the mound beneath it still sparsely new.

"He is here, near his father," Ingrid said.

Peter knelt beside the grave to read the Inscription in Gothic Swedish.

"Hokan Johannson, 1844—1902, A good man", it said simply. He closed his eyes and prayed aloud, "The Lord is my shepherd, I shall not want....." Ingrid's voice joined his, her pleasing alto blending with his rich baritone in the gentle cadence of the psalm. When he and Ingrid had finished, he was at peace. His tears for his father had fallen long ago, far away.

"I love you Father," he said.

It was something he wished he had said years before. But then, his Swedish family had never been demonstrative in their love for each other. It was almost as though they feared letting their feelings show, except for his mother, his patient, suffering, loving mother.

He and Ingrid walked quietly, their hands joined, until they reached the pond.

"Let's stop here a while," Peter said. "There's something I've been thinking about."

"I bet I can guess what it is."

"Can you now? Since when is my sister a mind reader?"

"I'm not, of course, but I am your sister yet, and that's almost the same. You're thinking of how you can get to see all of your old friends. I've already started plans on that."

Peter laughed. "You always could see through me, and I always got in trouble because of it. Like the time I stole

Mrs. Ingeborde's pie from her windowsill, and you caught me with it behind the stable. You demanded half of it."

Ingrid giggled at the memory. "At least I didn't tattle, like the other girls would have."

"No, that you didn't. But I am curious, what have you got planned?"

"Your birthday, dummy! Your birthday is almost here, and we're going to have a party for you. And we're going to have all of your old friends, and our cousins, and everybody."

"Everybody?"

"Sure, everybody...oh-h! I see what you're thinking. Not her!...Surely not her, after what she did to you!" Ingrid looked at Peter sharply.

He grinned. "I know it's crazy, but I'd like to see her again. Things are different now, but I'd still like to see her again."

Ingrid shook her head disbelievingly. "I guess it's your party, I'll invite Julia if you want me to. But I can't imagine why you'd want to see the little bitch, unless it's to make her envious of your wealth."

"There was a time when that was always in my mind. But it's not important anymore. I guess I just want to know how her life has turned out. Not knowing is like reading a book with a chapter missing."

"I guess I can understand that, Peter. Let's go home, we don't want to be late for supper."

"No wait...not quite yet. Where are we going to have the party?"

"Mary, Edith and I talked about that. Mom's house is too small—we thought we could have it here by the pond. You know, like we did when we were children."

"Is "The Sea Goddess" still open?"

"Why yes...you mean the ballroom?"

"Sure, isn't that what hotel ballrooms are for?"

"Yes, but it would be terribly expensive, only the rich and important people go there."

"Well, I guess you could call me rich, and all of you are important, so let's see if we can get it. This will be fun, I'll pay for everything and you girls can take care of the details."

Ingrid's eyes sparkled. "Tomorrow we'll see if we can get the ballroom, so we girls can start writing the invitations."

"No!"

"But, why not, Peter? You just said you wanted the ballroom."

"I didn't mean that, I meant the invitations, can't you have the invitations printed in time?"

"I suppose so, I just hadn't thought of having printed invitations." Ingrids eyes narrowed, then she grinned evilly. "Peter, you weasel, you had me believing how your feeling for Julia had changed. You want to jab her right where it hurts the most, don't you? You want to make that sissy husband of hers look like a poor bank clerk."

"Why Ingrid, the thought never entered my mind—now, let's go to supper." He took Ingrid's hand and walked down the street humming his favorite Swedish waltz.

The days that followed were glorious. Peter was beset by a steady stream of visitors who had heard that the young lumberjack son of Hokan, the cabinet builder, had returned from America. Gossip had it, on one count, that he had returned as an impoverished wretch to his father's house, just as the prodigal son of Biblical times. Another more optimistic story contended that he had found gold in northern Minnesota, and had chartered the Gravarne for his sole use to return to Goteborg. Both accounts drew great curiosity.

Consequently the list of invitations to Peter's birthday ball became longer, as people filed in and out of Helen Johannson's house to greet her young son. Helen seemed to thrive on the excitement, and when Peter purchased new gowns for his mother and sisters, and a new suit for Johann and each of the girls' men, she beamed with pride and happiness. "The old woman's retreated a good distance from the grave," one waggish observer put it.

Mrs. Elias Oberg put down the embroidery she was working on at the sound of the door chime, and hurried to open the heavy oak door. A young man with a bicycle stood outside.

"Special postal delivery for Mr. and Mrs. Elias Oberg," he said. "Are you Mrs. Oberg, Ma'am?"

"Yes, I am."

She took the envelope extended to her, and thanked the messenger. The envelope was addressed in a neat feminine script, and was of a good quality linen paper. Her curiosity aroused, she opened it on the broad stoop of her house. Enclosed was a folded card, printed in Gothic Swedish. On the cover was an imprint of Swedish and United States flags with their staffs crossed above "GREETINGS". She opened the card and read:

YOU ARE CORDIALLY INVITED TO ATTEND A BALL

at

THE SEA GODDESS H OTEL

on

SEPTEMBER 15, 1902 AT 7 PM

IN HONOR OF THE 24TH BIRTHDAY
of
MISTER PETER OLAF HOKANSON

Julia stared at the card in disbelief. Peter here in Huskvarna! And a birthday party for him in the city's biggest hotel! How could it be? The last I heard from him, he was working in a logging camp, she thought. I thought he might come back someday. But to have a ball at "The Sea Goddess"...surely a logger couldn't afford that, even in America. Julia was astounded, and she fidgetted at her embroidery until it was time to make supper for Elias. And indeed, she did poorly at that—because of her agitation, she burned the roast and scorched the gravy.

When she met Elias at the door, she pecked his cheek absently and launched into her news, as he put his hat and coat in the hall closet.

"You'll never guess what news I had today, Dear."

Elias sat down before the blackened roast. "It must have been very upsetting, judging from the condition of my supper."

She ignored the comment. "Peter Hokanson is back!"

"Peter who?" He began slicing through the charred meat.

"Peter Hokanson! You remember Peter."

"Oh yeah, the lumberjack you were seeing before we met. He left you and ran off to America, didn't he?"

"You don't have to say it that way, Peter loved me."

"Then why did he leave you?"

"Elias Oberg! He didn't leave me because he didn't love me. He had a dream about going to America and becoming wealthy."

"M-m-m-h-m-m, and now he's back with his dreams all gone, dragging his tail in the mud like a whipped dog, eh?"

"I don't know about that Elias, I don't know what to think. Here, look at this."

He took the card from her hand and adjusted his spectacles, which continually slipped down his prominent nose.

"My word Julia! It appears that your lumberjack has come on some money."

"He's not my lumberjack, he's probably got a wife and half a dozen children by now. But of course I'm curious. Do you think we might go?"

"Do you want to? Wouldn't you be a bit uncomfortable going to a party for an old suitor? After all, it is possible that he is still in love with you. And how do you think I'll feel? You're not going to say he never put a hand on you, are you Julia?"

"Oh Elias! Peter was just a boy when he was courting me. He was younger than me, and he thought he was in love with me. But he was still a boy, and he loved the thought of going to America more. By now he's grown up, and I have too. It'll be fun talking about how young and foolish we were then."

"Still, I'm not sure it's a good idea. But then, a free party isn't often to be had, especially one at The Sea Goddess. Do we have to bring a present?"

"Just a courtesy gift. If he has money, he doesn't need anything we could afford anyway."

"Yes, things have been a bit slow for a few years now. If only I could get father to be more progressive."

"Yes, I know Dear. But let's not talk about that now, it always depresses you so. We're going to a party to have fun, it seems like ages since we've done that. But I'll need a new gown, and all your suits are so shabby."

Elias rolled his eyes. "Why does a party always have to be a major investment? We might as well buy a new horse and carriage while we're at it."

Julia smiled, and the sparkle in her eyes washed away her husband's misgivings.

"Oh no, Dear, the new gown will be quite enough, we'll hire a carriage for the evening."

Thousands of miles to the west, it was mid-morning. Christian Halvorsen had just entered the office of Charlie LeBlanc. An unseasonal heat wave cloaked Minneapolis, and Charlie was sitting at his desk in rolled up shirt sleeves and open collar. He got up to take his friend's hand.

"Damn me, look what come crawlin out of the woods in this heat! If it ain't the sorry son of a Viking woman and a stud grizzly bear! Sit down, Christian. Charlie got some new brandy he like you to try."

"Thanks, could you maybe chip a little ice off the block in your ice box and throw it in the brandy with a little water? I gotta cut back a little on the spirits. You buy a bottle and you own it, you buy a dozen and they own you."

"You got trouble, Christian? You never been a drunk. Big difference between a man who like a drink, an a drunk."

"I haven't really got trouble, it's just that I got things that bother me. Thought maybe you could listen, maybe have some ideas about what I should do."

"For you, Charlie always got time to listen. Whatsa matter, your logging outfit going sour on you, eh?"

"Well, I guess that's part of it, Charlie. I've been running in the timber a long time. Things change, I'm thinking I should maybe shut it down after this season."

"If you need money, if the bank's on you, Charlie got money."

"Naw…it's not money. Like I say, I've been in the timber a long time. There's different parts in a man's life, parts when you're free to wander, parts where you're not. It's time I settle down. There's an old couple run a hotel in Grand Rapids. They want to quit. I'm thinking on buying them out. It would be a good place for my wife and kids."

Charlie's jaw dropped. "Mother of God! What did Charlie just hear you say! Are you saying you got a wife and kids, you old brushbuck, or you just wanna get em?"

"I got a wife an kids, real enough. Had them since the spring after Pete an Lucy got married."

"Why the hell you not tell Charlie? You been married over two years already an your friend don't know bout it? Charlie, he insulted. You shoulda let Charlie know, he throw party, we all celebrate."

"I'm sorry, Charlie. It just wasn't that way, I thought it was better to just get married quietly and not tell anyone."

"What you mean, 'it wasn't that way'? The bread was already rising? Lotsa women, they out of shape when they get married, eh? They get married anyway, an everybody snicker when the birthday a little early. That's nothing to worry about, life is that way."

"I know, but it's more than that. She had a little boy…named after me. He was three years old when we got married. Little Chris is five now, and David is a year and a half and Sarah is expecting next spring. We're a family now, though we wouldn't have been, if the truth had come out."

"What you telling me Christian, that the first little boy isn't yours? It not make a difference. Far as Charlie is concerned, he's your little boy, if that's the way you want it. What you say, when Pete gets back from visiting his folks in Sweden, we have a big party at my place? Pete and Charlie, they need all the company they can get, since Lucy died. We all get to know your wife and the little ones, eh?"

Christian twisted uncomfortably in his chair. "Dammit Charlie, give me one of your cigars to chew on, and maybe I'll tell you the whole story."

Charlie handed Christian a long black Cuban, then took one for himself, and deftly cut the tip with a razor sharp pen knife. Christian took a match from a little silver box that had been Wise Otter's. Sarah had given it to Christian on the anniversary of the old man's death, and he carried it always, as a remembrance of his old warrior friend. The two men drew on their cigars, it gave them something to do until they were ready to speak again.

"Damn it all!" Christian said. "We can't ever have that kind of party! I don't want Pete near Sarah and the kids! Pete knows Sarah already!"

Charlie launched a gust of cigar smoke, peering through it at Christian's agitated face. "There's only one reason I can see, you don't want Pete near your wife and kids," he said. "Pete…he's your little boy's daddy, eh?"

Christian nodded tiredly. "He was courting Sarah when he was up at the logging camp. Sarah got in a family way, and Pete didn't know about it. He doesn't know he fathered a son by Sarah."

"But, why she not tell him, Christian? I know Pete, he woulda made it right."

"We both know he would have. It was right when he was getting a start with you, Charlie. You know that would have blown his chances here."

"Maybe not, a nice girl, the boy make a mistake. It woulda been a little harder, but people always accept after they get tired of wagging their tongues."

"I don't think so, not this time,…Sarah's a half breed, Charlie."

"Holy Mother! That changes the situation, all right. You figured it would wreck Pete's chances,…so you got between them, eh?"

"Right."

"How you keep the girl quiet? She love him, she gonna go to him, eh?"

"I told her she would ruin him if she went to him about it. I made a deal with her grandfather. You knew old Wise Otter, the Chippewa medicine man."

Charlie nodded. "Decent Indian—so you took care of the girl and her baby?"

"Like they were my own, until the old Indian died. Before he died, he asked me to marry Sarah, I said I would if she'd have me. It wasn't hard, after taking care of them for all that time, I loved them both. I let her know that Pete was getting married. That made up her mind to not wait for him anymore. We got married in the spring, after Pete married Lucy."

"May God have mercy on all of us! Charlie, he can see why you don't want Pete and Sarah to get together, especially since Lucy's gone. Pete, he gonna hate your guts if he finds out. An maybe he be right, if he loved the girl. But you my friend, Christian. You say, 'Keep your mouth shut.', I keep it shut."

"Thanks, Charlie. But the problem is, am I doing right by little Christian? We can probably live out our lives up north without him ever hearing of Peter Hokanson. But is it right? The way Pete is going, he could be a millionaire some day. Little Christian is Pete's first born son. He's illegitimate, but he probably wouldn't be if I had kept my fingers out of it. Right now your grandchildren are Pete's heirs, but shouldn't little Christian be one too?"

"Damn me, but thatsa big headache," Charlie said. "But the way Charlie see it, the boy, he got a life with you. He got a papa, and a damned good one he can be proud of. Charlie, he say, if the Lord want Christian to find his real daddy, he gonna lead the boy to him. Telling Pete about the boy gonna give everybody lotsa heartache. Pete, he got a family to take care of, an he still grieving for Lucy. He don need anything else to fret about."

"So you think I should leave everything as it is?"

Charlie refilled his glass and Christian's. He raised his glass to Christian.

"Christian my friend, go live your life an raise lotsa kids to take care of you and your woman in your old age. An if you an your wife ever need anything, Charlie he here."

Christian drank the bottle of brandy with Charlie. But despite the warming flush he felt, he wondered if his was a secret that should be kept.

Chapter 15

Embers Not Dead

The ballroom of The Sea Goddess was resplendent with fall flowers and silk streamers in red, rust and gold. Huge tables were laden with food, and waiters were hurrying about, plying early comers with beer, wine and spirits. Peter's three sisters were greeting the guests as they entered, while Peter, his mother, and Johann drifted from group to group exchanging pleasantries. After a while, his mother grew tired and chose to sit and visit with an old friend. Peter and Johann went to renew their drinks.

"You have done just as you promised in those days as a boy in the woodshop," Johann said. "How does it feel to return to your home, a rich and envied man?"

"It feels good, in a way. There were many who thought I was a fool to go. And sometimes I felt the same, especially when I knelt by Sven Thorson's grave."

"I Thought you a fool too, little brother. But perhaps I was the fool."

"Why, Johann? The wood shop does well, does it not?"

"Aye, it does well enough, and could do better. But with father gone so soon, there is an emptyness about it—I should have gone to the new world when you did."

"But you liked the shop, and father was very proud of you. You are an excellent craftsman, Johann, and that is of great importance."

"And my little brother is a rich, important man at twenty-four. There is something missing in my life, Peter."

"You need a woman, Johann. I thought to see you married by now."

"The girls downtown have served me well enough for that," Johann smiled. "But I would like something more, to see something of the world, to test myself against it as you have."

Peter frowned, this was a part of his brother he had not seen before.

"Then, come to Minnesota—we can run the furniture factory together."

"I would like that, but I can't leave mother in her old age. It's strange, you were always her favorite, yet I must care for her."

"But what of the girls, surely they will see to her?"

"It is my failing, Peter, that I take my duty to heart. Or perhaps it is that I lack the courage to reach for my freedom. I wish that I had been born with your free spirit." He tipped his glass of spirits and beckoned a waiter for another.

"Do you look at your duty through the bottom of a glass, then? Ingrid worries about you."

"Aye, Ingrid worries about everyone, it is her nature. The spirits chase my demons away."

"And bring another in the morning."

Johann laughed, and Peter thought he detected a bitterness in it. "Aye, little brother, but then we all have our demons. Look to the door, one of yours has entered."

Julia and Elias had entered, and were receiving a diplomatic if not cordial welcome from Ingrid. Their greetings made, they walked uncertainly into the ballroom. An acquaintance of Elias's hailed them and they went to join the group. Peter tried not to stare, but his eyes seemed to have their own will, he stood looking at Julia, oblivious to Johann's presence.

"It seems your demon still plagues you, brother. Shall we go forth to meet the dragon?"

Peter was about to decline, thinking it would be best to make a casual meeting. But Johann was already striding across the floor. Peter hurried to overtake his brother, lest he appear to be a negligent host.

"Julia!," Peter said with great enthusiasm as he offered his hand, "it is so good to see you! And this must be your husband, I have long wished to meet you, Sir. I am Peter Hokanson, your wife and I know each other."

"Yes, so I understand." Elias offered his hand stiffly. "I am Elias Oberg, and this gentleman?" He noted that the two men before him were dressed in suits much finer than his own.

"My brother, Johann." Peter said. "We must get together and visit after all the guest have arrived."

His words were spoken not so much to Elias as to Julia, who smiled at him warmly.

"It would pleasure Elias and I greatly," she said.

"In that case, I would like you to join us at the family table for the banquet," Peter said. "There is much for us to catch up on."

His eyes fixed on Julia's. They were as blue as he remembered them, and her hair as blonde, perhaps even more so. She wore it trailing about her shoulders in a mass of ringlets. "Until later then." He took Julia's hand and brushed it with his lips, then walked away with Johann.

"A handsome woman," Johann said. "Is she as you remember her?"

"She was a pretty girl, Brother. She is an exquisite woman."

Johann laughed. "Such language from a lumberjack. You have changed much in seven years."

"Yes, and so has she, Johann, so has she."

Julia and Elias stood looking after the brothers as they walked away. The shadow of a smile touched Julia's face, then disappeared as Elias turned to her.

"It seems your lumberjack has become sophisticated since he left. I would never have known. Of course good clothing always makes an impression. Those suits had to come from LeChande's, they had the continental cut."

"Yes, he has changed…for the better. His brother too, they are quite the handsome pair. And so well mannered, his wife must have polished him."

"His wife?"

"Yes Elias, he wears a wedding band. I wonder where she is."

"I never noticed his ring, and I wonder that you would. His wife may be the kind that becomes seasick, or maybe they don't get on well, that sort of thing. But the man has money, I can see that. I'm curious to learn more of him."

"Why would you want to learn more of him, Dear?"

"The new world is where money is being made. One never knows, investments, that sort of thing. But, I don't want to bore you with man talk, Darling. Come, let's say hello to the Ericsonns."

Later, at dinner, Elias and Julia were seated across the table from Peter and Ingrid. The seating had been arranged by Ingrid, and the Obergs were to sit far from the family table. But Peter, with a grin, had requested that the Oberg's be placed near him. "You are such a weasel, Peter." Ingrid had complained, but laughed in spite of herself.

"Excellent food, Mr. Hokanson." Elias savored a slice of prime beef. "It is seldom that we get such tender beef these days. It seems the cattle farmers don't fatten their stock well anymore."

"Darling, we would have tender beef if I weren't forced to buy the cheapest cuts," Julia said. "Buy an armroast, you say. Just once I'd like to cook a loin. Not that we have beef that often. You always complain that pork is cheaper."

"Economy is insurance against want, Dear. But let's not bore Mr. Hokanson with such mundane quibbling. I'd like to hear about his investments in America. I've heard that you've done very well, Mr. Hokanson. Would you mind telling me what business you're in?"

Peter smiled. "Why, I'm just a lumberjack who's had a little luck. I had a chance to invest my savings in a little furniture factory. It went quite well, so we were able to build a new, larger one. That, and some elevators and a flour mill."

Elias looked at Peter with a calculating eye. "Yes, I suppose there is quite a demand in a new, developing country for furniture. You must supply much of your city... Minepolis, wasn't it?"

"Minneapolis is the name, it comes from the Sioux Indian name Minnehaha, or falling water. We supply much of the city, of course. And we ship east to Chicago, Cleveland and some as far as New York. The demand west and south is picking up too. The people in those states are making money on their grain, and they want to spend it."

Julia was listening intently, her blue eyes fixed on Peter. Now she spoke, her words coming out in a honey sweet gush.

"Oh, how grand, Peter! I always knew you would be a wonderful success in the new world. A factory, and a flour mill too! And what are these elevators? You know I'm just a Swedish girl who doesn't know anything about your wonderful country."

Elias looked at his wife in an irritated way. "Please Dear, we don't want to pry into Mr. Hokanson's business."

Peter grinned. "I don't mind, Mr. Oberg. It's been a long time since Julia and I talked." He smiled at Julia. "Elevators are tall buildings where we store grain that we buy from farmers in the west. It comes in by train, and we buy it. Then we sell it to markets in the east and south, or mill it into flour."

Elias was awestruck. "My God, you buy whole train-loads of wheat? How much is that in a year?"

"Well, we don't buy whole trainloads at a time, just ten or twenty cars a day. Last year we handled about a hundred and sixty thousand tons. It should be quite a bit more this year."

Peter laughed inwardly. The young banker was obviously calculating his worth. It would do no harm to let him. Letting these people see his success was satisfying to his soul.

"It must be a land of riches, just as you told me," Julia said, "for a man to make his fortune in such a short time. Here, it seems we cannot get ahead no matter how we try. But then, Elias's father is so backward, he won't let Elias progress."

Elias cleared his throat, embarrassed at Julia's revelation. "It's just that father is very conservative, he lacks the spirit to seize opportunity when it presents itself. He came up the old way and he is afraid of risk."

Peter smiled. "It is sometimes harder for those who have money to risk it than it is for those who have little. There are many in the new world who work hard and have nothing. I was one of the fortunate ones who had someone to help me. My timber boss got me a job with a wealthy lumberman by the name of Charles LeBlanc. Without his friendship, I would still be felling trees."

Elias looked at Peter intently. "Tell me, Mr. Hokanson, do you think there would be equal opportunity for a banker who is prepared to take risks, in your city?"

"Money paves the road of progress, Mr. Oberg. Right now there are great fortunes being made in Minneapolis. If a man has vision, is prepared to take calculated risks, he will do well. Do you know someone who wishes to go? I would be glad to introduce him to Charlie LeBlanc and some other businessmen."

"I was thinking of myself, Mr. Hokanson. I am growing restless with the stagnation here, and I would like a new challenge. I have some money, my share of the bank here. It might be enough to get a small start in...Minneapolis. That is, if my wife would consider leaving her home." He shifted his gaze to Julia, whose face mirrored her astonishment.

"I would have to think about it," she said. "It would mean losing all our family and friends."

"I guess I've heard that before," Peter said. "But, you were a girl then, Julia. We must all make hard decisions at some time, I made mine seven years ago."

Julia flushed. "It is easier for a man, Peter. Men thrive on adventure. Women have only their homes and families."

"You are right of course, Julia. Forget what I said. But enough business talk. You and Elias have children, I would expect?"

Elias cut in. "We have not been so blessed. I had a severe case of the mumps in early adulthood. The doctor's say it is not unusual to sustain damage that prevents having children. It is a cross we must bear, I'm afraid."

"Yes, I sometimes think it is some sort of cruel punishment." Julia said. "But that's silly, we have done nothing we should be punished for. What of you, Peter? Do you have a wife and family?"

Peter's expression changed abruptly, the happiness left his face and pain showed in his eyes. He was silent for a moment, as though words would not come.

"I have twin boys, Sven and Charles, and a baby daughter named for her mother, Lucille. My wife died at her birth, she lost too much blood."

"Oh! How sad! It must have been horrible for you," Julia said. "And the poor children, without their mother. I am truly sorry, Peter, I wish I could hold those poor children and comfort them."

"They have their grandmother, and the baby has a wet-nurse. But it is a sadness I must bear for them, and myself. Children shouldn't have to grow up without a mother."

"Yes Peter, all children should have a mother. Perhaps, when the pain of your wife's passing has lessened, you will find someone who will treat them as her own."

Peter looked at Julia and breathed a disconsolate sigh. "Perhaps, in time."

After dinner, the orchestra began playing a waltz, and Peter as guest of honor was obligated to dance the first dance. Formally, he rose from his seat, and extended his hand to his mother. She curtsied gracefully and took his arm, beaming with pride.

"I haven't danced in years, my son. But tonight I shall make these old feet of mine be gracefull once again. Your father loved to dance when he was young, and I was always fearful that another young woman would steal him from me on the dance floor." She laughed. "I need not have feared, he always had eyes only for me."

Peter danced carefully, fearful that his mother might miss her step, but she danced gracefully, if not energetically. Her pride in the moment seemed to smooth the lines from her face, and she talked as they danced.

"I am proud of you, Peter. I hated to see you leave, because I thought I would never see my son again. But you have come back for a short while, and my heart bursts with happiness. I only wish that your father could be here now, to see what you have done. We talked of you often, and when we got your letters he would say, 'By God, that boy is doing something! If I was younger, we would all go to join him.' He would have too, your father had spirit. He built the woodshop and our house with his own hands, with nothing but a few kronor. The spirit you have, you got from him."

Peter had never seen that side of his father, he had been too young, too caught up in his own dreams. But it was true, his father had built a business from nothing, just as he was doing. He had never discouraged Peter's dreams, and that must have been hard. Peter wished now, even more than before, that he could visit with him and tell him how grateful he was for the training his father had given him, and for his spirit. He held the frail old woman closer to him.

"I love you, Mama. I wish you could come back with me. I have a big house, and it would seem like a home again with you and my children."

His mother smiled at him with misty eyes. "You are a good son, Peter. I love you dearly, and I would like to be with you and your children. But my place is here with Hokan, even now. If God wills it, you may be able to come again with your children before I go to join your father."

Peter wondered, but he only said, "Yes Mama, I will bring them next time."

The next dance, a high spirited polka, Peter danced with Ingrid. There was little chance for talk, but when they left the floor Ingrid led him to the punch table.

"Elias shows more than a polite interest in your business success, Brother. You wouldn't seriously consider helping him move to Minneapolis, would you?"

"I don't know, I'm sure it's just a passing fancy of his. Still, it would be good to start a bank where we could invest some of our profits. The really big money is made in lending. I think that Elias has the ambition, and he has the banking knowledge."

"But you are ignoring the thing that could cause great problems for you, Peter."

"And what is that, dear Sister?"

"Julia,...the fire is low, but not out. She looks at you with renewed interest."

Peter laughed. "That is long over. It's true that she is a beautiful woman, and that is hard for me to ignore. But Lucille is still with me in my mind and heart—I am not ready for another. And besides, I'm sure Julia is a very devoted wife to Elias. You make problems where none exist, Ingrid."

"I wish I were as sure of that as you are, Brother. I know you will do what pleases you despite what I may say. But have care, Julia has no children. That is a thing that does not suit her fancy. The thought of gaining a wealthy, handsome, husband and children has already crossed her mind, I'll wager."

"You should write books, Ingrid, you have a wonderful imagination. Why are you so distrustful of Julia?"

"You may call it a woman's intuition, and you may scoff at it. But do you have reason to trust her, Peter?"

Peter flushed with the bite of the remark. "That was long ago, we were both barely more than children. Let's rejoin the group, I don't wish to be impolite."

When they returned to their table, a waltz was being played. Julia put her hand on Peter's arm.

"Would you like to ask a poor old married woman to dance, Peter? My husband doesn't care for it, and I would so like to waltz again."

Peter was acutely aware of Ingrid's eyes on him. "I would be flattered if you would consider dancing with me Julia—with your husband's permission, of course." He turned to Elias, who nodded his assent. "But I must warn you that I am a bit clumsy on my feet."

Julia smiled at him. "You are teasing me, Peter. I haven't forgotten that you are as graceful as the red deer. Come, let's dance before this waltz is ended."

They danced in silence at first, whirling around the floor in perfect harmony with the music. Peter felt a heady warmth rush over him. Julia's body in his arms, her silky golden hair against his face, the scent of her perfume, all were intoxicating to his senses. He was suddenly back in the past, as though there had been no time when they were apart. He thought of Ingrid's words, "The fire is low, but not out," and forced himself to think of Lucille and what a short while she was gone. He began talking to bring his senses back in his control.

"You dance as always Julia, as though a fairy has touched you with her wand and turned your feet to bits of cloud."

"And you have not lost your talent for flattery, Peter. I had forgotten how grand it feels to be in the arms of a gentleman. I want it to go on and on, I don't want it to ever stop."

"Doesn't Elias ever dance with you?"

"He does sometimes when etiquette demands it. But then he doesn't dance well, he is so stiff and wooden in his movement. He would much rather sit and talk about business with the men."

"I have noticed that, he seems every bit a banker. Was he serious about starting a bank in Minneapolis?"

"I don't know, he hasn't spoken of it. When it comes to business matters, he tells me very little. He thinks women have no head for business. But one thing I do know, if he makes up his mind there is no changing it. He's like you in that. If he decides to go to Minneapolis, he will go."

"How would you feel about that?"

"It would be hard,...there is no one I know there except you. Would that be awkward for you, Peter?" She looked at him, lines of concern showed about her eyes and forehead.

"Maybe,...in a way,...I'm not sure I've forgotten about us."

"I know, I haven't either. I miss you, Peter. I've never stopped missing you."

"Then why did you do it? Why did you leave me for him?"

"Because I was afraid to leave—I was such a little girl. My mother talked me into staying. Then she pushed me at Elias. I thought it was the best thing to do. But I couldn't bring myself to tell you, so mother did."

"That's what hurt the most, Julia. Because I was never really sure you wanted to leave me. I hated your mother,...and you, for that. But I found my way out of it, and I found a woman I could love. Then she left me too,...I still don't know exactly why. That's when I really started to work hard. I became successful, and when I had done that I started thinking about love again. I married Charlie LeBlanc's daughter. It wasn't for her father's money—we were very happy together, and she gave me three children. Now she's gone too. It seems that money comes easily to me, but love and happiness are always taken from me. It's a curse, I guess, because I'm too ambitious."

The music stopped, and they were left standing alone on the floor. Peter took Julia's hand in his and started walking back to their table. Midway, he stopped and spoke softly to her.

"If Elias decides to come to Minneapolis, I want you to come. Don't be afraid it will be awkward. I will be your friend, if nothing else."

After the party, Peter did not see Julia again. Elias had pressed him for more information on business possibilities in Minneapolis and had taken down his business address in the city. But that was all, and as the days rushed by and his departure approached, Peter dismissed the Obergs from his mind. Then, on the day before he was to embark on his return voyage, a covered carriage arrived at his mother's house.

Peter had been reading in the bright sunlight that streamed through the wide window of his mother's sitting room. He put the book down and watched curiously as the team of bays drew to a stop. The driver got down and opened the curbside door, extending his hands upward to assist his passenger down. Julia gained her footing, then adjusted her clothing before turning to walk up the pathway to the house. She carried a package beneath her arm, it was wrapped in white paper tied with a red ribbon. Peter dropped his book on table beside his chair and hurried to the door.

Julia hesitated before reaching for the brass lion's head knocker on the oak door. All of the anticipation she felt as she wrapped the package that morning suddenly melted and ran from her like hoarfrost in the morning sun. A tide of misgiving ran through her—she had been silly to come. She wanted to turn and run back to the carriage, but she could not. As she reached for the knocker, the door opened, and Peter was standing before her, smiling with a mischievous twinkle in his brown eyes. Despite her resolve to appear casual, she blushed like a schoolgirl meeting her first suitor. She had rehearsed a suitable greeting in her mind, but now she stood there dumbly trying to regain her composure.

Peter spoke first, saving her from the awkwardness she felt.

"Julia! What a wonderful surprise this sunny day brings. I had thought to call on you before I left, but I lost courage. I feared you might not wish me to come. Come in! Come in! But let us talk quietly, my mother is sleeping and I don't wish to disturb her." He took her hand and led her to the sitting room.

"You are a pleasure to my eyes, a woman who becomes more beautiful with each passing day."

"And your tongue becomes more beguiling, Peter. I fear it is improper for me to come, but I did wish to see you before you left. I wanted to give you a special present for your birthday—it would have been inappropriate to give it to you at your party. The gossips would make much of it, I'm sure."

She gave Peter the package, almost thrusting it at him in her embarrassment."

Peter took the package, then led her to his mother's brocade love seat and sat down beside her. He untied the ribbon clumsily, then began carefully unwrapping the paper, taking care not to tear it.

"Oh hurry up Peter!" Julia said a trifle too loudly. "I'll burst with suspense before you get it unwrapped!" Her eyes were aglow with regained anticipation.

He laughed and deliberately slowed in removing the pasteboard box from its wrapping. Julia reached over and tore the lid frome the box.

"There, smartie!"

The box held something knit from a luxurious angora fleece. Peter lifted it from the box, whistling softly at the beauty of the sweater. It was white with rust colored bands around the arms and a yoke of the same. On the chest a perfect picture of a buck red deer had been worked with the same rust colored yarn. He turned to Julia in astonishment.

"It's wonderful Julia, but much too beautiful to wear!"

She smiled happily. "But you must wear it, Peter. It's a peace offering from me to you. I made it in the hope that you might forgive me for what I did to you back then."

"I'll wear it on Sundays and holidays then. But you needn't have done it, I had already forgiven you."

"I wanted to, and I'm glad you've forgiven me, it will make everything better for all of us."

"What do you mean?"

"Elias and I have talked, we are coming to Minneapolis as soon as he can settle his affairs here."

Peter's mouth opened with surprise, then impulsively he gathered Julia in his arms, in a great hug that she did not resist. When he released her, he said, "Let me get a bottle of wine. This is something we must celebrate."

When at last Julia returned to her home, she felt a certain giddiness. It is the wine, she thought, only the wine."

The second trip to America was very different from the first for Peter. He was returning to a life that was promising and substantial. The waves of the Atlantic did not seem so gray and forbidding, the emotions within him were not fraught with ambiguous thoughts. He had put his father to rest. He was at peace with his feelings for his mother and family. Perhaps most important of all, he had shed the animosity he had felt towards Julia for nearly seven years. In its place the buddings of a friendship were growing.

He was returning to his home with a new feeling of confidence. His spirit was revitalized, and with it his ambition. A new and glowing future awaited him, and the need for work grew within him. Even the pain he felt when he thought of Lucille, had lessened. With each day at sea his eagerness to return home increased. He would return to his house with his children. After all, the four of them were still a family.

Chapter 16

Lightening Strikes Twice

Peter's homecoming was one of the most exuberant days he had known. It was as splendid as his homecoming to Sweden had been, perhaps more so, because everything was now right with him on both sides of the ocean.

The twins came running to him across the boarding platform of the depot as soon as they saw him. Charlie hurried along behind them calling words of caution, lest they trip and fall on the hard stone. Then he fell on Peter, pumping his hand and making a loud welcome. Elizabeth followed, carrying little Lucy. She glowed with pride as he hugged the boys, then deposited Lucy in his arms. The baby gurgled and cooed as all happy babies do. Peter grinned as he looked at the chubby face. He was looking for a resemblance to his wife in the tiny features.

"She looks like you, another Hokanson for sure." Elizabeth said, as though answering his thoughts. "She has done well with Ursala Wenning. Those German women always have such rosy, fat little babies."

Peter laughed. "And has Mrs. Wenning become less stout for her efforts?"

Charlie cut in. "She says it makes her hungry, so she eats more sausage and potatoes. It has been good for the woman, but it will be hard for her to give Lucy up."

"I've been thinking about that, maybe it won't be necessary for her to do that."

Elizabeth gave Peter a perplexed look. "Why, whatever do you mean, Peter?"

"Mrs. Wenning doesn't have children, does she?"

"No, the one that died was her first."

"And what does her husband do?"

"He's a fireman with the railroad, he's gone a lot. Why do you ask?"

"Because I'm moving back into my house, I thought Mrs. Wenning might like to be my housekeeper."

Elizabeth was horrified. "You don't need to move out, Peter. I love having you and the children. I don't know what I'd do with myself without them."

"I know you love the children, but we need to have our own home," Peter said. "They're right next door to you anyway, they can be with you as much as you like."

"Pete's right, Liz," Charlie said. "Even with Lucy gone, he an the kids still a family. An Charlie's not so young anymore, he needs a little peace an quiet sometimes."

Peter laughed. "Then it's settled. Now let's all go home, I need a bath and a good meal."

Later, in the comfort of Charlie's den, Pete and Charlie were enjoying a game of pool and a glass of brandy. As Charlie bent to shoot, Peter spoke.

"While I was in Sweden, I came on an interesting business possibility."

Charlie made the two ball, then missed a bank shot on the six. He straightened up and took the stub of a cigar from his mouth. "What kind of business would you be interested in in Sweden?"

"Well, the business would be here in Minneapolis. But the guy that wants to start it is in Sweden. He wants to move here, and start a banking business."

"That's nice, but Charlie's got enough bankers already. Them bloodsucking bastards don want to give you any interest on your money. But when you got to borrow, they charge you til the tears come."

"I know, that's why Elias Oberg's proposition is interesting. He's got some money, but he needs investors. It would be a chance to make a real return on our money."

"Oberg, huh! Charlie don't need to tell you how he feels about his kind. You invest money with them, an next thing you know...they own you, lock, stock an barrel."

Peter bent to shoot, deftly pocketing the five ball, then scratching on the seven. He placed the seven back on the table and turned to Charlie.

"I don't think Elias is like that. He's ambitious and wants to make his mark. But I think we could trust him. And I can't imagine anybody pulling the wool over the eyes of Charlie Leblanc anyway."

"Maybe not, but Charlie he's damned fussy bout who he does business with. You know this guy when you were kids?"

"No, he married an old girlfriend of mine. I met him through her."

Charlie snorted. "Women and Jews, the two worst kinds of people to have in a business. Did you make a deal with him, Pete?"

"No, I just told him I'd introduce him to some of the business people I know. You know I wouldn't involve us without talking to you first, Charlie."

Charlie sipped his brandy thoughtfully. "You did good, Pete. Tell you what, if this Oberg comes here, Charlie gonna talk to him an try to forget he's a Jew. If Charlie likes him, then maybe we talk business. Having a place to put money where it's gonna earn something would be good. An right now, the bankers are making money the way the loggers used to. I was thinking bout putting up another mill, but maybe we can make some money without investing so damned much first."

"That's what I was thinking, Charlie. The beauty of banking is that you invest your money, but you get it back, along with a profit."

"Just so long as you don't lend it to some dumb son of a bitch who loses it for you. Banks go broke too, Pete."

In the last week of January 1903, Elias and Julia Oberg arrived in Minneapolis, Minnesota. The sun had gone down, and the evening was a clear, windy, frigid minus10 degrees Fahrenheit as they stepped from the train. Elias pulled his wool scarf higher on his neck, and Julia shivered despite her fur coat, as a gust of snow crystals obscured the lights of the depot. A figure dressed in a Mackinaw coat and knit cap came running toward them. Peter halted in front of them, grinning broadly.

"Welcome to Minnesota!" he said, as he extended a gloved hand to Elias, then to Julia. "Let's get inside the station where it's warm. I've sent a porter to get your luggage, and I've got a driver and rig to take it to the house."

Peter led them to the warmth of the glowing iron stove in the station. "Here, this will take the chill out of you. But mind you, Julia, don't get too close or it'll singe your fur."

"Br-r-r, it got cold in Sweden, but not like this." Julia said.

"That's because you had the wind from the ocean. We have none of that here," Peter said. "But it's not always this icy, and it'll start warming in March."

"That's good, if we don't freeze to death by then," Julia giggled. "But never mind the cold, it's wonderful to see you." She hugged Peter and gave him a quick peck on the cheek. "Is this where you came when you arrived in Minnesota?"

"The same, it's a little bigger and grander now, but it's much like it was. The trains are warmer though."

"None too warm for me, my feet feel like they're frozen," Elias said. "I hope we're not too far from your house."

"Not far at all, I've got a covered rig with horsehide robes and some hot bricks on the floorboards. It'll be quite cozy."

Within the hour the Oberg's were sitting in the dining room of Peter's house. Mrs. Wenning was bustling about with a huge tureen of beef soup, ladling generous portions to her guests.

"You have a beautiful house, Peter. And how did you get such a wonderful cook?," Julia asked. "This soup is so good, just the thing to take the chill from one's bones."

Peter smiled, but waited until Mrs. Wenning had returned to the kitchen before answering. "Well, actually she was Lucy's wetnurse, and when I asked if she'd like to be my housekeeper, she jumped at the job, so she could stay close to Lucy. I had no idea she was also an excellent cook."

Elias spoke. "Obviously luck is with you, Peter. The last housekeeper we had was an abominable cook. We finally had to let her go."

"Yes," Julia said, "and I felt better doing everything myself. One can only do so much knitting and needlework. But Peter, where are your children? I do so want to meet them."

"They're at their grandmother's, I thought it would be a bit too much for Mrs. Wenning, what with guests and all. But, you shall meet them tomorrow. It's Saturday, and we can have a nice visit."

"I'm afraid there will be little time," Elias said. "We must find a suitable hotel to stay at until we can find a house."

Peter laughed. "You insult me, Elias. There is no need for that. This house has six bedrooms, of which we are using only three. I insist that you stay here until you find a suitable home. It may be some time, as it is the dead of winter and there will be little available, I fear."

"I thank you, but we wouldn't want to abuse your hospitality with such a long stay."

"Think nothing of it, we can fix one of the bedrooms as a sitting room, so you and Julia can have time by yourselves. The boys can be a trifle noisy at times, and you may want some peace and quiet. Besides, if we start putting together a banking business, it will allow us to do some of the work here."

"That is a good thought, Peter. It may be to everyone's advantage for now. I think we shall accept your offer, that is if Julia approves."

Julia smiled as though she had just received a grand present.

"Of course I approve, Elias. And I think it is wonderful of Peter to make the offer. I'll be able to help Mrs. Wenning around the house, and I'm just dying to spend some time with the children. Oh! This is just too wonderful. I hate those dreary old hotels. It'll be almost like being in a house of our own."

Elias shrugged. "Well, I guess it's settled then. Peter, you've got some boarders. When will I get to meet your mentor, Mr. LeBlanc?"

"Tomorrow, I thought. But I give you fair warning, Elias, Charlie isn't completely sold on the banking idea—I leave it to you to convince him. Though he never flaunts it, Charlie has considerable funds he could invest. He was about to build another flour mill. But he's a shrewd businessman, and he likes to diversify his investments. If you give him the right impression, I think he'll go along with the deal."

"And what would 'the right impression' be?"

"First, be completely honest. Then show him that you have a plan that will benefit him. Charlie likes aggressiveness, and he demands honesty, that's all."

"He sounds like my kind of man. He has to be, to have carved out a little empire in a new land. I think Charles LeBlanc and I shall get along just fine."

Peter didn't tell Elias about the one thing Charlie might hold against him. In the event that Charlie did decide to go along with the banking venture, it would be better that Elias didn't know about Charlie's prejudice against Jews.

The next afternoon Peter introduced Elias to Charlie. It went well enough, Peter thought. Charlie was cordial and invited them to his den, where he proceeded to offer his usual cigars and brandy. Elias was about to decline the liquor, but Peter shook his head ever so slightly, and Elias accepted graciously, taking care to express his appreciation.

"This brandy has an excellent bouquet, Mr. LeBlanc. Is it French?"

Charlie smiled. "No, Mr. Oberg. It's made by an order of Catholic monks in California. They have many talents, the brothers, and making good wines and brandies is one of them, eh?"

"Are you then, a Catholic yourself, Mr. LeBlanc?"

Charlie chuckled. "Charlie's mother, she try to bring him up a good Catholic. But in my younger days I fell away from the church. Then I met Liz, and after we were married she took me along with her once in a while. So I guess I'm a Presbyterian now. Charlie he figgers it ain't the label a man wears that makes him good or bad, it's what he does."

"Well spoken, Mr. LeBlanc. My father converted from Judaism when he married my mother. So here I am, a Lutheran Jew, or at least I'm half Jew. The other half is Swede like Peter. But, you'd be surprised how many people in the old country are predjudiced against people with Jewish names. I would guess that sort of thing wouldn't be as strong in a new country like America though."

Peter couldn't resist a grin in Charlie's direction. "Maybe there's less of it Elias, but some people brought their prejudices along from the old country."

Charlie gave Peter an indignant look, then offered Elias more brandy.

"Like Charlie says, it's what a man does, not the label he wears that counts, eh? Peter says that you are interested in starting a bank, Mr. Oberg."

"Yes, I've taken my holdings from my father's bank, and I intend to reinvest them in a new institution here. I've been thinking you and Peter might help me secure a position with a bank here, so I can learn the peculiarities of this country's banking system. Then, after I'm somewhat known by business people I might secure some investors and open a new bank."

"And take some of those business people with you, eh? I like that, you got a good head for business."

"Thank you. One must not put the cart before the horse. I must be known before I'd be accepted here as a banker, it is usually that way. But then, I must find substantial investors. They must be men that can be trusted and relied upon, men such as Peter and yourself."

"You don waste no time getting to the heart of the matter," Charlie said. "Charlie he like that. He got no time for assholes that beat around the bush. What you say, Pete? You think we might be interested in banking?"

"We might, but that would depend on the terms—what percent of the business we'd own, what say in the business we'd have."

Charlie nodded. "Pete's right, what kind of a deal are you thinking about?"

Elias looked directly into Charlie's eyes. "If you and Peter could supply sufficient funds to start with, say one hundred thousand dollars, I would be willing to give you forty five percent of the business. With that, you would have seats on the board of directors."

Peter shook his head. "That would give you complete control. How much do you have, to invest?"

"Sixty thousand dollars."

Charlie puffed a great cloud of cigar smoke. "Judas! You want us to put up a hundred thousand to your sixty, and you want fifty five percent of the business. Why don't you just ask us to give it to you?"

Elias sipped his brandy then gazed levely at Peter and Charlie.

"If I am to run a bank, I must have control. Otherwise I would just be working for two investors who act as one. Part of the money you invest will purchase a substantial share in the bank, and will secure a share in the bank's profits. The rest will draw interest as a loan to the bank, and will be paid back on an appropriate schedule. As the bank grows in value, your forty five percent investment will grow in value, and so will your profits. Really, it's a good investment, considering that you will have to do nothing for it except to sit on the board."

"By damn!," Charlie said. "This man's a banker to the marrow of his bones. Charlie was bout ready to laugh in his face, an now he's got me thinking I should run right out an get the money."

"Yeah, Charlie," Peter said, "I feel the same way. But I think there's time to consider this. Right now, I think we should have a party and introduce Elias to one or two of our bankers. They may have a place for a shrewd business mind."

Over the next few months, Elias gained a position of importance with one of the major banking interests in Minneapolis. Plans were drawn up, but not announced, for the establishment of First Home and Commercial Bank of Minneapolis. Charlie and Peter would be stockholders of the bank, Elias would be president. Additional funds were promised from Elias's father in Huskvarna as the demand should arise.

At the same time, a warm friendship that was nearly a family tie grew between Peter and the Obergs. Julia's presence was pleasant, though it sometimes caused Peter to dream fitful dreams from which he would wake in a state that mere friendship could not cause. She had become "Auntie Julia" to the children, and when Peter watched her playing with them or reading them stories, his mind formed visions of what could have been. Despite this, he kept his distance from her, treating her only as a dear friend.

Julia grew attached to the children. Their laughing, sometimes rowdy presence filled a void in her life that she had denied the existence of, until now. Because of this, she was dismayed rather than elated when one evening in May Elias came home with exciting news.

"Julia dear, you'll never guess what I discovered today!"

"Let me try. You've found the map to a hoard of gold left by a dying miser. Or perhaps a wealthy businessman wants to lend you money for your bank."

"No, nothing like that. It's even better, a vice president of the bank is going to New York for a year. He'll rent us his house for a very small amount. He says he wants someone in it until he returns, and he won't let it out to just anyone. We can move in the second week in June."

Julia looked at him as though he had announced a death in the family.

Elias was perplexed. "Aren't you happy? We can move out of here and have a home of our own."

"Well yes, it's wonderful Elias. It's just so sudden, I wasn't prepared for it. I guess I hadn't thought of leaving."

"We can't abuse Peter's hospitality, you know. Business and personal relationships don't mix well." He stopped talking and looked at her suspiciously. "It's not that you don't want to leave Peter,...is it? You're not falling for him again?"

She snapped at him angrily. "No, of course not! How can you say such a thing, Elias Oberg! It's just that I've grown attached to the children, I'll miss having them around."

"Oh well Dear, if that's what it is, don't fret. I'm sure Peter wouldn't mind at all if you take care of them sometimes on Mrs. Wenning's days off. That will let you assuage your maternal instincts."

"I suppose so. Elias, do you think we'll ever have children? I do so want a family of my own."

"I don't know, Darling. The doctors didn't give us much hope, you know. A thousand to one chance, they said. Still, miracles do happen and I want children for us as badly as you. It's just that I don't talk about it. A man doesn't like to admit that he can't give his wife a child. Pray for it, maybe God will give us a way."

"Yes, Elias. I will,...maybe God will give us a way."

As the day of their departure neared, Julia became distant and quiet. She still played with the children, but she seldom talked to Elias and Peter at the dinner table. Elias was concerned, and took the problem to Peter.

"Pete, have you noticed how out of sorts Julia is?"

"Yes, I've noticed. I thought that you might have had an argument."

"No,...it's not that. She's grown to love Sven and Charles, and little Lucy. She hates the thought of leaving them, and so she's distressed."

"Yeah, I know she loves them. And they love her. But, what can we do about it?"

"Well, I suggested to her that you might let her take care of them when Mrs. Wenning isn't here,...just until you get home, of course. But I know she won't ask you. I thought you might ask her if she'd do it."

"Golly,...I don't know about that, Elias. Elizabeth always takes them on those days, she'd have a fit."

"She can take them anytime, she's right next door. I don't know what Julia will do all alone at the house. I'm really afraid for her, Pete. There were a couple of times in Huskvarna when it really got bad. That was why I had to get a housekeeper, to have someone with her."

"You mean...she might...?"

"I don't know, she wants children and she gets awful melancholy when she thinks about it too much. Sometimes I fear for her."

Peter looked at him gravely. "I wouldn't want anything to happen because I didn't want to help. I'll ask her if she wants to take care of the children, then. If she does, I'll talk to Elizabeth. She won't like it, but she'll understand."

That night, after the children had gone to bed, Elias said he had some work to do and retired to the rooms upstairs, leaving Julia and Peter in the sitting room. Julia was working quietly on a piece of embroidery. Peter laid down the book he had been reading, "Julia."

"Yes, Peter."

"I've been thinking about your leaving, and something bothers me."

"Why, what would that be?"

"Oh, I guess it's nothing, really. But, I've been thinking about how the boys and Lucy love you."

"And I love them, Peter. It'll be hard to leave them—I hate the thought. But we've got to have our own home."

"I know, but I wonder if it's good for the children to have you torn out of their lives. I wondered if you might spend some time with them, at least for a while. Would you consider taking care of them some times when Mrs. Wenning isn't here."

Julia brightened. "You know I'd love that, Peter. But I don't want to intrude in your life. It's Elias…isn't it? He asked you to say that, didn't he?"

"No, why would he have? He didn't say a word about you and the children," Peter lied. "I thought it might be better for the children."

"And you really want me to come?"

"Of course I do, it'll make me feel better knowing you're with them at least part of the time. I'm asking you to do it for them…and me."

"Then I'll do it, Peter. For you and the children, because I love you all."

After the Obergs moved to their home, Julia stayed with Peter's children a day or two each week. She glowed with the sense of fulfillment it gave her, and she and Peter took to having a cup of coffee together, chatting happily until she left. On those evenings, the house seemed lonely to him, and the absense of his wife haunted him. He became painfully aware of the need for a woman in his life. But he couldn't bring himself to search the social life of his world for someone to take Lucy's place.

Those same nights Julia returned home to the silence of the big house on banker's row. Elias often worked late, indeed sometimes it seemed that he did nothing but work. As his plans for the new bank came closer to fruition, he became more distant with Julia. It was like he had a mistress, she thought. She almost wished he did—a mistress would give her a cause for complaint. His diligence in securing his future, and hers, did not. In her marriage she had been denied motherhood, which was one side of her nature. Now she felt that the other half of her being had also become empty. The only true happiness she now knew was with Peter and his children.

This Friday in August, the heat in Peter's office was particularly oppressive. The great fan on the ceiling turned lazily, but did little to ease his discomfort. The clock on the wall chimed once, and he looked up, its hands stood at 1:30. Hell, he thought, I might as well quit for the week. He picked up his jacket, stripped off in the early hours of the morning, and with a word to his bookeeper, left for home.

The children had been fussy with the heat, and Julia was finally able to coax them into taking a nap. It would be hours yet before Peter returned home. The heat was oppressive, and she felt sticky all over. A bath would help, she thought. She drew water into the huge cast iron tub and stretched out in it with pleasure. Oh God, she thought if I could just stay like this forever.

Her day hadn't been good—Elias had left early, saying he wouldn't be home until late in the evening. She had hoped to go to the theater, but now that was off. Why couldn't he be more like Peter? Peter was always considerate, and he was so attractive. If she had only known how things would turn out, she sighed aloud and reclined there, daydreaming.

She sometimes indulged in fantasies now, and most often Peter was in them. She imagined how he would look in bed. He was still lean and muscular, and still had his curly black mane. Elias was starting to go to paunch, and his hair was receding already. Julia wrinkled her nose when she imagined how he would look when he was forty, fat and bald with thick spectacles hanging on his prominent nose. She was lost in a particularly exciting fantasy when she heard the entry door close. Jarred back into reality, she scrambled from the tub and grabbed for a towel.

"Hello-o-o, is anybody here?" Peter's voice drifted up the stairway.

"Oh damn!," Julia said in a whisper. She grabbed Peter's big dressing robe from its hook by the tub and pulled it on.

"Hello, Julia are you here?"

Julia ran to the landing at the top of the stairs and put her forefinger to her lips. "Shush Peter, you'll wake the children."

Peter stared up at her with an incredulous grin. Julia stood there dripping water, her shapely legs and bare feet showing below the hem of his robe. Her face was washed clean of makeup and glistened with wetness. Her hair was pulled up under a towel exposing her slender neck and delicate ears. He thought that he had never seen anyone so madly provocative in his life. He took a step upward, then another. Julia pulled the robe closer.

"Wait a few minutes...while I dress." She said, but she stood still, looking down at him as he took yet another step up the stairs. He was smiling at her in a way she hadn't seen in years, his sweat dampened hair was a curly, unruly mane. His shirt was rolled at the sleeves and open at the collar, exposing hard muscled arms and a fringe of black chest hair. She retreated a few steps backward, then stood there mesmerized by this living fantasy. Peter reached the top of the stairs then stepped forward to her, placing his hands on her hips, searching her face, looking deep into her eyes.

Julia felt, rather than saw, his eyes burning into hers. The face before her was no longer grinning, it reflected a longing that she herself now felt. She placed her hands on his chest, feeling the tightening of his muscles as she did so. For long moments they stood there on the brink of something that was stronger than their virtue. Then Julia slipped her arms behind his neck, and he drew her to him in gentle submission to his love for her. Her body against his evoked the passion within him, and he kissed her hard, desperately, hungrily, finding her lips with his. Yet, when their lips parted, he went no further, transfixed between desire and the sense of morality that was ingrained in him.

Silently Julia dropped one hand from his neck and began to unbutton his shirt, then she slipped her hand inside and ran it over his chest, caressing him as though with fire and ice at once. Peter picked her up and carried her to his bedroom. They made love then, as only a man and a woman in an absolute joyous abandon of passion can, savoring each other as though the act of love could somehow wash away the years of their separation. And when their bodies were satisfied, they lay in each other's arms, knowing they must part, but denying it in their hearts, as if somehow the closeness they felt could wipe away the reality of their lives.

"Why?" Peter whispered, "why did it have to be this way?"

"Because we were too young, and too foolish," Julia murmured. "And now it can't be right for us…ever."

"Why? It could still be, if we cared enough."

Julia was about to answer, when they heard a gurgling sound down the hall. She jumped up and pulled Peter's robe on.

"Get dressed Peter, the children are waking."

Peter hurriedly pulled his clothing on and went down to the kitchen. He took the bottle of brandy from the cupboard and poured himself a good portion. Then he went out and sat alone on the front step. He wanted to go back to Julia, but now there were sounds of boyish voices clammering for attention from their aunt.

He couldn't bring himself to be with all of them together, it would be too much like a family. They were not a family and the chances were remote that they ever would be. Yet, he desperately wanted her with them—he sat alone with his brandy until a carriage came for her. His mood was no longer buoyant, instead he felt depressed. Today had been a mistake. Yet, as she was leaving, he touched her arm.

"Will you come again, like today?"

She looked at him, her face a mixture of love and confusion. "Yes, Peter. I know I shouldn't, but I will. Yes, I'll come when you want me to."

As the weeks passed, Peter and Julia continued to meet. Somewhat like a narcotic, their illicit relationship demanded constant renewal. They no longer questioned what the future held for them, but took their time together, ignoring the possibility of the terrible consequences it could bring.

Business matters continued, and the framing of Elias' banking venture was nearing completion. The relationship between Elias and Peter remained outwardly amicable, though within himself Peter's resentment of Elias was growing. Peter now saw the man as an obstruction in his life, that stood between him and happiness with Julia. Though Peter was sometimes curt with Elias, Elias gave no sign that he regarded it as anything but the normal ups and downs of a business relationship.

Then one day in November, Charlie appeared at Peter's office. He seemed troubled, and after shaking Peter's hand and drawing out a cigar he spoke.

"Pete, Charlie he got something that's bothering him. Maybe it's nothing, maybe it's something bad."

Peter looked at Charlie curiously. "It's not like you to be worried about nothing, Charlie. Tell me about it, and maybe I can help."

Charlie drew on his cigar and blew the smoke out slowly. "I stopped by here yesterday afternoon, an they told me you were gone."

"Yes, I had some business to attend to."

"What kind of business, Pete, eh? Liz said you come home early, said you come home early bout every week."

Peter flushed. "I didn't know Elizabeth was watching to see when I come home."

"Well Pete, usually she wouldn't. Liz ain't one of those busybodies that's always prying into other people's business. But she says it's always when Julia's taking care of the kids."

Peter reddened more. "Well, I guess that sometimes I get home early when she's there. We like to have a cup of coffee together and talk. She makes life a little less lonely for me with Lucy gone."

"Maybe that's all right, Pete. But maybe sombody's gonna get the wrong idea an take it to Elias. Charlie don need to tell you what that would do to the banking project, eh?"

"There's always someone that will make something out of nothing, Charlie. It's nobody's business when I get home, or who's there when I arrive."

"Maybe not, Pete. But Charlie, he's got an investment to protect. Maybe what you an Julia got going is innocent as a Mass in church. But if it wasn't, if you were doing something else with another man's wife, it wouldn't be good. An if that man was your business partner an Charlie's, it would wreck the partnership. We always been honest with each other, Pete. Charlie, he don't want to know what you got going. But Charlie he thinks it maybe be better if you don come home early when Elias's wife is there, eh?"

"And if I do, Charlie?"

"Then...Charlie gonna have to pull out of the bank deal."

"But, it's almost ready to go. What would you tell Elias?"

Charlie puffed out another cloud of smoke. "Maybe the truth, Pete. If that got out, it could hurt more than the bank deal. People in this city, they don like that kind of fooling around."

"You're threatening me, Charlie. I never question your life, even when you go down town."

"But that's something that don't involve business, eh? The businessmen in this town turn their backs on that. Maybe that's what you should do, Pete. Go down to Lola's once in a while. Or maybe you should start looking for another woman. God knows Pete's a young man, he needs to bed a woman. But we don need trouble, Pete."

Peter knew that his mentor was serious, but he had avoided confronting what he knew to be the truth. Now he was staring at the stark reality of it. He could not, now or ever, have Julia as his wife. He had invested too much of himself in his business to give it up. His spirit seemed to shrink within him with the knowledge he was forced to recognize.

"Yeah… you're right, Charlie. It doesn't look good, I'll quit coming home early, except for once. I'll have to tell Julia."

Charlie saw the despondency in Peter's face, and he felt sorry for his protege. Yet, there were business and social considerations that were being violated, and that he could not tolerate.

"I know it's tough, Pete. The right woman can do things to a man that makes him forget what he's gotta do, eh? But one day, you just gonna smile about it. You know Charlie's right, now do what you gotta do."

The rest of that week Peter was withdrawn and irritable. Though he was at his office, he was almost indifferent to the demands of business. When his long time friend

Gus stopped by to go over sales plans for the developing western furniture market, Peter was vague and inattentive.

Gus was perplexed. "You got a problem, Pete? I haven't seen you this way since you got the letter from Sarah, when we were both just starting with Charlie."

Peter looked at Gus soberly. Here was what he needed, his friend, his confidante. "Try going back a little further, Gus."

"The only other time was in the logging camp, when Julia's mother wrote you."

"Yeah. Lightening does strike twice in the same place."

"Oh shit! I knew she was here, but I thought it was long over between you. You mean that you and Julia..."

Peter nodded dismally. "For a few months, now."

"Damn! I didn't think you'd ever look at her again, after what she did to you. You got to be out of your head, Pete."

"Tell me, Gus. I'm in real deep, I love her and I have to give her up."

"Her husband...what's his name? He find out about it?"

"No, Oberg doesn't know, at least he hasn't given any indication, but Charlie suspects. He threatened to pull out on the bank deal."

"Oh shit! It's bad enough to get kicked in the teeth once, but you're the winner. You oughta learn to keep your pants buttoned, Pete. That thing of yours is gonna get you killed one day."

"I know that already Gus, you don't have to rub salt in the wound!"

"I'm sorry, Pete. But what am I supposed to say? You know she dumped you for this Oberg guy, and now you go right back to her. I guess I should be more sympathetic, but you're thinking with your pecker, Pete."

"Damn it Gus! Is that all you can think of? It's a lot more than that, I guess I never quit loving her, it just came back now that she's here."

"All the more reason for you to get your ass away from her. She's married Pete, and there's nothing you can do about it. Did she say she'd leave him for you?"

Peter shook his head. "She said it couldn't ever be right with us."

Gus was incredulous. "Damn it, there it is! You got to be the dumbest guy I know as far as women are concerned. She's never gonna be yours, and still you're mooning like a school boy. I'll tell you what, let's go out and get drunk, that always helps."

Peter laughed. "I guess you're right Gus. I'll buy, if you listen."

"You better buy the best, if I have to listen to more of this shit."

The two friends went out, and the next day Peter felt better, despite a nagging hangover. His resolve had strengthened. The next day he would talk to Julia.

Julia was worried. Elias was becoming resentful of the time she spent with Peter's children. This morning he had become angry when she told him she was going. Could it be that he was suspicious of her and Peter? Julia thought so, and now there was this, she had always been very regular but she had missed her time. What if she was with child? If she was, and she told Peter, he would insist that she leave Elias and marry him. Her affair with Peter was exhilarating, and she truly thought she loved him. But she always knew she couldn't marry him. She had told him that, if not in those exact words, the meaning had been clear. She couldn't break up her home and bring disaster on all of them, not when she was just becoming accepted into society here in Minneapolis.

She liked being part of the new, vital community. As Elias progressed in his position at the bank, the need to attend social functions became more frequent. She had become part of the circle of women who hosted those functions. When Elias had his own bank, she would automatically achieve the upper strata of society. To give that up would be unthinkable. And, if she did bear a child, Elias would think their prayers had been answered. Her life would be beautifully complete. She sighed, but what of Peter?

Peter walked up the steps of his house later then he usually did when Julia was there. He had steeled himself for this encounter, but still he had no heart for it. After all the years they had been apart, they had come together with a passion that set fire to his spirit. To stop it now was going to be very difficult.

At times like this he cursed his ambition. Must a man sell everything, his very being for the sake of power and wealth? He looked at himself and didn't like what he saw very well. Still, what he had with Julia wasn't right, and he must pay the piper some time. It might as well be now, before all else was destroyed. He hoped she wouldn't cry, it would make him feel worse than he already did. He opened the door and smelled fresh coffee. Julia must be feeling domestic. He didn't really like it when she did that, it brought out visions of her by his fireside.

"Hi, is that you Peter? Her voice came from the kitchen, it was cheery and inviting. She appeared, a cup of coffee in her hand. "I've been waiting for you Peter, you're late."

"I know, a little unexpected business. Where are the children?"

She smiled. "They're still sleeping, we can have some coffee and talk.

"That's good, there's something I need to say."

"About us?"

"Yes, about us." Peter swallowed against the tightness in his throat. "We need to talk about us, Julia."

Julia motioned for him to sit down at the table, then poured him coffee and pushed a plate of cookies to him. "Oatmeal and raisin, Elias loves them. You look so serious, Peter. Is something very wrong?"

"Not horribly, it's just that I've been thinking about us. I love you Julia, I always have, except when I was hating you for quitting on us. But it's not going anywhere, we can't be married, and I can't do this forever. It's not right for me or for you, and not for Elias. I envy him, but he didn't come between us back then, not really. It was the distance we were apart, it was me leaving, it was you giving up on me."

"Are you saying it's over between us, that you don't want to see me any more?"

"Yes…I'm sorry,…I am.…You don't seem surprised."

Julia started to laugh first in giggles, then louder and stronger until she had to catch her breath.

"Am I being a fool? Is that what's so funny?"

"No, dearest Peter, you're not a fool at all. I was thinking the very same thing this morning, about splitting up, I mean. I was afraid of telling you, because I thought you wouldn't take it well. That's why I was laughing."

"You mean you were going to quit seeing me,...again!"

She smiled. "Yes Peter, it's funny, isn't it?"

"I don't know, it's kind of insulting, don't you like making love with me? Am I that bad?"

"You are a fantastic, virile, man. And I'll daydream about you for the rest of my life."

Peter grinned ruefully. "Golly, I wish you hadn't said that."

"Why?"

"Because I was all set to be mad at you again. That would make it easier to quit seeing you. Now I'll be dreaming about you again."

"Oh Peter! You are such a hopeless romantic."

"Gus says I'm dumb as far as women are concerned."

"You didn't tell him about us?!"

"I had to talk to somebody."

"Oh God,...what if he tells someone else? Peter, that was dumb!"

"Don't get excited. Gus is my best friend, except for Charlie. He'd never breathe a word."

"Just the same, I think it was dumb of you to talk about us. I didn't talk to anyone."

"That's only because your mother's in Sweden."

"Peter Hokanson, you're infuriating."

"No more than you. What made you decide to quit me anyway?"

"It was wrong, and I finally came to my senses. I realized I could never leave my husband."

"First you couldn't leave your mother, now you can't leave your husband. I wish to hell you would have worried about leaving me half that much. I thought you loved me, you said it in bed."

"That was in the heat of the moment.... Oh Peter! You know I love you. That doesn't mean it would work! There's Charlie and Elias, and your children...and our friends. They wouldn't let us be together, our lives would be ruined. Then finally we'd be hating each other as well. Isn't it better to part while we still love each other?"

"Oh damn it anyway! I know you're right, and Gus is right, and Charlie is right. But my head tells my heart that, and my heart won't believe it. I came over here to tell you we're through, and I did it. So how come I don't feel like I've done the right thing, Julia?!"

Julia got up and walked to Peter. She cradled his head against her breasts and spoke to him gently, like a mother consoling a child.

"My sweet, darling Peter, I hate it too, but there's nothing else to do, so I must go." She bent and kissed his forehead, then walked quickly out of his life.

Chapter 17

A Letter from Kat

Charlie LeBlanc took the solitary letter from his mailbox and stood studying the envelope. It was addressed to Mr. Charles LeBlanc, and bore the return address, K. Rousseau, 27 Saint Charles Ave., New Orleans, Louisiana. He frowned at the unfamiliar name, then his face lit up and he ran into the house.

"Liz, Liz, come here quick! We got a letter from Kat!"

As Elizabeth came running, he tore open the envelope and withdrew the letter. It read:

December 10, 1903

Dearest Papa and Mama,

I fondly hope that you both are well and happy. I have missed you, and all our family and friends terribly. I would have written much sooner, but my pride and shame would not let me. I am deeply sorry for the way I left, and I beg your forgiveness.

Though I know that I have done nothing to deserve it, I need your help, not just for myself, but for your granddaughter. Little April will be three years old on the twenty-fourth of March. We named her April because it is the beginning of spring, the time of newness and promise. And she is that, a sweet little girl whom I dearly love, and the only promise in my life.

It does not go well with Girard and me. Almost from the beginning he drank too much, and because of it, there often was not enough money for the rent and food for us. But then, he was always kind and loving to our baby and me when he was sober. But now, he has taken to using opium, and he has become unstable. He has changed from a loving husband and father to something I no longer recognize as Girard. His need now, seems to be only for the substance that rules him. He uses all the money he makes as a musician to buy the vile drug, and flies into a viscious rage at me when I will not give him the money I earn cleaning at his club after it has closed. The hardship of our poverty is hard to bear, but now I also fear for the safety of my child.

I beg you to send me enough money to return home, so I can start a new life for April and me. Papa, I know that your first impulse may be to come and get me, because you always were protective of me. Please do not, because I fear that Girard might do something terrible if he sees you come for us. He always carries a knife now, because of the dangers we live with. And with the drugs and liquor, he cannot be trusted.

If you send money, please send it to Henry Gibson, #14 Basin Street, New Orleans, Louisiana. He is an old, black gentleman who has been my friend since I came here. He is kind, and can be trusted. If you send it to me, Girard might get it, and it would be bad for me.

I love you both dearly, and I ask you to tell Lucy that her sister is coming home. I cannot wait to see you all. I will count the hours until I can leave here.

With sincerest love,
Kathryn

"May the devil take him! Charlie, he go and kill that bastard himself!"

Elizabeth was sobbing, streams of tears began making little rivulets in the powder on her face.

"No Charlie! You saw what she wrote, you can't endanger her more! Oh-h-h, my poor baby trapped with that monster! And that little child!...To have such a beast for a father!...Charlie, you've got to send her money now, right away! We've got to get them home, away from there!"

"You right, Liz! Charlie, he send them lots of money. He buy the damned railroad if he have to! My poor little Kat,... she so hard headed, but she not deserve no son-abitch like that. Charlie ever see that bastard, he gonna kill him. Come on Liz, get your coat. We gonna get Kat an her little baby home!"

Elizabeth dried her eyes as best she could, though she wasn't finished crying. "There's just one thing, Charlie."

"What's that?"

"She doesn't know about Lucy. What are we going to tell her?"

Charlie thought for a moment. "We ain't gonna tell her anything, not now. Kat got all the grief she can bear right now. But by our Holy Mother, when the time comes, Charlie don't know how he gonna tell her that Lucy's dead."

"Hello! Is anybody home?" The voice was accompanied by a hearty knocking on the front door.

"It's Pete," Charlie said, "we gonna tell him bout this?"

"Oh yes! We have to Charlie. Kathryn and Peter were close before he married Lucille. He might be able to help."

Elizabeth ran to open the door. "Peter, do come in. We have such news, so wonderful and yet frightening at the same time."

Elizabeth paused to blow her nose and dab at her eyes, which were starting to ooze tears all over again.

Peter looked at her, and then at Charlie, who was still flushed with anger. "What kind of news? You both look like there's been a death in the family."

"It's Kathryn,...she's got a baby...and they don't have any money...and Girard is a terrible brute!" Elizabeth started wailing.

Charlie put an arm around his wife. "Liz, you jus calm yourself. You don need to explain to Pete, he can read the letter for himself."

Peter took the letter from Charlie and began to read, his face became grim. When he had finished he looked up and his eyes were black with anger.

"I'm going to get her," he said quietly.

"But she said not to....Girard..."

"She was writing to Charlie, Liz. And she's right, Charlie shouldn't go. But I will...today,...on the first train out."

Charlie shook his head. "It's not your concern, Pete. Charlie is Kat's old man, it's Charlie's place to take care of his little girl, eh?"

"No Charlie, we're family and you're not as young as you were back in your logging days. If something happened to you, Kat would never forgive me, and I wouldn't either."

"Charlie he's not afraid to fight any man, specially that damned, horn blowing drunk."

"I know that for a fact Charlie. But Girard is half your age, and he'd probably use a knife if it came to fighting. You have to let me do this, I can't help but think she wouldn't have left except for me."

"Kat's leaving was her own doing, Pete. But if that's the way it is with you, go...go get her back for her mama and papa. An,...Charlie ain't much for praying, but he gonna pray for you an Kat,...an for that little girl that Charlie's never seen."

Pete nodded. "I'll go pack a few clothes. And Liz, you'll take care of the boys and Lucy?"

Elizabeth hugged him. "Of course I will! And Charlie will tend your factory. Go get Kathryn home for us Peter, and God bless you and keep you safe!"

That Friday night Peter was once again on a train to Chicago. But this time he wasn't on a holiday. He thought of Kat and her abuse at the hands of Girard. What sort of man was he? A drunkard, a user of drugs, ill tempered and unpredictable, a man who would not hesitate to use the knife he carried? Peter touched his hand to the 38 caliber Bulldog tucked under the waistband of his trousers. He had never had to use it for protection in the logging camp, but now the feel of it was reassuring.

On Sunday morning, Kat was preparing to clean the club later than usual. She hated Sunday especially much because the Saturday night parties seldom ended before three or four in the morning. This morning the revelers had stayed until five and Girard had not returned home until after six. As usual, he was drunk and in a foul mood, scowling at her when she met him at the door.

She hated leaving April in his care when he was like that. But she had no other choice, she had no other place to leave the child at that hour, and she needed every cent she earned just for food and shelter. There was nothing left to pay for the child's care, even if someone would take her.

Girard threw himself face down on the bed without a word, and was instantly asleep. He seldom spoke to her when he came home now. But it was terribly late, and April would be waking soon. Kathryn sat down on the bed beside him, hoping he wasn't too drunk to care for her. He reeked of whiskey as usual. But now he also smelled strongly of cheap perfume. It was too much for Kathryn, she began pummeling him with her fists, beating on his back with a fury she had never known.

"You bastard!" she screamed. "You stinking, drunken, whoring bastard!

Waking from his stupor, Girard turned over onto his back and seized her pounding fists. Surprise gave way to anger as he began to realize what was happening.

"Hold now, bitch! Is this how you treat your husband? I've had a long night, and you wake me by pounding me like some insane bar maid! Stop it now, or I'll teach you to have more respect for me!"

Kathryn tore her arms from his grip, and stood up screaming at him.

"Respect?! You want me to have respect for you?!…You leave your wife and child penniless so that you can have drink and drugs, and now you're bedding some whore!

You want me to respect you?! Who is she, that red headed slut that carries drinks like a peasant woman feeding the pigs?"

Girard staggered to his feet, his face a mask of drunken rage.

"Marie isn't a peasant—she's more woman than you'll ever be! But, I'm not bedding her, we just had a few drinks together! And what if I was, do you expect me to come home and bed a slovenly bitch like you?"

"You are bedding her you drunken bastard, that's why you don't love me anymore, isn't it!?

Girard looked at her and his rage turned to an expression of evil glee.

"So that's what this is all about, my bitch wife is jealous! Well, come here, and I'll show you there's enough of me left for you."

He grabbed her by the wrist and threw her to the bed. Crushing her with his body, he held her head in his hands and kissed her hard. For the second time in her life, Kathryn bit a man, this time it was with complete rage and hatred. Girard jumped up, grabbing his mouth in pain. Kathryn followed him, raking his face again and again with her nails. Then, he hit her hard, again and again, not stopping until she fell into oblivion.

Kathryn slowly gained her senses. Somewhere in the darkness of her mind she heard a sound, dimly at first, then louder and more urgent. A child was crying—then awareness came to her, it was April. Slowly she forced herself up from the floor, fighting the dizziness that engulfed her. She stumbled haltingly, then almost fell, catching herself on the bureau near her, her face inches from the mirror. Kathryn drew back in horror, the image she saw wasn't her, surely it was her eyes fooling her. She blinked, feeling pain around her eyes as she did so, then looked again.

The face bore little resemblance to hers. The eyes squinted out through purple swelling, and crusted blood formed a hideous streak down the left side of her face. Her nose was swollen and crooked, and the rest of her face was a mass of bruises. She stood there in shock, the dizziness threatening to engulf her again. Slowy the weakness she felt gave way to anger, and with anger her strength returned. She looked about her—he was gone and only the insistent crying of her child remained. Kathryn dragged herself to the storage room that served as April's nursery. The little girl was standing in her packing box crib. She stopped crying as her mother appoached and looked at her quizzically.

"Mama owee?"

Katryn cried and laughed at the same time.

"Yes Sweetheart, Mama has owee."

She laid April down and changed her diaper, thinking remotely that the child should have been potty trained by now, then she dressed her and gave her some milk and porridge. That done, she picked the little girl up and walked to the door down the hall. A large, matronly, black woman opened the door—she stared at Kathryn with horror.

"My lands! Missus Rousseau, is dat you?"

Without waiting for an answer, she took the child from Kathryn's arms and helped her to a threadbare couch. Then she hurried to her kitchen and came back with a bowl of water and a cloth. She began swabbing the blood from Kathryn's face.

"My lands! It was dat husbun of yours, wasn't it?"

"Um-hmm."

"I heard the commotion going on, but I didn't 'spect he was beatin you. If'n I did, I woulda come over an' give him a few swipes. Ain't no man oughta beat his woman. Dis old woman had a man like dat once. I got to thinking dat one day he gonna kill me, so next time he started on me I hit him wit' a piece of stove wood an chased him out wit' a butcher knife. He nevah come back, left his clothes an' all. An you know what? Dis woman nevah missed him at all—ain't nobody needs to get beat on."

Kathryn giggled, despite the pain in her face.

"You laughin', Missus Rousseau, dat's good. But you gotta get away from dat man. Once they start beatin' on you, they don't stop."

"I know, Nellie. I'm going home as soon as Papa sends me some money. But I was wondering if I could stay with you until then."

The motherly black woman shook her head. "I'd sure nuff like to have you, Missus. But dat man comin' back, an dis gonna be too close, no tellin what he gonna do. Ain't you got someplace away from heah you can go to? I'll sure nuff help you."

"There might be, an old man over on Basin Street. But we used to live there, and it's close to where Girard works, he might look for me there."

"Well it's sure nuff better'n waitin' for him to come heah an maybe beat on you agin. Get a few things you need together an' I'll help you outta heah. Den we gonna have a doctor look at dat nose. My lands, he done squooshed it 'bout off'n your face."

"But, I don't have any money to pay for a doctor."

"Don't you fret 'bout dat, Missus. Dis doctor do 'bout half his fixin' for nothin'. Reckon one more bit ain't gonna bother him."

Doctor Weinberg was a chubby, balding bespectacled little man who exuded good humor despite the dingy unkemptness of his office. When Nellie and Kathryn arrived he had just finished setting a broken arm on a skinny, black boy.

"Best stay away from your paw when he's drunk, Billy," he said.

Then he waved away the handful of change the boy's mother offered.

"You need that for food, Corrie. You can pay me something when your man finds work again."

He turned to Nellie and Kathryn and his face became grim momentarily.

"By the beard of Elijah, doesn't anybody just get sick anymore? Let me guess, your husband got drunk and beat you up, didn't he?"

"Uh—huh."

"Well, he did a good job of it. Come into my examining room and we'll see what I can do for you. I wish the police would do something about these brutish men. Talked to the chief about it once. He said a man's home is his own, and what he does there is no concern of theirs, as long as he doesn't kill somebody. Fact is that happens all too often. They drag the rascal away, and they bury the poor woman. Shouldn't be that way. Now let's see what we can do about that nose, the bruises will heal on their own. You don't faint easy, do you? It's going to be a little painful."

Henry Gibson forced himself up on his arthritic legs and hobbled, grumbling to the door of his shabby apartment. He opened it a crack and peered out, then threw the door wide with appalled concern.

"My lands! Miz Rousseau, what happened to you? Come into the house an' sit down, yo'all look purely awful."

"Her no good bum of a husbun done beat her proper." Nellie spat out the words.

"Mister Girard? I never woulda thought it. He always looked to be a decent sort when yo'all lived here."

"He was," Kathryn said, "until he started using drugs. It changed him."

"Always knew he liked his likker, but that's a different pot of beans. That other stuff is purely evil, Miz. No suh, old Henry likes a spot of booze now an agin, but they ain't no way he's gonna touch that other stuff. Makes a man into a beast, sure enough."

"Fact is, Henry Gibson, dis poor gal needs a place to lite for awhile. Her pa's gonna send her some money so's she can go back home. But ain't no way she can go back to her place. How 'bout you put'n her up for a spell?"

Nellie looked at Henry with the demeanor of authority, her words were more a demand than a request.

Henry squirmed under her imperative gaze. "I dunno, I got my grandson Jesse stayin' with me while he looks for work. Wouldn't look fittin' for a white woman to be stayin' here."

Nellie was unrelenting. "Mistah Gibson, ain't you got no Christian feelin's? Dis poor chile done fall on bad times, we gotta help her or we is as bad as her husbun."

"Please Henry, it's just for a few days until my money comes," Kathryn implored, "I'll stay out of sight, and I'll pay you for your trouble. I don't have any other place to go."

"I ain't one to be messin' in other folks doin's, Miz Rousseau. But bein' that you was always decent t'me, I'm goin to take you in. But if that man of yours comes around, I can't stand up to him,...no ma'am!"

"You won't have to Henry, I don't think he'll come here as long as nobody saw me here. And if he does, I'll leave."

Kathryn was safe for the moment, but her mind was not at ease. She prayed that her father would send her money soon, but she didn't know, and that was very hard.

Peter arrived in New Orleans at noon on Monday. He immediately hired a hack to take him to 27 Saint Charles Avenue. He was apprehensive. What would he find when he got there? Would Kat be there alone? If Girard were there, would he let Kat go without a fight? Peter wished he had brought Gus with him, it would be better if there were two. He dismissed the thought, he was alone and there was no help for it now. At last the carriage drew up in front of a shoddy stucco building.

"This is it." The driver said. "Would you be wanting me to wait? It'll cost you extra."

"Yes, wait. I won't be long, and there'll be two more passengers for you. Here's a dollar for now, I'll double that for the return."

The last vestiges of paint were peeling from the sagging door, which scraped protestingly on its sill as Peter opened it. He stood at the bottom of a worn staircase. A feeble light fought through an accumulation of grime on a single small window high on the wall. The thought that Kat lived here sickened him. Anger at the man who had brought her to this pitiful condition rose in him hotly, unleashing a tide of adrenalin into his bloodstream. He stepped briskly, noisily, up the stairs to a narrow hall. There were two doors, both scarred and cracked from age and abuse. He pounded on the first, there was silence for a moment, then the sound of a man swearing. The door opened enough to reveal a haggard, unshaven face and bloodshot,watery eyes. The mouth opened, revealing smoke-yellowed teeth.

"Who the hell are you? If you're here to collect the rent, forget it, I'll have it for you next week!" The door started to close, but Peter stopped it with his foot.

"I don't give a damn about your rent—I'm Peter Hokanson."

"Who the hell is that?" The door opened further, Girard stood there naked, except for his wrinkled trousers. He was dirty, smelly, unkempt and annoyed.

"Kat's brother-in-law, I've come to see her."

The eyes narrowed. "Oh yeah, you're the big shot that married her sister. Well, you can go back to where you come from, Kat's gone."

"You're lying!"

"Nobody calls Girard Rousseau a liar, get your ass out of here before I kick it down the stairs."

Girard kicked Peter's foot out of the doorway and started closing the door, but Peter drove his shoulder against it, sending Girard staggering across the room.

"I said, I'm here to see Kat, where is she?"

"She's not here, asshole! I don't know where the damned slut is! If I did, I'd slap the shit out of the bitch!"

Peter's anger turned to fury. He lunged at Girard and drove him up against the wall, his hands instinctivly finding a hold on the Frenchman's throat.

"You worthless bastard! You'll tell me where she is! And when you do, I'm taking her out of this shithole!"

The statement infuriated Girard. He drove a fist hard into Peter's stomach, then grabbed him by the hair and brought his head down to a smashing blow from his knee. Peter staggered across the room and crashed into the iron stove, then fell to the floor amid a clatter of rusty stovepipes and falling soot. He slumped against the stove, his senses dimming, pain exploding in his face. He struggled to see his adversary through the darkness in his mind and the blackness of the soot in his eyes.

Girard was laughing, a rasping, vicious sound, then he was kneeling in front of Peter. He was a shadow, an indistinct form slowly materializing into a face that was the essence of evil. He was grinning, and in his hand was a knife, its slender blade waving in arcs bare inches from Peter's face. Girard began speaking, his voice an ominous whisper that was terrifying in its softness.

"You aren't taking Kat anyplace, bigshot. Because you're going to be dead. I'm going to slit your throat, then watch you pump out your blood. Then I'm going to find Kat and show you to her, and maybe if she begs hard enough, I'll let her live."

Fear cleared Peter's mind and drove the paralysis from his body. Desperately he grasped Girard's wrist, forcing it up and away. It wasn't enough—Girard forced the blade back slowly, deliberately, laughing his rasping laugh. Peter's right hand found the revolver in his belt—with the strength born of terror he pushed Girard back once more and fired. With an expression of complete surprise Girard lurched backward and the knife flew from his hand, making little rattling sounds as it skidded across the room. Then he crumpled to the floor and lay still.

Peter remained slumped against the stove, gasping for breath, fighting to clear the chaos of his mind. He stared at Girard lying supine on the floor at his feet. Blood was oozing from a small hole a few inches below his neck. His eyes were closed as though he were sleeping. Peter pulled himself to his knees and bent over the man, feeling the side of his neck, just below his jaw. There was a pulse, but it was rapid and light. Shakily he rose to his feet—only then was he aware of the revolver in his hand. Wearily he placed it back in his waistband and turned to the open door.

A large black woman was standing in the doorway, her eyes wide with horror. She screamed, a piercing, ear-shattering scream, then fled down the stairs. Peter heard shouting voices in the street below, then the clattter of shod hooves on paving stones. There was no need to summon help, that had already been done.

He turned back to Girard, blood was still oozing from his wound. He took a folded handkerchief from his pocket and pressed it down on the wound, then looked for something to bind it with. The bedroom…he got up and went to the bed. He stripped off a dingy sheet and tore two strips from it. One he folded into a thick wad, and pressed it down over his handkerchief. Then he wrapped the other strip over one of Girard's shoulders and under the other and tied it tightly over the compress. Girard was still breathing but he was pale, and his skin was cold. Peter found a worn blanket in the bedroom and covered him.

Damn, what a mess, he thought. What if Girard dies? I could run now, and hope I make it back home. But I must be a mess—he looked at the front of his shirt. It was spattered with blood. His nose was bleeding and swollen from the blow it had received. He hadn't noticed it in his shock, but now he tore another piece off the sheet and tried to stanch the flow. He might as well wait for the police, he wouldn't get far in this condition. The revolver…he thought, it would be better if it isn't on me. He pulled it out of his waist band and removed the four unspent cartridges. Then he laid it on the kitchen table and sat down tiredly on a wobbly chair. Damn, what a mess. He was dimly aware of the clattering of horses' hooves and wheels in the street, then voices, followed by the stamping of feet on the stairs.

Inspector Cousteau stopped in the doorway and surveyed the scene before him. Two other policemen peered over his shoulders.

"What have we here?" he asked, addressing no one in particular. He looked at the man on the floor, then at Peter. "Did you kill that man?" His face showed something like recognition, then quickly returned to a professional demeanor.

Peter shook his head. "He's still alive, he needs a doctor."

Cousteau turned to one of the policemen. "Get Bremmer." Then he knelt beside Girard and felt for a pulse. "Just barely, I'd say, you do this bandaging?"

Peter nodded. "He was bleeding."

"But you shot him? Never have I seen an assailant bandage his victim." Cousteau fastened ice blue eyes on Peter, his thin line of mustache twitched. "It goes contrary to the reason for shooting someone."

"We had a fight, he tried to knife me."

"I can see you had a fight, and your face says you were getting the worst of it. Do you still have the gun?"

"On the table."

Cousteau went to the table and picked up the revolver by its barrel, noted the empty cylinders, then wrapped it in a handkerchief. He smiled at Peter's questioning look.

"There is a new technique of investigation I have been studying. One can determine who last held an object by the marks his fingers leave. While it is hardly necessary in this case, it will be an interesting experiment. And where is the knife this man attempted to use on you?"

"Someplace in the room, it flew from his hand."

"Officer Bertrand, would you be so good as to find the instrument for us?" the inspector said. Then he whispered something in the man's ear. He turned back to Peter.

"Where were you when this man attempted to stab you?"

"There on the floor against the stove. I was stunned, he was kneeling in front of me waving the knife in my face. He said he was going to slit my throat, then bring Kat to see my body."

"And who is this Kat?"

"His wife, my sister-in-law."

"And what has she to do with you?"

"I'd come to take her home. She wanted to leave him, and I came to get her."

"And from where have you come?"

"Minneapolis."

"That is a long way to come to interfere in another man's affairs."

"She was afraid of him and asked for help, she had no one else."

"So you came, her knight in shining armor. And when this man objected to having you take his wife from him, a fight ensued and you shot him. Is that right?"

"Yes, but I wouldn't have if he hadn't tried to knife me. He is filth, he brought Kat from a good home and brought her to this…this shithole!"

"Mister…what is your name?"

"Hokanson, Peter Hokanson."

"Mister Hokanson, most people here believe that a woman marries a man for better or worse. Fighting a man who attempts to violate that vow would be considered justifiable. If he had killed you because of it, a jury might also find that justifiable. However, I feel I should warn you that if this man dies, you are on much shakier ground."

"But I didn't shoot him because of Kat, it was because he was going to kill me!"

"Yes," Cousteau said dryly, "and when we find evidence of that your troubles will be less serious, not over, but less serious. Officer Bertrand, what success do you have?"

The policeman, who had been rummaging around the room, shrugged and shook his head. "Nothing so far Inspector, shall I keep searching?"

"Please do, it is essential that we find the knife," he glanced at Peter, "if there is one."

The first policeman had returned. "I sent the hack driver for Doctor Bremmer."

Cousteau nodded. "Is the woman still down there?"

"Yes Sir, she's awful excited though, she wants to go home."

"She may return home in a little while, we must interview her when this situation is fresh in her mind. Please bring her up."

In a few moments the black woman appeared. She looked at Peter and Cousteau apprehensively.

"Is this the man you saw?" Cousteau asked her.

"Yassuh!"

"What was he doing?"

"He was kneeling over Mistah Rousseau. Den he got up an stuck a gun in his belt. Dat's when he saw me."

"And what happened then?"

"I screamed, an I ran like de devil himself was after me!"

Cousteau turned back to Peter. "And that's when you decided to stay, wasn't it? When you knew someone had seen you."

Peter looked at Cousteau without saying anything—Cousteau had already formed an opinion, it showed in his eyes and face.

Bertrand had quit searching, he shook his head. "Nothing, Inspector."

Cousteau turned to the first policeman.

"Grover, I want you to turn this place upside down. If there's a knife laying around, I want it. Bertrand, take the woman and the hack driver down to the station. Mr. Hokanson, you'll come with me." He drew a pair of handcuffs from his belt and snapped them on Peter's wrists.

Inspector Cousteau questioned Peter all afternoon. It was obvious that he was trying to exact a full confession from him. Again and again he came back to the missing knife, and always, Peter insisted that there had been one.

"We have searched thoroughly," the inspector said, "but there is nothing, save a few old blades in the cupboard. It is doubtful the wounded man could have returned a knife there, is it not? You have said that you were stunned, perhaps you imagined it—Is that not possible?"

"He had a knife, inches from my face. It has to be there."

"Why don't you make a clean breast of it, Peter?" Cousteau was sympathetic now.

"You were losing a fight, and in your pain and fear you acted in a way you would not have if your head was clear. A jury might understand that, a judge would be more lenient if you admitted to that."

"I can't because it isn't true, dammit! He was going to stick me like a pig in a slaughterhouse."

Cousteau sighed. "Very well, think about it for a while. We'll talk about it later." He turned to the officer at the door. "Make Mr. Hokanson comfortable in his new quarters."

Peter sat on his bunk, a plank affair with a straw matress. His head throbbed, his nose was a swollen blob of hurt. He was in the worst trouble of his life, and no one even knew he was here. And what of Kat? Where had she gone? Peter wished he had believed Girard and went to search for Kat. Now he couldn't help her. Hell, she didn't even know he was here. He supposed that eventually the police would let him send a message to someone. "All in due time." Cousteau had said. Did that mean tomorrow, or next week, or a month from now?

"Tme fo' beans an bacon!" A cheerful black face appeared at the bars of the iron door and pushed a tin plate through the slot. " You sho nuff look like a mule done kicked you, mistah. Reckon you could use a sawbones."

"That and a lot more. But I suppose they wouldn't let me have one."

"Oh they'll let you have one, they jus' won't pay fo' it. Reckon you could pay though, you don't look like no bum. Got some dollahs?"

"I did when I came in here, they took it from me though. I guess they'll steal it."

"Did 'specter Costoo bring you in?"

"Yeah, Cousteau."

"Then you got no cause to fret on that count, mistah. He tough as hell, but he ain't gonna let nobody steal from you. Tell you what, you give ol' Jebadiah a coupla bucks, he gonna get you a sawbones sho nuff. Deal?"

"You bet it's a deal, Jebadiah. My nose feels like that mule of yours kicked it, alright. Can you maybe find someone else for me?"

"Depends, who you lookin' fo?"

"A young woman I know. She used to live on Saint Charles Avenue."

"She got yellow hair, an a little girl?"

"Yes, and she's pretty, with blue eyes."

"Don know 'bout that, mistah. Cuz the gal I saw had a plaster on her nose, an' she was all black an blue. But she sho nuff had a cute little gal with her."

"Well tell me where you saw her, Jebadiah! Was it out on Saint Charles?"

"Hell no, mistah, it was right here. She was talkin' to 'Specter Costoo."

Peter's heart seemed to lurch within him. Could it have been Kat? "Could you hear what they were talking about?"

"One thing you don't do aroun' here, that's evesdroppin' on 'Specter Costoo. But she kinda screamed once, can't rightly remember what it was. Something like regard, but that don't make no sense."

"Regard?…No Jebadiah! Was it Girard?!"

"Yeah, that's what it was! It was like 'Specter Costoo said something to her, an' she kinda screamed out, "Girard!". That's all I know, mistah. Best eat your beans, afore the rats do. I gotta go."

"No wait! Is the woman you saw still here?"

Jebadiah shook his head. "She left jus' afore I brought your beans. Poor gal was cryin' fit to break the heart of a field boss."

Peter sat down on his bunk with the plate of beans. They were cooked to an unappetizing mush, but he hadn't eaten since morning and his stomach was complaining, so he spooned them into his mouth. He thought of the beans at the logging camp years ago. They had been good, cooked with molasses and salt pork. God, he thought, how I wish I were there now. He had made his mark, he had money, but it seemed that he paid for it with a continuing set of trials. Oh well, better to have money and trials, than to have trials and no money. He wondered if Kat knew he was here. Had Inspecter Cousteau asked about him? He must have… His thoughts were cut short by a jailer who unlocked the door and beckoned with his hand.

"Come on Bub, the inspector wants to see you."

Inspector Cousteau was standing beside the table in the little interrogation room. His face was smiling, but his eyes were calculating.

"Good evening Peter, I trust you have had your dinner. I would imagine you are accustomed to more palatable fair, but on our limited resources we must make do with inexpensive food. Please sit down."

Peter sat down at the table. "Inspector Cousteau, I have a question."

"Yes, I would imagine you have many questions. But the purpose of this meeting is for me to ask questions of you. I think that in due course your own questions will thus be answered."

Peter was surprised and dismayed. It was the first time in his life that he had been refused the privilege of asking a simple question. He leaned on the table, hand to chin and waited.

"No, no Peter, that is not the way we do it. I find that an erect position is more conducive to proper attitude in conferences of this sort. There, that's better, now I can see I have your full attention. Now Peter, I trust that you have thought about the proposal I made to you this afternoon. Have you decided to make a clean breast in this situation?"

"I have already told you the whole story, nothing has changed."

"You maintain that Mr. Rousseau was about to set upon you with a knife, and so in fear of your life you shot him?"

"That's the way it happened."

"It is regretable that you choose to hold to that description of the events that took place. In our continued and very thorough search of the premises we could find no knife. It is our conjecture that no such weapon exists. I must advise you that the absence of a weapon in Mr. Rousseau's possession greatly weakens your claim of self defense. Furthermore, it presents the possibility that you deliberately undertook Mr. Rousseau's destruction. In which case a charge of attempted murder might be brought against you, rather than assault with a deadly weapon, which would otherwise be the charge. Now, before I continue, does what I have just said change your remembrance of this incident?"

Peter was aghast, the thought that he might be charged with a deliberate attempt on Girard's life had not occurred to him. Cousteau was building a case against him based on that premise, it horrified and infuriated Peter.

"Damn you Cousteau, what I said is the truth, I can't help it if your apes can't find the knife. It's there somewhere and I'll find it if I have to have the house torn down."

Cousteau smiled in the way Peter was beginning to hate. It was a smile designed to disarm him, to make him say what Cousteau wanted him to say.

"There, there Peter, becoming angry will achieve nothing for you. I am merely pointing out the dire straits you will be in if Mr. Rousseau dies."

"You mean he's still alive!"

"He hovers between life and death—there is no harm in telling you that. We too would prefer that he gains consciousness. We have a number of questions we would like to ask him. There is something else,…late this afternoon I had an opportunity to speak to the young woman who seems to be at the heart of this matter. In the course of our conversation, I was able to procure bits of information I find interesting." Cousteau stopped talking and took a drink of water, assessing Peter over the rim of the glass.

Peter grew rigid with apprehension. Now what the hell was Cousteau about? He smothered the urge to strangle the man—he had to be calm, he couldn't give the inspector more than he already had.

Cousteau continued. "It seems that she wrote to her father asking him to send her money. She was adamant in her assertion that she cautioned him not to come,...because she knew the volatile nature of her situation. In that she showed good sense, judging from her appearance when I talked to her. It seems Mr. Rousseau beat her quite viciously a few days ago. That fact is beneficial to your case, in that it shows he is quite capable of violence. She also denied any knowledge of your attempt to rescue her from her husband.

However, there are other factors that I must consider in my investigation, factors that do not shed a favorable light when they are combined with the hideous condition of Mrs. Rousseau's marriage....Mr. Hokanson, is it true that you were once romantically involved with Mrs. Rousseau?"

The question caught Peter off guard, just as Cousteau had intended.

"I...in a way...it was a long time ago,...before she married Girard. I married her sister, Lucille. It was never very serious between Kat and I."

"She seems to feel otherwise, she was very worried about you. How did your wife feel about you coming to get her sister?"

"Damn it! You don't have to bring her into this, Cousteau—Lucille died in childbirth!"

Cousteau regarded Peter for a moment, then he spoke again. "My condolences, it must have been difficult for you. Did her death occur recently?"

"Nearly two years ago."

"Ah,...then your pain has diminished somewhat. Mr. Hokanson, the fact that you came to save your sister-in-law from her abominable circumstances may be very honorable and charitable of you....But there will be those who would say it was something entirely different." Cousteau paused, letting the tension build in Peter's mind.

"It might be conceived that you and Mrs. Rousseau had been in communication with each other. It might also be hypothesized that you were lonely since your wife's untimely demise, and that Mrs. Rousseau was discontent with her marriage. It follows that considering your previous romantic involvement, a resumption of that romance would be entirely possible."

"That's a lie! You can take your hypothesis and stick it! I haven't heard from Kat since she left Minneapolis."

"Calm yourself, Peter." Cousteau was smiling again, and Peter wanted to smash the smile off his face.

"I am merely pointing out what some people might think. People like the parish attorney, the judge and a jury. You see Peter, if you and Mrs. Rousseau are lying about the true state of your relationship, and evidence was found to support the contention that you are, then this case will take on an entirely different aspect."

"What are you saying, Cousteau? How Kat and I feel about each other has nothing to do with it, Girard and I fought, and I shot him. There's nothing more to it!"

"Oh, but there is. If you and Mrs. Rousseau wished to be together, there would be an obstacle,... Mr. Rousseau!

Considering his disposition, you would know he would never consent to letting her go. The only way that would ever happen would be if he died.

It could be conceived that you communicated through the mail, and that you came here with Mrs. Rousseau's knowledge and support, for the sole purpose of killing Mr. Rousseau and taking Mrs. Rousseau back with you. And that, Mr. Hokanson, is conspiracy to commit murder. It would also implicate Mrs. Rousseau, making her a codefendant.

Now, wouldn't it be better if you simply got in a fight with Mr. Rousseau, who was obviously better than you? It would be understandable that a man who is being beaten would shoot his assailant, out of fear, even though he had no weapon. Juries in this country tend to look at fights as natural, and they shrug at the consequences. And taking care of your kin is considered an obligation. Messing with another man's wife—that's something they're downright intolerant about."

"You're a stinking bastard, Cousteau!" Peter's voice was shaking with anger and hatred as he spoke.

"You might send me to prison, but your pack of lies can't touch Kat. If you've got an ounce of decency, you'll help her get free of Rousseau and go back home!"

The smile left the inspector's face. "I have to follow every possibility, Hokanson. I'm not interested in increasing that poor woman's sorrows—but I think you shot Rousseau because you wanted his wife. And I'm going to put you in prison for it."

When Peter returned to his cell, Jebadiah and a doctor had arrived. The doctor shook his hand, a bare touch of palm to palm. "Weinberg is my name. Jebadiah says you need my services and I'd say he was right. Second nose like that I've seen in these last few days. The other was a woman...pretty too if she hadn't been beaten so bad. When will people stop destroying each other? Never mind, sit down and hold still, this is going to smart a bit."

It did, it hurt like hell. But when the doctor left, Peter's nose was reshaped to something resembling its original form, save for a flatness of the bridge that would remain with him.

The inky darkness of his cell did little to help Peter sleep that night. He lay on the hard bunk staring upward into the blackness, a blackness that was both physical and psychological. And in it, he prayed as he had never prayed in his entire life. But despite his fervor, he found little consolation in prayer. It would take a miracle bestowed by a guardian angel to deliver him from the hands of Inspector Cousteau.

Early the next morning the jailer came. "You've got a visitor, Bub. It ain't visiting hours, but Inspector Cousteau give her special permission." He led Peter to the interrogation room, which apparently doubled as a visiting room. Kathryn was seated at the little table.

As he entered she rose and ran to throw her arms around him. "Oh Peter! Oh Peter!"

He hugged her tight. "Kat! I'm sorry, I made an awful mess of things."

"This is very touching, it seems you both retain a certain affection for each other, but you must separate and sit on opposite sides of the table."

Inspector Cousteau stood in the doorway, smiling his half smile.

"I gave Mrs. Rousseau permission to see you, Peter, since you have no one else to act in your behalf. It would be adviseable to retain an attorney, since you are scheduled for preliminary examination before a magistrate this afternoon at three o'clock. Until then, I suggest you use your time wisely." He turned abruptly and left.

"Peter, what happened?" Kathryn asked. The swelling of her face had diminished somewhat, giving way to ugly blue and greenish yellow marks. She still wore the plaster on her nose, which was smudged under her eyes by the wiping of tears.

Peter felt the anger rise in himself again as he looked at her. "That miserable, stinking bastard, I hope he dies!"

"Oh no Peter! Pray that he lives. He has friends here, you don't. Can you tell me what happened? Inspector Cousteau told me what he thinks happened, but I can't believe you'd shoot an unarmed man, not even Girard."

"I can only tell you what I've already told Cousteau. He had a knife, and he was going to kill me. The problem is that they couldn't find the knife."

"And if he dies?"

"They'll charge me with premeditated murder."

"But they couldn't, you had no reason."

"They'll say I did. You told them about us, the way it was long ago."

"Oh no! He thinks that you and I…I was trying to tell him how good you are. And now,…he's twisting everything!"

"He's got a talent for that alright. But now, I need you to help me, Kat. Send Charlie a telegram, I need him, and Gus too. Tell them to find a good lawyer and bring him along. Then see if you can find a lawyer here, for now."

"But, I don't know any."

"There's a black man, Jebadiah, who works around the jail. Find him, he may be able to help you. Now go, you haven't much time."

A few hours later, the jailer brought a middle aged, cadaverous looking man to Peter's cell. He looked at Peter with empty eyes.

"Jebadiah says you need an attorney, says you aren't from here, but you can pay for my services." He grinned a deathly grin. "That'll be a welcome change from the usual business he brings me."

He held out his hand, it was lifeless and clammy to Peter's touch. "J. B. Higgins, at your service."

"Yeah, I need a lawyer alright. I shot a man. He's a worthless, mean son- of-a-bitch, and he had it coming. But I guess that doesn't matter, does it?"

Higgin's face contorted into its hollow grin. "Not in the eyes of the law, son, though such shootings might sometimes be considered a service to mankind. Now suppose you tell me all about it."

Peter told him the whole story, then waited for the lawyer's comment.

"You want to know the truth?"

"Of course."

"You don't stand much chance of getting clear of this without that knife, if there is one."

"You don't believe me?"

"Doesn't matter if I do or not—my job is to defend you regardless. The hearing today is to decide whether or not to charge you. They'll say you shot this man with the intent of killing him. We'll say it was self defense, that you had no choice. The magistrate will bind you over for trial."

"It's that sure?"

"Sure as Christmas comes every year. There is no question that you shot him. The question is why. They have to go to trial to decide that."

"So what happens next?"

"If the man dies, they'll go for an indictment by a grand jury to decide whether there is probable cause for trying you. Otherwise, there'll be an arraignment hearing where the prosecuting attorney for the parish will bring formal charges against you."

"How soon will this all happen?"

"Within a few weeks, most likely. Unless there's some reason for waiting."

"There's just one other thing. Do you object to me bringing in an attorney from home?"

"Not at all, two heads are generally better than one. You're going to need all the help you can get. I'll leave you now, I'll be at the courthouse just before three."

Chapter 18

A Desperate Situation

The preliminary hearing took less than twenty minutes. The magistrate ruled that a crime had occurred, but that the circumstances were unclear as to whether Peter was the instigator of the incident, since his own injuries were evident. For that reason the magistrate set bail for Peter at 10,000 dollars despite the parish attorney's protest that Peter might flee.

"There is evidence that Mr. Hokanson is a man of stature in his own community." The magistrate said. "It is doubtful that he would not answer the charges against him, knowing that he could be extradited for trial, and then face charges under less favorable circumstances."

That afternoon Kathryn sent another telegram to Charlie: Charles LeBlanc 1029 Nicolet Mpls Minn / Send authorization for bank cheque / $10,000 Kathryn Rousseau / bail Peter / State Bank of New Orleans.

Charlie and Gus were waiting for their train to Chicago when an out of breathe stableboy brought Charlie the telegram. "Mother of mercy!" He exclaimed, then he hurried to the telegraph desk.

By noon on Wednesday Peter was a free man, at least for the moment. He, Kathryn and April were checked in at the Continental Hotel in the heart of New Orleans. The desk clerk had looked at Peter and Kathryn strangely because of the plasters on their noses and the bruises on their faces.

"Fell down a stairs." Peter said with a grin, as he opened a roll of bills.

"You should be more careful." The clerk smiled. "Thank goodness your little girl didn't fall with you. We have a nice room on the second floor with two beds. It is very comfortable, and it has a balcony over the street."

"That'll do fine. Is there a good clothing store near here?" Peter asked.

"There is a good establishment for women and children just a block west." The clerk said, glancing at Kathryn and April in their well worn dresses. "Millelands, they specialize in the latest attire from Europe. Shall I call a carriage for you?

"Later, we'd like to freshen up and rest a bit, we've had a trying day."

"Very well, Sir. I do hope your day improves."

After Kathryn, April and Peter had bathed and changed clothes, they lay down on the two big beds. Peter sprawled out on one, while Kathryn and April snuggled together on the other.

"I had forgotten what a soft, clean bed feels like," Kathryn said. "Thank you Peter. I just wish there hadn't been such trouble."

"Me too, Kat. I didn't intend for it to happen, I hope you believe that."

"I do, but God will help us, I feel it in my soul."

"Maybe,...but that Cousteau, he wants to send me to prison. He'll try his damnedest, you can be sure of that."

"But we've got to have faith anyway. We've got to believe we'll be back home soon. I can't wait to see Mama and Lucy."

Peter sat up and put his feet on the floor. He'd forgotten that Kat didn't know. Damn, damn, he thought, all this trouble, and now another heartache for her.

"Peter,...is something wrong? You look like you've seen a ghost."

Peter looked at her sadly. "Come here and sit beside me, Kat. There's something I have to tell you."

Kathryn got up carefully to avoid waking April, who was now sleeping peacefully. She sat down beside Peter. "What's the matter Peter? Is it Mama, is she ill?"

Peter shook his head. "Elizabeth is fine, she's taking care of the boys and little Lucy."

"The boys and little Lucy! You've got three children?" Kathryn's face lit up with delight, then it clouded. "But you said Mama is taking care of them. Is Lucille ill? Is that it Peter? Is Lucy very sick?"

"No,...it's worse than that. Lucy died, Kat. It'll be two years ago, come April. We didn't know where to reach you, Kat."

"Kathryn's face became blank with shock. She stared at Peter, hoping she had heard him wrong. But the sadness in his eyes confirmed what she heard. The knowledge could not be denied—she seemed to crumple before Peter, collapsing into a creature that was completely desolate. Her face contorted and two large tears traced their way down her cheeks. Then there were many more, and Peter drew her to him as she began to cry in violent, wrenching sobs. As he held her, Peter wept silently, not for himself or for Lucille—that grief had passed. His tears were for the poor creature he held in is arms. A young woman whose life had gone so terribly wrong. A woman whose troubles had drawn him into the same web of misfortune. He wondered if their lives would ever be safe and sane again.

Two days later Charlie and Gus arrived—Kathryn flew into Charlie's arms, holding April in her own.

"Daddy! Daddy, I've missed you so!"

Charlie held his daughter and granddaughter as though he would never let them go.

"My little Kat, Charlie dreamed a tousand dreams of this day."

"Can you ever forgive me, Daddy? I was so stupid and so stubborn."

"That's because you're Charlie's little girl. You got a hard head like your daddy. There ain't nothin' to forgive, Kat. Charlie loves his little Kat, an that's all that matters. An besides, you brought me another little girl."

He released Kathryn and took April from her. "You look just like your Mama did when she was little. You gonna give your grampa a hug?"

April looked at Charlie in the tentative way of little children. Then she smiled and threw her arms around Charlie's neck. "Grampa!"

As a carriage took them to the hotel, Kathryn took Charlie's hand in hers. "Peter told me about Lucy, Daddy. I'm sorry I wasn't there with her, I'll always be sorry for that."

"That's over and done with, Kat. She died peaceful. She was proud she gave us a little girl, an she died peaceful. It was real hard, but we went on, an you gotta too."

"Yes, I know. But now Peter's in trouble because of me. If something happens to him, I'll never forgive myself."

"Pete wanted to come, Kat. What he did, he did, and you couldn't prevent it. Now we gotta do our damnedest to help him. An we gotta pray."

"I do Daddy, every minute of the day."

Girard Rousseau regained consciousness on the fifth day after he was shot. He blinked awake and stared at his surroundings. A hospital, I'm in a damned hospital, he thought. Why? He tried to remember but everything was fuzzy, then slowly it came back to him. That damned Hokanson! The son of a bitch had a gun, he shot me! Girard remembered kneeling in front of the man, then there was this little nickel plated thing in his hand. Oh shit! What kind of trouble am I in? he thought. He put a hand over his eyes. I've got to get out of here, got to get my clothes and get out of here. He tried to sit up and swing his legs to the floor, but nothing happened. He tried again, his waist muscles and legs ignored his command—Girard swore loudly.

A nurse came running. She took one look at Girard and disappeared, then returned with a doctor in tow. He towered over Girard, a tall man with spectacles hanging low in front of his eyes.

"I see you're back with us, Mr. Rousseau. We were afraid you might not make it."

Girard's face displayed confusion. "You're a doctor?"

"Yes, I am. How do you feel?"

"Feel? I can't move my damned legs!"

The doctor's brow wrinkled with concern. He took Girard's right foot and poked at it with something.

"Did you feel that?"

"Feel what?"

The doctor repeated the procedure on Girard's other foot, the results were the same.

"What the hell is the matter with me, Doc?"

The doctor looked at him gravely. "When you were shot the bullet passed very close to your spine. There were some bone splinters. One of them may be pressing on or may have penetrated your spinal cord. It is interfering with nerve responses to your legs."

"So what the hell does that mean, Doc?"

"It means that you are paralyzed in your lower torso, your lower back and legs."

"You mean I can't walk...ever?"

"You can't move your legs now, whether it is a permanent condition I can't tell you. Your condition is grave, but there is a bright side."

"What the hell is that?"

"If the wound had been a few inches higher your arms would have been paralyzed too."

Girard began laughing a wild, mirthless laugh, then he cursed with a foulness that appalled the doctor and nurse. They turned and walked from the room.

With Girard out of imminent mortal danger, the parish attorney petitioned for an arraignment date for Peter. As required by law, it was to be prompt. The date was set for the following Tuesday at 9 o'clock in the morning.

On that day Peter, Kathryn, Charlie, Gus and Peter's two lawyers were seated in the straight backed wooden benches of the Orleans Parish Court House, Courtroom #2.

At 9 o'clock the bailiff adressed the gallery. "All rise! The court of Louisiana, Parish of Orleans is now in session, the most honorable Judge Hewitt P. Justice presiding.

The judge banged his gavel and the gallery seated themselves. He turned to the court secretary and nodded, whereupon the man rose.

"The people of Louisiana versus Peter Olaf Hokanson."

Peter and his attorneys presented themselves before the Judge, as did the prosecuting attorney.

"You are Mr. Hokanson?" The judge looked at Peter in an appraising way.

"Yes, Your Honor."

"And you have legal counsel?"

"Yes, Your Honor."

"Very well. Mr. Rogette, are you prepared to read the charges for the court?"

"Yes, Your Honor, we are."

The prosecutor launched into a statement of legalese defining the offices involved in the investigation and prosecution of the case. Then he got to the heart of the matter.

"The Parish of Orleans, and the duly elected attorney thereof, do contend that Peter Olaf Hokanson did, at approximately 1 p.m. on December 16, 1903, assault one Girard Rousseau with a revolver, causing him great bodily harm. We do further contend that the assault was of a premeditated nature on an unarmed man. Therefore we do, as Attorney for the Parish of Orleans, State of Louisiana, charge Peter Olaf Hokanson as follows:

Count one, assault with a deadly weapon.

Count two, attempted murder in the first degree.

Count three, conspiracy to commit murder in the first degree.

We do petition the court to set trial, whereat Peter Olaf Hokanson shall defend himself against the aforenamed charges."

The judge turned to Peter and his attorneys. "Mr. Higgins, you represent the defendant?"

"Yes, Your Honor, with the able assistance of Mr. James Whitmore of Minneapolis."

"Is Mr. Whitmore licensed in the State of Louisiana?"

"No, Your Honor, he is serving as a consultant."

"Very well, do you have any petitions for the court at this time?"

"Yes, Your Honor. We petition that the case be dismissed on the grounds that no crimes stated in the charges occurred." Higgins handed the judge a written petition, which the judge scrutinized.

"Mr. Higgins, the defendant claims that the incident in question was self defense, and that no wilful assault by his person took place?"

"Yes, Your Honor. Mr. Hokanson contends that Mr. Rousseau attacked him with a knife and threatened to kill him."

The judge looked at Peter. "Is that true, Mr. Hokanson?"

"Yes, Your Honor, it is."

"Mr. Rogette, what have you to say about this?"

"The defendant did indeed make that claim, Your Honor. However, a careful search by investigating officers failed to disclose a knife that could have been used against the defendant. The absence of the instrument in question, or any substantiating testimony by someone having witnessed the incident, make the charges we have filed mandatory."

"I see, and the charge of conspiracy, that would require a codefendant. Has your office arrested another person?"

"No, Your Honor, not at the present."

"But you wish the charge to stand against Mr. Hokanson?"

"Yes, Your Honor, we feel that additional evidence of conspiracy will be uncovered as we examine witnesses before the court."

The Judge turned to Peter.

"Mr. Hokanson, while it is incumbent on the investigating officers to find all available evidence pertaining to a case, their responsibility in that regard ends with a thorough search. It then becomes the responsibility of the defense attorneys to procure whatever supporting evidence they can, to defend you. For that reason, I must reject your petition to dismiss on the grounds of self defense. You have heard the charges against you. How do you plead?"

Higgins whispered in Peter's ear, and he faced the judge squarely. "Not guilty of all counts, Your Honor."

"Very well. Do you have anything further, Mr. Rogette?"

"Yes, Your Honor. We move to rescind Mr. Hokanson's bail and return him to incarceration, on the grounds that he is likely to leave this jurisdiction."

"Mr. Higgins?"

"Your Honor, if Mr. Hokanson had any intention of leaving New Orleans, he would already have done so. He is a responsible businessman of considerable means, he can ill afford the implication of guilt that skipping bail would bestow upon him."

"I think you are correct in that assertion. Mr. Hokanson, I am releasing you on your own recognizance. You will stand trial on a date set by the court. Failure to appear to answer charges will result in your immediate arrest. That is all."

The trial date was set for the second Tuesday in January. Peter met with his attorneys in the run down office of J. B. Higgins. Charlie looked about and whispered to Peter.

"Look at this place, Pete. You can afford a better lawyer than this."

"It's a rathole all right, but I think Higgins knows the ropes, and we've got Whitmore."

"Yeah, but this guy gotta do the talkin'. Has he got what it's gonna take?"

"I guess we're going to find out, aren't we? Come on Charlie, let's sit down with them."

J. B. Higgins started the discussion. "Rogette thinks he has a solid case. He's got an admission by Peter that he shot Rousseau, and he's got the gun. He also has an eye witness who saw Peter standing over Rousseau with the gun in his hand. What we need is the knife that Rousseau had. Can we get it?"

"It has to be there somewhere," Peter said, "maybe it fell in a crack or something. The place is falling apart. We'll have to go and search for it."

"An if we find it, how we gonna convince the police it belongs to Rousseau?" Charlie asked.

"That's true Pete." Gus said. "They'll think it's something you put up, even if you have us for witnesses."

"And that would create a poor aspect at your trial." Whitmore said. " If a jury thought you concocted one piece of evidence, they wouldn't believe anything you said."

Peter frowned. "There must be some way…There is a way! Cousteau!"

"What you mean…Cousteau? He's on their side, he's the one wants to put you in prison!" Charlie said.

"I know that! It's something he said when he took my gun. He said something about how he could tell who last held something by the marks the person's fingers left."

"You're dreaming," Gus said, "fingers don't leave marks, not even on an axe handle."

"Wait a minute." Whitmore said. "Have you ever noticed the smudges your fingers leave on a glass?"

"Yeah sure, but that's all they are, just smudges."

"Not quite, look at your fingertips. You see all the little ridges on them?

Every one of them shows up in those little smudges if you look at them with a magnifying glass. And everybody's are different. That's what Inspector Cousteau was talking about. It's called fingerprinting, they're using it for identification in England and soon it will be the vogue here."

"Mr. Whitmore is right," Higgins said. "It might help if Cousteau cooperates. But can we find the knife?"

"I don't know, but we start looking today," Peter said.

"What about the neighbor that saw you, Peter? Did she see the fight?" Whitmore asked.

"I don't know—Cousteau didn't tell me anything. But she's friendly toward Kat. She helped Kat when Girard beat her."

"Good! Then she'll be a sympathetic witness. Talk to her and see if she knows any more. Did she see Girard with a knife then or at any other time? What kind of a person was he? Things like that."

"There's something that really bothers me," Higgins said. "It's the thing about premeditated murder, and conspiracy. You've told me that you and Kathryn were friendly a few years ago. Was it any more than that? Is there anything that Kathryn might have told Cousteau that would lend credence to his hypothesis, that you planned Rousseau's murder?"

"They were two kids, they went to a party together, it didn't turn out," Charlie said. "Pete, he fell in love with Kat's sister an' they got married."

"And that was all, Peter? If there was more, we have to know."

"That was it. But Kat was really mad at me for a little while."

"Was she mad enough to want to do you harm?"

"Then, maybe. But now,...never!"

Higgins leaned back and stared at the ceiling. "I wonder what set Cousteau off on this. He's not the kind of man to fabricate an idea like that without something to go on. I'll have to talk to Kathryn, find out everything she told him. Have her stop by."

"I'll bring her." Peter said.

"No, I'd rather talk to her alone. Sometimes it is easier for people to remember certain things that way."

Whitmore was drumming his fingers on Higgins desk. "What of this Rousseau? Will he be well enough to testify?"

Peter nodded. "But they'll have to carry him into the courtroom. He's paralyzed from the waist down."

Whitmore looked glum. "That's the worst kind of witness we can have against us. The jury will feel sorry for him. Is there even a slight possibility this man will tell the truth?"

Charlie spat out the answer. "That damned, worthless tinhorn will lie like it was his own trial!"

"Will he be openly hostile, Mr. LeBlanc?"

"The bastard is too smart for that. He's gonna look like he never done nothin' to harm nobody in his life."

The room became silent, everyone knew that Peter faced a desperate fight.

"I guess that's all for now." Higgins said.

Peter, Charlie and Gus went to Girard Rousseau's place. A board had been nailed across the door, and a notice affixed. It read: CRIME SCENE UNDER INVESTIGATION. DO NOT ENTER.

"First we talk to the neigbor," Peter said. He walked to the second door and knocked.

The door opened a crack, and Nellie peered out.

"Oh! It's you," she said, and opened the door a little further. "Kat, she done tole me 'bout you. If'n I had knowed who you was, I wouldn't a called de police, nosuh!"

"It's all right," Peter said, "but we'd like to know a few things. Did you see the fight between Girard and me?"

"Nosuh, I jus' heard some hollerin', couldn't rightly make out what was said. Den dere was dis crash, shook the floor in my kitchen. I heard Mistah Girard laughin' dat awful laugh of his. Makes my hair stand up straight when he does dat. Den dere was dis pop, kinda like when a home brew blows de cork. Dat's when I ran down the hall an saw you wit' de gun. Sakes alive, it skeered me, I thought you was gonna shoot me for sure."

"You heard Girard laugh, though? You were sure it was him?"

"Sure nuff, I heard dat laugh nuff times to know it, sounds like de devil hisself."

"When did you hear it before?"

"Lotsa times, mostly when he got to fightin' wit' his missus. Dey be yellin at each other, an' den things would go quiet. Den she'd go to cryin', an he'd laugh like dat. I don't no what he done to her, but it wasn't no good, I'll tell you dat."

"Well thanks, you've been a help. Can you tell me who takes care of this building?"

"Sure nuff, old Orvis. He's de old man lives down below me."

The three men went down to the street and huddled together.

"What we gonna do now, Pete?" Charlie asked.

"See if we can get into Girard's place."

"Oh shit!" Gus said. "The police have it sealed. You go in there you'll be in more trouble."

"Can't get much worse than it is. Wait here, I'm going to see this Orvis."

Peter walked to the next ramshackle door and knocked. An old, gray haired man opened the door and looked at him sourly. He spit a stream of tobacco juice into the path.

"What you want?"

"You Orvis?"

"Maybe so."

"I need to get into Kathryn Girard's place, she left some things."

"Can't let you in, police got it sealed. Go see them."

"I don't really want them to know." Peter took a ten dollar gold piece from his pocket and held it between his thumb and forefinger."

The old man looked at it with interest. "There's a fire stair out back. I reckon I couldn't see anybody went up that way, if they were quiet."

Peter put the gold piece into the old man's open palm and walked to the back of the building. Charlie and Gus followed him up warped, rotting steps to a window of Girard's bedroom. With the combined strength of Peter and Gus the sash slid up grudgingly.

"Damn! This place is a rathole." Gus said.

"Sh-h-h, we've got to be quiet."

"Okay, but it stinks of vermin."

Charlie was shaking his head sadly. "I can't believe Kat was living here."

"We can talk about it later. Help me look for the knife."

Peter walked into the kitchen. The stovepipes still lay where they had fallen and soot was smeared across the floor.

"I fell there against the stove, and Girard fell here when I shot him." A dark red brown blotch marked the spot. "The knife flew back, away from here."

The men started searching. A few minutes later Gus motioned to Peter.

"Look here Pete." He was on his hands and knees in front of an old cupboard that stood against an outer wall of the building.

"Have you found it?"

"No but look at the leg of this cupboard, there's a new mark on it, like something sharp hit it. And look there."

Gus pointed under the cupboard—Peter bent low and looked. There, about a foot to the right of the cupboard leg there was a six inch wide hole gnawed in the wall.

"A damned rathole!" Peter said. "Help me move this cupboard. Quiet now."

With the cupboard aside, Gus dropped to his knees and put his hand in the hole. "It goes straight down into the wall, the knife is down there someplace, it has to be."

Peter sighed. "Now what?"

"We find the owner, we buy the place if we have to," Charlie said. "Then we take it apart a stick at a time if need be. Lets go talk to the old man again."

"Sure, I know the owner's name," Orvis said, "deposit the rent in his account when I can get it. He owns a bunch of these crappy old wrecks. Name's Willis, Martin Willis—won't do you any good though. He's gone, went to France, took his whole family with him."

" You know where in France?" Charlie asked.

"Nope went on some fancy tour. Going to France, Italy, Spain. Gonna be gone for two, three months. Wish to hell I could go someplace, instead of tending these rat infested places of his."

"Does he have a lawyer, or somebody that takes care of his business?" Peter asked.

"Naw, don't believe so, old Willis is too tight fisted for that. I put his money in the bank, he takes it out."

"Then you're in charge of this building?"

"This and a couple others, I collect the rent, an fix things, like if a door falls off. Old Willis don't hold with doing much."

"I can see that—I've got a problem. You see, something very valuable dropped down in a wall of this house. I'd like to open it up and see if I can find it."

"Haw! That's a good one! Ain't nobody lives here got anything valuable. And there ain't no way I'd let you tear open the wall to look for it."

"Not even if we paid you well? Say, three hundred dollars."

Orvis looked at Peter suspiciously. "You'd pay three hundred to open a wall?"

"Tomorrow, as soon as we can hire a crew."

Orvis took a chew off a piece of plug tobacco, he was thinking hard.

"And you'd fix it up again, like it is?"

"At least as good."

"Don't rightly know how it'd do any harm. But you gotta do it fast, it's downright chilly in this old barn as it is."

"It'll be done by evening tomorrow, we won't have to open very much."

The following evening a somber group was gathered at Peter's hotel room. Peter was pacing the floor. "It had to be there, it had to be in the rathole," he said.

"I could see all the way down to the street from that rathole," Gus said. "If it was there, we would have found it. Are you sure Girard had a knife? What with being hit in the face like that… "

"Dammit, Gus! I know what I saw, he had a knife and he was going to stick me with it!"

"Ain't no use us fighting between ourselves," Charlie said. "We ain't gonna find it, so we might as well forget it."

"Yeah, you're right, Charlie." Peter heaved a heavy sigh. "I just don't know how I'm going to defend myself without it."

"It's a bitch all right," Gus said. "You try to help Kat and you wind up in a pickle like this. You shouldn't have taken the gun along, Pete."

"What kind of shit is that, Gus? If I hadn't, you'd be looking at my corpse right now."

"I suppose that's right, but I wish you'd taken me along."

"You're great on hindsight alright. But right now we don't need that. There're other things we have to think of. Look, there isn't any use in both of you hanging around waiting for the trial. Somebody has to run the furniture plant and the mills. Gus, can you run the factory for me? Charlie has his hands full with the rest of it."

"I guess I can see to the manufacturing and sales. But somebody else will have to oversee the business end of it. How about George Riebeck?"

Peter thought a moment. "He's a good bookkeeper, but I don't think he'd be able to handle the finances. I need somebody who specializes in that."

"How 'bout your friend?," Charlie asked.

"Who?"

"Oberg."

"Hm-m, yeah I guess he might do it until I get back. I'll send him a telegram."

The next morning Peter sent a message to Elias:

NEED YOU TO OVERSEE BUSINESS FINANCES UNTIL MY RETURN / CAN YOU / GIVE IMMEDIATE REPLY / PETER.

Within hours Peter received his answer.

YES / NEED POWER ATTORNEY / DOCUMENT TO YOU FIRST MAIL / ELIAS.

Peter was reluctant, but he could trust Elias. When the document arrived a few days later, he signed and returned it.

CHAPTER 19

TRIAL IN LOUISIANA

The second Tuesday of January arrived and Peter's fight for his freedom began. Legal machinery moved rapidly in the court of Judge Hewitt P. Justice. By the end of that day the preliminaries were completed, including the selection of a jury. Peter viewed them uneasily, twelve men from the bastions of New Orleans society. A serious, no nonsense group, with not a smile among them. The prosecuting attorney was Rogette, and sitting next to him was Inspector Cousteau. A chill ran along Peter's spine.

On the second day, Rogette delivered his opening statement.

"Gentlemen of the jury, we are here to decide the guilt or innocence of Peter Olaf Hokanson. We will prove to you, beyond a reasonable doubt, that this man did maliciously and with careful deliberation seek to end the life of Girard Rousseau. And that in so doing, he committed the felonies of assault on an unarmed man with a deadly weapon, attempted murder in the first degree and conspiracy to commit murder.

Because of the compelling evidence in this case, and the deplorable circumstances surrounding it, you must find the defendant guilty of each and every count. The pitiful condition of the man who was so fouly attacked demands it. Indeed the spirit of justice that is inherent in the citizens of Louisiana demands it."

As Rogette took his seat, J. B. Higgins confronted the jury.

"My friends and neighbors of New Orleans, I applaud you for the sense of duty that brings you here. It is a thing that cannot be taken lightly, for a man's life hangs on the scale of justice which you hold. The prosecution will ask you to believe that a man acting out of compassion for a family member whom he loves, would subvert his very character in a deliberate act of violence.

Peter Hokanson is a man much like you. He is a man who came to this country with empty hands and a dream. Through hard work and diligence he has become a successful business man, a man who is a credit to himself and every man of this nation. Out of fear for the life of a loved one he became entrapped in circumstances beyond his control.

We will show that Peter Hokanson is not a callous criminal, but a man who stands for the defense of those who are endangered and cannot defend themselves, even at peril to himself. He has done nothing more than commit an act of self defense necessary to quell the attack of a madman. And that is a right we all possess. You must free this man out of your sense of justice, conscience and compassion."

Predictably, Rogette's first witness was Inspector Cousteau.

"Inspector Cousteau, did you investigate the incident at the home of Girard Rousseau?"

"Yes, I did."

"And what did you find?"

"The injured man was lying on the floor, unconscious from a bullet wound. The defendant was sitting on a chair. The gun used in the assault was laying on a table."

Rogette walked to the prosecution's table and picked up a revolver.

"Is this the gun that was used to shoot Mr. Girard?"

"Yes it is, it's an octogon barrel, nickel plated Bulldog. They're fairly rare."

"The prosecution marks this gun as 'state exhibit A', Your Honor. Now Inspector Cousteau, did the defendant admit shooting Mr. Rousseau?"

"He didn't deny it, he said they'd had a fight, and Mr. Rousseau tried to knife him."

"Inspector, was there evidence that what he said was true?"

"My men conducted a thorough search for the knife he said Mr. Rousseau had. They found nothing."

"And what was the defendant's condition at this time?"

"He had been struck in the face, his nose appeared to be broken and there was blood on his face and shirt."

"If there was a fight—would you say that the defendant was getting the worst of it?"

Higgins spoke. "Defense objects, the question calls for a conclusion by the witness."

"Inspector Cousteau is qualified to answer, Your Honor, we seek to show motivation on the part of the defendant."

"Objection overruled, you may answer the question, Inspector."

"I would say he was getting the worst of it—he had fallen against a stove, causing the pipes to fall to the floor."

"Did someone see that happen?"

"The defendant made that admission."

"So the defendant was knocked to the floor in a fight, and that is when he shot Mr. Rousseau."

"That would appear to be correct."

"Did anyone witness the incident?"

"No, but a neighbor heard a disturbance and went to see what was happening, it was she that sent for the police."

"Thank you, Inspector Cousteau. I have no more questions of this witness at this time, Your Honor. However the prosecution reserves the right to call him later."

Higgins rose and stood before Cousteau. "Inspector, what was the condition of Mr. Rousseau when you first saw him? Wasn't there something peculiar about him, other than that he was unconscious?"

"Yes, he had been bandaged, a compression bandage had been secured over his wound."

"Who applied that bandage?"

"The defendant, Mr Hokanson."

"Wasn't that a peculiar action for a man who allegedly was trying to commit murder?"

"Very, it was the first time I'd seen it in my career."

"Inspector Cousteau, wouldn't that indicate to you that the defendant did not wish Mr. Rousseau to die, that he had acted in self defense?"

"Objection!," Rogette said. "Mr. Higgins is asking the witness to make a judgement on the guilt of the defendant."

"We are trying to disprove Mr. Rogette's allegation of motive, Your Honor."

"You go too far, in that the witness has no way of knowing what the defendant wished. Objection sustained—the jury will disregard the question."

"Very well, Your Honor, I will rephrase the question. Is it normal for a murderer to apply medical treatment to his victim, then wait for the police to arrive, Inspector?"

"No, but the defendant knew he had been seen. He may have done it to make it look like self defense."

"Your Honor, the witness is now hypothesizing on the defendant's motivations. We ask permission to treat him as a hostile witness."

"That goes too far, Mr. Higgins. I refuse to put a muzzle on professional witnesses. The jury will disregard the witness's statement. Inspector, keep your answers within the bounds of fact."

"Inspector, you testified that Mr. Hokanson told you that Mr. Rousseau attacked him with a knife. You also testified that your search did not disclose the weapon. What was the condition of the room in which the alleged fight took place?"

"It was run down, in very poor repair."

"And were there not one or more large ratholes on the walls, next to the floor?"

"Yes, there were."

"Inspector, is it not possible that the knife in question, may have fallen into one of those ratholes?"

"It may have been possible, but unlikely."

"But it is possible, is it not?"

"Yes."

"I have no more questions for the witness at this time."

Rogette returned to the floor.

"The prosecution calls Mrs. Nellie White to the stand."

Nellie lumbered down the aisle, and was sworn in.

"Mrs. White, you were present at the scene of Mr. Rousseau's shooting, were you not?"

"Yassuh, I was."

"Tell us in your own words what you saw."

"Well, I heard a commotion down de hall, an' I went to see what it was. An when I got to de door, I saw mistah Peter wit' a gun."

"You mean the defendant, don't you?"

"Yassuh."

"And, where was Mr. Rousseau?"

"He was layin' on de floor."

"What happened then?"

"Mistah Peter turned aroun', he was an awful sight, sho nuff. His face was all bloody an he looked scared. I screamed an run down de steps."

"And then, you called the police?"

"Yassuh, dere was a hack driver waitin for Mistah Peter, I sent him."

"Mrs. White, did you know the defendant at the time?"

"Nosuh, didn't know him from Adam."

"And, did you find out who he was later?"

"Yassuh, Missus Rousseau said he was her brudder-in-law, she said he come to get her."

Higgins spoke. “Objection Your Honor, that’s hearsay.”

“Objection sustained. The jury will disregard that statement.”

Rogette turned from the witness stand. “I have no more questions, Your Honor.”

Higgins smiled reassuringly at Nellie.

“Mrs. White, you said that you heard a commotion down the hall. Would you explain just what you meant by that?”

“Well, Suh,...de first I heard was men hollerin’ at each other.”

“Could you tell what they were saying?”

“Nosuh, jus dat dey was hollerin.”

“Very well, go on.”

“Den dere was a loud crash an a rattlin’ sound. Few seconds later I heard Mistah Girard laughin’....“

Rogette stood up. “Objection! Mrs. White said she couldn’t tell what the voices were saying, yet she claims to know that it was Mr. Rousseau who was laughing.”

“We will make this clear in a moment, Your Honor.”

“I hope you do, it seems questionable at the moment. Objection overruled.”

“How did you know it was Mr. Rousseau who was laughing?”

“Cuz I heard it so many times before. It’s a skeery kind of laugh, sends chills up my backbone.”

“What were the circumstances when you heard his laugh before?”

“Objection!” Rogette said. “This line of questioning is not pertinent to the question of Mr. Hokanson’s guilt.”

"It is pertinent Your Honor, it goes to identify who was laughing, and sheds light on what actually happened prior to the shooting."

"Very well, but keep it brief, Mr Higgins. Objection overruled. Answer the question, Mrs. White."

"I done forgot what de question was."

Higgins smiled. "When had you heard Mr. Rousseau's laugh before?"

"When he an' his missus fought. He'd laugh like dat after he smacked her."

"Did you actually see him strike his wife?"

"Nosuh, but I could tell, on account of I could hear her cryin'."

Rogette was standing again. "Objection, Your Honor! The witness is making an assumption!"

"I'm not hard of hearing, Mr. Rogette. The jury will disregard the statements regarding the striking of Mrs. Rousseau. However, the identification of Mr. Rousseau's laugh is adequate for the jury to consider. Go on, Mr. Higgins."

"Mrs White, were there any other sounds, following the laugh you heard?"

"Yassuh, I heard a pop, like I tole 'Spector Cousteau, it sounded like a home brew poppin' its cork."

"Thank you, Mrs. White. I have no further questions."

The rest of the morning was spent questioning the two officers who helped investigate the scene of the shooting, and the hack driver who had called the police. Nothing was gained from their testimony except to affirm the presence of ratholes in Girard's home. The court was recessed until the afternoon.

"So far, it's a toss of a coin," Whitmore said. "They haven't proven anything except that a shooting took place."

"Yes, but I've gone up against Rogette before, he saves the power for the last," Higgins said. " It makes me uneasy, he's got something up his sleeve. Do you suppose it's Rousseau?"

"Rousseau? We can expect him to lie. But if we can trip him up, we've got a chance of turning him in our favor," Whitmore said.

Higgins nodded. "He'll still be damaging. The jury will look at him in his wheelchair or whatever, and they'll feel sorry for him. I just hope Rogette hasn't got any surprises for us."

"Do you think we should let Peter testify?"

"Only if it looks like there's no other way," Higgins said. "He's too honest, he might give Rogette something we don't want him to have."

"Without him, we don't have anything, except Kathryn Rousseau."

"She can't give us anything except that her husband beat her, and that would provide motivation for Peter to kill him. No, we don't have anything except Nellie White and Rousseau's laugh. Too bad they couldn't find the knife." Higgins shook his head and sighed.

"Do you really think there is a knife?" Whitmore asked.

"I don't know, it doesn't matter anymore. We may have to put Peter on the stand and hope the jury believes him."

At two o'clock Rogette levelled his big gun at the defense.

"The prosecution calls Girard Rousseau to the stand."

The courtroom became deathly silent as all eyes turned to the aisle. The twin doors opened, and Girard appeared, gaunt and pale in the wheelchair an officer pushed.

"Damn!...look at them." Higgins whispered to Whitmore.

The jury members were watching intently. One could see a softening of features, as the first wave of sympathy hit. The wheelchair proceeded slowly down the aisle. When it reached the stand, the officer turned it around. For the first time since the day at Girard's home, the eyes of Girard and Peter met. Peter looked at his adversary stolidly, Girard returned a gaze of pure hatred, his lips curled momentarily in a sneering smile, then it was gone.

After the swearing in, Rogette walked to Girard and touched him on the shoulder momentarily, then backed away sadly. It was almost as though he was a war hero, and Rogette was about to bestow a medal for valor. He began to speak.

"What do you do for a living, Mr. Rousseau?"

"I am a musician, or rather, I was." Girard spoke softly enough so that the jurymen leaned forward to hear.

"Could you speak a little louder, Mr. Rousseau?"

"I'm sorry...it's difficult, since...it happened."

"Of course, we understand—Your Honor, could an officer repeat Mr. Rousseau's testimony for the benefit of the jury?"

"I scarcely think that is necessary, Mr. Rogette. I think that with a little effort on the part of Mr. Rousseau we shall hear him quite well."

"Very well, Your Honor. You said that you 'were' a musician, Mr. Rousseau. What were you doing at noon on December the sixteenth?"

"I was sleeping, I was accustomed to sleeping into the afternoon, since I used to work into the early hours."

"And on this day, you were disturbed, were you not?"

"Yes, a knocking at the door woke me."

"Who was at the door?"

"It was Peter Hokanson."

"What did he want?"

"He said he was Peter Hokanson, and that he had come to see my wife. I didn't remember the name, since I'd never really met him, so I asked him who he was."

"Then what happened?"

"He became quite abusive, it was very embarrassing."

"What exactly did he say?"

"I'll never forget that. He said, "You stupid bastard, you don't remember me? I'm the man who had your wife before you did! "

There was a buzz of astonishment in the courtroom. Peter stood up angrily. "That's a lie! I never said that!"

The judge pounded with his gavel. "Order! Order! Mr. Higgins calm your client. Another display of that nature and I'll have him removed to a holding cell."

Rogette smiled faintly. "What happened next, Mr. Rousseau?"

"I was rather upset, I told him that I thought he was a liar and that Kathryn wasn't home. I told him that I wouldn't permit him to see her if she was. He got very angry and forced his way past me into my home."

"So he intruded into your home to see if your wife was there?"

"That's right, I asked him politely to leave. I sensed there was something wrong with the man, and I didn't wish to agitate him further."

"How did he react to that?"

"He was furious, he said that he'd come all the way from Minnesota to get her, and he wasn't going to leave without her. I told him that she was my wife, and that he wasn't taking her anyplace. When I said that, he must have lost whatever control he had. He grabbed me by the throat and began strangling me—I was terrified."

"So he forced his way into your home and proceeded to throttle you. Did he then release you?"

"No, I managed to break his hold and delivered a blow to his face. It apparently set him off his balance, since he fell backwards against the stove and then to the floor. The stovepipes fell, and there was soot everywhere, that's when he began laughing."

"Mr. Hokanson started laughing?"

"Like a maniac, I thought he had become completely insane. I reached to help him up. And then…." Girard's voice became husky with emotion, he paused for a moment to regain control. "Then…he pulled out a revolver, and just as calmly as if he were killing a chicken, he shot me!"

"Just one other thing, Mr. Rousseau. Did you know at any time of an involvement between your wife and her sister's husband?"

There was an audible gasp from the gallery.

"I am correct, am I not, Mr. Rousseau? Mr. Hokanson was married to your wife's sister."

"Objection!," Mr. Higgins said. "Mr. Hokanson's personal family relationships are not relevant."

"The relevance will become apparent, Your Honor."

"I think I know what you're getting at, Mr. Rogette. You may answer the question, Mr. Rousseau."

Girard seemed to sag together. "Yes he was, I just found out that his wife had died. I didn't know of any involvement between Kat and Peter—I thought her coolness to me was the others."

"Others, Mr. Rousseau?"

"Yes, Kathryn occasionally had a dalliance with someone, another musician, a bartender, it was her nature."

"I have no further questions of Mr. Rousseau at this time, Your Honor. The prosecution reserves right of redirect."

"Damn him!" Peter whispered to Higgins. "He made the whole thing up from beginning to end. The jury's sucking it up."

"I know," Higgins said. "We've got to blow some holes in his story, or you'll have to take the stand. Let's see what I can do."

"Mr. Rousseau, did you mean to imply that your wife and Mr. Hokanson were in communication with each other?"

"It seems reasonable to believe that. She kept things from me."

"Do you also believe that she told him about the beating you administered to her shortly before he arrived?"

"I…do I have to answer that, Your Honor?"

"Mr. Rogette opened your affairs to question, Mr. Rousseau. Answer the question."

"I don't know."

"You admit to the beating? Yes or no, Mr. Rousseau. Bear in mind that there may be testimony on this subject."

"Yes, I hit her once or twice. But she asked for it."

"How did she 'ask for it,' Mr. Rousseau?"

"She woke me up by pounding on me, then she started to claw me."

"And so, you beat her into unconsciousness, did you not, Mr. Rousseau?"

"Objection!," Mr. Rogette said loudly. "Mr. Rousseau is not on trial!"

"We are only trying to discover the cause of the 'agitated state' that Mr. Rousseau claims Mr. Hokanson was in."

"I'm going to overrule the objection. But please conclude this line of questioning quickly, Mr. Higgins. Answer the question, Mr. Rousseau."

"I don't know if she was unconscious, she was lying on the floor when I left."

"You beat your wife and left her lying on the floor, because this small woman pounded on you. What caused her to be angry enough to attack you?"

"She thought I was carrying on with a barmaid."

"And were you?"

"No, we only talked at the club where I work."

"Mr. Rousseau, if Mr. Hokanson had known about his sister-in-law's beating, wouldn't that be reason for him to come and rescue her?"

"Ojection! Mr. Higgins is asking the witness to draw a conclusion!"

"Objection sustained. That's enough of this line of questioning, Mr. Higgins."

"Very well, Your Honor. Mr. Rousseau, you stated that you were sleeping when Mr. Hokanson knocked on the door at Monday noon. You said it was because you work late as a musician. But isn't it true that your club is closed on Sunday night?"

"Ah…yes, I had forgotten."

"You forgot, or you lied? Wasn't it because you were drunk, as you are much of the time? Isn't it true, Mr. Rousseau, that you drink so much that your wife is forced to clean your club to support herself and your infant daughter?"

"Objection! Your Honor, Mr. Higgins is placing Mr. Rousseau on trial again."

"Objection sustained. Mr. Higgins, you are going too far in that direction. The jury will disregard Mr. Higgins' last question."

"Very well, your honor. I have no more questions of this witness."

"You didn't ask him about the knife, or about his laughing." Peter whispered.

"He would only have denied it. Every time the jury hears it from him they will be more likely to believe him," Higgins said.

Whitmore nodded. "If you know a man is going to lie, don't ask him the question unless you can prove it's a lie."

"The Prosecution calls Kathryn Rousseau," Rogette said.

"Why are they calling Kat?," Peter asked. "Won't she be damaging to them?"

"That damage is already out in the open," Whitmore said. "They are trying to prove the motivation for you to kill him."

Kathryn took the stand, she was pale and obviously nervous.

"Mrs. Rousseau," Rogette began, "Mr. Hokanson is your brother-in-law, is he not?"

"Yes."

"We realize that this is difficult for you, since it involves two people whom you love. You do love them both, don't you?"

"There are different kinds of love."

Rogette smiled. "We are well aware of that, Mrs. Rousseau. How do you love your husband."

"I...loved him as a husband and the father of my child."

"You used the past tense, Mrs. Rousseau. Don't you love him any longer?"

Higgins stood up. "Objection! Your Honor, whether Mrs. Rousseau loves her husband has nothing to do with the case at hand. It is completely irrelevant.

"We will presently show the relevance, Your Honor."

"Please do so quickly, Mr. Rogette. Answer the question, Mrs. Rousseau."

"No, he is no longer a loving husband and father. I do not love him."

"And how do you feel toward Mr. Hokanson?"

"He is kind, and a dear friend."

"Was there not a time when he was more than that? Isn't it true that you were romantically related?"

"It was a long time ago, and it was nothing."

"He took you to a party, did he not."

"Yes."

"And at that party, you caught him in the arms of your sister, did you not?"

"Yes."

"How did you feel about that?"

"I was angry with him, but we made peace later on."

"So then, you were on good terms when your sister and Mr. Hokanson were married."

"Yes, we were."

"Is it not a fact, Mrs. Rousseau, that you were on very good terms? So much so that Mr. Hokanson tried to make love to you when you were alone in the house. And that is why you so precipitously left with your husband-to-be?"

"No! It wasn't like that, it wasn't his fault. I...seduced him,...because I was still angry with him."

"You stated that you were at peace with him—now you say you were still angry with him. Which was it?"

Kathryn was sobbing quietly. "I...was still angry."

"And so you seduced him, your sister's husband. Then you went away, and married Girard Rousseau. And some time later, when your sister had died and your own marriage was failing, you started writing to Mr. Hokanson."

"No!...I didn't!... I didn't even know my sister had died."

"Didn't you? Isn't it a fact that you and Mr. Hokanson were in love, and that you conspired to kill your husband, so that you could be married?"

"No!, No!, I never wrote to him!" Kathryn began crying with anguish and misery.

"I have no further questions of this witness, Your Honor."

Peter was stunned. "Why did she tell Cousteau about that?"

Higgins shrugged. "She was probably trying to convince him that there wasn't anything between you anymore."

"But they've twisted everything!"

"M-hm-m, did a damned good job of it too. Try to sit tight, I've got to ask Kathryn a few questions." He walked to the stand and waited for Kathryn to compose herself. Then he spoke.

"Mrs. Rousseau, I have just a few questions, I will not bludgeon you with suppositions. The episode that has been described was that of an impetuous young woman getting even with a suitor who jilted her, was it not?"

"Y- yes."

"Did you continue to communicate with your family after you left?"

"No."

"Did you ever write to Mr. Hokanson, or have any other communication with him?"

"No."

"Did you write a letter to your father in December of 1903?"

"Yes. I wrote to Daddy asking him to send me money."

"For what purpose?"

"So that I and April, she's my daughter, could go back to Minneapolis. Because we didn't have anything, sometimes not even enough to eat. And I was afraid for April."

"Why were you afraid for her?"

"Because Girard was often drunk, and he had started taking opium and other things. He had become someone I no longer knew—he hit me on several occasions—I was afraid he might hurt April."

"And so you asked your father for money, did you ask him to come for you?"

"No, I told him not to, because I was afraid Girard might do something to him."

"Did you know that Mr. Hokanson would come?"

"I had no idea he would want to, because of what I had done to him."

"Did he know about the beating you received at the hands of your husband?"

"No, he couldn't have. It happened after I wrote the letter."

"Do you have that letter now, Mrs. Rousseau?"

"Yes, I have it right here, Daddy gave it to me after Peter was arrested." Kathryn gave Higgins a rumpled envelope.

Higgins took the letter. Your Honor, the defense wishes to enter this letter as evidence. It is dated December 10, 1903, and is postmarked on that date. It is addressed to Mr. Charlie LeBlanc, Mrs. Rousseau's father, and substantiates the testimony she has given." He handed it to the judge who perused it.

He offered it to Rogette, who scanned it quickly. "Does the prosecution have any objection?"

"We do not, Your Honor."

"Very well, the bailiff will carry the letter to the jury for their attention."

Higgins turned to Kathryn. "I have one more question, for the record, Mrs. Rousseau. Did you conspire with Mr. Hokanson to kill your husband?"

"No! I could never do that!"

"I have no more questions for this witness, Your Honor."

The judge turned to Rogette. "Does the prosecution have any more witnesses?"

"No, Your Honor, the prosecution rests."

"Mr. Higgins?"

"Your Honor, defense petitions that the court direct the jury to find for acquittal. The prosecution has not shown sufficient evidence for conviction on any of the charges."

"Mr. Higgins, I have anticipated your request, and I must rule against it. The prosecution has shown some rather compelling evidence in some areas that should be weighed by the jury. Is the defense prepared to call a witness?"

"Your Honor, the defense requests a recess, so that I may consult with my colleague."

"Very well, Mr. Higgins, court recesses until one o'clock."

Kathryn joined Peter and the two attorneys at their table. She looked at Peter sorrowfully.

"I'm sorry I told Cousteau about what I did to you before I left, Peter. I thought it would show him that you had a reason for hating me, and that you would never be interested in me. But he took it and twisted it to make it look like like we were lovers, instead."

"I know, Kat. The man is evil, despite his badge. He isn't interested in justice, he just wants to put me in prison. The thing is, what do we do now?"

"We can put the doctor on the stand—tell the jury how badly Kathryn was beaten." Whitmore said.

Higgins shook his head. "I don't think we'd get far with that, Rousseau has already admitted to the beating. And Rousseau has already testified about Peter's condition at the time of the shooting. We may use him later. But I'm afraid that Peter will have to take the stand, otherwise Rousseau's story will be the only one the jury will hear."

"I don't understand why Rogette accepted the letter so easily, they could have objected to it, since it was opened already. The original could have been replaced with another letter," Peter said.

"That's true," Higgins said, "but the envelope was addressed to Charlie LeBlanc. I don't think they ever expected to make the 'conspiracy' charge stick. They think the jury will throw that out and settle for a lesser charge."

"Yes," Whitmore said, "they have a weak case on the 'conspiracy' charge. They are hoping that the jury will believe Peter did it on his own, that he went to Roussea's place with the intent of killing him."

"But, isn't the 'attempted murder' charge just as weak?" Peter asked, "They don't really have any evidence on that."

"Technically, you're right," Higgins said. "But these men are used to looking at women as passive creatures incapable of the type of scheming that conspiracy requires. They are used to crimes of passion, where a man sets out to acquire the love of a woman, using any means. And that is the way they'll be looking at you, unless you can convince them that he shot Rousseau out of fear for your life." Higgins turned to Whitmore. "That's why Peter has to testify, it's his only chance."

"But, won't they think it was a fight between two men, and both were responsible?" Peter asked.

"They might, if it were two ruffians fighting over a bar girl. But Kathryn is his wife, and he's in a wheel chair, not you." Higgins replied. "You have to be adamant in denying a love relationship with Kathryn. You were just a man who was trying to take care of his kin. They understand that, and they'll respect it."

At one o'clock court reconvened, and Higgins called Peter to the stand. The jury was alert with anticipation.

"Mr. Hokanson, did you go to the home of Girard Rousseau on December the 16th, 1903?"

"Yes, I did."

"What was your purpose for going there?"

"Kathryn's father, Charlie LeBlanc, received a letter from Kathryn. She said that she feared for her daughter's safety, and asked for money to return to Minneapolis. When I saw the letter, I was afraid that Girard might not let her go. I came to aid her, if necessary."

"What type of relationship did you have with Mrs. Rousseau?"

"None, since she left in February of 1900. She hadn't written to anyone until Charlie got her letter in December of 1903. It really hurt Charlie—he and I have been very close—I owe everything I have to him. So when he got the letter from Kathryn, I felt I owed it to him to help his daughter."

"So, you had no feelings of a romantic nature for her?"

"None whatever, it was the farthest thing from my mind."

"How did you feel toward Mr. Rousseau?"

"I had no feelings toward him, because I'd never had any dealings with him. But after I read Kat's letter, I was appalled—I think that a man who doesn't care for his family is the most despicable creature in existence."

"Mr. Hokanson, when you knocked on Mr. Rousseau's door, what did you expect?"

"I expected Kat to come to the door, I didn't know that Girard had beaten her, and that she'd left."

"What did you do when Mr. Rousseau answered the door?"

"He thought I was a rent collector. I introduced myself, but he didn't remember who I was. I told him I was Kat's brother-in-law and that I wanted to see Kat."

"What happened then?"

"He was unpleasant, he called me a 'big shot'. He said she wasn't there and said I should go back to where I'd come from. I thought he was lying, and I told him so. He told me, 'get your ass out of here before I kick it down the stairs.'"

A chorus of snickers ran through the courtroom, and the judge banged his gavel.

"What was your responce to that?"

"I pushed him out of the way, and entered the room. Then I asked where Kat was, since she wasn't there. He called me an asshole and said he didn't know where she was. He said, 'I don't know where the damned slut is. If I did, I'd slap the shit out of the bitch.'"

A tremor of excitement ran through the gallery.

"Those were his exact words?"

"Yes, his exact words."

"Mr. Hokanson, how did you react to that reply?"

"I guess I lost my head. He was dirty, he stunk of whiskey and he was altogether vile. When he said those things about Kat, I grabbed him by the throat and demanded that he tell me where she was. I told him I was going to take her out of that shithole."

"What was his reaction?"

"I misjudged him in my anger. He hit me in the stomach hard, then smashed his knee into my face. I crashed into the stove and fell to the floor. The fight was over then, because I was blinded with the pain in my face and the soot from the stovepipes."

"You are saying that you were disabled, and couldn't continue to fight?"

"Yes, I was finished."

"Mr. Hokanson, Mr. Rousseau testifyed that at this point you started laughing, drew a gun, and shot him. Is that what happened?"

"No, not at all. Girard was laughing at my helplessness. As I started to regain my sight he was kneeling in front of me—he was waving a knife in my face. Then he started talking real low, with this awful grin on his face. He said I wasn't going to take Kat anyplace because he was going to slit my throat and watch my blood pump out. He said that he was going to find Kat after I was dead and show her what he'd done. He said that if she begged hard enough he might let her live."

There was a loud buzz of excitement in the courtroom. Higgins paused while the judge gavelled for order, then he resumed.

"You were nearly helpless, and Mr. Rousseau was threatening you with a knife? How did you react?"

"I grabbed his arm and tried to push the knife away, but he was stronger and he forced the knife back toward my throat—he was laughing as he did it. I remembered the revolver in my belt and somehow I was able to pull it out. I pushed him back with the last strength I had and fired. He fell backward and lay there."

"What happened then?"

"After I'd recovered myself I felt his neck for a pulse to see if he was dead. Then I got up and was about to go for help when Mrs. White screamed and ran down the stairs. I knew she would call the police, so I put a bandage on Girard to stop the bleeding. I hadn't meant to shoot him, and I didn't want him to bleed to death. Then I waited for the police."

"Thank you, Mr. Hokanson. I have no further questions of the witness, Your Honor."

The judge turned to the prosecution. "Mr. Rogette?"

"I have only a few questions, Your Honor."

"Mr. Hokanson, by your own admission, you initiated the violence that occurred by grabbing Mr. Rousseau by the throat, did you not?"

"Yes, it was in a fit of anger."

"It was in a fit of anger, yet you testify that you didn't mean to shoot Mr. Rousseau. Had your anger cooled, after he hit you to defend himself from your attack?"

"No, I didn't want to shoot him. I had to, because he had a knife."

"Oh, I see. You shot him because he had a knife. But, Mr. Hokanson, if you didn't want to shoot him, how was it that you so conveniently had a gun in your belt?"

"I...I was carrying a large amount of money–I carried it for protection."

"How prudent of you. You have explained everything except for one minor problem. How is it the police were not able to recover the knife that you said Mr. Rousseau had?"

"Objection!, Higgins said. "Your Honor, the defendant could not possibly know why the police did not recover the weapon in question."

"He could know, if he knows that it does not exist, Your Honor," Rogette shot back.

"The existence of the knife has not been proven, nor has it been disproven, Mr. Rogette. Objection sustained."

"Very well, Your Honor. Mr. Hokanson, after the police failed to discover the knife in question, did you not perform your own search?"

"Yes."

"And did you not go so far as to remove a portion of the building exterior?"

"Yes."

"Did you find the knife?"

"No, the building is rotten and full of holes, it may have fallen out on the street."

"Once again, you have a laudable explanation, Mr. Hokanson." Rogette said sarcastically. "I have no more questions, Your Honor."

"The witness is excused. Do you have further witnesses, Mr. Higgins?"

Higgins glanced at Whitmore who shook his head glumly. Higgins said, "No, Your Honor, the defense rests."

"Very well," The judge said, "Mr. Rogette, are you prepared to make your summation?"

"Yes, Your Honor."

He stood, then walked to face the jury—his face was a picture of gravity.

"Gentlemen of the jury, a crime has been committed. It is a crime that is terrible in its result to the victim. For it has taken something from an innocent man that cannot be replaced, the use of his legs! Girard Rousseau was awaked from peaceful slumber by the defendant, and soon after, he was crippled for life. For what reason did the defendant come to Mr. Rousseau's home? For what reason did the defendant grasp him by the throat, throttling the breath from him? For what reason did the defendant finally shoot Mr. Rousseau with a gun that he carried concealed in his belt? The sole reason was to take his wife from him. It was to violate the holy admonition, 'What God has joined together let no man put asunder.'

"The defendant claims he was on a mission of mercy to protect his sister-in-law, Mr. Rousseau's wife. If that were indeed true, why did he not go to Mr. Rousseau's home in peace, instead of with a weapon? Why did he not implore Mr. Rousseau to see the error of his ways, giving him wise counsel to return his marriage to its sacred state? The answer, Gentlemen, is that Mr. Hokanson did not want the marriage to survive. Why? Because the defendant wanted Mr. Rousseau's wife for himself!

"And so, he sought to divide them. When Mr. Rousseau objected, the defendant used his ace card, a thirty eight calibre revolver. He would have suceeded in his plot, had providence not intervened. A witness appeared and summoned help. Mr. Hokanson had been seen, his face was damaged and bleeding as a result of Mr. Rousseau's desperate attempt to save himself. He could not escape, so he bandaged his victim and manufactured a story about an attack by the victim, an attack with a knife, which incredibly could not be found!

"The defendant knew exactly what he was doing, he knew what he would do before he arrived at the victim's home. And that, gentlemen, is attempted murder in the first degree!

"He used a gun to do harm to another, in a fight he initiated. That is assault with a deadly weapon.

"What of conspiracy? Look at the testimony and weigh it carefully. The defendant had once been involved romantically with Mr. Rousseau's wife. Mr. Rousseau's wife was unhappy with her marriage. Mr. Hokanson's wife had died. Suddenly Mr. Hokanson appears to take Mr. Rousseau's wife back to Minnesota. They both knew that Mr. Rousseau would not permit that. Were they innocent of planning the death of Mr. Rousseau? Or did they conspire to eliminate a problem in their plans to resume a lost romance?

"Judging the balance on the scales of justice is a difficult task. It is a task which must be taken seriously, without emotion. You must consider the evidence diligently, weighing for truth the words that have been spoken here. Then you will deliver a verdict on each of the charges. And when you do, you will tell the court that Peter Olaf Hokanson is…guilty as charged!"

When J. B. Higgins approached the jury, it was with a trace of smile. He exuded good will and sympathy.

"Members of the jury, I sympathize with Mr. Rogette. He has one of the meanest jobs in the world. It is his job to take a man who is suspected of committing a crime, and prove that he has done it. He cannot subscribe to our belief that a man is considered innocent until proven guilty. Shadows of doubt do not exist within his mind, the defendants he prosecutes are guilty,…at least in his mind. And it can be no other way for him—if he felt compassion or respected anything other than the absolute letter of the law, he could not function as a prosecutor.

"You and I are different, we can seek the hows and whys of human behavior. We can take the blacks and whites of the prosecutor's lawbooks and find that in reality they are varying shades of gray. And that is what justice is gentlemen, deciding if the gray falls more to the side of the white of innocence or the black of guilt. If in your mind, the evidence leans even slightly toward the white of innocence, there is a shadow of doubt. And no matter how much the prosecution theorizes to the contrary, you must find that man innocent. You cannot judge a man guilty on the basis of a theory built by the prosecution. You must decide on the basis of fact, and failing to find that, you must find for the white of innocence.

"The other factor that we may use is compassion. If we are to render a verdict in which we also render a sentence, we must first decide in our minds if the man is guilty. If he is guilty, then we must look into the man to see why he acted as he did. That is where justice is tempered with compassion. A man who murdered his wife with an axe in a fit of jealousy would not be as worthy of compassion as a man who killed another to protect a loved one.

"Let us examine the charges against Peter Hokanson, taking the most odious one first. The prosecutor would have you believe that he and Kathryn Rosseau conspired to kill Girrard Rosseau. Mr. Rogette extends nothing but theory and innuendo on this charge. He has not one credible witness, not a letter or telegram or any other piece of evidence to substantiate that allegation. I will not insult you by suggesting you would even consider a guilty verdict.

"Then we have 'attempted murder in the first degree'. Mr. Rogette must have proven to you—beyond a reasonable doubt—that the defendant went to the home of Mr. Rosseau with the single purpose of murdering him.

"Peter Hokanson is an intelligent man who came to this country as a boy of seventeen. He put together business holdings that most men never realize, before he was thirty! If you were Peter, and you wanted to kill a man, would you yourself go to his home to do it,…or would you perhaps, hire a thug?… No, he expected to find Kathryn there, and what happened was a complete surprise to him.

"His reason for carrying the gun was prudent, just as Mr. Rogette said. He had it to protect himself and the money which he carried, on a long trip far from home. And if you believe what Peter said, you will realize that it was that weapon that saved him from a violent death!

"Last, we have 'assault with a deadly weapon'. Here the prosecutor must prove that the defendant used the weapon with the intent of doing bodily harm. The law is explicit in the differentiation between assault and defense against an overwhelming threat.

"Peter testified that he was defending himself against a knife attack by Girard Rosseau. Mr. Rogette claims there was no knife, simply because the police did not find one. Mrs. White testified that she heard Mr. Rousseau laugh a 'scary' kind of laugh. Why was he laughing if he didn't have control? Certainly he wouldn't be laughing if Peter were holding a gun on him. No, he had a knife, or he was certain he could destroy his adversary by other means. In which case, Peter had a perfect right to fear for his life. And,…if he feared for his life, the shooting was self defense.

"Peter Olaf Hokanson fell into a horrible situation, Gentlemen. He was moved by compassion for a member of his family, Kathryn. She is a poor woman who was living in poverty with a husband who drank and used drugs. Bravely she supported her child and herself, until it was too much to endure. She cried for help, and her brother-in-law came to her aid as kin should, as you and I would. Use compassion gentlemen, use compassion."

Higgins returned to his seat beside Peter. "The die is cast," he said. "Now all we can do is pray."

Peter nodded in agreement. Of late he had become very spiritual.

The judge charged the jury and they filed out of the courtroom to another smaller room where they would begin their deliberation.

Peter and the attorneys talked quietly for a while. Then the attorneys drifted off to visit with colleagues in the court area. Peter was surprised to see Higgins and Rogette shake hands and talk with obvious pleasure. It is not so strange, he thought, remembering how he visited with competitors of his own. It is their business, and the lives of those they deal with have nothing to do with their own. He moved next to Kathryn, who had borrowed a Bible from the bailiff and was reading intently.

"Kat, how are you? I mean are you all right, inside?"

He looked at her and could see lines around her eyes and mouth. Her life had aged her too soon, he thought.

"I don't know, Peter. It's all too much. First my trouble with Girard, and now this. I'm worried for you Peter."

"Don't worry, Kat. I'll survive, regardless of what happens, I'll survive."

"I know you will, Peter. But what if you go to prison?" Tears were forming in her eyes, and Peter reached gently to brush them away.

"Then you must do something for me, Kat."

"Anything, Peter, oh yes,...anything at all."

"If I'm convicted, I want you to go home and live in my house. I want you to take care of my children and talk to them about me every day. I don't want them to forget they have a father if I have to stay here. Elias will see that all your needs are taken care of. And I want you to write to me every week. Will you do that?"

"Oh yes, Peter. But you are talking as if you think you will be convicted. You don't, do you?"

"I hope I won't, but I'm tired and my life rests with twelve strangers. It's hard to be optimistic. Don't expect too much, Kat."

They waited the rest of the day. At six o'clock the bailiff came and told them there would be no verdict that day. They went back to the hotel and a night of sleeplessness.

In the morning they went back to the courthouse. Nothing had changed—the jury was still closeted—they resumed their vigil. Kathryn and Peter were tired and drawn, the attorneys were fresh and rested. At ten o'clock Higgins came to the bench in the hallway where Peter and Kathryn were sitting.

"The jury is coming in," he said.

"All rise!" the bailiff cried. "Court of Justice, Parish of Orleans is now in session. The honorable Judge Hewitt P. Justice presiding."

The judge banged his gavel. "This is the case of the people of Louisiana versus Peter Olaf Hokanson. Mr. Foreman, has the jury reached a verdict?"

A stout, red faced man rose. "We have, Your Honor."

"Very good, the defendant will stand for the verdict."

Peter rose with the two attorneys. His hands were clammy, his throat dry, he swallowed nervously.

"How do you find, Mr. Foreman?" The judge peered at the foreman.

"On the count of 'Conspiracy to commit murder in the first degree', we find the defendant,—not guilty. On the count of 'Murder in the first degree', we find the defendant ,—not guilty. On the count of 'Assault with a deadly weapon', we find the defendant,—guilty as charged."

Peter stood there stolidly—it was what he had expected, worse than they had hoped for, better than it could have been. At least Kathryn will be free, he thought.

The judge was thanking the jury and dismissing them. Then he turned to Peter.

"Mr. Hokanson, you have been found guilty of the charge of 'Assault with a deadly weapon'. You are remanded to the custody of the bailiff until sentencing at one o'clock this afternoon. Court is recessed."

As Peter was led to the holding cell, his eyes met Kathryn's, she was crying and she seemed very small and helpless. It was strange, he thought that at a time like this he should feel more concern for her than for himself.

Judge Hewitt P. Justice sat alone in his chamber. He had listened to this man who was obviously not a common criminal, and Hewitt doubted that he should have been convicted at all. His sympathy was not with the victim of this tragedy, but with his wife. He wondered that there were not laws to bring the wrath of justice on vermin like Girard Rousseau.

Still, Hokanson had been found guilty by a jury of his peers, and now it was the judge's duty to sentence him. The man had attempted to help that poor woman—Hewitt was comfortable with that. After years on the bench he could sense a liar, he could see it in their eyes. Hokanson was honest and truthful, maybe too much so for this world. He had blundered into a situation that led him to a prison sentence. At least it was only assault.

He wondered why Cousteau and Rogette had brought the conspiracy and murder charges. They were such assholes sometimes. Rogette had his eye on the attorney general's office. Cousteau was groping his way upward too.

Power corrupts, and the quest of it corrupts even more, he thought.

Well, he would impose a light sentence, and parole. There would be the possibility of parole for good behavior. The thought improved the picture and Hewitt's mood lightened. The judge was a good man, he enjoyed bringing the wrath of justice on the scum of the earth. But he had no stomach for sending good men to prison.

When court had resumed, Judge Hewitt P. Justice looked sternly into the eyes of Peter Olaf Hokanson.

"You have been found guilty of 'Assault with a deadly weapon', he said. "Do you have anything to say before sentencing?"

"Yes, Your Honor, I would like to say that I am sorry that I shot Girard Rousseau. It was fear for my life, not anger, that made me do it. I could not be angry enough to take a man's life deliberately or to cause him to be crippled for the rest of his life. That is all I wish to say."

"Very well, the court notes your contrition, and passes sentence. You, Peter Olaf Hokanson, are sentenced to confinement at the Louisiana State Penitentiary at Angola, Louisiana, for a period of not less than two years, nor more than five years. You are remanded to the custody of the Sheriff of Orleans Parish for transportation to the penitentiary."

Chapter 20

New Beginnings

Kathryn and April returned to Minneapolis and settled into Peter's big house with Charles, Sven and the toddler, Lucille. Despite the absence of Peter she was happy to be home again. The children had quickly accepted April, and the house rang with their laughter. True to her promise she spoke often to the children of Peter. She explained to them that he could not be with them now, but that he would return. She didn't tell them that he was in prison, they were too young to understand. To the questions of Charles and Sven, she replied that he was working in another state and that he would return when he was finished.

Every week she wrote to Peter, and it was her letters that sustained his spirits. Charlie, Gus and Elias kept the businesses running. The new bank was open, and had been received enthusiastically by the people of the city. Elias sent money to Kathryn every other week for the maintenance of Peter's household—she and the children lacked nothing—for the first time since she left home, Kathryn was at peace.

Peter soon fell into the monotonous rhythm of prison life. Because of his experience he was placed in the penitentiary carpenter shop. He found that working with his hands relieved the otherwise grinding oppression of his confinement. Other than that, he kept to himself, finding solace and strength in Kathryn's letters. Higgins had filed an appeal with the Louisiana State Court of Appeals on Peter's case based on predjudicial evidence brought forward by the prosecution. It was denied.

In September of 1904 Peter had a visitor. When he was ushered to the visiting room, he was surprised to find Elias Oberg waiting for him. They exchanged greetings, and Elias assured Peter that all was well, but that he had come on a matter of business. "It has to do with the bank," he said.

"Why?" Peter asked. "Is it not doing well?"

"It's doing very well, your investment is quite safe. There is a small difficulty, though."

"What kind of difficulty?"

"It concerns your present situation, Peter. It seems that it is illegal for a convicted felon to serve on the board of directors of a financial institution."

The words,"convicted felon" struck Peter hard. He had never thought of himself in that light—he considered himself a victim of circumstances. It was true, of course. He was now a convict, and there were certain things society would deny him.

"Does that mean that I have to take my money out of the bank?"

Elias smiled reassuringly. "Your investment is quite safe, Peter. It is vested under the power of attorney you granted me. However, you must resign from the board. I have the papers here, all that you need to do is sign them." He slipped the resignation and a pen beneath the wire screen that separated them.

Peter looked at the papers briefly, then applied his signature. "I'm damned lucky to have you to take care of my business," he said. "I don't know what would happen otherwise. Charlie can't handle everything."

"I'm glad to do it Peter. You helped me get a start in this country, I owe you. And you're right, Charlie has all he can do. He's sold the lumber mill, so that will help. I'm afraid it was a little late, he didn't do well at all on it. Actually, after his payable accounts were cleared he just about broke even."

Peter was perplexed. "That's strange, it was all free and clear. He should have made a lot."

"Yes, we all thought that. Frankly, I think Charlie's slipping. Timber is getting scarce, and he was paying too much for it for some time. Then, he was forced to sell lumber too low to meet competition from the west. I did the best I could do for him on the sale, but the mill went low, very low."

"You arranged the sale?"

"Yes, since the bank was involved in the finances of the mill, Charlie turned the whole thing over to me."

"But the flour and grain business is okay, isn't it?"

"It's doing very well, and so is the furniture factory, despite the rising competition. Gus is pushing it hard and it's making money, even if the profit margin is a little slimmer. You have nothing to worry about, Peter. When you get out of here you can step right back into things."

"Time's up," the guard said. "You'll have to leave now, Sir."

"Very well." Elias rose from his chair. "Oh, by the way, Peter. Kathryn plans on coming to see you at Christmas. But don't tell her you know, she wants it to be a surprise."

That night Peter made a calendar from a large sheet of paper a guard gave him. Every morning he marked off the date with an "X". The coming of Kathryn was marked with a big circle.

Peter threw himself into his work, and by the end of November he was put in charge of the bookwork for the carpenter shop. It gave him a sense of accomplishment, though he was chafed by the rigid restriction of confinement. Every day brought Christmas closer, and work shortened those days.

At one o'clock on the day before Christmas Peter was called to the warden's office. Peter stood at rigid attention as was required. The warden was smiling.

"Peter, you have been a model prisoner. As a reward, I have something special for you. A lady has arrived from your home to visit you. Since it is Christmas, I am going to lift the one half hour visit restriction. You may be together for four hours today, and also on Christmas day."

Peter was astonished, a four hour visit was unheard of, much less two of them. "That's wonderful, Sir. When will she come?"

"She's here now, Peter. You can visit in the reviewing room."

Peter wanted to run as he plodded along with the guard. Not only did he have a long visit with Kat, it would be without a wire fence between them! The guard opened the door, and suddenly Kat was in his arms hugging him. It was beyond his dreams.

At last he released her. He held her at arms' length looking at her. The worn look that she had at his trial was gone. She had gained weight, but not too much. The light was back in her eyes.

"You look wonderful, Kat! God!,…how I've looked forward to this day."

"Me too, Peter. Are they treating you well? You're a little thinner. And look! You've got some gray hairs!"

Peter laughed. "It must be the lack of sunshine. But they treat me as well as one can expect. I'm busy, and that's the main thing. How are Sven and Charles, and little Lucy and April?"

They are fine, the boys are growing like weeds. Sven looks just like you, and Charles looks like I would have if I'd been a boy. Lucy is talking like a grownup, and she's a picture of Lucille. And April is happy, at last. She's so proud of her cousins, they are so wonderful together."

"God, how I wish I were with them. That's the hardest thing about being here, being separated from my family. But I won't talk about that. How are Charlie and Elizabeth?"

"Mama's fine, she spends more time at your house than at her own. I fear she's spoiling her grandchildren terribly." Kathryn became serious. "Daddy seems healthy enough, he still charges around like an old warhorse. But he's different somehow. He's forgetfull, and that's not like him. Mama wants him to go to a doctor, but of course he won't."

Peter frowned. "Does he have trouble running the business?"

"I don't think so, Elias helps him. Maybe it's just a passing thing, he misses you of course. He has a lot of things on his mind. I suppose he's preoccupied."

"You're probably right. I miss him too, Charlie is like a father to me. Only he's my friend too, he's done more for me than anybody I've ever known. Speaking of friends, does Christian come around anymore? I haven't seen him in ages."

"Not since I've been back home. He's quit the logging business. Daddy said he and his wife have a hotel in Grand Rapids."

"Christian married!...That's wonderful! Who did he marry? Do I know her?"

"I don't know. Daddy said he'd never met the woman, but that she was from up there. I guess they have children too."

Peter shook his head incredulously. "So the old brushbuck is a family man. I would never have thought it could happen. It just goes to show, you never really know people as well as you think."

Peter and Kathryn visited all that afternoon, and too soon their four hours were up. Peter returned to his cell feeling renewed. He would live through this experience, and when he was free again he would be a stronger man for it.

On Christmas Day, Kathryn brought him a fruitcake and a box of cookies. The warden had been skeptical of allowing it, but when Kathryn gave him a box that she'd prepared for him, he relented.

"It's too bad they won't let me have a bottle of Charlie's brandy." Peter teased. "Or some of his cigars."

"Look in the bottom of your box of cookies," Kathryn said.

Peter dug to the bottom of the cookies. There was a wooden box of Cuban cigars. "How in the world did you manage that?" Peter asked.

"I gave the warden a box too. He didn't search your package, he just winked."

For the rest of their four hours Kathryn and Peter talked happily and played cards with a pack that was secreted in Peter's package. They munched on cookies as they played. Kathryn hadn't wanted to, because the cookies were for Peter, but he insisted. When, too soon, they had to part, he hugged Kathryn tight. Then she was gone, and Christmas was over.

The days turned to months and soon it was spring. It was the hardest time of the year for Peter. As he walked in the prison yard during his excercise hour, the warm spring air and the songs of birds beyond the walls beckoned to him. It was his second spring behind the gray walls of the prison, and his spirit longed for freedom.

Each time an inmate disappeared, Peter knew he had gone beyond the walls, and Peter would sink into depression. It was especially hard when the man in the adjoining cell left. The man had spent four years there for robbery, and Peter had come to know him. Suddenly he was gone—he'd been paroled. He and Peter had talked of it, but the man hadn't really believed it would happen. Peter sank to a new low.

The following week, a young man with a hideous scar down his right cheek took up residence in the empty cell.

He was talkative, unlike most of the inmates. His voice came to Peter from behind the wall that partitioned them.

"I say there matey, what brings you to this miserable cottage?"

Peter was depressed and he didn't feel like talking, but he answered. "Assault,…with a gun."

"The hell you say, you're in fine company then. Same rap as me, only mine was with a knife."

"The guy I shot had a knife."

"Hm, it's gun over knife everytime. You didn't kill the guy then?"

"No, just crippled him."

"You don't say. Bet it was over a woman, wasn't it?"

"Yeah, only it wasn't that way."

"Hah, it's always that way. I knew a guy was crippled, just like that. He was the bastard that gave me this scar a couple of years ago, damn his soul. I don't hold no grudges, especially since we was both drunk, and fightin' over a bar girl. So we still drank together, even after he was shot."

Peter said nothing.

"You still there, Matey?" The man laughed at his joke. "Anyway, this guy had a fight with some guy that was messin' with his wife. He tried to knife the guy, and wound up gettin' shot. Had to get around in a wheel chair after that. But he bragged that he got the guy put away. He laughed because the cops said they couldn't find his knife. Thought it was a good joke on the poor bastard he tried to stick."

Peter had been slumped dejectedly on his bunk. Now he sprang to his feet and grabbed the bars next to the adjoining cell. "What was that guy's name? Do you know his name?!"

"I oughta, knew him for a coupla years. His name was Rousseau, Girard Rousseau."

"Where is he now? I have to know!"

"I can tell you where he is. Don't know as how it'll help, though. Why you gettin' so fired up?"

"Because I'm the guy who shot him, and he can get me out of here!"

"No he can't, been stuck in a wall of the cemetery, three, four months now."

Peter went back to his bunk and sat down.

The voice behind the wall continued. "Well damn me to hell. Here I am talking about that worthless cuss, and you're the one that put 'im down. Awful shame, bein stuck in this hole when all you did was keep him from sticking you."

"What happened to him?"

"Drank all the time when he wasn't blowin' his horn, drank then too, cept the last week or so. Still drank, didn't blow his horn. His system just gave out, pickled his gizzard, I guess."

"Did he tell anyone else about what happened between us?"

"Told it to anybody that'd listen. 'Bout everybody on Basin Street. Why, you think you can get outa here?"

"Maybe, if enough people tell the law what he said. Do you think the people down at his club would talk?"

"Don't know why not. It can't hurt him, and he wasn't real well liked anyway. Say, who was the cop that put you away?"

"Cousteau, Inspector Cousteau."

"Whooee! You couldn't have picked a worse one. He used to hang around the club once in a while, liked Girard's playing. They was friendly."

Suddenly it all fit. The relentless attempt of Inspector Cousteau to convict him of charges that couldn't be proven, the disappearance of the knife, everything!

That night Peter wrote a letter to J.B. Higgins.

Higgins listened intently as Peter told him the story of Girard and Cousteau. He could see that Peter had built up hopes that it would free him. He also was encouraged by the story, but the possibility of improper conduct by a police inspector caused grave concerns. When Peter had finished his recitation of the conversation with his neighbor convict, Higgins spoke calmly and seriously.

"What you have told me sheds light on many things, Peter. It tells me why Rogette filed the charges that he did. It also seems to explain the absence of the knife. It would appear that Cousteau was attempting to punish you for crippling his friend. It also appears that Rogette was in league with him. I may be able to get depositions from some of the people who knew Girard Rousseau that will support what this convict...what's his name?"

"Nichols, John Nichols."

"Yes, that would support what Mr. Nichols told you. However, you must realize that this information would likely be regarded by the court as hearsay. Normally this type of testimony would not be admitted by the court. And without corroborating evidence, say the reappearance of the knife, or a confession by Rousseau, the chances of getting you a new trial are not too good."

Peter's face fell. "You mean I'll have to stay in prison even though Girard bragged that Cousteau's charges were false?"

"It would be very difficult to prove that to a court. Especially if Cousteau and Rogette have friends in high places."

"Are you saying it isn't worth trying?"

Higgins was thinking hard, his fingers were drumming the table top.

"I didn't say that,…there may be another way. I'm going to get as many depositions as I can. Sit tight Peter, don't get your hopes too high, but don't give up hope either. I'll be in touch."

Spring turned to summer, and Higgins had not returned. Peter was depressed. Had Higgins given up? How much longer would he be here—a month—a year—more? It was July, would he spend another Christmas in prison? He thought of his last Christmas, and Kat.

She had been his anchor, he read and reread her letters. When he could, he wrote to her in return. He was allowed to send one letter a month, and he had used one precious letter to call Higgins. He hadn't told Kat about Girard's death. She was free, and she didn't know it.

He wondered if this whole thing had a purpose. He had been attracted to Kat once, but it was a long time ago. A lot had happened and he wasn't sure of how he felt about her. He loved her now because she was all he had. But was there anything more? He would write to Kat that night. He would tell her that Girard was dead, it would ease her mind after the first shock. Then, when things were normal again, something might evolve between them.

On the last Monday of July, Peter was summoned to the warden's office. Peter was apprehensive, his work had not been as good as it should have. Was he going to be taken from his job and put back with the rest of the workers? That would be hard. Many of them resented his rise from the work floor, and they could make his life miserable. He entered the warden's office and was startled to see Higgins with the warden, they both were smiling.

"Sit down, Peter." The warden said. "I have something for you."

Peter was mystified, one never sat in the presence of the warden. He obeyed hesitantly.

The warden handed him a piece of paper. "Read this," he said, still smiling.

Peter read, and his face registered concern, then unbelief, and finally, absolute joy.

"It's a pardon! It's a pardon from the governor!"

"Yes Peter, it's a full pardon. It acknowledges that you were wrongfully imprisoned and restores all your rights as a citizen," the warden said. "You are a free man, Peter."

He extended his hand, and shook Peter's vigorously. "I extend the apologies of the State of Louisiana for the time you've spent here. Good luck!"

Higgins and Peter went to collect his clothing and belongings.

"How did you do it?" Peter asked. "It was so long I thought you'd given up."

"I didn't want to get your hopes up and then have them dashed. I had a hard time getting to Governor Blanchard. But when I did,...well, the governor is a fair man, and here you are. What are you going to do first?"

"First I'm going to buy my lawyer the best dinner he's ever eaten. Then I'm going to buy some new clothes, these smell of mildew."

That night Peter was on a train north. He slept soundly despite the lurching of the Pullman car. For the first time in nearly two years he was at peace. In the morning, when he awoke he looked out on the countryside, never had it looked so green, never had his heart been so glad.

It was early morning, Kathryn had just picked a bouquet of roses from the bushes beside the house. She loved the scent of them, and now she cradled them in her arms, enjoying the sweet aroma. A carriage was coming down the street, its horse trotting rapidly. Kathryn frowned as it approached. Didn't the driver know enough to drive more slowly in a residential neighborhood? The carriage stopped and the passenger leaped to the ground, he stood looking at the house and at her, then he started running up the pathway. She stood, not believing what she saw, then she threw the roses in the air and ran to his arms.

"Peter! Peter! Oh my God, it's really you!"

He held her close and smelled the scent of roses on her.

"Yes Kat, I'm free and I'm home!"

"Oh Peter!, it's the most wonderful thing in the world. How did you do it? I was afraid you'd be there for a long time yet."

"Higgins got me a pardon from the governor. A full pardon, I'm not a convict anymore. I'll tell you about it later. Where are the children?"

"They're still in bed. Come, we'll wake them."

Peter went first to the room that Lucy shared with April. He looked down at his little girl sleeping peacefully. She had been a baby when he left, now she had nearly doubled in size and was a little girl. He saw her mother in her, the same delicate face, the same flowing dark hair. She was an angel, as her mother had been. He bent and kissed her tenderly. Her eyes flickered open with the touch, and he sat on the bed to gather her in his arms.

"It's your daddy." He said tenderly. The small forehead wrinkled as she looked at him. Of course, Peter thought, she was a baby when I left, she doesn't know me. But then the lttle face took on a look of joy, and she threw her arms around his neck. "Daddy! Daddy!"

Kathryn had awakened April, and led her to Peter.

"Would you like to give your Uncle Peter a hug?" She asked.

The little girl, fully a head taller than Lucy, smiled at Peter shyly. Then she went to receive his hug. She looked up at him tentatively.

"Thank you for letting me live here, Uncle Peter. Are you going to stay home now?"

Peter drew her close to him along with Lucy. "Yes, April. I'm going to stay home forever."

He looked up. Two tousled heads were watching from the doorway. Svens' and Charles' eyes grew large with surprise. Then they ran, jumping on the bed with Peter. "Daddy! Daddy! " They shouted in unison.

Kathryn stood watching them, her eyes misty with tears. For the first time in too long, they were tears of happiness.

After the children had run out of questions and things to tell Peter, Kathryn prepared breakfast for the family. They ate happily and ravenously. That done, the children went to play. As is the way with happy children, they made the adjustment of having their father home, quickly. Peter and Kathryn sat over the luxury of a second and third cup of coffee on a happy summer morning.

"I'm anxious to see Charlie and get back to work." Peter said.

Kathryn looked at him strangely.

"Why are you looking at me that way? Is something wrong?"

"It's Daddy," she said, "I didn't want to worry you. He's not well, Peter."

He looked at her with concern, waiting for her to continue.

"You remember how I said he was getting forgetful, but that he wouldn't go to a doctor."

Peter nodded.

"The doctors said it was because he'd had a little stroke."

"Then, he finally did go to a doctor?"

"Not then, he had a big one Peter. He's paralyzed on one side, and…he can't talk!" She blurted out the end of the sentence as her face contorted and she bit her lip to hold back the tears that welled in her eyes.

Peter was stunned. The thought of jovial, irrepressible Charlie being without his voice was more then he could accept.

"You mean…not at all?"

Kathryn sniffed. "He tries, but everything comes out all garbled, then he gives up. He needs you, Peter. More than ever, he needs you."

Peter stared out the window. Will it never end? he thought.

"Where is Charlie now?"

"At home, Mama and the stableman take care of him. He still goes out, Aaron gets him into the carriage and takes him for rides. Otherwise he's in a wheelchair—he hates that. We built a ramp to the side door so Mama can take him outside, but when he's outside he wants to walk, and he can't do that. He's angry Peter, and it's eating him up inside."

"I'll go and see him, do you want to come along."

Kathryn shook her head. "I think you should see him alone."

Peter walked out and across the lawn to the steps of Charlie's house. Elizabeth came to the door—her jaw dropped, then she threw the door open and hugged him.

"It's really you Peter! Oh! I'm so glad, we need you so! Let me look at you. My, you're as handsome as ever! Those gray hairs do you good, you look so mature." She lowered her voice. "Kathryn told you about Charlie?"

He nodded solemnly.

"He's in the sitting room reading, he can still do that, though he can't speak clearly. Come in to see him, but don't pity him, he hates that."

Peter followed her into the sitting room. Charlie looked up as they entered. His face broke into a one sided smile and he laid the book down in his lap, and extended his good arm. Peter went to him and took his hand. The grip was strong and pulled Peter downward. Peter knelt on one knee and put his arm around his mentor. Charlie slapped his back with his good hand, then he pushed Peter to arm's length and and motioned to his mouth while shaking his head.

Peter didn't know what to say, how to begin visiting with this man who always liked to talk, and now could not. He nodded. "I know, Charlie, Kat told me. We're going to get you up again, Charlie. Up and back to work."

Charlie shook his head slowly. Then he put his finger to his temple and made a twitching motion with his thumb.

"No Charlie, don't even think it. You might be down now, but you'll get better. And I still need you to advise me on business affairs. You can read and we can do a lot of work here, even if you're not at the office every day. And hell, we can take you there too, just need a couple of ramps like you've got here. How does that sound?"

Charlie looked at Peter with an unsure expression and hunched up his good shoulder, putting his hand out palm up to signify acquiesence.

"Good! We'll start as soon as I get broke in again at work. It's been a long time, and I won't know what's happening."

Peter stayed with Charlie and Elizabeth for several hours. Then he went back to his house. Tomorrow would be soon enough to go back to work.

After the children were in bed, Kathryn and Peter were talking quietly on the loveseat that faced the spreading window of the sitting room.

"How long has Charlie been like that?" Peter asked.

"Since last March."

"Who's been taking care of Charlie's business for all that time?"

"Elias hired a manager, Daddy gave him power of attorney so he could see to the things that needed to be done. That's why he's so glad to see you back. Elias knows finances, but not much else in a business sense."

"I'm glad I helped him get started here, we'd have been in a pretty fix without him."

"Just the same, I'm glad you'll be taking over the businesses again, your own and Daddy's."

"And I can take my seat on the bank board again. I had to resign when I was convicted. But now that I have a full pardon, I can go back on."

"But wouldn't somebody else have taken your place?"

"It doesn't make any difference, as a major investor I was guaranteed a seat."

"Wonderful! It's going to be so nice with things back to normal. And if you're going to include Daddy in business dealings, that will help him. I think what made him so angry and hopeless is that he couldn't work anymore. We're going to be a happy family again, Peter."

"Yeah, I thought a lot about that in prison. And it's great with our children together. I thought about that too, Kat. Have you?"

She drew her knees up under her chin and stared dreamily at the orange-yellow moon climbing up from the horizon.

"I have, I've had fantasies of how it would be if we were all together, for life. But so much has happened, we're not the people we were back then. Can we just be like we are for now, friends?"

He looked at her in the soft glow of lamplight and thought she had never looked better. The impetuous beauty of her teen years had been destroyed by the trials of her life. In its place was a regal beauty, and a graciousness of manner that put Peter at ease. She did not set him ablaze with passion, their relationship had become one of a gentler nature, they were friends, and for the moment that would be enough.

Chapter 21

Betrayed

In the morning Peter went to the furniture factory and was surprised by all the new faces.

"Where's George?" He asked a young man at an accounting desk.

The young man looked up in surprise. "There's no George here. If it's something of importance, you can see Mr. Hurst." He pointed to the office that had been Peter's.

Peter strode to the door, where a brass plaque announced: "Manfred J. Hurst, Manager". A blocky man of about Peter's age sat at his desk, reading a newspaper. Damn, they're at it again, he thought.

"You the manager here?"

The man lowered his newspaper. "Yes, I am. Is there something I can do for you? I don't remember having an appointment this morning."

"You can get out of my chair, for a start. I'm Peter Hokanson, I own this plant."

The man gaped, then jumped to his feet. The newspaper scattered itself on the floor.

"Oh, pardon me, Sir. If I'd known you were coming I would have vacated your office."

"Vacate it now," Peter said, "I'm going out to the plant."

He turned and went to find Curtis. As he walked through the plant he saw few of the old faces. The men were working, but the pace was casual. Here and there pairs of workers were talking. The foreman's office was in the center of the plant, a closure of brick with large panels of glass. Peter didn't see Curtis, another stranger was sitting at the foreman's desk. He went in anyway.

The man looked at Peter. "Salesmen go to the front office."

"I'm not a salesman, I'm Peter Hokanson, the owner."

"You own this place?"

"Every inch of it. Who the hell are you, and where's Curtis?"

"If you mean the old foreman, he's gone."

"Gone?"

"Yes Sir, Mr. Hurst fired him. I'm his replacement."

Peter turned on his heel and left. He needed to talk to Elias Oberg.Elias extended his hand rather cooly.

"Well, I'm certainly surprised to see you back, Peter. Julia and I were talking about you just the other night. Did they give you a parole so soon?"

"No, not a parole. The governor gave me a full pardon for wrongful imprisonment. The slate is clean, Elias. I can go back to business as if nothing had happened."

"That's great Peter, I'm sure Julia will be glad to hear it."

"How is she, and your baby?"

"They are both fine, the little guy is toddling now. I didn't realize you knew about him."

"Kat wrote to me while I was in prison."

"Oh yes, I've barely met her. There hasn't been much socializing what with you gone, and Charlie's condition. Sad, that."

"Kat tells me you have power of attorney for him."

"Yes, I reluctantly took on that yoke. Somebody had to, with his mind being the way it is."

"I saw him yesterday. I didn't find anything wrong with his mind. He can't speak clearly, but he can read and think. He should be taking part in his business."

Elias raised his eyebrows. "Really, I didn't realize he'd improved that much."

"Speaking of business, I'm ready to take over my affairs again. We can have your power of attorney rescinded this week. And, I'd like my place back on the board of the bank."

"Yes, I'll certainly be glad to vacate my power of attorney. Lord knows I don't need the extra strain. But your seat on the bank board is a different matter entirely."

"What do you mean?" Peter asked. "Our contract guarantees me a seat on the board."

"The contract reads that you shall have a seat on the board until you voluntarily vacate it. You resigned, Peter."

"I was forced to, you said I had to."

"Just the same, you did vacate the seat legally by your own judgement. There was no court order requiring you to do it. And actually, it's a moot point, since the bank's charter calls for five director seats, all of which are now filled."

"Well dammit, Elias, change the charter."

Elias smiled thinly. "You don't understand that these things are not so simply done. The charter can only be changed by a unanimous vote of the directors, and a two thirds vote by the investors at the annual meeting."

"Well. you can try, can't you?"

"Yes, I suppose I can. But for now, you are an investor with one vote at the annual meeting, Peter."

"If I can't be on the board, I want to withdraw my investment, and my share of the profits."

"You are entitled to your share of the profits, of course. and they will be paid to you at the annual meeting in March. However, you cannot withdraw your investment. In your absence the board of directors saw fit to incorporate the company. The investors approved, and your investment has been converted to stock in the corporation. You can sell those stocks, of course. If you can find a willing buyer."

"Damn, all that in less than two years?"

"It was the prudent thing to do, Peter. These are changing times, and to retain a large company under a partnership is risky for everyone."

"What about my company? I found a guy I'd never met sitting on his butt in my office. And the plant is barely moving, it looks like everybody is on holiday."

Elias looked pained. "You understand that I had to hire a manager in your absence. If you no longer need him, I suggest you relieve him of his duties. As for the men, I too noticed a slight slowdown in production since they organized."

"Organized? What the hell do you mean, Elias."

"Your employees organized, they formed a union."

"A union? Why?"

"They felt their pay and benefits were inadequate. They formed a union and threatened to walk off their jobs. Mr. Hurst and I negotiated and reached what we felt was a reasonable settlement."

"How much more am I paying them?"

"It's all in the contract in your office, Peter. I suggest you read it at your leisure. Now, if you have no further concerns, I have much to do."

Peter left the bank feeling as though he'd been in a poker game and lost, without knowing how much. When he returned to the factory, his office had been cleared, and Manfred Hurst was waiting for him anxiously.

"I'm sorry I gave such a bad impression, Mr. Hokanson. I was catching up on business events in the city. I suppose that now that you're back, you won't be needing me any more."

Peter appraised the man. It was too early to fire him, there would be questions to be answered.

"No, let's continue as we are for a while, Mr. Hurst. We'll see what develops. I'll want the union contract first, bring it in to me."

"It's already on your desk Sir, along with the ledgers. I thought you'd want them."

"Okay, thanks. Don't go too far."

Peter sat down at his desk and selected the folder marked "UNION CONTRACT". He opened it and read with intense concentration. When he had finished he sat thinking. The pay that his employees were receiving had increased by about twenty percent. Moreover, the contract guaranteed them annual raises over a period of three years. On top of that, they would receive wages without working at Christmas and Independence Day. Those who had worked for two years would also receive a week of vacation with pay each year. What was the world coming to, when people wanted to be paid for not working?

He put the folder aside and picked up the sales ledger. He turned the pages to December of 1903 and started scanning the figures. The figures rose slightly, then declined in January and remained fairly constant for several months. In early summer, when sales should have been up, they dropped sharply for a month then regained slowly and reached a plateau lower than the previous year.

"Mr. Hurst!," he called. "Come here!"

Hurst appeared, with an appearance of apprehension. "Yes, Sir?"

"What's this drop in production in 1904?"

"It was a slowdown, when the men organized."

"And they didn't get back to full production?"

"No, Sir."

"They got higher wages for less work?"

"I guess so. Sir."

"But they always worked well for Curtis."

"Yes, Sir. But Curtis left. He disagreed with Mr. Oberg on the terms of the contract. He thought the pay increase was too much. He said he couldn't go along with robbing you, Sir."

"So what happened?"

"Mr. Oberg told him that if he didn't like it, the door was open. I believe he went to Morrison's, Sir."

"Damn! Where was Gus Svenson when all of this was happening, and where is he now? He was supposed to be minding production and sales for me."

"I don't know, Sir. I've never met him. He must have left before I came."

"When did you come?"

"In May of four."

"Where were you before?"

"Swanberg's in Saint Paul."

"I don't know of a Swanberg in the furniture business, are they new?"

"No, Sir. They make packing boxes."

Peter breathed a heavy sigh and rubbed his eyes. "I should have guessed, you can go for now."

Peter wondered what had happened that caused Gus to leave. It must have been serious. Gus had been his first friend in this country, and he was a good salesman. He'd have to talk with him, maybe he'd come back. Never let a banker run a manufacturing business, he thought ruefully. He scanned down the sales figures until the last entry. They showed a slow, but continuous decline. Dammit! he thought, we're selling less than we were three years ago. The receivables were in bad shape. There were too many uncollected accounts.

In disgust he threw the sales ledger aside and picked up the payables. They had risen in January, then at the time of the union organization they rose sharply and remained high until the last entry. Peter understood the second rise. But why had they risen by a thousand dollars a month in January? He looked more closely. The difference was in wages and salaries. That doesn't make sense, he thought. Then he compared the receivables with the payables. By the end of 1904 the two sets of figures had crossed each other. He had been losing money since then!

Worried now, Peter picked up the payroll ledger. Among the list of names every month was E. Oberg, and each check was for $1000. He had a balance of nearly $15,000 when he left, more than enough for two months wages for his entire company. The deposits and balance of the payroll account diminished as sales went down. Until at the end of 1904, the account was dry. Then there was a deposit showing, $15,000—First Home and Commercial Bank of Minneapolis. Peter shook his head and frowned—a loan, Elias made a loan to the company. After that, the slide continued. In the next six months the account again lost ground. At the end of June there was another deposit of $15,000, again from First Home and Commercial Bank of Minneapolis. He picked up the payable ledger again, and looked more closely at the figures for June, 1905. An entry was listed as interest on loan, First Home — $1125. That's double the normal interest rate, Peter thought. The bastard's bleeding me dry from all sides. Damn him, I had more than enough to pay him back, but it's locked up in bank stock. He was going to have a talk with Elias, but first he'd talk to Gus.

That night Peter went to Gus's house. Gus opened the door—surprise showed on his face, but friendliness did not.

"They let you out already?"

"Yeah, governor's pardon." Peter smiled and extended his hand.

Gus ignored it, and stood in the doorway, unsmiling. "What do you want, Pete?"

Peter dropped his hand awkwardly. "I thought we might talk."

"We don't have anything to talk about, Pete."

"Whoa! What's going on here, Gus?"

"Christ, you oughta know!"

"Hey! I just got back to the plant and I find you gone. Don't you think you should at least tell me why?"

Gus looked at Peter oddly. "You really don't know, do you?"

"You've been my friend since I came here, Gus. I want to know why you quit on me."

Gus motioned for Peter to enter, then went to the stove and poured two cups of coffee from a big enamel pot.

"Sit down Pete, I thought it was funny when it happened. I didn't think you'd fire me without talking first."

"What do you mean, fire you?"

"It was a couple of months after you went to prison. Elias and I weren't getting along very good. I wanted to print a new catalog and send it out to our customers. Curtis and I had come up with a new line of inexpensive furniture, tables and chairs, chests of drawers and things like that. It was priced so that young people starting out might afford it. We were all set to put it into production."

"Sounds like a damned good idea," Peter said. "Most of our stuff has been aimed at people who have money. The low priced stuff would open a whole new market. Didn't Elias like the idea?"

"He said that business was going into a downturn, and that it wouldn't be wise to expand into a new line. He said we should just sit tight. I said that a downturn would be a good reason for trying to expand our market into lower priced furniture. He wouldn't budge, and he was holding the purse strings. I said I'd write to you and find out what you thought of the idea."

"Why didn't you? I would have agreed with you."

"Elias said he was running the show, and that he would write to you himself. Then about two weeks later he came up with the letter."

"What letter?"

"A letter from you. I've still got it somewhere, I was going to burn it, but I saved it." Gus went to a drawer in the kitchen cupboard and started rummaging through a pile of papers.

"Here it is." He handed it to Peter. "I should have thought at the time that it was funny it was typed, but it made me mad and it had your signature on it."

Dear Mr. Oberg,

With regards to the plan you communicated to me concerning a new line of low priced furniture, I believe that it would only reduce our profit margins further. Our best plan of action is to aim for greater sales of the higher priced furniture. We have only one factory, and it should be affording us the highest profit margin possible. The printing of a new catalog will only increase our costs.

With respect to the current sales figures reflected in your letter, I think it may be time for drastic action. Gus Svenson is a long time friend, but it is evident that he is dealing in areas beyond his capabilities, rather than concentrating on improved sales of our very good furniture line. I reluctantly suggest that you terminate his employment with us, and pass his position on to someone who will pursue our interests more vigorously.

Yours with sincerity,
Peter O. Hokanson

"Damn! What a crock of shit this is!" Peter exclaimed. "Does this letter sound like me, Gus?"

"No, I guess not. Too polite and full of nice words, sounds like a bookeeper."

"Or a banker! The son of a bitch had my signature on papers. He forged it!"

"But why would he fire me? I was doing a good job."

"For the same reason he got rid of George and Curtis. He wanted the company to fail, I just don't know why."

"But the company is solid, isn't it? I know we had a little downturn before I left, but that's normal in winter."

Peter shook his head. "As of this minute I owe Oberg's bank $30,000 and I'm losing money every day. I don't know if I can turn it around. I need your help, Gus. The first note is due in December, and I'll bet Oberg won't renew it."

"You want me to come back?"

"If you can. I know it's risky, but we can do it together."

"Damn, Pete. I've got a good job now, I'm making more than I did before."

"I'm going to incorporate, Gus. I'll give you a bigger commission and stock in the company."

"I don't know, Pete. I'll have to think about it, talk it over with my wife."

The next morning Peter told Charlie what was happening to his business.

"I think we better look at your books too," he said. "I think it might be wise to rescind Elias's power of attorney."

Charlie nodded his head vigorously, and pointed at Peter.

"You want me to take it over?"

Charlie nodded again.

"Okay, I'll bring the books tonight, we'll have a look at them together. Then I'm going to have another talk with Elias."

That day Peter took the control of his business back into his own hands. And that night he brought the books of the flour mill and grain shipping company to Charlie's house.

The first thing they found was that the volume of business had dropped greatly. The second thing they found was that loans against the company that had been with another bank were now with First Home and Commercial Bank of Minneapolis. The interest rate had risen by five percent.

"It's the same thing he did to me," Peter said. "And look here." He pointed to the column of wages and salaries. Every month there was a check to E. Oberg for $2,000.

Charlie's face was red with anger. He pounded his good fist on the table.

"Yeah, he's letting sales slip, and he's bleeding you white at the same time. Pretty soon your cash reserves will have depleted so that you'll have to take a loan to stay in business. He wants it all, Charlie, your business and mine."

The next day Charlie and Peter rescinded Elias's power of attorney over the mills. Then Peter paid a call on Elias.

"What the hell were you doing, Elias?" Peter said angily. "You were running both my business and Charlie's into the gutter. Sales are down, and costs are up. Another year like this, and we'll bankrupt.

Elias took his spectacles off, and folded them carefully.

"I can't be responsible for a downturn in business, Peter. Business is going into a recession. I've tried to offset it by avoiding unnecessary risk, but your fixed costs are too high. I suggest you cut back on employees, and service your loans."

"If our fixed costs are too high, how is it that you transferred our loans to your bank, and made new ones at a higher rate than we were paying?"

"Interest rates are rising, Peter. The transfers were a matter of convenience."

"And why were you charging us those damned high salaries?"

"The salaries were not out of line with the responsibility involved."

"The hell they weren't. It looks to me like you were deliberately trying to make our businesses fail. Why? We got you started in this country, Elias. We've all been like family. Why would you try to wreck us?"

For the first time, Elias lost his banker's composure. His face colored with anger, anger that had been restrained and now was forcing its way out.

"So we've all been like family, have we? And does that kinship extend to Julia, also?"

"What do you mean by that?"

"Did you really think I didn't know, Peter? Did you really think that I would believe Julia's pregnancy to be some sort of miracle, like the virgin birth? You violated my marriage, Peter. And now, I and Julia are raising the fruits of that violation."

Peter was dumbfounded. There it was, the reason for Elias's actions against him. He fully intended to bring about Peter's ruin. Peter could say nothing that would appease Elias. No apology was adequate, no matter how penitent it was. He had done Elias a wrong that he could not right. And now Charlie was suffering with him. Their investments were intertwined, and what might happen to Peter would also happen to Charlie.

"If it's any help, I'm sorry," Peter said lamely. Then he got up and left.

In the weeks that followed Peter worked desperately to bring the enterprises that he and Charlie shared back to a profitable state. Gus had declined Peter's request that he return.

"Back in the old days I just had to take care of myself," he said. "But now I have a family and I have to take care of them first."

Peter understood, but it was still a blow to him. Gus had always been beside him, he would be missed in the years ahead.

One night in the end of August Peter was talking with Kathryn. It was a thing he had grown accustomed to. Though they were not lovers, Peter talked to Kathryn as though she were his wife. She was his safety valve, providing a means for him to release his frustrations and fears. Tonight she was withdrawn, doing her needlework quietly as they sat together.

"Is something wrong, Kat?"

"Not terribly."

"But there is something?"

"Yes Peter. It's a small thing really, I…I can't live here anymore."

"Why, is it something I've done?"

"No, of course not. It's the neighbors, Peter. They are saying things about us, things that aren't true."

"Like that we're lovers, living in sin?"

"Yes."

"I don't care what they think, Kathryn. I like having you here. I need you."

"I know, I feel that way too. But it isn't just us, the other children are teasing April and the boys. I don't care what they think of me, but I won't let them hurt April. I have to go back to Daddy's house, Peter."

"Damn those gossips! They're tearing our home apart."

"I know, but what can we do?"

Peter looked at her thoughtfully. "We could fix it so they couldn't talk. We could get married."

"No Peter, we couldn't do it for that reason. I'm not ready to marry again. I don't know if I ever will. I love you as a friend, Peter. I don't know if it could ever be otherwise between us."

"Do you mean I won't see you anymore?"

"No, I'll still take care of the children if you want me to. And we can still visit, but I can't live here."

The next day, Kathryn and April moved back to Charlie's house. In the evening, Peter sat on the loveseat staring out of the window. Despite his children, he felt bereft. The anchor that gave him a feeling of security was gone, and he felt utterly alone. The loss of Gus and the loss of Charlie's blustery conversation had struck deep into Peter's being. The loss of Kat as a daily confidante took from him the last outlet for his problems. Depression stalked Peter, and his ability to fend it off weakened.

Inch by inch Peter brought the businesses under control. By November both the furniture factory and the milling business were showing gain. Peter at long last was able to sell his stock in Elias's bank. He had lost money on it, but there was enough to pay the first note for $15,000 that was due in December. Things were looking better.

The Christmas holidays came and went. They had been glorious, a time of much needed celebration that brought Peter's circle of family and friends closer than they had been in years. Peter was again invigorated, and he again pursued work with gusto.

On the night of January 6, 1906, Peter was awakened by a banging on his door. It was Merle, the plant boiler-man, and he was excited.

"Come quick, Mr. Hokanson, the factory is burning!"

Peter pulled on his clothes and ran to the carriage with Merle. In the east there was a glow against the winter sky. They arrived at a confused mass of horse drawn pumps, hoses and grim faced men attempting to contain the blaze. The figures cast eerie shadows in the ruddy light as they arced streams of water on nearby buildings.

Flames were roaring from the wide windows of the factory, spitting great tongues of smoke and sparks into the night. Peter watched, transfixed with horror, as the roof collapsed in an inferno of fire and sparks that rose a hundred feet in the air. Then gradually the holocaust receded. It was as if it were a monster glutted by consuming his property, and so sated, was content to leave his livelyhood and his future in smoking ruins.

Peter watched until all that remained was a fire blackened corpse of brick and stone, its gut filled with the twisted remains of machines that had been his pride. Then he left, his shoulders hanging, his eyes hollow with shock. He walked alone down the snow windrowed street, as new flurries drifted in a gentle wind, as if to throw a cloak over the ashes of his life. He looked back, as the snow increased, a column of steam was rising high in the air from the place where he had built his dreams.

He turned away and walked on to the railroad station where his life here had begun. He sat for hours amidst the busy throng of people, thinking of the boy of seventeen who had stepped off a train here. He was full of ambition then, he had a vision of great things he would do. He had fulfilled his vision, and now it was gone, wiped out in a few hours by the hand of fate. Finally Peter got up, he walked out into a driving blizzard and went home.

The winter storm roared with fury for two days, piling up huge drifts of white in every sheltered place. Peter stared at the swirling snow through the window of his sitting room. Kathryn sat beside him speaking consoling words, and brought him cups of hot chocolate which set, barely touched on the table beside him. She had never seen him so despondent. He had drawn within himself, and she feared for him. When he spoke, it was with the voice of a beaten man, and then it was only of what he must do to straighten up the chaos left by the hostile hand of fate. There was no mention of rebuilding his life, and that worried Kathryn. It was as though he had reached the end of life, and must only arrange the details leading to his expiration.

In the weeks that followed, Peter forced himself to attend to the duties so abruptly thrust upon him. There was insurance on the factory, and Peter paid Elias with it. Then he gave each of the people he had employed a small sum to tide them over until they could find another job. He did not venture near the ruins of his factory, or speak of rebuilding. Instead he used his remaining money to set up a trust fund for his children.

Kathryn watched him day by day as he sank deeper into depression, and she could do nothing. She had taken to sitting with him in the evening, but he seldom talked. When he did speak, it was of times past, never of the future. It was as though the fire in his spirit had died with the flames of his factory. There was a coldness in his soul, as bleak and unrelenting as the Minnesota winter. Kathryn hoped for an early thaw. Perhaps a bright sun and a diminishing of the frozen snow would reawaken his spirit.

Chapter 22

Redeemed

One biting cold evening in February, Kathryn gave Peter a letter after he'd taken off his coat and hat. He looked at the envelope casually, then looked at it again with more interest. Hurriedly he slit the envelope with his pen knife and drew a letter out, then began reading it with intense concentration. As he read, his face took on an incredulous look, and when he had finished he started at the beginning and read it again. When he had read it the second time he spoke to Kathryn excitedly.

"Will you take care of the children for a few days, Kat? I have to make a trip."

"Why certainly Peter, is something wrong?"

He looked at her and shook his head—for the first time in weeks there was a light in his eyes.

"No Kat, but I can't tell you about it now. I'll be leaving right away, if there's a train."

Later that night Peter was listening to the sound of iron wheels on steel rails. He smiled as shadows of trees on the snowy landscape flew past. He remembered his first trip into the north, and the faces of young Gus, braggy Sven and the stalwart Christian joined him. The tall pines crashing to the frozen earth, and the mighty draft horses pulling their huge sleighs passed through the scenes in his mind. So did the wolves trailing along behind him, and Wise Otter the old medicine man. And then, there was Sarah, walking beside him and telling him about her people. Peter grinned and fell into a peaceful slumber.

In the the first light of northern morning, when the sun grudgingly crept above the horizon, the train slowed for yet another stop.

"All off for Grand Rapids," the conductor shouted.

Peter woke with a start, then remembering where he was, he got up and hurried from the train. He stepped onto the frigid, squeaky, frozen snow and looked about. Little had changed since he was last here. Turning his fur collar up against the cold he began walking briskly. The crisp air invigorated him, and once again he was filled with a sense of anticipation. He had been gone too long, he thought, and he realized that he had missed this primitive land. His roots in this new country were here, planted with the swinging of an axe in his sinewy hands. He felt joy at being back, a deep throbbing joy that clutched at his throat and quickened his heart. He hurried on through the streets just now awakening, and smelled the wood smoke from newly fired stoves. The few first risers were already entering the doors that drew him, and he joined them, stamping the snow from his boots.

She turned, coffeepot in hand to serve the early morning men as they clustered at the counter, not noticing the newcomer as he took a seat. Peter watched silently as a young boy with curly, black hair brought a stack of hotcakes to a man in a Mackinaw jacket, then returned to the kitchen for another. It was then that she turned to Peter for his order. She drew up with a gasp and the coffee pot fell to the floor, the remainder of its contents splashing on the dry wood.

"My God! Peter!...here...in Grand Rapids?" Sarah stood speechless, then as though it were something of great importance she bent to pick up the coffee pot.

"I'm sorry, it's just that I never expected to see you again. Are you hungry?"

He smiled. "You bet I am, I'd like a ton of pancakes and a cord of bacon."

"Will you settle for a stack and a pile?" Her shock was easing, and she managed a smile. "My goodness, what brings you here, Peter?"

"Do you suppose you could get somebody to take over here while I tell you about it?"

"All right, we're not busy yet." She called to the kitchen. "Emma take over, will you?"

"Could we go someplace private?" Peter asked.

"If it's really necessary. We live in the back." She led the way to a comfortable parlor, and sat down with him. "How have you been, Peter?"

"It's a long story, and I don't want to talk about it right now. But the reason I came is you, Sarah."

She looked at him questioningly. "Me? I thought...you didn't write for such a long time. It seems like a lifetime ago, Peter."

"I wrote to you twice. You never got the first letter. I didn't know that."

"Oh, my God! I thought you'd leave a letter, and at first I thought that Lone Man threw your letter away. But then when I didn't hear from you…I thought you didn't care. Then when Christian brought a letter from you, he said it would be better for you…without me."

"And that's why you wrote me the letter saying it was over between us?"

She nodded. "But it doesn't matter anymore, does it? Your wife…"

"My wife died nearly four years ago, Sarah."

Sarah looked at him, her face reflecting surprise and confusion. "I'm sorry Peter, I didn't know. When you got married, I…"

"I know, Christian wrote me a letter. He had his lawyer hold it for six months before he mailed it. He told me everything."

"Then, you know about young Christian?"

"Yes, that's him out there, isn't it? He's a fine looking boy, Sarah."

"Yes…our son—but there are so many things I don't understand."

"Christian said to let you read his letter if I came to you. Here it is, it will explain everything."

Sarah took the letter from Peter's hand as though it would burn her if she touched it. She slowly unfolded it and began reading.

Dear Pete,

My doctor says that I am on my death bed. What I did to you rests heavy on my soul. I have confessed it to Father Goebel, and he tells me I must confess it to you and Sarah so that my soul can rest in peace. I freely make confession to you, and hope that you will find it in your Swedish heart to forgive this Norwegian sinner. But I can't tell Sarah of it and cause her pain that would follow her to the grave. She loved you dearly and I don't know what cards life has dealt you. So I am asking my lawyer to mail you this letter six months after my death. If you are free, and want to go to Sarah, show her this letter. It will help her understand what happened between you. If not, I ask you for the sake of the love she has given me in these years, to keep my secret.

In the days when you worked for me, I thought of you as my son. And I didn't ever expect to have a son of my own. I wanted you to be a success, to be a greater man than I was. When you left your first letter to Sarah, I didn't give it to Lone Man, but burned it instead. I gave her the second letter, but I convinced her that you didn't have a chance to succeed with a half breed wife—I was wrong, and I deserve to burn in hell for it—but because she loved you, she wrote you a letter calling it off between you. As my part of the bargain, I promised Wise Otter that I'd take care of Sarah and her coming child. She was pregnant with your son, and I didn't have any idea of what was going to happen, I swear it by my mother's grave.

Shortly before you were to marry Charlie's daughter I went to visit Wise Otter. He was on his deathbed, and he was worried about Sarah. He asked me to take her as my wife, Peter. By that time, I'd come to love Sarah and the boy. So I told Wise Otter I would marry Sarah, if she would have me. I could tell by her look that she was still thinking about you. So I showed her the letter you sent me, announcing your wedding. It was a bad thing to do, but I loved her. We got married that spring, and Sarah has given me a son and a daughter, and the best years of my life. I only hope that she doesn't hate me, for the sake of our children and the years that we had.

Christian Halvorsen

Sarah's face was pale with shock, that slowly turned to anger as she realized what Christian had done.

"It was Christian all the time! He deliberately planned to keep us apart! And I thought I was doing what was best for you! I married him when I had no hope we'd ever be together."

"I know, and when I married Lucille, I thought you didn't care about me anymore. I never suspected that Christian was the cause of it, he was my friend."

"It hurts when you find out something like this about someone you've loved, Peter. I was a good wife to him."

"And was he a good husband?"

"Yes, the best. Christian was always kind and gentle, and he was a good father to all of our children. Young Christian misses him terribly, he's at the age where he needs a father. And I miss him too. I look at my bed every night, and I imagine his big raw boned frame lying there. At first, when he died, I cried all the time. It's better now, but I still miss him terribly."

"You loved him deeply, didn't you?"

"Yes, with all my heart. It wasn't like it was with you and I, Peter. It happened gradually, in a comfortable way. He'd smile at me in that way of his, you know how he smiled with his eyes. And he'd tease me about some little thing and slap me on my bottom. And I knew he was a man I could always depend on. But he left us ,Peter! He got sick, and he died, and I thought my world had ended!"

Sarah started crying then, and Peter held her gently. He was remembering his anguish at Lucille's death. His grief had diminished through the years. But hers was still fresh and poignant. In his last act on earth, Christian had used the wisdom that Peter had so respected. He knew that Sarah would need a time of grieving alone, and so he had withheld his confession to Peter. But then, at his death he had given them a second chance. Peter could not feel ill toward him because of it.

"It must have broken his heart to leave you, Sarah. Even though he came between us, he took care of you, and he loved you. He was that way. I've seen him kick a man with his caulked boots when he had it coming. But he gave me a start I wouldn't have had on my own. I'll always remember his grin, and his hand on my shoulder. He was a wonderful friend and a terrible enemy. And when he was wrong, he couldn't leave without making it right."

Sarah nodded her head against Peter's shoulder. "I'll always remember him with love, Peter. Just as I'll always love you."

Peter took Sarah by both shoulders and held her at arms length.

"Do you mean that, Sarah? Do you mean what you just said?" His eyes looked deep into hers, just as they had done so long ago.

"Yes, Peter. I never stopped loving you. You were always in my prayers."

"Do you think that...would you..."

"Would I what, Peter?" Her eyes sparkled in contrast to the tear smudges on her face.

"Well, damn it all. I thought that since you are alone, and I'm alone, we might think of getting married."

"That's not a very good reason for getting married, Peter." She was laughing now, gently and melodiously.

Peter started laughing too. He dropped to one knee. "If I must, I must. I love you, Sarah. Will you marry me?"

"Yes Peter, I will."

"That's wonderful!" He rose to take her in his arms, and kissed her soundly.

"We can get married, then we'll build a big resort on one of the lakes here. We'll have our kids all together, and I can go fishing with the boys. And you can do woman things with the girls. And I'll bring Charlie and Elizabeth up in the summer. And Kat can bring April too.... "

"Just a minute Peter."

"What?"

"Don't we girls get to go fishing too?"

Sarah and Peter were married in June in Peter's church in Minneapolis, and were blessed with a son and daughter. Peter and Charlie closed out their business dealings in the city, and Charlie retired. Peter and Sarah built a resort on Lake Pokegama at Grand Rapids, where Charlie and Elizabeth summered every year until Charlie's death many years later.

Kathryn married again and had two sons. She and her family continued to live in Minneapolis, in the house Peter had built. She was devoted to Charlie and brought him much happiness in his retirement. Elias became a powerful banker, and raised his son to follow him. Julia happily became part of Minneapolis society, and founded a children's home.

Peter's ambition led him to acquire several businesses in the Grand Rapids area. But he never again let his ambition control him. He built strong ties with his sons, Christian,

Charles and Sven, and his son and daughter by Sarah, Peter Hokan and Kathryn Sarah, that would endure in later years. He was a good father to Christian and Sarah's son, Louis, named for Sarah's father, and to their daughter Ingrid, named for Christian's mother. Thus he returned the care that Christian had provided for Peter's son, Christian. Though he lavished affection on his entire family, 'Little Lucy' was rather his favorite, his remembrance of Lucille. He and Sarah were happy and content. And the girls all got to go fishing.

About the Author

Richard Grabmeier lives in a lakes region of central Minnesota. The grandson of Swedish and Austrian immigrants, he enjoys reading historical literature of all types. Now retired from his career, he raises terrier dogs and writes historical fiction. The youthful immigration of his Swedish grandfather inspired *Peter Olaf.*

9 780595 157440